FATHOMLESS

TOR TEEN BOOKS BY ANNE M. PILLSWORTH

The Redemption's Heir Series

Summoned

Fathomless

FATHOMLESS

ANNE M. PILLSWORTH

TOR®
TEEN

A Tom Doherty Associates Book
New York

FATHOMLESS

A Tor Teen Book
Published by Tom Doherty Associates, LLC
175 Fifth Avenue
New York, NY 10010

www.tor-forge.com

Tor® is a registered trademark of Tom Doherty Associates, LLC.

The Library of Congress Cataloging-in-Publication Data
is available upon request.

ISBN 978-0-7653-3590-6 (hardcover)
ISBN 978-1-4668-2658-8 (e-book)

Our books may be purchased in bulk for promotional, educational, or business use. Please contact your local bookseller or the Macmillan Corporate and Premium Sales Department at (800) 221-7945, extension 5442, or by e-mail at MacmillanSpecialMarkets@macmillan.com.

First Edition: October 2015

Printed in the United States of America

0 9 8 7 6 5 4 3 2 1

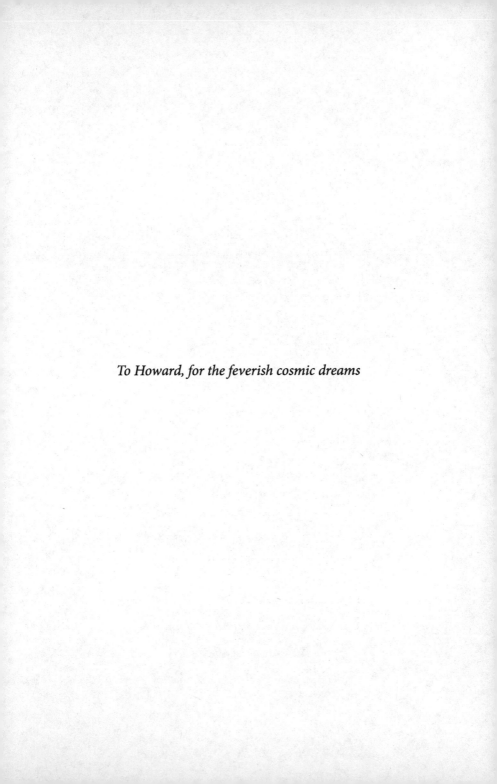

To Howard, for the feverish cosmic dreams

FATHOMLESS

AFTER THE FIREWORKS

Arkham's Independence Day festivities had drawn thousands of souls to its harbor, including Redemption Orne, who looked for a single soul of peculiar quality. To conserve magic, he'd dropped his customary illusion and walked as the young man who'd escaped mortality centuries before. The candor posed little danger; in Arkham, only two living men knew his true face, and the dead he disregarded.

He had started hunting at noon. With nightfall, the barges in the harbor began to vent their pyrotechnic cargoes, goading the crowd to an exhilaration that deafened his psychic "hearing." Redemption retreated from the boardwalk to the comparative peace of Saltonstall Park. Where benches afforded a view of the fireworks, gawkers still clustered. He walked deeper under the trees and leaned against a trunk to regain his bearings. After the show, he could work the throngs milling homeward. Except—

Except . . .

Except he might not have to. Though the din of the fireworks continued, a far subtler vibration rattled the bones of his inner ears. Ambient energy ebbed as someone nearby drew upon it. The person was no magician—they took too little energy for that—but they had the spark Redemption needed.

He traced the ebb to a clearing where Captain Saltonstall, in bronze, defied King and customs men. Present-day patriots had deserted their Revolutionary hero and left the clearing empty except for a boy not much older than Sean Wyndham, who'd last summer answered Redemption's ad for an apprentice. The sparse beard he'd managed to raise emphasized rather than disguised his youth. Youthful, too, even childish, was his hunch over the artist's pad on his knees. To observe unobserved, Redemption paused beyond the glare of the sodium lamps that allowed the boy to draw. On the bench beside him slumped a scarred leather backpack. Equally scuffed were his work boots, and the knees and cuffs of his jeans were frayed. Add to these signs of rough travel a Mohawk lapsing into all-over carrot-red stubble, and the boy hadn't seen home for some time.

Nyarlathotep clearly favored Redemption, to send him such a perfect donor.

Before entering the light, he took out his phone and feigned conversation. His ploy had the desired effect: the boy looked up, wary but unstartled, read him as harmless, and returned to his drawing. As Redemption approached the boy's bench, he channeled magic into his voice, warming it to a trust-inducing balm. "Okay, I'm off. Tomorrow, lunch. Don't forget."

The boy's hunched shoulders relaxed. He sat up, blinking.

Redemption halted in front of the bench. "Hey," he said. "Somebody else who doesn't like fireworks?"

"They're all right." The boy flipped his pad shut. "I was going to check them out, but I got distracted."

"Drawing?"

The boy hesitated before nodding.

"Cool. I draw some. Can I have a look?"

Another hesitation, but Redemption's balmed words affected this target strongly. The boy's spark explained part of that susceptibility. More, though, his simultaneous shrug and grin belied a hunger for contact. "I guess so. If you like scary stuff."

"I think I can handle it," Redemption said. He sat to receive the pad. Handing it over, the boy said, "The base sucks. I blew the perspective."

The minor errors in Saltonstall's statue were unimportant; the strength of the sketch lay in the creature coiled around the monument. Its upper body was human, female, lissome. However, its smile revealed viper fangs, its eyes had slitted pupils, and from the neat waist down, the body turned into a python that constricted Saltonstall's bronze legs and granite pedestal, then trailed off into the grass. It wasn't a novel concept, but the execution showed conviction. In some remote country of his soul, the boy knew monsters existed.

At his age, Redemption's demons had been the trite ones of woodcuts, easily vanquished by God's Word. Well, Redemption had learned better, and he'd teach the boy better, too, though with mercy, so he remembered nothing of the monster's clasp.

"Hey, come on," the boy said. "Don't shit me that you're really scared."

Redemption stilled the hand tremor the boy must have seen. "Not scared. Maybe jealous. This is damn good. You been to art school or what?"

"High school's all, so far."

The boy's slight breathlessness signaled that honey, too—praise—would work. "What's the 'GL' here? Your signature?"

"Stands for Garth Lynx." Who cleared his throat and confessed, "Not my real name. It's what I'm gonna go by, drawing comics."

"That's what you want to do?"

"Yeah. I got this series idea, too. Apocalypse, but not with zombies. Zombies been run into the ground."

Redemption tapped the sketch. "So, with lamiae instead?"

And with that remark, he had set the hook. Garth said, "You know what lamiae are?"

He didn't laugh—irony would have introduced an errant note into his vocal snare. "Vampires or succubi. Snaky, like yours."

"Snakes rock. I had two before I ditched my mom's place, a reticulated and an albino Burmese. Had to give them to my friend."

"Why'd you ditch your mom's?"

Garth's eyelids sank to half-mast. "Her boyfriend's a dick. He burned one of my sketchpads. Said drawing's gay, get a real job. I'm, what, mowing lawns like you? Big fucking man. He busted me for that." Garth pulled back his upper lip to display a broken incisor. "So I busted the headlights on his truck. I had to leave then, but I wanted out anyway."

The duller the man, the more he wanted to stamp out any spark of magic he encountered. Redemption might *use* this boy's spark—he *would* use it, now that it was practically in his hand— but he wouldn't destroy it. Into the balm and honey of his voice, he trickled molten iron, compulsion: "You were right to get out of that, Garth."

"Tony," not-really-Garth murmured.

"No, *Garth*, because that's the name you've picked for your work. It'll be good work. You'll do all right."

"How d'you know?"

Redemption flipped through the sketchpad. "I'm looking at these, that's how. But you're tired."

"Kind of."

"Tired right through."

Garth's eyes finished closing. Redemption reached for his

backpack. He slipped the pad inside. "You need sleep. I'll take care of you until you wake up. Then you can go wherever you need to."

"Where's that?"

"Maybe you'll dream the answer."

Garth smiled. His eyes opened, unfocused.

"Stand up."

Garth stood, and Redemption eased the backpack onto his shoulders. "Follow," he said.

On the main path through the park, they joined revelers pressing toward the parking lots. The fireworks were spent, and only the smell of gunpowder remained, a scorched phantom that would haunt Redemption and his prize all the way home.

Number Five Lich Street was a modest Gothic Revival facing Arkham's oldest cemetery. The boneyard was full of ghosts Redemption had known in the flesh, but the hubbub of celebration must have driven them underground, for not even good Pastor Brattle poked out his spectral head to murmur about lambs bound for unholy sacrifice.

Inside the house, Redemption ordered Garth to shower, put on a hospital gown, and walk to the basement. The boy obeyed magical instruction until he reached the subcellar stairs. The balk was understandable, given his sensitivity to the uncanny. She who lay below gave off no odor save the attar of rose with which Redemption tried to sweeten her dreams. Usually the attar failed, and the spiritual fetor of nightmare, exquisite and (by her) exquisitely enjoyed, thickened the subcellar air.

Words of adamantine sternness brought Garth down the last steps and onto the waiting gurney. Restraints dangled from it, but Redemption relied instead on Geldman's Powder of Lethe, a bottle of which stood on the cart beside the gurney. He poured fine white dust onto his palm and gently blew it into Garth's nostrils.

The boy's face contorted for a sneeze, then slackened again. Self-awareness flared in his eyes, then faded. His lids drooped closed. "Sleep," Redemption said, so his words would drift with Garth into the deep waters. "I'll watch out for you, no worries."

Garth sank beyond reach. Except for the slow heave of his chest, he lay motionless. For the next two months his dreams would be the kind one yearned to live in forever. Geldman guaranteed it.

Geldman had also helped devise a procedure to make one donor do the job of dozens. A rare occurrence, they'd agreed on the morality of the project, for who could argue with less hunting, no killing, even no lasting harm? Geldman's Resanguinary Tonic would accelerate donor blood production, if one could keep the donor hydrated and fed. Redemption had tried IV lines, but they needed frequent replacement and monitoring beyond his scope. Less troublesome were Geldman's "reverse leeches," larvae of the between-spaces he'd long been molding to sustain unconscious patients.

He'd lent Redemption the one that lolled in a tank on the lower shelf of the gurney. It looked like a jaundiced maggot swollen to watermelon size. Its sole feature was a ropy proboscis that stretched like rubber as Redemption pulled it from the tank and looped it around Garth's left wrist. Its tip nuzzled the boy's inner arm, then flattened into a suction cup and gripped tight. Redemption didn't see it thrust a hollow harpoon into the vein it had selected, but its slow throb told him the leech had begun to pump water and nutrients into Garth's undernourished body. It had absorbed them from the clear broth of its bath, Geldman-calculated to sustain both leech and man. With a precision Redemption couldn't approach, the leech would also administer the Lethe and Resanguinary Tonic he'd periodically mix into the bath.

Efficient. Elegant. Geldman.

Redemption next rolled Garth to an alcove curtained off from the rest of the subcellar and set a stool between alcove and gurney. Light-headed, he sank onto it. Ensorcelling Garth had drained him, and it was a month since he'd taken time to feed himself. It was unlucky Patience's reawakening coincided with Sean's arrival, but Redemption couldn't let her luxuriate in trance until fall. She'd been walking the dream realms for two years; any longer, and she'd wake in a fury of starvation, uncontrollable.

From the inner pocket of his sport coat, he withdrew an implement Garth would have admired. The handle of the ladle was merely beautiful, silver chased with dimensional efts. The shallow bowl, with half the rim ground to a razor edge, was both beautiful and practical. Redemption probed Garth's right wrist. He ran the razor edge over a shallow vein and tapped a ladleful of blood, which he set aside while he pressed the cut with his thumb and muttered a stanching spell he'd heard first when Patience was alive. In those days healers would bleed the sick for their supposed good, while she had done it for her secret sustenance. He withdrew his thumb from a scar already paling, and then he drank off his ladle.

Astonishing, how rich the least magical spark made a person's blood. He swallowed the full two ounces the ladle held but refrained from licking the bowl. The last drops he'd need for her.

Redemption reached through the alcove curtains and drew out first a padded bench and second Patience's left arm. He rested her forearm on the bench, then arranged Garth's right forearm beside it. Two velvet ribbons sufficed to bind the limbs, the tanned to the bleached, the warm to the marble cold. Patience's hand lay palm up, fingers furled, nails a steely blue. Despite the proximity of prey, not a finger twitched. Though magic might detect the dream-flicker in her brain, she remained dead to any medical test. With careful management, she would wake gradually, breaking from trance only when he permitted it. Just prenourished enough to prevent hunger-rage, she'd remain weak and docile. He would even love her again, until lamb reverted to lioness. Then? He'd love her still, but hate himself all the more for it.

As always at this point, Redemption hesitated. As always, he unfurled her fingers, poured the last of the ladle onto her palm, chafed the blood into her skin. Slowly the skin budded; slowly the buds bloomed into five fleshy tubular petals, sea anemone feelers. When they'd grown a foot long, he guided them to Garth's forearm, where they opened lamprey mouths and battened onto the boy. In seconds, the translucent ivory tentacles turned pale pink, then rosy, then a pulsing scarlet.

On one side the reverse leech, giving. On the other side Patience, taking away. In the middle Redemption, balancing gift with sacrifice.

He looked down at his watch and let the proper number of minutes pass.

After separating Patience and Garth, Redemption climbed to his attic study and looked through Garth's backpack. There wasn't much: briefs and T-shirts and socks; charcoal pencils and worn erasers; a wallet guarding a driver's license, seven dollars, and one photograph of a girl in a prom dress. The girl appeared again in Garth's sketchpad, naked but with crossed legs and arms that rendered her touchingly modest. The caption named her "Stace," and though a frequent subject, she never appeared as one of the lamiae that dominated Garth's bestiary.

Redemption repacked all but the sketchbook. It wasn't likely that the authorities would trace Garth to this house or, indeed, that anyone had reported him missing, but he put the pack into a cubbyhole behind a bookcase. Garth's other clothes he'd already fed to the furnace. He'd supply the boy with a new wardrobe when he woke him.

The most telling evidence, the sketchbook, he'd hide later. For now, he flipped to the naked Stace and hovered his fingertips above the page. The energy lingering in charcoal and paper was faint. Even when Kate Wyndham had been as unschooled as Garth, her magic was much stronger. He looked at the painting above his desk. Though he'd hung it within hand's reach, he didn't need to touch the canvas to feel its energy—that was like sunlight arrowing through breeze-stirred leaves, only not intermittently, irregularly, but with the steadiness of a healthy pulse, warmth and then warmth and then warmth again. Sunlight itself was the subject of the piece: sunlight on sea and sand and Sean—Kate's son, four or five, who crouched at the tide line with dunes behind him. In Kate's pigments and brushstrokes, everything lived more vividly than in life, and Sean's chubby hands were miracles of arrested transience as they pressed shells into his sand castle and fortified its ramparts with the spiny tails of horseshoe crabs.

While Redemption still gazed at painted Sean, Raphael returned from his surveillance of the original. The aether-newt melted through the skylight and corkscrewed to his shoulder. He put his ear to its feathery antennae. *Is the boy ready to come, nothing's gone wrong?*

His things in the car. His things, many things, and his father's gone away.

Go back and let him see you, then. Let him know I'm still watching.

Raphael departed as it had come. Soon Sean would be in Arkham for two full months, and every day, whatever Patience's situation, Redemption would see him. And perhaps, one way or another, they would meet. Finally, knowingly.

Face-to-face.

1

Sean and Eddy had hoisted their kayaks onto the roof of the Civic. They'd stuffed suitcases into the trunk, strapped bikes to the trunk rack, crammed the backseat with paddles and life vests, bike helmets and beach umbrellas. Now Eddy had gone home to pack books. She'd promised to limit herself to a single backpack, but even that was like shipping Coke to the Coke factory. She'd be working in the Miskatonic University Library, plus the Arkwright House had its own library, plus Horrocke's Bookstore was five minutes from campus. Good thing the Civic could handle her fear of getting stranded on a bookless desert island between Providence and Arkham—Dad had made sure the car was in top shape before he handed Sean the keys.

Sean had expected to drive the Civic more after Dad got his new Accord, but for Dad to give it to him? That was the (forest green) cherry on top of a whole summer studying magic, another gift he hadn't dared take for granted, even with Helen Arkwright and Professor Marvell arguing for it. The Servitor incident was a year behind them. Things had returned to normal, pretty much.

So why would Dad risk Sean plunging them in another magical shit-storm?

Reason One: Dad would be in England all summer on a big restoration job, while Aunt Cel and Uncle Gus would be in Italy from mid-July on. Better Sean go to Arkham than poke around home alone. And Reason Two: Whether Sean pursued magic or not, the shit-storm that was Redemption Orne still rumbled over Sean's head.

At Marvell's request, an Order magician had come to Rhode Island to determine whether Orne still watched Sean. Right off, Afua Benetutti had felt brushes of too-sentient air, fluctuations in ambient energy, and with a puff of the dust that gloved her brown hands in sparkling silver, she'd revealed an invisible spy: a sinuous wisp of legs and feelers that cavorted around Sean, flicking its longest tail as if to chuck them an ethereal bird. Though the aether-newt had shaken off the dust and vanished from sight, Benetutti had continued to sense its energetic signature. Dad had exploded: Orne promised he'd leave Sean alone! Zap the thing! But Benetutti had said dispelling the newt would be wasted effort; Orne could simply resummon it. Better to ward the places where Sean spent the most time, his own house and his aunt's. The newt couldn't pass through the wards, so inside their perimeter, Sean would be safe from Orne's observation.

Not the scorched-aether solution Dad had wanted, but he let Benetutti weave the defensive webs. Every month a paramagician— someone who couldn't do spells himself but who could energize spells already in place—needed to reinforce the wards. Marvell and Helen had done the job. They'd have come anyway, because their other job was counseling Sean and Dad and Eddy, even Gus and Celeste, through their transitions from blissfully ignorant to people who could face the reality of magic without going nuts.

Far as Sean could tell, Gus and Celeste had needed the least counseling, Dad the most. Eddy, hard to say. She liked hanging with Helen—they talked about everything, not just the scary truth of the worlds. Obviously Helen thought Eddy was cool, or she wouldn't have offered her a summer internship at the MU Library. But pre-Servitor, Eddy had never had trouble sleeping. Now, when Sean was staying at Cel and Gus's, he'd look next door and see her "office" lights burning long after midnight. A couple times the blinds had been up, and he'd seen Eddy tilted back in her desk chair, clutching a book like a shield.

Sean dropped his tennis racquet through the Civic's rear window, afraid if he opened the door, he'd unleash a junk avalanche. Eddy had better stick to the one-backpack deal, but he wouldn't grouse if she didn't. He got why she'd want to bring comfort books to Arkham; in fact, he'd stuck comfort books of his own under the driver's seat. One was his duct-taped *Lord of the Rings*. The other was Marvell's *Infinity Unimaginable*—the matter-of-fact way it treated magic had helped him chill whenever he started thinking too much about the Servitor or, worse, the god who'd sent it.

Sean backed the Civic out of the driveway. After that he had nothing to do but sit on the porch steps until it was time to drive Dad to the airport. Maybe he'd stowed *Infinity* too soon, because he lapsed into thinking about how, Servitor-possessed and mentally delivered to its creator, he'd come that close to teaming up with Nyarlathotep, the Master of Magic himself. If Dad hadn't called him back. If Helen hadn't broken the Servitor's psychic grip by ramming a pitchfork, and herself, into its gut. Even now Sean could close his eyes and see the poison-green sky with its three black suns, the obsidian shore lapped by a protoplasmic ocean of shoggoths, the crystal-shard palace of a pseudo-Pharaoh who smiled because he understood the freaky hollowness inside a speck like Sean, a speck that longed to suck in the universe, to own the magic. He couldn't do that unless, to earn the Outer Gods' favor, he became their servant—

Servant or *slave*, like Orne. For everything Nyarlathotep promised, he wanted everything in return.

Everything was too big. Better to break magic down into speck-
sized nibbles Sean could handle without divine intervention.
Since dismissing the Servitor, he hadn't done any magic. He'd
been afraid to try, and besides, *Infinity*'s descriptions of spell-
casting didn't amount to much more than Obi-Wan telling Luke
to use the Force. Marvell had explained that since *Infinity* was
written for the general public, its vagueness was a deliberate precaution. Besides, Sean shouldn't attempt further magic until he'd
been properly trained. In Arkham, Marvell would handle theory,
and the Order would assign Sean a magician mentor to handle
practice.

This time tomorrow, Sean would know his mentor's name.
Maybe it would be Geldman—Helen had mentioned he sometimes took Order students. Geldman would be amazing, but
Sean would be happy with any legit magician other than Orne.
And maybe he wouldn't have to wait until tomorrow, because Dad
came onto the porch with his cell phone ringing, and when he
dropped his suitcases to answer it, he said, "Oh, hello, Helen."

Good old Helen. She must've gotten the advance scoop on
Sean's mentor and was calling with the news. He jumped up and
walked over to Dad, to be ready to take the phone. But Dad didn't
offer it. In fact, he turned away, frowning. "Yes, my flight's not
for a couple hours, I can talk."

Talk about what? "Hey, Dad."

Dad shook his head, phone to ear.

"Let me say hi to her."

Dad walked into the house and shut himself in his study.

It was either squash his ear to the study door or wait for bad
news in the comfort of a porch rocker, and, yeah, Helen's news
had to be bad to drive Dad into seclusion. Sean opted for the
rocker and speculation. His summer in Arkham was off because

no Order magician would mentor him, and that was because the Servitor had been a fluke—Sean wasn't magician material, after all. Or else he was, but in so hazardous a form that the black helicopters were coming to take him to Area 52, Magical Miscreants.

Half an hour later, the helicopters hadn't arrived. Dad had left the study, though, and gone to the carriage house. Following, Sean watched lights come on in Mom's old studio while Dad's stayed dark. Not an encouraging sign. He dithered in the garden for a few minutes, then sucked it up and finished the pursuit.

Dad stood under the window he'd made while Mom was sick, eyes fixed on the Madonna who sat painting in a walled garden. Sean climbed the stairs as if he were sneaking into church after the funeral had started, but Dad heard him, and he said, "I was talking to Helen."

"I know. I was there when she called, remember?"

Dad sat on a worktable and nodded at the stretch of unoccupied tabletop beside him. His hair was a pawed-through mess, and the jaw muscle that twitched when he was pissed off looked like it was jumping rope. Sean stayed put at the top of the stairs. "Something's wrong about Arkham, right?"

"No, if you mean something to keep you from going. Helen's still expecting you and Eddy tomorrow."

"So everything's okay."

Dad looked him in the eye. "As long as you can study magic, all's right with the world?"

"I didn't say that!"

"But that's how you feel?"

"No, because there's still wars and climate change."

"I'm glad you take a global view."

"What did Helen say, Dad?"

The jaw muscle got tired of jumping. In fact, Dad half smiled. "Sean, you haven't done anything wrong, and nobody's mad at you."

That was a first.

"What's come up, it's something Helen thought I should know before I went to England, but we agreed she and Professor Marvell should be the ones to tell you about it."

"Why them?"

"Well, because magic's about the same to me as quantum mechanics. I know it exists, but hell if I can explain it. Helen, Marvell, they'll explain things the right way."

"So, whatever made you come up here, it's about magic in general?"

Dad heaved off the tabletop. "Why do I come up here sometimes, Sean?"

"To hang with Mom, when you're worried."

"And you do the same thing, except you can actually feel the part of her that's still around. I'm glad we know that's real now."

He meant the buzz of her energy, in the cabinets. Sean looked up at the Madonna. In the halo that circled not her head but the tip of her paintbrush, Dad had tried to paint Mom's magic onto the glass, and he'd made the window years before learning magic was real. "I always knew she was different. You did, too, Dad."

"Yeah, I did." Dad walked over and gripped his shoulder. "Look, Sean, you're all right. That's all you need to know before Helen and Marvell explain the rest." He stood. "I've got some last things to pack. Ready for the airport run?"

"Whenever you are."

"Okay. Hit the lights when you're done here."

And Dad knew what it would take for Sean to be done, which was why he ran downstairs and closed the carriage house door with thump enough to signal his exit. It was a shy and private thing to approach the cabinets where Mom's unfinished canvases lived. *Lived* was the right word, too, because without opening the cabinet doors, just by resting fingertips on the cheerfully paint-freckled wood, Sean felt the low hum of magic. As magic had vibrated in her skin and breath, not pulse, not respiration, steadier than either, so it hummed in all her paintings, *her*, like no other sensation in the world. Yet the hum was strongest in the work she'd had to abandon, as if the residual magic knew there was more for it to do—it had to persist until she came back and directed it. No other artist, even Dad, could reproduce her brush-strokes or her sense of color and light. No other magician, even Sean, could match her hum—according to *Infinity*, each magician's energy was genetic code unique, an absolute signature.

Sean sagged forward until his forehead pressed a door and absorbed its vibration. These days he rarely did more—he certainly didn't throw the cabinet doors wide, as he'd done at age six or seven, weirdly unafraid, actually hoping to catch her ghost curled up in the linseed-scented dark.

It wasn't that now, at seventeen, he was afraid to open the doors. He was cautious, that was all, because what if her energy were to burst out, to disperse, the last of her gone right when he was about to study magic? At the end of summer, he wanted to come back and demonstrate the legacy she'd given him. However unconscious her witness might be, he wanted it.

Dad yelled from the garden, time to go.

Going up to the studio hadn't cured Dad's unease over Helen's call. Preflight, he'd tried to transmute it into standard Dad warnings, don't drive like a nutcase, don't spend your whole summer allowance the first week, but a deeper anxiety had kept his jaw muscle hopping. Plus he'd told Sean to call England anytime, not just when it was normal-human hours over there. After Dad's plane had cruised, Sean considered calling Helen and teasing out the magical secret. He'd held off until he drove to Cel and Gus's for the night, and then he'd had to wedge Eddy's books—a backpack *and* three bags full—into the Civic, and then Eddy's parents had taken them out to dinner. By the time they got back, it was too late to bug Helen.

Eddy doused her lights by eleven thirty. They stayed doused—Sean knew because he was too wired to sleep. The dark windows next door gave him a postapocalyptic chill: Sean Wyndham, last human on earth. Around one, he wandered down to the kitchen. Warm milk was supposed to be a natural sedative, but to avoid gagging, Sean took his cold, flopped on the living room couch. No dice. The mantel clock chimed two, and he remained wide awake, thinking of Mom's energy in the cabinets, and how she hadn't even known she had magic, it had just poured out of her, while he didn't know his mentor yet, and now there was this other thing Dad wouldn't tell him. Also, why didn't brains come with an OFF switch?

He stared into his empty glass. Lattes were mostly warm milk, right? Maybe it wouldn't kill him. But when he sat up, pursuing sleep became irrelevant. Something moved outside the living room windows. Flash back a year, to his own house and to Sean glimpsing enough of the Servitor to make him run, animal-intent on escape. He almost ran now, but before his shock-frozen legs could thaw, he realized this creature was no Servitor. For one thing, it was much smaller. For another, no one's blood had solidified it into flesh—it was only a hint of a being, an elongated wisp that floated from window to window, then took a lazy U-turn and shimmied back as if swimming through air.

It was the spy Benetutti's dust had revealed, an aether-newt. It wouldn't eat him. It couldn't even get into the house, thanks to her wards. Sean set down his glass, then sidestepped slowly into the window bay. The *Necronomicon* said that aether-newts rendered visible appeared to have glass or soap bubble skin. This one was more glassy, but with swift chromatic slicks that washed over it like the rainbows on bubbles.

As he reached the windows, the newt executed a tight figure eight, passing through itself at the juncture of the two loops to settle on the screen inches from Sean's nose. No, not on the *screen*. The suction cups at the end of its stumpy caterpillar legs rested on an invisible surface farther out, the ward-barrier. In spite of its many-jointed skeleton, glass within glass, the newt's body was also more caterpillar-plump than newt-sleek. Caterpillars didn't have obvious necks, though. The newt had one it could stretch longer or corkscrew shorter; on it bobbled an egg-shaped head without mouth or nostrils, just two fan-shaped appendages like fleshy feathers. Ears? Organs of an obscurer sense? The eyes were more obvious: two bulging hemispheres with diamond pupils, and maybe those glossy winking spheroids on its sides and underbelly were eyes, too. The back sported more fleshy fans, the butt five tails, long one in the middle. The shorter tails had tiny waving hairs—what had they called those in Bio Lab? *Cilia.* The long tail ended in a wicked barb. If the newt weren't ethereal, it could put a person's eyes out with that.

What it did right now was flick the barbed tail at Sean. Again, like it was chucking him the bird.

He chucked it one back.

Impressed? Probably not—it kept flicking.

Sean pushed up the screen and leaned out past the ward-barrier—as always, he felt its mild sting as he broke through. "How come I can see you now?" he demanded.

The newt retreated a couple feet. Flick.

"Your boss Orne must want me to see you, right?"

Flick.

"Like, you must've heard me and Eddy outside the wards, how we're going to study with the Order. So he knows I don't need him to study magic."

Double flick, plus a wave of the feathery head fans.

Yes? No? "Not that I care if he knows. It'll be the last thing he finds out, because I bet the Order has kick-ass wards you'll never get through. So yeah. He can fuck off. All right?"

The flicks stopped.

"All right?"

The newt retreated. Shimmying from head to tail-tip barb, it began to fade.

Sean watched until it was gone, or at least invisible again. He was breathing too fast, but it was because he was as pissed off as Dad had been when they first glimpsed the newt. Orne had promised to leave Sean alone, but instead he'd been spying, and now he was rubbing the spy in Sean's face.

He ducked inside, pulled down the screen, slumped onto the arm of Gus's favorite chair. His hand brushed his backpack, ready to go in the morning. In it was his wallet, and in his wallet was a much-folded printout, Orne's last e-mail. Sean didn't need to get it out. The text was stuck as deep in his head as the first poem he'd memorized for school. *Sean, I can't apologize enough for what's happened.* Got that right. *I meant you and yours no harm.* Bullshit. *In time we'll meet face-to-face, and you'll know me better.* That was so not happening, and time Orne knew it.

He carried his pack to the back porch. Night was all he could see beyond the screens, but the newt had to be out there. He fished Orne's message from his wallet, unfolded it, and pressed it to a screen, so the newt could take a good look. Then he tore the thing in two, four, eight, easy enough along the worn creases. Cel kept candles on the porch table, protected from wind inside jars. He thumbnail-struck a match, lit the largest candle, and fed its flame the scraps of e-mail. Brief stink of paper mixed with vanilla, then there was just the vanilla, and Orne was officially gone. Maybe Sean was crazy to give orders to the night, but he knew for sure now that it had ears, or close enough. "Tell your boss what I did," he said.

And maybe burnt paper and vanilla were better sedatives than milk, because when he flopped again on the couch, his eyelids finally slid closed and stayed that way.

2

Next morning, his near-sleepless butt dragging, Sean handed Eddy the Civic keys and reclined in the shotgun seat, armed with a quadruple-shot latte. By the time they hit Route 128, the caffeine had revived him enough to tell her about the aether-newt. "You think Orne showed it to you on purpose?" she said.

"Hell yeah, to prove he's still stalking me."

Without taking her eyes off the road, Eddy shrugged.

"Plus it kept flipping me the tail," Sean added.

"Maybe that's how it talks. One flick 'no,' two flicks 'yes.'"

"Maybe, but how am I supposed to know the code?"

"Experiment. Ask, 'Are you an aether-newt?' and see if it flicks once or twice." She spared him a microsecond's glance. "I'm not sure you should've told Orne off."

"He deserved it. How'd you like an aether-newt hanging around all the time?"

"I wouldn't get naked anywhere without wards, that's all."

Sean thanked her for putting that idea into his head, a few months too late. "Anyhow, so what if I told Orne to fuck off? He's been a dick for more than three hundred years. He must've heard it before now."

"Probably." Eddy pulled around a refrigerator truck emblazoned with the neon yellow message SHOP SAL'S DOCK-FRESH SEAFOOD. They had to be getting close to Gloucester. "But how many people have lived to brag about it?"

"I wasn't bragging. I was just telling you what I did."

Eddy shut up and concentrated on passing other trucks. It looked like time for a subject change. "I still can't believe Dad's letting me do this. And your mom and dad, letting you."

"Really."

"And Greg. Wasn't he sorry you'd be gone all summer?"

"You know how many times I dated Greg?"

"No."

"Twice."

"Well, Joaquin, then."

"Way old news. I haven't even texted him since prom. And what's with the sudden interest in my love life?"

"It's not sudden."

"It's not?"

Conversationwise, he should have stuck with the aether-newt. "I mean, I couldn't help noticing you went out a lot more this year. I was thinking you might go normal on me."

"What's that even mean? Wait—there's our exit."

While Eddy negotiated the ramp to the Gloucester bypass, then the sub-exit to the coastal highway, Sean tried to figure out for himself what he was getting at. His bad, running off at the mouth when he should have been snoring. "You know, *normal*. Like, not interested in geek stuff and magic."

Eddy frowned at the innocent car in front of them, which meant she was really frowning at Sean. To give her space, he leaned out his window and caught the first salt breeze of their trip. Weird how much today's drive was like their first to Arkham, down to the cloud-free sky and blue-green ocean lapping the seawall to their right. What if they really could go back a year, go back and change one thing? They could skip going to Horrocke's Bookstore, where Orne's advertisement for an apprentice had ambushed Sean. Maybe that would have discouraged Orne. Maybe he would have tried to lure someone else into magic—

"Sean."

A fleet of cormorants paddled and dived among the mild waves. That meant there was a run of fish along the shore.

"Sean."

He let the shoulder harness pull him back into his seat.

"I'm a born geek," Eddy said. "That's not going to change even if I do go all twu lub over someone."

"Yeah, I guess you can't change your genes."

"Plus, how could I *not* be interested in magic? Like, I'm going to see something like the Servitor and go, 'Oh, that was weird, now let's forget about it'?"

Sean supposed Eddy saved her major angsting for Helen, like he saved his for Marvell, but he knew the Servitor had shaken her to the ground. Scary to think that the coolest person he knew was in the same boat as him. "No. You can't forget. Unless someone hits you over the head."

"Amnesia plots suck. Besides, we *shouldn't* forget. I mean, a Servitor, a Geldman's Pharmacy, you being a magician. Everything's different. The whole universe, how it runs."

What she was talking about, Marvell called a "paradigm shift": a radical mental makeover that could inspire people to jump off bridges or drive cars into seawalls. Eddy would never crash a car, though. She'd be afraid of surviving and getting a ticket.

And sure enough, as the cliffs between Gloucester and Kingsport forced the road into climbing curves, she didn't let the Civic swerve an inch from its lane. "Some people would go into denial about magic, though," Sean said.

She snorted. "That's hard where 'magic' equals a monster almost eating you."

"Well, kind of."

"And if you were in denial about magic, I guess you wouldn't be going to Arkham to study it."

"And you wouldn't be going to work in the Archives. Whatever you tell your mom and dad about deciding whether to major in Library Science."

"I don't tell them that."

"But you said—"

"That was my story before Helen came last week. We decided I better tell them the truth."

"You told them about the *Servitor*?"

Eddy's hands had slipped from the three and nine o'clock positions on the steering wheel. She quickly corrected the Driver's Ed infraction. "We told them everything. Professor Marvell even joined in over Skype. Next day they went to Arkham to meet Dr. Benetutti."

"She did magic for them? They must have freaked."

"Not as much as I thought they would. And Mom's all into the link between magic and math, which is one of Dr. Benetutti's things."

"And they're still letting you go."

Eddy nodded at the cresting road. "They know I've got to learn to deal with this."

"Man, Eddy, you *did* deal with it. Better than me."

"You got rid of the Servitor. You didn't go over to Nyarlathotep."

"Barely."

"And you're not too scared to study with the Order."

"I'd be more scared not to."

"Me, too, exactly," Eddy said. "So shut up about me going normal on you."

"Mouth officially shut. You're deeply abnormal."

Eddy pulled a huge fake smile, as if she were accepting a third-runner-up trophy. She accelerated over the crest, and summer dropped into place below them: antique Kingsport climbing the leafy westward hills, sailboats plying the harbor and ducking under the long bridge that spanned its mouth. Across the bridge, the coastal highway leaped up the cliffs between Kingsport and Arkham. Perched on the tallest was the cottage Lovecraft had called the Strange High House; below it, on Orange Point, was the Witches' Burial Ground and a parking lot that glinted with excursion buses.

Beyond the lot was an overgrown path that led to Patience Orne's grave. Last year he and Eddy had laughed about how crazy people used to be, thinking Patience was such a badass witch that she had to be buried apart from the others. They didn't know anything yet about her husband, Redemption, but maybe his aether-newt had already been hovering around them, listening to their snark.

Sean hoped not, but maybe they'd better not stop at the Witches' Burial Ground to use the restrooms, just go straight on to the Arkwright House, where, Helen claimed, the wards could bar a lot more than peeping newts.

＜＝

The Arkwright House was on the corner of West and College Streets, facing the Miskatonic University Green. It stood on a walled terrace six feet above the sidewalk, a mansion of reddish brown stone three floors and an attic high. Eddy's Arkham guidebook said it exemplified the Italianate style, what with its hipped roof and square cupola, its bracketed eaves and pedimented windows. Sean wasn't sure which thingies were brackets and which pediments, but anyone could see the place was crazy historical, even if they missed the plaque on the gate that read:

THE ENDECOTT C. ARKWRIGHT HOUSE
ARCHITECT: THOMAS TEFFT
COMPLETED 1854

At over 150 years old, in a town famous for hauntings, the place had to have collected a ghost or two. Sean hadn't noticed any when he had helped Dad take out the library windows last year, but that had been in broad daylight. Come nightfall, old Endecott might show up. Maybe Mrs. Endecott, dragging a gauzy train and a ghost-pug. Or did magical wards repel ghosts, too? If so, the Arkwright House would be spirit-free; an invisible barrier started a foot from the terrace walls, and an experimental probing had given Sean a hair-raising tingle on the verge of painful.

Inside the house, an unseen hand twitched lace curtains from a window. No ghost: Helen Arkwright emerged, and with her shorts and flip-flops, she was about as far as you could get from a Victorian specter. She ran down the steps and through the gate to join them. "You guys made good time!"

"Pretty amazing, with Eddy driving," Sean said

Eddy was too busy hugging Helen to protest, but afterwards she punished him: "I had to drive. Sean was hungover."

"Bull!"

Helen hugged Sean. If she was sniffing for alcohol, he couldn't tell. "I vote bull, too," she said.

Eddy clarified: "I meant from no sleep because he was talking to aether-newts all night."

Would it have killed Eddy not to mention the sighting out on the sidewalk, where any lurking invisible familiar might hear? Helen must have read Sean's mind, because she gestured them inside the gate and thus through the ward-barrier before saying, "Aether-*newts*?"

"Not plural," Sean said. "Just the one we think is Orne's. It let me see it last night."

"Away from your house?"

"It was outside, I was in."

"Did it communicate anything?"

"Flicked its tail, whatever that means. Then I kind of yelled at it, and it went invisible again."

Eddy raised her eyebrows.

Helen asked no more. "We'll talk about it later. Let's have lunch first."

Because the Arkwright House had been built way before it was fashionable for rich people to cook, the kitchen was in the basement. Luckily the basement was mostly above ground level, so Helen had been able to install a whole wall of windows to brighten up the long room. They ate chicken salad at a breakfast bar overlooking the back garden, which for now grew only Dumpsters and stacks of plywood—the carriage house was being remodeled to provide offices for the Order.

Lunch done, Helen led them through the first floor. Last summer it had featured stepladders and plaster dust and the frayed guts of knob-and-tube wiring. Now the marble floors, walnut woodwork, and plaster moldings looked like new. Eddy was impressed by the grandeur of the parlors and dining room, but when they walked into the library that took up the rear third of the floor, she went into near shock. At the east end were tall windows and a conference table with chairs as ornate as thrones. At the west end was a fireplace fronted by a leather couch and armchairs. Directly opposite the doors was a dais like an oversized pulpit or the upper deck of a ship. Computer stations ringed it, but on top was a massive antique desk, and above the desk were the stained glass windows Dad had restored: *The Founding of Arkham*.

Every other inch of wall space, from floor to fifteen-foot

ceilings, featured bookcases, and every inch of every shelf was crammed with books.

Eddy came out of her bug-eyed catatonia and walked around the room, trailing her fingers across the book spines. "God, Helen. This is in your *house*."

Someone who didn't know Eddy might have mistaken her awe for horror, as if she'd opened a closet, and it had spilled out a horde of rats. Helen knew her well enough to say, "It's great, isn't it? None of my doing, except for the new workstations. Endecott Arkwright was the first collector. That's his desk on the dais. My grandfather Henry and uncle John took over on the scholarly side. Theo Marvell says they built the biggest private collection of arcane literature in the country. The oldest and rarest books are in the Archives now, but still impressive."

While she joined Eddy among the tomes, Sean climbed the dais to try out Endecott's desk. The top was an acre of mahogany, with an inlaid monogram—*ECA*—wreathed in laurel leaves. It was more showy than useful, since once he'd sunk into the cushy desk chair, he'd have to stand to reach anything. He spun the chair toward the stained glass triptych and tilted back to look at it. Dad's "after" photos hadn't done *The Founding of Arkham* justice, but photos never did. You needed to see a window on-site, struck to life by the sunlight passing through it. He kept tilting until the chair back rested on the edge of the desk. The center window, twice as wide as the side ones, showed the future Arkham Harbor, with two *Mayflowery* ships on the water and Puritans on the foreground hill: a governor or mayor (he had fancier clothes than the rest), a minister on his knees praying, and soldiers with breastplates and helmets and muskets. The soldiers were the only ones who noticed the Indians approaching from the right window. No problem, they came in peace. The foremost Indian had his hand up, fingers practically in the Vulcan V-salute, and the other Indians toted a deer carcass and strings of fish.

Nobody in the center or right windows looked toward the dense forest in the left one. Sean didn't either until disgust at his cowardice made him shift his gaze. The figure under the eaves of the wood had onyx skin and all-amber eyes. Add its Pharaoh getup, and it was totally out of place in a seventeenth-century scene on the planet Earth. And yet could Nyarlathotep ever really be out of place? Master of Magic, Soul and Messenger of the Outer Gods, wearer of a million skins—maybe a million skins simultaneously! He could be anywhere, at any time, doing business for his cosmic bosses and looking for dumb magicians to enslave. Or dumb *potential* magicians, like Sean.

Dad had restored the Dark Pharaoh down to the enigmatic faintness of his smile, but after all, this Nyarlathotep was harmless glass, not a true avatar of the god. Sean could look away, no problem, and he did, lifting his eyes to the crow-familiar Nyarlathotep tossed skyward. Pre-Dad, it had been a winged black blob. Now Sean could see every feather, every claw, the whiskers around its beak, the inky buttons of its eyes; though a minor detail, the crow dominated the *Founding* by sucking in sun until the excess brilliance seeped out its edges like one of the subliminal haloes in Mom's paintings.

Mom's paintings? And did it—?

To get a closer look, Sean got up and stood below the left window. The wall beneath was still under his palm. So was its wooden frame and the bit of glass he could reach, just the wildflower-studded turf of the foreground. To touch the crow and check for a Mom-like hum to match that halo, he'd need a ladder.

In addition to the ladders that slid along bookshelves on steel rails, the library had stepladders that looked tall enough to reach the crow. But when Sean turned back to the windows, the crow had already lost its halo. It must have been the effect of a fleeting angle of sunlight, nothing magical after all, optical illusion, wishful thinking—

"Sean?" Helen said. She and Eddy stood at the library doors. "We're going upstairs."

"Coming." After a last glance at the crow (no sneaky return of the halo), he jumped the three steps off the dais. It was time for real concerns, like whether Helen would stick him in a bedroom so museum-like, he'd be afraid to touch anything.

3

Helen's bedroom was on the second floor, at the front of the house. She'd given Eddy the guest room opposite, which had a canopy bed and cushioned window seat and million-drawered writing desk straight out of *Jane Eyre,* or so Eddy gushed. Sean's room was another flight up. "Originally the whole third floor was a ballroom," Helen said. "Since the Order doesn't host a lot of dances, we've remodeled it for students—four beds, two baths, and the common room."

Sean had his pick of the bedrooms, and he picked the left front, which had furniture way less *Masterpiece Theatre* than Eddy's: simple oak bed, simple oak desk, simple oak wardrobe, everything he could want except a TV. He hadn't seen any TVs downstairs either. Maybe the Order wanted to make the house distraction-free.

That fear evaporated when they entered the common room. Like the library, it was at the back of the house, but the new bathrooms in the east and west corners made it smaller, and the furniture was comfortably modern: braided rugs, vinyl couch and recliners, game table, and a kitchenette with fridge and micro-wave. Over the gas fireplace hung a mantel-wide flat-screen TV.

Helen pointed out the empty bookshelves on either side of the fireplace, then winked at Sean and said, "Eddy, I put those in es-pecially for you."

"I didn't bring *that* many."

Instant pants-on-fire rating. "No," Sean said. "It'll just take a week to haul them all up."

"We'll get your stuff in a minute," Helen said. "First I've got a quick heads-up for you two."

Eddy parked on the couch, Sean on a recliner, while Helen stepped back into the hall and cocked her head as if listening. What with the Order's wards, she couldn't be checking for Orne's newt. Could there be human spies? "Hey, Helen. Something wrong?"

Helen closed the door. She took the other recliner but kept her feet on the ground. "No. It's just I didn't know about this myself until last night. Not for sure, or I'd have mentioned it to your father, Sean, when I phoned yesterday."

The excitement of arriving had shoved the mystery of the Helen-to-Dad call to the back of Sean's mind. He opened his mouth to ask for the solution, closed it as Helen continued: "We're going to have another student this summer. He came this morning."

"Another magician student?" Eddy said.

"Yes. He's gone out with Theo, but he'll be back for dinner."

Eddy scooted down the couch toward Helen. "Dish. How old is he? Where's he from? Are you afraid we're going to hate him or something?"

Helen gave a nervous laugh. "Eighteen. New York. And why should I worry you'd hate another student?"

"Because you're making such a big deal of warning us about him?"

"Direct hit," Sean said.

And Helen laughed like her usual self. "No fair double-teaming me, and really, that's the point. You guys *are* a team, you've been friends so long. That could make a new person feel like an outsider, and I don't want that to happen to Daniel."

"That's the new guy's name?" Eddy said.

"Yes, Daniel Glass."

"So we shouldn't be like, 'We're supertight, but who are *you*, dude?'"

"I know you wouldn't do that deliberately."

"He might just take it that way?"

To rescue Helen from Eddy's rapid-fire interrogation, Sean jumped in. "What's his deal, Daniel?"

"Well, Theo says he's been isolated the last few years. Home-schooled, no real social life. He was badly hurt in a car accident, and he's been through a lot of reconstructive surgery."

So did he look like the Elephant Man? Sean searched for a more delicate way to ask. "So he's a little funky looking?"

Helen shook her head. "All I noticed were a few scars on his hands. He did have neck surgery lately, so he's wearing a brace. Otherwise, he looks ready to get back out into the world. You and Eddy could help him."

Helping this Daniel guy could be either a big assignment or no big deal. No telling which until they met him. Eddy said, "We'll be cool, Helen. And I'll have your back if the guys act up."

"My assistant dorm monitor? You're on."

"So should we drive around back to unload?"

"Yes, to the garage."

Eddy, who still had the Civic keys, bolted for the stairs. It gave Sean a perfect opportunity to address that mystery phone call, so he stayed put and cleared his throat. Always quick on the uptake, Helen stayed put, too. "Something else, Sean?"

He got right to it. "Dad acted kind of weird after you called him yesterday."

Helen's smile went out like a blown bulb. "I'm sorry he was upset."

"Yeah, I thought I must have screwed up somehow, so forget about my internship. But he said I was in the clear, and you'd explain the situation because it was magical and he didn't really get it."

"I see." The corners of Helen's lips twitched.

"So?"

"So, tomorrow Theo and I are going to meet with you and Daniel individually. We'll talk about your study plans, any concerns. Any situations. For now all I can say is you're part of our program for as long as you want to be."

If he had to wait, he might as well be cool about it. "Okay, great. You'll tell me about it tomorrow. And you'll tell me about my mentor, too? Like, is it going to be Mr. Geldman?"

Helen stood up. "Tomorrow, Sean."

"I bet it is."

"You're not teasing anything out of me."

Nope, because she was out of the common room before the Civic's horn blatted down by the garage. Geldman, yeah. Helen had blinked, so it would probably be him, which cheered Sean up for the unpacking ahead.

It took an hour to stow the bikes and kayaks and haul their suitcases to their rooms. Then Eddy had to hang up half her clothes, refold the other half, and arrange everything in this monster armoire Sean hadn't noticed before. Seriously, if he had that in his room, it would keep him awake expecting its mirrored doors to creak open and Nosferatu to float out, all rat teeth and raptor claws. When he shared this perception with Eddy, she said, "How about you go unpack your own clothes?"

"Done. Let's take a walk."

"I've got to take my books upstairs."

"They're *books,* Eddy—they're not going to get wrinkled or anything. Come on. Just across the green and back."

"Or to Geldman's?"

"It might not be open. Not if you rush up to it."

"Even if it's closed, I want to see it."

They walked across the MU green, over the Garrison Street Bridge with its view of Witch Island, and up Gedney Street. The old barbershop and the ratty newsstand and the Portuguese grocery were the same as the first time Sean had passed them. Nothing like that first time was Geldman's Pharmacy: it was in closed mode, bricks and trim corroded, canvas awning like shredded skin on a rusted skeleton, windows boarded over or caked with grime. They rubbed themselves spy-holes and peered in at the hanging urns, empty except for spiderwebs; at bottles scattered in dust as thick as snow; at a doctor's scale lying on its back, round face shattered.

Across the street at Tumblebee's Café, Eddy put a happy latte-swilling face on her disappointment. Maybe that earned her a reward. On their way back down Gedney, they turned together and saw Geldman on the sidewalk, same air of unaging middle age, same unruly aureole of young Einstein hair around his placidly amused face, same spotless lab coat. He was painting fresh grime over their spy-holes, and he saluted them with his brush. A whisper tickled Sean's inner ear: *Come another time, with the young lady. Welcome back to Arkham, Sean.*

Tightness left his chest. It would have majorly sucked if Geldman's had been closed for good.

At the Arkwright House, they found a note from Helen. She'd be at MU until seven, and then they could all go out for pizza. Eddy went up to deal with her books. Sean went to check on the carriage house reconstruction. They'd gutted the place and were starting on interior framing—Joe-Jack would have been impressed by the probable cost of the job. Helen said the Order was paying for it. Where'd it get the deep pockets, just private donations and secret government funding, or did it have a third revenue stream? Part of the foundation was so new, it was still damp: steel-reinforced concrete three feet thick, like the walls of a vault meant to house all the treasure the Order had unearthed and all the artifacts it had recovered from cultists, or worse.

Eddy had to come see the vault. Lucky for Sean, his run up to the third floor left him too breathless to yell something stupid before he realized Eddy's wasn't the only voice coming from the common room. The other was a guy's voice, and then a guy's laugh, followed by Eddy's "No, you've got to read it."

Sean waited until he'd stopped panting to walk to the common room door.

Eddy knelt at one of the fireside bookcases, surrounded by her sacks of books and her backpack of books, and the books she'd already stacked on the floor. The guy at the other case had one backpack still crammed full and another lying eviscerated on an ottoman. He wore a foam collar-brace-whatever around his neck, and so he had to be Daniel Glass.

Talk about being way off. Sean had imagined the other magic student as a pale skinny dude with hollow eyes, an invalid. Instead he was slim and swimmer buff, only about Eddy's height, but not because he was humpbacked or spine-twisted. He dressed sharp, too, in loafers and khaki trousers and a red polo shirt that screamed high-end prep. Maybe his hair was a wig, though. It looked like the one Elijah Wood had worn as Frodo, dark brown with curls going in every direction. Hobbit hair.

"I thought I heard someone coming," Eddy said.

The guy turned to the door, and Sean. "I think you were right."

Not to look like a total lurking loser, Sean stepped into the room and said, "Hey."

"About time you came up," Eddy said. "I figured you'd impaled yourself on construction equipment or something."

"So when were you coming to check?"

"After I put my books away."

The guy started to laugh again, caught himself, dropped his eyes from Sean's. His face *was* pale, without the swimmer's tan to match his swimmer's build, and it showed a flush with brutal clarity.

Eddy got up. "Introductions. Daniel, that's Sean Wyndham. Sean, this is Daniel Glass."

Trying not to be obvious about looking for a fake hairline, Sean crossed the room. Daniel Glass offered a fist bump instead of a shake; too bad he blew his hipness factor by wearing cologne. Sean knew only one guy their age who did that: Mitch Chafee, another preppy jock from school. At least Daniel's cologne wasn't an olfactory deflector shield, just a light scent of cut grass and herbs, faintly familiar. Did Dad have an aftershave like it? "So," he said. "You got here this morning?"

Daniel lifted his eyes. They were Frodo-like, too, blue and protuberant. "First thing."

"Did you come from far?"

"Not so much. New York City."

"Cool. You live there?"

Daniel nodded. "In Chelsea."

Sean didn't know Chelsea from Swansea, but he nodded, too.

Eddy saved him from whatever lame conversational gambit he would have tried next. "Hey, check this out—I'm not the only one who brought books. And we brought a lot of the same ones. *Perdido Street Station* and *Gormenghast* and *Jonathan Strange* and what else?"

"*Franny and Zooey*," Daniel said.

"Oh my God, *Franny and Zooey*! I can't believe that. And it's your favorite book, too?"

"Pretty much," Daniel said, and looked from her to Sean, and dropped his eyes again. "My father gave it to me because we have the same last name as the characters."

"I've never had anyone to discuss it with before."

Because Sean hadn't even gotten through the first part, all that soul-searching in restroom stalls.

"How many times have you read it?" Eddy went on.

"Around five, I guess."

"Four here. That bathroom scene, where Bessie sits on the toilet and talks to Zooey? I'd have to drown myself if my mom did that."

There was a *bathroom* toilet-sitting scene in addition to the *restroom* toilet-sitting scene? Sean stifled a snort. Salinger dude had a one-track mind.

"Zooey's behind the shower curtain, though," Daniel said.

"Yeah, but still. Your mom."

Daniel hesitated, then agreed: "Yeah, your mom."

Anyhow. "It must be time for Helen to come back," Sean said.

Eddy chucked her stacked books onto the lowest shelf. "Hope so. I'm starving. You, Daniel?"

"I could stand some pizza."

"Well, I'll finish the books later—better go change."

As usual when on a mission, Eddy was through the door like a house cat escaping into the forbidden outer world. Eyes wide, Daniel turned to Sean, who had to laugh.

Which turned out okay, because Daniel laughed, too. "She's on the track team, right?"

"Track team *and* cross-country *and* swim."

"I should have known. This place we're going for pizza? Do we have to change?"

"*You* don't," Sean said. He checked his T-shirt and shorts. There was sawdust on his right sleeve, but it brushed off. "And I don't feel like it. I think I'll crash until Helen's ready."

He fell into a recliner. Daniel pushed his empty pack off the ottoman and perched there. "Ms. Arkwright asked me to call her Helen, too. I was surprised when I got here. I thought she'd be older."

"So'd I, when I heard she was an archivist at MU. Well, assistant archivist. Professor Marvell's the boss."

Daniel's teeth, perfectly aligned, gleamed movie-star white. Whatever else they had in Chelsea, they had killer orthodontists. "You don't call him Theophilus?"

"No way. He's definitely Professor to me."

"Me, too."

"Not like he'd get mad, but anything else wouldn't sound right. He's got like this—" Sean hunted for the right word.

"Authority?" Daniel suggested.

That's what you got for reading as many books as Eddy: a quick-draw vocabulary. "Yeah, authority. Where'd you go with him today?"

Daniel foot-scrabbled his empty backpack into reach, then folded it. "I've never been to Arkham, so he was showing me around."

"Did you go to Horrocke's Bookstore?"

Daniel nodded. "That back room's amazing."

"Where the tomes are?"

"Exactly."

Should Sean ask about the real secret of the North End? Why not. "Did you go to Geldman's Pharmacy?"

Not satisfied with his first go at the pack, Daniel shook it out and straightened the straps. "Yeah, we walked by."

"Was it, you know, open?"

Daniel nodded. "But we didn't go inside. He was out sweeping the sidewalk. He said he'd seen you earlier, and a young lady. That must have been Eddy?"

Like Sean hung with a few dozen young ladies. Still, nice of Daniel to give him the benefit of the doubt. "We went to Tumblebee's. The pharmacy looked closed, but he let us see him when we were leaving. So we wouldn't worry he'd kicked or something."

Daniel shelved his pack and rested his hands on his knees. They *did* have scars, thin red lines on the inner sides of the fingers. "Mr. Geldman can't, can he? Die, I mean."

"I don't know. I think he's super old, at least."

"Like Redemption Orne?"

Hearing the name from someone who had no reason to know it made Sean kick the recliner leg rest down too hard, *smack.* "You've heard about him?"

Daniel blinked. "A little, from Professor Marvell."

Heard about Orne *and* how he'd gone after Sean? But chill: After all, Helen had told him and Eddy personal stuff about Daniel. "Orne's been around for three hundred thirty-eight years. Maybe Geldman's been around even longer, if you can believe it."

"I can believe a lot more than I used to." Daniel took a deep breath. "What Professor Marvell said about Orne wanting you for an apprentice and sending you that spell? I was like, this Sean guy's incredible, summoning a familiar the first magic he ever did. That's major league."

Sean felt a cheeks-to-neck burn of gratification. "But, see, I summoned the *wrong* familiar."

"You got rid of it, though."

Marvell must have left out all the shit that had gone down between the summoning and dismissing. Maybe sometime Sean would tell Daniel the whole cautionary tale. "Well, after a bunch of other people helped me. So. Anyway. What did you do to get here?"

"Nothing much. No real magic."

"Then why's the Order think you're magic-capable?"

"More because of my family. They say there've been a lot of magicians on my mother's side. Including my mother."

"I get it from my mom, too! Not that I knew for sure until last year. Did you know about your mom all along?"

"No, not really." Daniel went to the door. "Eddy's calling us."

The guy had good ears—Sean heard her only when he followed Daniel into the hall, and by the time he'd grabbed a hoodie from his room, Daniel was swinging around the second-floor newel post and onto the last flight down.

4

Helen drove them to Mama Jo's in Kingsport, Sean's favorite pizza joint east of Providence. Afterwards they hung out in the common room, where Helen and Sean played cutthroat Scrabble and goofed on how Eddy and Daniel, busy at the shelves, kept discovering they'd read the same book.

With so little sleep the night before, Sean crashed early, and if any ghosts visited him, he slept through the electromagnetic field fluctuation. He'd have slept through breakfast if Eddy hadn't pounded on his door. Daniel, on the other hand, had been up long enough to make a mushroom frittata. Seriously, a mushroom frittata, plus home fries. Helen and Eddy had brunch-gasms, and Sean had to admit that the guy could cook. Nobody was going to be impressed on Sean's days to fix breakfast, but at least Daniel wasn't all *Iron Chef* about it. Helen's compliments turned his face tomato red, and he snuck apologetic glances at Sean like, *Dude, did I overdo it?*

Yeah, but chowing on his third slice of frittata, Sean could forgive him. Besides, he was too stoked about the meeting with

Helen and Marvell to work up a good surge of resentment. Pretty soon he'd know who his mentor was (had to be Geldman). Maybe the mentor (Geldman) would even pop in. Plus Helen would reveal what she'd told Dad on the phone, which wasn't that Sean was getting expelled before he started, so how bad could her big secret be?

Marvell arrived as they came up from the kitchen. Eddy immediately went fan girl on him: "Whoa, Professor! That's an awesome tan."

Marvell's white-toothed smile made his skin look even darker. "Thanks, Eddy. Two months in Greece helped."

"Were you on an archaeological dig?"

"No, just visiting relatives."

Oh, right, because Marvell's mother was Greek, which explained his dark brown hair and eyes and that scary first name of Theophilus. To poke at Eddy, Sean asked, "Your relatives aren't archaeologists, Professor?"

Marvell must not have realized it was a joke, because he didn't smile when he turned to Sean. "I'm afraid not, Sean. Glad to see you arrived without incident."

"No problems. Eddy drove."

"Ah, that explains it." Marvell smiled again, at Daniel. "Good morning. All well?"

"All well, Professor."

"To business, then. Let the tyranny of the alphabet prevail, Glass before Wyndham."

"I'll warm up the rack for you," Daniel whispered before following Marvell and Helen into the library.

Eddy curled up in a front parlor armchair and started rerereading *Franny and Zooey*. Apparently, Daniel was also rereading it, so they could analyze the book together at lunch. That sounded like so much fun that Sean went out to watch carpenters lay the carriage house subfloor. He'd helped Joe-Jack lay floors, but the foreman here gave him dirty looks if he drifted near the work zone. His loss—Sean would have worked for nothing to pass the long hour before Daniel came outside, his pale skin flushed. "Was it that bad?"

"No. It was good. You better go in."

After a pit stop to wash off secondhand construction grime, Sean slipped into the library. Marvell sat at the head of the conference table, with Helen to his right. The chair to Marvell's left was askew, so Daniel must have sat there. Good enough for Daniel, good enough for Sean. "So," Marvell said as he settled in. "How's the carriage house coming? The crew must have arrived by now."

They hadn't heard the nail guns? Come to listen, Sean didn't hear them either, even though the windows were open and the chirrup of sparrows drifted in from the side garden. "Yeah, and they're making a racket."

"But not in here," Helen said.

"Is it magic?"

"A ward that filters out unwanted noise," Marvell said. "Too bad we can't ward away the mess, but it'll be worth it once the Order's housed in one building instead of scattered around campus."

"And the basement, Professor? Looks like it's going to be a vault."

Marvell's eyebrows arched. "Part of it will be. We've collected many irreplaceable items, some dangerous. That area will be closed to students, of course."

In fortune-teller singsong, Helen added, "But someday you'll have a key to all the mysteries."

"Nobody has that key," Marvell said, so totally serious that Helen got busy with the canary yellow binder in front of her. To Sean, he said, "You saw Orne's aether-newt the other night?"

So the small talk was over. "Yeah, Professor. But it didn't bring any message. Not unless the way it wags its tail means something."

"The gestures probably have meaning for its master and his regular contacts. Helen says you spoke to the newt. Do you think that was a good idea?"

Marvell had borrowed Dad's you-screwed-up voice, and his Back Bay accent made it sound even more ominous. "I didn't think it would matter. I mean, I didn't tell it any secrets."

"What did you say?"

"I asked why it was letting me see it. All it did was flick its tail, like it was flipping me the bird." Marvell gazed at him unamused, but there was no going back. "So I told it and Orne to fuck off."

As if Marvell smelled something nasty, his nostrils flared. "In those exact words?"

"Uh, yeah. Then the newt disappeared."

"I don't suppose it did any harm, Theo?" Helen put in. "Orne did provoke Sean, showing him the newt."

Sean nodded. "Like he did it to prove he'd keep stalking me even though I'd picked the Order over him."

"And how would Orne know you'd picked the Order? Have you talked outside the warded houses about studying with us?"

"Ah, maybe. Probably. Just to Eddy, anyways."

"Indiscreet. When Dr. Benetutti put up the wards, we discussed keeping talk about magic inside them."

The seat Daniel had warmed up really was starting to feel like a rack. "I guess I screwed up. I'm sorry, Professor."

"I don't need an apology, Sean. I need you to take our precautions seriously. Orne's pursuit has always worried me. Why single out Sean Wyndham to be his apprentice?"

Sean looked at the *Founding* windows and the figure in the forest shadows. "It wasn't Nyarlathotep that sent Orne after me?"

"Nyarlathotep's certainly *aware* of all magicians, actual and potential. However, I think Orne's interest preceded his Master's."

A tray on the conference table corralled a carafe of ice water and four glasses. Sean reached for a glass; Helen, closer, poured the water, then said, "Remember how Orne was surprised when Nyarlathotep appeared to you at the summoning?"

Sean rolled the cool glass between his palms. "Like Orne thought, 'Hey, I'm the only one supposed to be messing with this kid'?"

"Exactly. Again, what made Orne pick you to mess with? Until recently, we didn't know."

"That's changed," Marvell said. "As Helen told your father yesterday."

The phone call at last. On Marvell's cue, Helen coughed, then started talking. "Jeremy agreed we'd better be the ones to tell you about it, since we had the data." She patted the canary yellow binder.

Sean vacillated between hoping she'd open it and willing her to toss it out the window.

She did neither, instead winkling out a legal-sized sheet of paper, which she smoothed under her palms, blank side up. "Recently I was helping an Order member research magical lines—families that have produced magicians. That made me think about researching your genealogy."

Sean had one? Duh, everyone did, even if it wasn't drawn up on paper. "My granddad Stewie's into that."

"Jeremy told me, and your grandfather was good enough to send me his notes. They're detailed on the Polish side, the Krols and Dudeks. On the English side, he didn't have anything earlier than the 1850s. A friend of Theo's at the New England Historic Genealogical Society made it to 1715 before he hit a wall at Thaddeus Howe, whose mother was a Constance Cooke from Boston. The other Cooke children appear in the usual records, but not Constance. Before her marriage, her only appearance is in the Cooke family Bible, as 'Constance, taken in, 1693.'"

"She was adopted?"

Helen had cut her hair short, so when she reached for the lock she used to worry during the Servitor crisis, she had to settle for rubbing her cheekbone. "But adopted from whom? Then I remembered where I'd seen the names Constance and Cooke before." She paused, as if waiting for Sean to have his own eureka moment.

Nothing, though "Constance" did tease his memory. "Where was that?"

"Redemption Orne's journals, the ones you and Eddy read last summer. I looked at them again and saw that Orne had an uncle in Boston named Cooke." Helen fingered the sheet of legal paper. "And that Orne's daughter was named Constance."

Helen was right about the daughter. "Yeah, but *that* Constance died. It's in the Arkham Witch Panic book. Redemption and Patience's baby died right after they hanged Patience."

"That's what I thought, too. Except it was too big a coincidence. Redemption and Patience had a baby named Constance. In 1693, when Constance Orne would have been a year old, Redemption's uncle adopted a Constance of about the same age."

From the concerned look Helen gave Sean, she must have noticed the break of sweat that chilled his face. But she plowed on: "I checked the archives of the Third Congregational Church and found a record of Constance Orne's burial in 1693. Then I found a collection of letters at the Arkham Historical Society. They'd belonged to Nicholas Brattle, who was pastor of the Third when Redemption was its teacher. One letter was from Alden Cooke, Redemption's uncle. He wrote to thank Brattle for helping free an innocent from the infamy of her parents, a convicted witch and fallen minister. Cooke didn't name the innocent, but I've got to conclude it was Constance Orne, and that what Brattle did to free her was to fake a burial record."

First Sean had to close his mouth so he didn't look like a landed trout gaping for oxygen. Second he had to make sure he'd heard Helen right. "Like, Constance Cooke was really Constance Orne?"

Helen kept her voice level but her gaze sharp, like a doctor giving bad news to a patient who might flip: "Yes, Sean."

Sean swallowed. "Constance was Patience and Redemption's daughter."

"Yes."

"So, if Constance is my ancestor, they are, too."

Helen slipped him the legal sheet, print side up. It didn't show a whole family tree, more like one branch split off the trunk by lightning. At the left margin were the names PATIENCE BISHOP and REDEMPTION ORNE, yoked together, then an arrow to CONSTANCE (ORNE) COOKE, then more arrows and names all the way over to the last twigs, which were a yoked KATHERINE KROL and JEREMY WYNDHAM, shooting an arrow into SEAN WYNDHAM.

Sean pushed the sheet away. "What's that make Orne to me?"

Starting at REDEMPTION, Helen counted forward to SEAN. "He's your ten-times-great-grandfather, right, Theo?"

"That's how I counted it."

That was an insane number of *great*s. For the first time, Orne's 338 years took on weight for Sean, became an overloaded backpack digging straps into his shoulders and chest, because what was at the end of all those years? *He* was. SEAN WYNDHAM.

"Sean? You okay?"

The straps of his ancestral burden cut his breath short. He'd never had an asthma attack, but this had to be what it felt like.

Marvell stood, but it was Helen who urged Sean to his feet and made him walk. The panicky suffocation eased, and by the time they'd traversed the library and returned to the table, Sean was breathing fine but burning hot. "Sorry," he began.

"Don't be," Marvell said, and weirdly, there was approval in his voice. "I'd be more worried if you didn't have that kind of reaction. Sit down. Finish your water."

"Here's some colder," Helen said, pouring him a fresh glass.

The water cleared his head without extinguishing his embarrassment. "This is what you told my dad, Helen?"

"Yes."

No wonder he'd holed up in the studio, studying Mom's image and trying to gut down the fact that she was Redemption Orne's nine-times-great-granddaughter. Say that Dad could get his last-summer's wish, and kick Orne straight out of the world. Orne would remain part of their lives, tangled up in Sean's DNA. "I guess Orne's been watching his line? Looking for magicians?"

"That would make sense," Marvell said. "Doubtless from Constance on forward."

"Was Constance magical?"

"We have no record of it, and the same's true for Orne's other descendants. But magicians tend toward secrecy, and many magic-capables never realize they have the knack."

If it hadn't been for Orne, Sean might not have realized it, either.

"And magic-capability's a complex genetic trait," Helen said. "No one's worked out the exact mechanics of transmission, but it looks like magic often skips several generations."

"Is that what happened with my line?"

"All we know for sure is from Mr. Geldman. He and Orne are friends of a sort."

Marvell rolled his eyes. "Of a very odd sort, but we're not here to wrestle with that enigma. Orne told Geldman that none of his previous apprentices have been related to him. You'd have been the first."

"Does it make a difference, Professor? If a magician's apprentice is related to him?"

"Possibly. Master and apprentice establish a psychic bond that allows them to exchange energy. At its most extreme, the bond can merge them into a single acting unit, a synergy greater than the sum of its parts. Am I making sense?"

"The strongest kind of bond is this synergy thing?"

"Precisely. Even married couples—Redemption and Patience, say—are unlikely to achieve a true synergy. Virtually all known cases have been between magicians related by blood. And I'm afraid that explains why Orne's pursuing you."

"So synergy's bad?"

From Marvell's scowl, Sean had asked the world's stupidest question. "The term may imply equal partnership, but in practice, the master dominates. Picture his hold over an apprentice as a small-scale version of the one Nyarlathotep exerts on allied magicians."

Which would suck. "Orne never said we were related."

Helen said, "Maybe he was afraid of spooking you."

"And would he have?" Marvell asked.

The library was cool—no visible air-conditioning, so more magic?—but not cool enough to account for Sean's goose bumps. "Well, yeah."

Marvell brought his hands together in a single emphatic clap. "Stay afraid, then. Never let your relationship to Orne make you trust him. He's out for himself and, necessarily, his master. Give him the chance, and he will, for all practical purposes, enslave you."

Helen had nodded at every beat of Marvell's warning. "Remember what Geldman said about Orne: He's like Satan in the Bible, a lion seeking someone to devour."

And Geldman was Orne's friend? Frenemy was more like it. Sean glanced at the Satan in the *Founding* window, Nyarlathotep actually, no devil. The Outer God was real. His servant, lion-Orne, was real, and still lying in wait for Sean. Yeah, like any ten-times-great-grandfather would do, could you blame him?

He pushed damp hair off his forehead. "I understand, Professor. And, I mean, he's not a close relative. Not somebody to get all mushy about."

Cold as a judge, Marvell said, "He's somebody who should have died centuries ago."

That was harsh, as if simply breathing for so long were a crime, but Sean wasn't about to stick up for Orne. "I didn't want to sign up with him before, and being related makes it even creepier. Forget about him."

"Don't forget," Marvell said. "Avoid."

"Right. Exactly."

"That also means remember about Orne's spies and don't talk about your magical business in unwarded places."

"Okay, Professor."

"And if you see the aether-newt again, get into a warded place."

"Okay."

"And if Orne tries to contact you in any other way, tell me or Helen immediately."

"No problem."

As if talking about Orne had given Marvell an anxiety attack as bad as Sean's, he rose and paced the library. Sean leaned toward Helen. "Is the meeting over?"

"No," she whispered back. "But don't worry. We've dropped our big bomb."

"You're sure about me and Orne?"

"I wouldn't have told you otherwise."

"But what should I do about it? Should I tell anyone else?"

She smoothed the mockingly cheerful hide of her binder. "You could tell Eddy. I'd wait on Daniel, since you're just getting to know him."

"Yeah, it might scare him off, how I'm the spawn of an evil wizard."

He'd expected Helen to laugh. She didn't. "You are going to take this seriously, Sean?"

"Yeah, I just meant—" Nothing, that was what he'd meant. "I was just kidding."

"All right. And you're not a spawn."

"Don't count on that."

His usual composure regained, at least outwardly, Marvell returned and seated himself on the broad sill of the east windows. He leaned out and waved at someone. "Daniel and Eddy are in the garden. It looks like they're waiting for you, Sean, so let's finish up. Helen, Eddy will be working at the MU Library weekdays, nine to two?"

Helen nodded.

"So Sean and Daniel will have class the same hours. We'll meet in the library here. You'll have reading, but no papers or tests. The weekends are all yours."

"Sounds great, Professor."

"You will have a curfew. Ten o'clock, unless you're with an Order member."

Ten was too early, but if they wanted to hit a midnight movie, Eddy could talk Helen into playing chaperone.

"One more thing, which I hope won't disappoint you."

Sean sat as straight as his chair allowed, which was straight of the ramrod variety. This had to be about his mentor. If there was disappointment involved, he might not get Geldman, or even Benetutti, but a magician he didn't know yet. Still, that could be cool—

"I've been thinking about last summer," Marvell went on. "How one day you thought magic was a pleasant fantasy, the next you found out it was real and potentially deadly. An extreme introduction, do you agree?"

He'd be an idiot not to. "Yes, Professor."

"Facing not just the Servitor but an Outer God? People have been staggered by much milder exposure to the truth of the Mythos. I'm impressed by how well you've handled it. However—"

However, the Death Star of words. Sean held on for the blast. Marvell fired. "We need to pull you back a few steps. You started with advanced practical magic, which is exactly the wrong way to start. Theory should come first. Without it, a student's magic remains wild. So for now you'll concentrate on theory."

That disappointment Marvell had been worried about? A big old fist of it hung in the air ready to punch Sean in the gut. Maybe he could still dodge it. "Okay, but I'll still learn a little practical magic?"

"No. You won't learn any."

The big old fist nailed him, right in the solar plexus. "But what will I do with my mentor?"

"Since you won't be practicing magic, you won't need a mentor this summer."

Big old fist nailed him again, lower.

Helen jumped in. "Sean, I know you were looking forward to studying with a magician. But, believe me, theory will keep you plenty busy for two months."

"And I hope to make it interesting," Marvell said.

He and Helen—Helen, especially—looked like the parents of a kid on the brink of a tantrum because the expensive present he'd unwrapped wasn't exactly what he'd wanted. Sean had to remind himself that these were the people who'd helped save his butt last year. They were offering him a huge opportunity right now. Spoiled-brat behavior was not an option, even though Marvell had never talked about going backwards before. "I guess it makes sense, theory first." It almost choked him, but he added, "And so waiting for a mentor makes sense, too."

"I'm glad you see that," Marvell said with a brisk finality that cut off any further discussion. When he came around the table, right hand out, what could Sean do but shake it and seal the deal? Then Marvell checked his watch. "I'm late for the acquisitions meeting," he told Helen. To Sean, he said, "I'll see you and Daniel tomorrow at nine."

After he'd left, Helen collected glasses and notes. "It's a load off my mind, Sean, telling you about Orne. Are you okay with it? Well, reasonably okay?"

To tell the truth, the no-mentor announcement had smacked him so hard, he'd half-forgotten about Orne. "I guess. Orne was stalking me before. Only change, now I get why."

"Look, if you want to talk, I'm available. So is your father. He said to call him whenever you want."

"Yeah, I will. But it's not an emergency. I don't have to get him up in the middle of the night or anything."

Helen passed him, binder under one arm, tray in her hands. She still managed to give him an elbow-to-elbow bump. "Better get back to Eddy and Daniel before they decide we've thrown you in the dungeon."

"You've got a dungeon?"

"Haven't found it yet, but there has to be one in a house like this."

Sean opened the library doors for Helen, but didn't follow her out. Instead he turned back toward the *Founding* windows. Since he couldn't flip off Orne to prove the big reveal hadn't freaked him out, he flipped off Orne's boss, Nyarlathotep. The Dark Pharaoh didn't react, of course, but his crow familiar—did it flare out a halo like the one he'd glimpsed yesterday? Any extra brilliance was gone before he could focus on the stupid bird, and the more impressive window phenomenon was Eddy, bobbing and flailing in an east wall casement as if doing jumping jacks. Her mouth worked without producing a peep; the ward that squelched obnoxious exterior noise must have considered her one.

Eddy would love hearing that, so Sean headed for the garden to tell her.

5

Dominating the side garden was a copper beech so massive, it must have been planted the same year the house was built. Eddy swung on a low branch. Far above, a loafered foot dangled before disappearing into the canopy. "That's Daniel?" Sean asked.

"Yeah, he's a freaking squirrel." Eddy left the under-tree shade and sat on a marble bench otherwise occupied by copies of *Franny and Zooey*. She took them onto her lap to make room for Sean. "I was worried he couldn't climb with his hands scarred, so I'm like, 'Helen's going to kill me if you fall.'"

"I saw the scars. They're pretty weird."

"I asked him what happened. He said his hands were burned so bad, they couldn't save any of the skin. So they took skin off another part of his body—"

"Which?"

"He didn't say. Probably his butt. Anyhow, they sewed the new skin on his hands like gloves, which is why the scars look like seams. His toes are the same way, he said."

Loafers dangled again, followed by khaki legs. The khaki butt didn't look big enough to provide skin for two hands and ten toes, though couldn't they stick balloons under your skin and slowly pump them up to stretch it? If Daniel had gone through that, two burgeoning cheeks and nurses always checking on the progress, he deserved major sympathy.

The rest of Daniel appeared. He waved at them before continuing his descent.

"Did he say anything else about the car wreck?" Sean asked.

"No, except that it wasn't the wreck that killed his mom."

"Wait, what?"

Eddy scooted closer, her voice dropping. "I know! Helen didn't tell us about her. But she died before the accident, when he was eight."

"Died how?" But when Eddy shrugged, Sean knew. "Cancer, right?"

"Leukemia."

Was there a curse on moms who passed magic-capability on to their kids? "That sucks."

"Big-time."

Daniel had dropped neatly to the ground. He walked toward their bench, calling, "That's an awesome tree. On top there's a place you could string hammocks. Or you could build a flet, like the elves."

In Lothlórien, he meant. "Maybe Helen would let us," Sean said. "With leftover construction lumber."

"I'm going to check it out," Eddy said.

"Um, how about lunch?"

"Tree first, lunch second. We decided on the Mexican place at the harbor."

That was a *we* that hadn't included Sean. It was hard to argue against Mexican, though, especially since Eddy had already swung up into the beech. He expected Daniel would follow her.

Instead he took her place on the bench, right down to cradling the sacred Salinger books. "I think Eddy wants to give us a chance to talk shop," he said. "I already told her how our schedules match. And about Mr. Geldman."

"What about Mr. Geldman?"

"You know, how he's going to be my mentor."

No, Sean had not known that. In fact, he was so blindsided, he almost slid off his end of the bench. "Your *magician* mentor?"

Daniel's grin lapsed into an uncertain frown. "Is there some other kind?"

He had to stay cool so he didn't scare Daniel out of talking. "Not that I know. Anyhow, Geldman's yours? Solomon Geldman, from the pharmacy?"

Daniel's frown deepened. "Right."

Good thing they hadn't eaten yet, the way Sean's stomach clenched. "That's great. How'd they pick him?"

"I guess the Order thinks he'd be the best match for me."

"To start right now, this summer. Him teaching you practical magic."

Daniel shoved Frodo curls from his forehead, hard enough to have pushed a wig askew, if he'd been wearing one. "Are you—?" he began. He gave the curls another shove. Still no slippage. "Did you want to work with Mr. Geldman?"

Eddy had summited the beech and was on her way down. If she caught them in the middle of a drama, she'd blame Sean, and in this case, she'd be right. Unfair as it was for Daniel to get a mentor (Geldman!) while Sean had to wait (a whole year!), the situation wasn't Daniel's fault. "Sure, who wouldn't want to work with him? But I'm good with—"

Right, with whom?

Eddy shinnied along a branch that came close to overhanging

their bench. As it dipped, she rolled off into a cat-soft three-point landing. "What've you guys been talking about?"

Daniel cleared his throat. "I told Sean about Mr. Geldman."

"I'm still geeking out over that. Who's your mentor, Sean?"

With Daniel still looking worried, Sean made do with a kinda-sorta truth: "I don't know yet. The Order's still thinking about it."

"But Daniel's starting with Geldman on Monday. Every Monday, Wednesday, Friday, three to six. You'll get behind."

"No, he won't," Daniel said. "I've never done magic, and Sean has. I'm the one who'll be playing catch-up."

Sean almost said it out loud: *Dude, stop trying so hard to be nice. We're going to be your friends—Helen made us promise.* Then he remembered what Eddy had said about Daniel's skin grafts and his mother dying of leukemia, and he was glad he'd swallowed the snark. It came from the Gospel of Joe-Jack: *You think when you kick crap at somebody else, you're making your own pile smaller, but karma just doubles your crap allowance, and everybody ends up buried.* "You're right about that," he told Daniel. "The Order's only trying to give you a fighting chance."

"Not that it's a contest," Eddy said.

But Daniel was smiling again. "No, the contest's who's going to eat the most tacos. If you guys are ready."

Daniel borrowed Helen's bike, and they pedaled to the harbor, a tree-shaded ride along the old residential streets to the east. They passed the Third Congregational Church, where Orne had preached, and Daniel said he'd like to check it out sometime. Sean made a mental note to skip that outing, but in Arkham it was hard to escape Orne. On the way back, they stopped at a cemetery on Lich Street, and next to the spiky iron fence was a lichen-coated

mausoleum on which the Historical Society had stuck a shiny
new plaque:

THE REVEREND NICHOLAS BRATTLE, 1655–1731,
FIRST PASTOR OF THE THIRD CONGREGATIONAL CHURCH

Good old Brattle, who'd faked Constance Orne's death so
she could become Constance Cooke, no questions asked. Sean
looked for her fake infant-sized grave, but unless it was beneath
one of the many stones worn illegible, he didn't find it.

Back at the Arkwright House, Sean went to the library and
Skyped Dad. He was in his workshop, shoulder deep in glass
samples, with cartoons of the St. Anselm windows pinned to
the corkboard behind him, and so he was in an excellent mood.
Sean filled him in on the new guy, Daniel. Then he said, "Helen
and Professor Marvell told me."

Dad pulled his laptop closer. "About Orne."

"About how he's my grandfather. Times ten. Mom's times
nine."

"Were you thrown as hard as I was?"

Sean skipped over his panic attack. "A little, but we already
knew Mom had some magic. I wonder if she could have become
a magician. You know, with training."

"Helen thinks her magic wasn't as strong as yours, or else Orne
would have contacted her first."

Sean had a scary new idea: "What if Orne *did* contact her?"

"Something like that, she'd have told me."

"Even if it happened before she knew you, and she figured
Orne was just a nutcase?"

The breeze from an unseen window stirred Dad's cartoons,
making their stiff medieval saints shimmy. "You could be right,
but does it make any difference?"

"Guess not. Except maybe I'd feel better if he *had* gone after Mom."

"Why, Sean?"

"Because if Orne went after her, and she turned him down, that means I can turn him down, too. Like, I don't have evil overlord genes or bad blood or something."

Dad shook his head. "There's two things I know for certain: Your mother wasn't crazy or evil. You're not crazy or evil. If the Professor or Helen suggested—"

"No, Dad. No way they'd say anything like that." Though since the meeting, Sean had been worrying about how down Marvell was on Orne—didn't he have to at least wonder about Orne's great-et cetera-grandson? "It's only, what if they don't trust me, now that they know I'm related to the Reverend? Before today, Professor Marvell said I'd have a magician mentor this summer. Now he says no mentor until next year. He says I started too fast. I have to backtrack."

"That sounds reasonable to me."

It would. "But the Order's assigned Daniel a mentor. And you know who it is? Mr. Geldman!"

"Well, you said Daniel's eighteen. Doesn't that put him a year ahead of you?"

"Not in magic. He told me he hasn't done any yet."

If Sean was being held back in any other subject, Dad would be ticked off. With magic, relief glowed off his face. "I can see why you're frustrated," he began.

"It's not that."

"No?"

"Okay, it's a little that. But what if I was going to get a mentor before they found out who my magic comes from? And then Marvell changed his mind because he's afraid I'll turn out like Redemption Orne? Or like Patience—she was even worse. She *ordered* her Servitor to kill people."

Head bowed, Dad seemed to chew over his reply. "Your uncle Gus would know the exact quote, but the Bible talks about the sins of the fathers being visited on the children only to the fourth or fifth generation. Sixth, tops."

"You don't believe that stuff."

"No. *I'd* say the fathers' sins aren't visited on anyone."

"I'm not talking sins. I'm talking genes."

"Okay, genes. Helen would've told me if yours had evil overlord cooties."

Without wanting to, Sean smiled. "You think she'd tell you about overlord cooties?"

"I think she'd tell me the truth about anything concerning you. If she and Marvell were afraid of your ancestry, they didn't have to let you come to Arkham. Take what they said at face value—you just need to start over right."

"But right for Daniel—"

"Daniel's a different person. Look. That last phone call, Helen wasn't worried about you personally. She was worried about how Orne's likely to keep chasing you."

"Because, us being blood relatives, he could use me to get stronger?"

"That's my worry. Him getting some kind of mental control over you."

Would a psychic bond with a human be as will-crushing as the bond the Servitor had forced on Sean? Maybe it would be worse. Much less impersonal, for one thing.

"You've got to be a lot more careful now," Dad went on.

"I know. They told me."

"Did you listen?"

"Totally, Dad."

"You're going to keep listening?"

"A hundred percent. Far as I'm concerned, Orne is so not an option."

Dad rubbed his lower lip. "And you're not going to do any spells?"

"Who's going to teach me spells if I don't have a mentor?"

Someone knocked on Dad's door. "I'll be over shortly," he called, then turned back to Sean: "Okay. Anything else?"

An overhead flare jerked Sean's eyes to the *Founding*. The sun had dipped behind the huge old oaks that lined Pickman Street, leaving the windows dim, except for Nyarlathotep's crow. Its halo had returned, brighter than ever in contrast to the darkened glass around it. He blinked. It stayed bright.

"Sean?"

He looked down at the screen. "No biggie, Dad, but your crow?"

"What crow?"

"The one in the *Founding*. That Nyarlathotep's throwing. Did you do something special to it?"

"No, just some repainting."

"You didn't paint it to glow, like you painted Mom's brush, in her window?"

"That would have meant changing the original design. Is there a glow?"

"You know, halo-ish."

Dad sighed. "That could be a light leak. Do me a favor. Check the putty around the crow. See if it's shrunk."

How could you have a light leak if there wasn't any light hitting the glass? But Sean said, "Sure, Dad. Should I fix it?"

"No. As long as the glass isn't about to fall out, I'll deal with it when I come back. Anyhow, tell Eddy and Helen and the Professor hi for me. And don't forget I'm here whenever you want to call."

"Middle of the night, your time?"

Dad groaned but nodded. Then he was gone.

Sean hauled one of the library stepladders onto the dais, under the left window, and climbed. Nyarlathotep remained inert glass, didn't try to grab him, didn't even wink in recognition, and four rungs up, Sean stood eye to eye with the crow. The putty that held it in the lead came was intact, so its halo wasn't a light leak. In fact, it was an aura a lot like the ones in Mom's paintings, where the closer he got to the canvas, the less he saw it and the more he *felt* it, a faint warmth and vibration. He rested his fingertips on the crow's breast. No mistake, there was a Mom-like hum.

He could only come up with one explanation for how Mom's energy had gotten into the crow. Dad had restored the *Founding* windows in his carriage house studio, right next to the one where Mom's unfinished paintings lived. Sean had half-persuaded himself that the hum in the paintings was magical residue without consciousness, but maybe his younger self had been right, after all. Maybe Mom was a less abstract ghost, more willful, capable of breathing her unfading magic into a glass bird. Did she often "help" Dad with his work, or was this the first time, because Sean was going away and she wanted a bit of herself to follow him, a surrogate guardian spirit?

It was shocking how unshocked he felt. Or was it just reasonable? If the universe could hold Servitors and immortal wizards and state-shifting pharmacies, why get his shorts in a wad about ghosts, especially one he ached to believe in?

By climbing one more rung, Sean was able to lean over the top of the ladder and press his forehead to the crow. The humming against his skin didn't strengthen into words or anything, into Mom's voice, but that was okay. He communed with it until Helen came home, and Eddy and Daniel thundered downstairs to greet her. Then he hustled the ladder back into its wall niche. Helen couldn't have noticed anything special about the crow, or she'd have mentioned it to Dad. Come to think about it, Sean had never seen its halo when anyone else was looking at the windows. He'd have to watch, and if he truly was the only one the glass glowed for, that was more evidence the glow and hum came from Mom, were there for Sean, and were meant to be their secret, why not, who could it harm?

He joined the others in the hall.

6

That night Eddy and Daniel huddled over *Franny and Zooey*. If they had to get all book-clubby, they could have picked *The Catcher in the Rye* at least, which had that awesome part about the ducks and the sore cabdriver. Sean lurked behind his laptop, one eye on Twitter, the other on the couch—he'd have to catch Eddy alone to tell her about his connection to Orne. If he even wanted to tell her right now. Dad had already depressed him by endorsing Marvell's no-magic, no-mentor plan, and Eddy was such a Marvell fan girl, she'd probably endorse it, too.

So when Eddy cruised, he stayed in the common room and talked to Daniel. He'd tell her in a day or two.

Or three or four.

Or more, as it turned out, because they fell into a routine too comfortable for Sean to risk upsetting it. Mornings Eddy went to the Archives, Sean and Daniel to class. Marvell had kicked off with a reminder that *Infinity Unimaginable* had presented the Outer Gods as myth, a benign lie to protect interested "civilians." As potential magicians, however, Sean and Daniel had to learn the truth. The first truth, because he was the first entity, was Azathoth: the Demon Sultan who roiled at the center of the cosmos, chaotic and amorphous, blind and mindless. Some magic scholars equated Azathoth with the Big Bang. Others believed he existed in steady state, involuntarily spawning the singularities that inflated into bubble universes around him.

That was cool beyond Sean's previous standards of coolness, and beyond Daniel's, too, from the excited questions he asked. Next among the Outer Gods was Yog-Sothoth, Keeper of the Gates and their Keys. Marvell called him a sort of universal memory, perhaps time itself. Next, Shub-Niggurath, referred to as "she" because, well, she was the Mother through whom energy became matter, so calling her "he" would be pretty rude. Not that she'd care. The only Outer God who paid much attention to lesser beings was Nyarlathotep.

Whenever Marvell mentioned Nyarlathotep, he bestowed a brief scowl on Sean. Among the god's seemingly countless avatars were the Dark Pharaoh, the Three-Lobed Burning Eye, and the Howler in Darkness. But Soul and Messenger of the Outer Gods was Nyarlathotep's proper title. Also, the Master of Magic.

Daniel noted every word of Marvell's wisdom on his laptop. Sean didn't want to look like the only slacker in a class of two, but he couldn't keep up with Daniel's high-speed typing. Besides, he had to sneak glances at the *Founding* windows. Intonation of the god's name didn't summon Nyarlathotep out of the glass, good. Better, the crow kept its halo doused whenever Marvell was in the library, or Helen or Eddy or Daniel, for that matter, which could be more proof the glow was of Mom's making. Several times since his call to Dad, Sean had climbed the stepladder and touched the crow's breast. Energy pulsed within it, a steady heartbeat that felt more and more like Mom's magic. It had to be hers, a ghostly gift, sacred in its obscurity, hers and Sean's alone.

Marvell dismissed class at two. Eddy usually stormed in to change out of her library clothes by three. Some days they snagged a tennis court at the university sports complex; Daniel hadn't played much since his accident, but Eddy was a good coach. She soon had him up to besting Sean one out of three matches and even to besting her on the occasional long volley.

Other afternoons they bicycled in town or on the Miskatonic River Trail. Daniel had bought a Jamis road bike that must have cost a couple thousand dollars, but that was no big deal since (as Eddy had learned) his dad was a corporate lawyer. Sean couldn't hate on him—Daniel let one of them ride it half the time, a favor Sean returned by being the go-to guy for drives to the beach.

The biggest beach was in Kingsport, but Eddy and Sean liked the smaller one between the Arkham Harbor jetties. It was decent for swimming; the jetties hosted enough sea life to make snorkeling worthwhile; and kayak access was easy. Under normal circumstances, Sean would have opted for swimming every day, and Eddy the mermaid would probably have lived at the beach every second she wasn't basking among the Archives' tomes.

The problem was that Daniel had a phobia of water, especially the ocean. Before their first beach trip, he'd told them about a rip current that had grabbed him when he was a toddler, how it had sucked him away from shore and almost drowned him. Since then he hadn't set foot in surf or even the shallow end of a pool. It blew in hot weather, but he didn't mind hanging out near water, or even out on one of the jetties, as long as there weren't high waves that might pull or knock him in.

Privately, Sean and Eddy agreed they'd do most of their water stuff on the afternoons when Daniel was with Geldman. Whatever he said, it had to be a drag to stand around while they had fun. It was also a drag for Eddy. The phobia was Daniel's one flaw in her eyes. In a selfish way, it was good to know there was one thing Sean could do better than him. Even if it wasn't practical magic.

On their second Monday at the Arkwright House, over a Sean-made breakfast of Cheerios and strawberries, Daniel relayed Geldman's invitation to visit the pharmacy that afternoon. Eddy nearly exploded pink milk in her rush to accept. Back from work, she spent an hour trying to figure out what you'd wear to meet the most awesome wizard in Arkham and ended up back in formal library gear, a white blouse and navy skirt. Then she started nagging Sean to change. "Show up looking sharp, maybe Geldman will take you on as a student."

"I bet he can only have one at a time, like a Sith master."

"Then maybe he'll give you a letter of recommendation."

Sean changed into a fresh T-shirt and genuine leather flip-flops. He considered raiding Daniel's room for a squirt of his cologne, but since Eddy knew how much he hated cologne, she'd have realized he was mocking Daniel's superior prepitude, and she probably wouldn't have appreciated the joke in her current state of pre-Geldman nerves.

They arrived five minutes early, to find the pharmacy was "closed." Standing in front of the sooty display window, Eddy looked ready to bawl. Sean got her to walk around the block, slowly, and the next time they approached it, Geldman's Pharmacy was open for business. Its bricks were buffed to a sunflower yellow, its trim painted a fresh leaf green. Snowy lace curtains billowed from the windows of the second-floor apartment, and the scale sunned itself outside the shop door. Eddy stared at the fabled urns, upside-down teardrops again hanging level on their chains, the right brimming with emerald liquid, the left with ruby. Sean looked beyond the urns to shelves holding bottles and tins and drawstring bags, to the mahogany counter topped with frosted glass panels, to the candy-cotton-pink and spearmint-green soda fountain. No one was in sight unless he counted the shadows wavering across the counter panels, and he did count them, and there were three.

Eddy pointed across the street, where the owner of Tumblebee's Café hustled drinks to the outdoor tables. "Is it true what Daniel said? If you're standing next to the pharmacy and it looks open to you, you're invisible to people who see it as closed?"

"Right. If you can see it like it really is, you're covered by the same ward of illusion. Check this out." Sean waved an arm and yelled: "Hey! How about a couple iced mochas over here?"

"Shut up," Eddy hissed, but when no one outside Tumblebee's glanced their way, she waved, too. "Yo! Want to see Sean drop his shorts?"

No one reacted. "Class act," Sean said.

"Yeah, but I proved no one can see or hear us." She walked to the door practically on tiptoes, as if she might scare the pharmacy closed again. When she came up to the scale, she started.

It had protruded a square of blue cardboard from the slot beneath its face. "That must be for you," Sean said.

"Why?"

"You're closer to the scale than I am."

Eddy plucked out the square. It was a sort of clamshell, from which she extracted a slip of onionskin paper. During the Servitor crisis, Sean dreamed he'd gotten a Geldman scale-fortune crimped into infinite folds, unreadable, but Eddy opened hers easily, and scanned it, and flushed. "What's it say?"

Flush deepening, she read it again. "I'm supposed to come in."

Through the onionskin, Sean saw there was a lot more message than that. "What else?"

"Never mind. Put in a nickel and get your own." Eddy refolded the fortune and slipped it into her skirt pocket. Then she pushed into the pharmacy.

Sean didn't have a nickel, so he followed her inside and across the glossy tiles to the counter door through which Geldman stepped. Instead of shaking the hand Eddy extended to him, Geldman took it between his and bowed over it. "A pleasure to meet you, Miss Rosenbaum. Helen Arkwright tells me you're a promising scholar in my favorite field."

Eddy hadn't even started to blush outside. "Thanks, Mr. Geldman. I've wanted to meet you since Sean told me about the pharmacy."

Actually, her initial opinion had been that Geldman was a nutcase quack who ought to be arrested for selling dangerous drugs to minors. But why spoil the moment? When Geldman released Eddy's hand, he gave Sean's a hearty shake, none of that bowing stuff. "And you, Sean, studying magic with the Order of Alhazred! I'm glad."

"And I'm glad I can say thanks in person, Mr. Geldman, for how you helped Helen find the dismissing spell."

"I couldn't have done otherwise, since my Powders helped you summon the wrong familiar."

Daniel came out of the hidden regions of the pharmacy, fiddling with his neck brace. "You guys made it," he said, like anything short of a Category 5 hurricane could have stopped them.

"Actually, we got here early," Eddy said. "While the pharmacy was still—do you call it closed, Mr. Geldman?"

"Or asleep, or even dead."

"It gives me the chills when it's shut down."

"As it should."

"This way, open, it's—"

Eddy wordless was an unnatural phenomenon. Daniel threw Sean an anxious look, but Geldman watched her with placid attention, as if she were still speaking. "Exactly," he said. "But allow me to introduce you and Sean to my ward."

He meant the girl who'd stepped out from behind Daniel. Had she stood there all along, unseen? Possibly, because she was only about ten, shorter than Daniel and super-slender. Yet shouldn't

Sean have noticed her glow? The whole girl shone, from her cascade of pale blond hair to her bare feet. In between were a heart-shaped face, arms exposed from shoulder to wrist, and a white dress plain as a pillowcase—a pillowcase draped over a lamp burning 200-watt bulbs. He blinked, squeezing out tears. When he'd swiped them away, the girl had spun her dimmer switch to low, because she looked normal. Well, pretty much. Her eyes remained the inhuman blue of forget-me-nots, and radiance still seeped from her slim feet, of all places. Feet!

Daniel smiled at the girl as if she was his kid sister, nothing special yet totally special, and she gazed at him with the corners of her delicate lips uptilted. Eddy looked at her as she'd looked at the revived Geldman's Pharmacy, wedged between wonder and terror.

Except for the reflection of the girl's glory that lingered in his eyes, Geldman remained the same old Geldman. "Miss Edna Rosenbaum—," he said.

"Please, Mr. Geldman. Just Eddy?"

"Eddy, then, and Sean. This is Cybele."

Eddy extended her hand, so Sean stuck his out, too. Cybele didn't shake their hands; instead, she touched her fingertips to theirs. Magic happened, the transfer of a cool spark and the passage of a breeze scented by flowering grass. Weird how Sean knew the scent from somewhere, from more than one somewhere, in fact.

The smell dissipated before he could remember. Cybele was speaking in a voice as high as a young girl's but much more measured, mature: "You're welcome here as Daniel's friends, but you're also welcome for yourselves." She looked at Geldman. "Aren't they, Guardian?"

Geldman bowed his head.

Guardian, so was she as young as she looked, after all? With magicians, appearances could deceive. Cybele might be the older of the two, and Geldman already struck Sean as much older than Orne.

"Cybele, Daniel," Geldman said. "Could you show Eddy around? I'd like to have a word with Sean in back."

In back were the hidden regions Daniel—and Helen—had always squirmed out of describing, as if a taboo against telling fell on the few lucky beholders. Finally Sean would get his own look! On the other hand, words from authority figures were usually bad news. And inescapable, like now, as Geldman directed him to the counter door with a gesture that subtly twisted invitation into command.

Daniel raised one hand, forefinger and thumb joined into an O. Well, he'd been with Geldman more than a week—he had to know whether a torture chamber lurked in the depths of the pharmacy.

Sean followed Geldman into a white corridor with white doors to either side. At the end of the corridor was an equally bland and antiseptic door that Geldman swung open to another world, or was it to another time? Candles lit a large parlor, Victorian to the max with its red wallpaper and curvy-carvy furniture. Candles in a triple octopus of a chandelier, candles in candelabras and candlesticks and jars. Candles on the mantel, in the fireless fireplace, scattered on every flat surface except the floor, which boasted a carpet animated by the candlelight into a jungle of coiling vines and skulking beasts. Beside the stairs to the second floor stood one of those desk-bookcase combos that antiquey people called secretaries. The back wall featured two heavily curtained windows, or at least Sean supposed there were windows behind the curtains; not a photon of outside light made it through the layers of lace and velvet. Opposite the stairs were the fireplace, and two armchairs, and a tea table, and a bird on a brass perch behind the chair Geldman had taken. Helen *had* told Sean and Eddy about Geldman's familiar, an African pied crow, "pied" not because he was baked under a crust with twenty-three other blackbirds but because he had this white bib, and his name was?

"Boaz," Geldman said.

Sean approached the perch. The crow eyed him, head thrust forward, beak open. "Does he, ah, bite?"

"Not very often."

Better not risk it. Sean retreated to the armchair across from Geldman's. The hem of his shorts brushed candles, and he jerked around, sure he'd set himself on fire. He hadn't. As if to demonstrate why, Geldman lowered his palm into a dozen flames, all the way to the wicks. When Sean fingertip-prodded a flame, he found it gave off no heat. If anything, it was cold. That also explained why none of the candles was dripping wax. He sat, and when the chair cushions swallowed him up comfortably, he didn't even wince. Magic lived everywhere in the room, and it felt like?

It felt like home.

"So, Daniel," Geldman said.

"Daniel, sir?"

"Cybele said he's your friend, so it must be so. You don't resent him for becoming my apprentice, while you've yet to find a master?"

"No. It's not his fault if the Order doesn't think I'm ready. Professor Marvell says I'll get a mentor next year. Not you, though, I guess?"

"Not me. My skills and Daniel's needs are a better match. Cybele is also here, with talents that can benefit him."

"That's great, Mr. Geldman. And, really, I'm okay."

Boaz flapped his wings. "Sour face can't lie," he screeched.

He obviously meant Sean. "I'm okay with *Daniel*, anyhow," he told the bird.

Boaz sidled over to a food cup attached to the perch and

pecked out peanuts and apple chunks. Apparently he was done, for the moment, with Sean.

Geldman? Nope. "May I take it that you question the Order's management of your studies?"

Sean shrugged. The armchair thoughtfully plumped up behind his shoulders. "No. Well, yes. Daniel's starting practical magic right off. That proves there's more going on with me than, 'Oh, it's your first year, so theory only.'"

"What else could be going on?"

He gazed into the candle flame nearest him. "Did Orne ever tell you about a connection between us?"

"He told me you were his descendant."

How long ago had he told Geldman that? Before Sean's first visit to the pharmacy? "Professor Marvell just found out. Maybe he's having second thoughts about training Orne's ten-times-great-grandson."

"I see."

"Like, would you give a pyro a box of matches?"

"Or even one match."

Geldman understood. Sean lifted his eyes to the wizard's. Heavy lids half obscured them, but beneath the lashes, a hundred light motes glinted, reflected candle flames. "Now, I may be wrong, Sean."

But?

"There may be something to your concerns."

Since Sean had expected Geldman to toe the Order line and dismiss his worries, that answer was a mild shock: mild because something that would have upset him elsewhere had little sting in the parlor. While most of the candles were white, those on the tea table were green; they gave off a fragrance like the one that had accompanied Cybele's touch, flowering grass and herbs newly mown. He remembered where he'd smelled it before. After the

Servitor's ichor had burned Helen, Marvell treated her with a balm labeled CYBELE's #1, and Sean had often snuck whiffs from the jar, because the smell alone was enough to loosen the knot of guilt any glimpse of Helen's bandages had tied in his midsection. Whatever made the smell, in balm or candles, acted like magical Valium.

"Sean?"

"You think so, too, Mr. Geldman. They don't trust me."

"If you mean the entire Order of Alhazred, I can't speak to that." Geldman made a tent of his hands by pressing his fingertips together. "Helen Arkwright, on her own, wouldn't think to distrust you. However, she goes rather in awe of Theophilus Marvell. In her heart she might not share his reservations, but she wouldn't oppose any precaution he took."

"So Professor Marvell doesn't trust me."

"Remember, Sean, I could be wrong."

"But can't you read minds, Mr. Geldman? Like when I was trying to remember Boaz's name? And when Eddy was trying to say what she thought about the pharmacy, and she couldn't, but you said, 'Exactly'?"

"I can catch unguarded thoughts, but a person's strong intention to shield his mind is enough to defeat me. As a paramagician, Marvell can deploy such a shield."

"So you can't read his mind."

"No. And if I could, would it be right to tell you his private thoughts?"

"You're telling me what you *think* he thinks."

"Speculation is another matter. And you haven't answered my question."

Boaz swallowed a last peanut, then, head cocked, joined Geldman in watching Sean. Except for the white bib, he could have passed for the crow in the *Founding*, Nyarlathotep's minion. "We haven't done magical ethics yet, but I guess it would be like reading someone's secret journal and then tweeting about it. Only worse."

"Oh, very well said for a milk-teeth pup," Boaz squawked.

"Be still," Geldman said.

"But it is a pup, so it is."

"Be still."

Boaz launched himself off his perch and dive-bombed Sean's head, pulling up at the last second, so his claws only grazed hair. Then he flew up the staircase to the second floor, where he chattered to himself. His distance-muted rant wasn't like any language Sean had heard, unless you counted the grunts and squeals of movie Orcish.

"It's not only blood-spawn Servitors that get unruly," Geldman said.

"No problem. Eddy's dog is worse."

The way Geldman's eyes narrowed robbed his smile of real amusement. "I'd have thought Marvell would address magical ethics at once. It's one of his obsessions."

"Is that why he hates Redemption Orne?"

"Does he hate him?"

"Well, he said Orne should have died long ago. You wouldn't say that about someone you *liked*."

"It depends," Geldman said. He struck his finger tent by dropping his hands into his lap. "Some believe that immortality or even significant life extension is a misuse of magic. Marvell's often taken me to task for my longevity. Yet we remain colleagues."

A whipcrack of incredulous anger lashed Sean, unsoftened by the green candles. "That's freaking rude, though! Like asking, 'how come you haven't dropped dead yet?' "

Geldman laughed, the candle-flame motes jittering in his eyes. "I assure you, Sean, I don't let the Professor offend me. He has strong objections to immortality, which the Order largely shares.

It tolerates me because I commit the lesser sin of living beyond a normal human span."

"You're not immortal?"

"Not as Orne is. Eventually I'll get tired, my magic will wane. There's only one way for a human to gain immortality, and I decided against that long ago."

Orne had named the way during his first chat session with Sean. "The Communion of the Outer Gods."

"The Communion of Nyarlathotep, to be precise. But isn't it odd how our talk has wandered to that? I only wanted to know you wouldn't let Daniel's apprenticeship push you two apart. You ought to be friends, I think."

Sean had no objection to that.

It was a loud thought, because Geldman said, "I'm glad to hear it. But to go back to Professor Marvell. It's actually Orne he distrusts, and so your relationship to Orne can't help but trouble him."

"So I shouldn't worry about being held back?"

"Accepting the situation would wear less on your nerves."

"Or about him thinking immortality sucks?"

"Are you in favor of immortality, Sean?"

"I don't know, but I don't like him coming down on you."

"You're kind to take my part."

"What's so terrible about living a long time, anyway? Or even being immortal?"

"No doubt you'll ponder those questions when you study magical ethics. Right now I imagine Cybele has led the tour to the soda fountain, so—"

The word *soda fountain* conjured Boaz, who flapped downstairs and lighted on Geldman's right shoulder. As they walked the white corridor to the shop, the crow made a perilous clinging transit to his master's left shoulder and pivoted to Sean. "Learned your lesson?" he inquired.

"I guess," Sean said.

"Good boy. You get a drink. Lemon or root beer or chocolate. No? Like it red? Cherry's red, and strawberry's red, and blood's red. But no blood for you."

"Nonsensical bird," Geldman said with surprising severity.

7

When Boaz asked Sean if he'd learned his lesson, Sean said yes mainly to avoid a dive-bombing. But he *had* learned two important things during his visit to the pharmacy. One, that Marvell didn't trust him, now that he knew Sean was Orne-spawn. Also, that living a very long time had made Geldman so chill, he could shrug off Marvell's prejudice against people who lived a very long time. And come on, as long as a magician didn't hurt anyone in the process, why shouldn't he extend his life?

Going into class Tuesday morning, Sean was all set to ask the question, but Marvell went straight to the dry-erase board and wrote *EIDOLON* on it. "Eye-*doe*-lin," he pronounced the word. "Greek for 'image' or 'idol.' In English, for our purposes, it means 'ideal.' An ideal is an abstraction, a perfect *idea* about something. In magic, *eidolon* has special meanings."

Under *EIDOLON*, Marvell drew an amoeba radiating yellow squiggles. "Azathoth, who emits pure but chaotic energy, blind force."

To the amoeba's right, he drew a bat-winged eye with three

slit pupils. "Nyarlathotep, who imposes order on blind force. The result is what we call creation-eidolons—ideal patterns for creating particular types of energy or matter. You could call them the blueprints for everything."

The creation-eidolon he drew issuing from Nyarlathotep was a neat black box. He connected it via arrow to a clump of blue bubbles: "Yog-Sothoth," Marvell named the bubbles. "Who acts as guardian for the creation-eidolons, a sort of cosmic library."

Daniel typed like a madman. He and Sean had decided Daniel should take notes for them both, while Sean, the better artist, should copy drawings. He embellished his version of Marvell's diagram with letters, an *A* in Azathoth's "stomach," an *N* crowning Nyarlathotep, a *Y* protruding from Yog-Sothoth like the legs of a stick figure plunged into the acid seething of the librarian god.

Marvell droned on. "Only Nyarlathotep can fashion creation-eidolons, but all magicians impose will on force, *intending* it to do one thing or another. Some intentions *direct* energy, while other intentions *substantiate* it, making it material or changing one material into another. Daniel, some examples of directed force?"

Daniel reeled off, "Telekinesis, telepathy, precognition, illusion, clairvoyance, pyrokinesis."

"Sean, of substantiated force?"

The first one was easy: "Summoning, Professor, if you give the summoned thing an actual body in our plane."

"And?"

"Um, alchemy, and shape-shifting."

"Yes. And?"

There was a major one with a name he couldn't remember under the stress of Marvell's gaze. "Some psycho-thing. Shub-Niggurath does it."

Marvell cocked an eyebrow, then drew in red a tree trunk with toothy mouths and flailing tentacles. "Shub-Niggurath, who transforms creation-eidolons from idea to reality. We call the process?"

Psycho, psycho, psycho-something from the Bible—

But Marvell waited only seconds before asking, "Do you know, Daniel?"

Cornered, Daniel had to answer: "Psychogenesis, Professor."

Okay, Sean wouldn't have come up with that anytime soon. Still.

Marvell gave Daniel an approving nod. "Correct. But psycho-genesis belongs solely to the Outer Gods. Let's return to the kind of intentions that have practical applications in human magic—"

Practical applications, finally. Sean jumped in: "Professor? I was wondering—so, I formed a magical intention when I summoned the Servitor?"

Marvell had begun to erase the board. He didn't turn back to the table until he had finished. "No, that's exactly what you didn't do. Orne gave you a spell devised by Enoch Bishop, and the intention to summon a certain familiar is inherent in its symbolism and incantations. To put it bluntly, Sean, you borrowed Enoch Bishop's intention. His will formalized."

"But I was the one who intended to call *this* Servitor, so doesn't that count?"

Marvell gazed upward; when he spoke, it was to the distant ceiling: "I'm concerned, Sean. You always drift back to the summoning. It strikes me you're trying to make one act of second-hand magic into your claim to fame."

The ice water always on the table during class remained on its tray, but Sean felt as though a poltergeist had poured the whole pitcher down his back. Daniel's chair creaked. Sean didn't dare look at him, so he kept looking at Marvell.

And Marvell kept addressing the ceiling: "That's not necessary, you know. The Order acknowledges the potential that allowed you to act as an extension cord between Enoch's intent—the spell—and the energy Enoch's Master gifted you. But you didn't shape the intent or independently gather the energy, and it will be some time before you learn how. So slow down, please. Stop dwelling on last summer and keep to the task at hand."

"I didn't mean it like that, Professor."

"Perhaps not, Sean."

Daniel's chair hadn't creaked again. Was he still there? Yeah, but he was posing for a statue of *Dude Totally Absorbed in His Laptop.*

"Well," Marvell said, and smiled as if he hadn't just delivered a swift nut-kicking. "We'll continue tomorrow. I have a seminar in Boston. You two have enough reading to get you to two o'clock?"

Daniel said, "Yes, Professor," for both of them.

In his wake, Marvell left an oppressive silence. The library clock read eleven thirty, not too early for lunch, but Sean already had a gutful of humble pie to digest.

Daniel closed his laptop and dutifully got out a book Geldman had given him. Its catchy title was *On the Mysteries of the True Atlantis off Novo-Anglia, and of its Origins and Denizens,* and its author was everyone's favorite, "A Gentleman of Boston in the Massachusetts Commonwealth." On the cover was a woodcut of two Puritan guys in a boat surrounded by mermaids and mermen, though the merpeople seemed to have frog legs, not fish tails. Frog faces, too, and Sean had probably looked as goggle eyed as them when Marvell had let him have it.

Instead of opening the book, Daniel tugged at his neck brace as if it chafed him. It probably did, hot as the last week had been. Glad for any distraction, Sean said, "Dude, you really have to wear that thing all the time?"

"What?"

"Your brace. I mean, your neck doesn't seem to bother you much."

Daniel dropped his hand from the foam collar. "My neck feels okay. But my doctor said to wear this for two more months."

"Sucks. That's the rest of the summer."

"I can deal." Daniel nudged his book aside. "Look, Sean. I believed you."

Sean blinked. "Believed me what?"

"That you didn't ask Marvell about the summoning to brag."

It was a relief for the elephant in the room to stomp center stage. "I just wanted a straight answer."

"I figured. You did kind of interrupt his lecture, though."

"So I pissed him off."

"Yeah, but it was still harsh, saying you didn't do anything magical on your own."

"What if he was right?"

"In that case, would Redemption Orne still be after you? Anyway, I never heard Marvell talk like that."

"That's because he thinks you're great."

Daniel drew in a sharp breath.

Damn. "And you are! You and Eddy. Plus he doesn't have to worry you'll do something stupid."

"He's right about Eddy." Daniel smiled weakly. "Me, who knows? But why should Marvell think you'll mess up?"

It had been more than a week since Sean discovered the deep-down reason for Marvell's uneasiness, and he hadn't even told Eddy yet. She had to be the first to know about his connection to Orne, because ever since their pirate–spy blood pact in the third grade, Eddy had been his secret-keeper, and a blood pact had no expiration date. But maybe he could make Daniel understand about Marvell without going into his crazy ancestry. "It's because of Orne," he said.

"What about him?"

"Marvell's worried about why Orne wants me for his apprentice. Like, does Orne sense I have dark-side potential? Like, I might sign up with Nyarlathotep after all?"

Daniel shook his head. "Marvell said all that?"

"Well, not exactly, but he did say I have to go slow with magic. And Geldman said yesterday, the way Marvell feels about Orne is probably the reason I'm not getting a mentor until next year."

"You're not?"

Oh right, that was another thing he'd kept to himself. "Nope. I'm not even allowed to do any practical magic until then."

"Did you tell Eddy?"

"Not yet."

Daniel worked fingers under his brace and scratched like his neck was the enemy. The way he grimaced, it had to hurt.

"Hey—"

At Sean's matching wince, Daniel abandoned the self-assault. "Eddy figured you were mad about something Geldman had told you. That's why she went to her room early last night, in case you wanted to talk. I think she was bummed when you didn't show up."

Surprised, anyway. "It's—we've been tight so long. Did you ever hear what she did during the Servitor mess?"

This time Daniel's smile was anything but weak. "Helen says Eddy talked to you to keep the Servitor from taking over your mind. Then she beat on it with a baseball bat and kept it from killing your dad."

"You so want Eddy on your side."

"I do, man."

"I *was* wanting to talk to her. But a lot of it's about Marvell, and she thinks he's Professor Perfect."

"Fan girl."

"Exactly."

Again Daniel went to attack his neck beneath its foam barricade. He checked himself. "It's not fair you aren't getting a mentor and learning practical magic, same as me. Maybe not to do the big-ass stuff you did before—"

"You heard Marvell say how big-ass that was."

"He was trying to pop your swelled head," Daniel said, face sober but eyes gleaming.

The gleam freed Sean to laugh until laughing loosened the springs in his chest that Marvell had wound aching tight. "He wouldn't pop my head in Helen's library. Blood on old books, bad."

"Important safety tip—thanks, Egon."

Was that a Perfect Movie Moment from the new guy? "I guess Eddy taught you our game. *Ghostbusters,* by the way."

"Busted. Five points or ten?"

"Should be five, but because you're a noob, I'll give you ten."

Grinning, Daniel stood. "I'll waive the points if you'll make lunch."

"Deal."

Without Helen or Eddy around to enforce reasonable nutrition standards, Sean made his infamous Sky-High sandwiches, bologna and cheese with potato chips squashed between the layers. After that belly bomb, he was thinking nap, not the next chapter of Henry Arkwright's *History of the Cthulhu Mythos.* Daniel, on the other hand, was alert to the point of drumming his fingers on the breakfast bar. "Maybe we could do something besides read," he said.

"Does this something include moving?"

"No, you can sit."

"Good enough. What's the plan?"

Daniel went to close the kitchen door. Back at the bar, he said, "Since the Order won't give you a mentor, maybe we can share Geldman."

"How?"

"I can teach you what he's teaching me."

"Magic?"

"What else?"

Candlemaking? Victorian home décor? "What about Marvell not wanting me to do practical magic?"

"I don't think that's fair. Do you?"

"No, but I don't want you sticking your neck out."

"I'll only stick it out when there aren't any guillotines around."

Sean straightened from his stuffed sprawl and scanned the backyard. If Marvell was lurking behind a stack of plywood, he was doing a good job of it. "I guess you could just *show* me the stuff you're learning."

"Sure." Daniel swept their paper plates into the garbage can, clearing the decks for action. Sean got a paper towel and wiped the bar down, his heart picking up speed at the prospect of real magic.

Resettled, Daniel said, "What Marvell was talking about, creation-eidolons, psychogenesis? That's great, we've got to know theory, but Geldman puts things a lot plainer."

Geldman *would* talk like a normal person, even though he had to know way more about theory than Marvell. Not to derail Daniel's lecture, Sean kept the opinion to himself. "He doesn't use—" Jargon. "—technical terms?"

"Not much. It's more than style, though. See, most of the Order are Source magicians. Geldman's an elementalist, which is like going off the grid."

"Not using electricity?"

"Not using the blind force Marvell talked about. Geldman calls that Source energy, capital *S*, because the Source is Azathoth. Almost no one uses *pure* Source energy, though. It only gets to earth through a few portals or rifts—good thing, because it would fry most people's brains. A few magicians allied with Nyarlathotep can use it. Not even all of them."

Could Orne? "So if you can't use Source energy—"

"You can't use it pure. But mostly it filters through lots of interdimensional fabric first. That weakens it down to *ambient* energy, which is everywhere, all the time."

"And that's what most magicians use?"

"Right, but elementalists go a step further. They use energy that's seeped into earth or air or water, or that's coming back out of material as fire. They believe the nature of that energy's different, changed—now it belongs to whatever element absorbed it, not to Azathoth. I guess there's a controversy about whether the elementalists are fooling themselves about getting away from the Outer Gods, but anyhow, going elemental is advanced magic, so Geldman's teaching me Source magic to start."

If Geldman would teach Source magic, and most of the Order used it, it had to be okay. Even considering the Source. "So there's magical energy all around us, here in the kitchen."

"Everywhere."

"And you can feel it?"

"Not all the time. Only when I channel it to do magic."

"What's that even mean, though? Channeling, intentions. How's it *work*?"

"It's different for each magician."

"I was afraid you'd say that."

Daniel laughed. "Right, why can't there be one easy method? But it's all about symbols. Human brains don't like abstractions, so to channel energy, you have to come up with your own symbolic complex for doing it."

Sean slumped again. "Symbolic complex. That's as bad as creation-eidolons!"

"If I can figure it out, you can."

"So you have? You can do magic?"

Daniel checked the kitchen door, then the clock over the sink, before nodding. "A little."

"Seriously?"

"Lame stuff. But I'll show you." From his breast pocket, Daniel extracted a pencil stub two inches long, which he set on the countertop. Parallel to the stub, he arranged a slip of notepaper, and then he scooted his stool back. "So check me. I can't touch the bar even with my feet."

Sean checked. Nope, with his legs stretched straight out and his toes pointed, Daniel still came up inches short.

"And you can see my hands."

"Ah, yeah."

"I just don't want you to think it's a trick."

"I trust you."

"Then shut up."

"The Great Glassini requires silence!"

"Shut up."

Sean obeyed and waited for Daniel to draw pentagrams in the air or mutter incantations. He did neither, didn't even look at his pencil stub. Instead his protuberant eyes flicked from side to side until they went glassy, fixed on nothing Sean could see. His body was still except for his shoulders, which rotated like he was trying to swim without moving his arms from his sides. Was he even breathing? Could you concentrate so hard, you forgot to? Though the kitchen AC was on, the atmosphere in the room thickened; Sean felt pressure in his ears, mildly painful.

He managed not to break silence or squirm on his stool.

The pencil stub moved.

Sean didn't see it, but his straining ears caught the slide of wood on quartz countertop. He looked down in time to catch new movement, the stub's pivot from parallel to the notepaper to perpendicular across it.

Though his shoulders kept rotating, the trancey glaze left Daniel's eyes. He leaned forward, breathing, avid.

Inch by inch, the stub scooted toward him across the paper.

Then it pivoted to aim its lead point at Sean. What if Daniel (turn-ing out to be an evil wizard) fired that sucker right between his eyes?

Cool in theory, better in practice that Daniel straightened, shoulders stilling. "That's it," he said, throaty.

"I saw it," Sean said.

"Hope so. I'm done for a while."

"No, I mean, I *saw* it, and before that I *felt* like something was happening. The air changed. No way that wasn't magic."

"Telekinesis."

"Telekinesis counts."

"You've seen magic a lot more impressive."

Sean had seen a Servitor birthed out of flaming briquettes. He'd seen Geldman's Pharmacy age decades in a second. He'd even seen freaking Nyarlathotep, who could be in innumerable places simultaneously, and so no problem for him to drop in on Sean. "But it's different with you. That other stuff looked too easy. Like Geldman shrugs, and the pharmacy's open or closed, and fortunes pop out of the scale, and candles burn forever."

As if trying to erase his scars, Daniel rubbed the pencil stub between his fingers. "You're not surprised with Geldman, be-cause you figure he can do about anything. With me, you don't expect it."

"You're a normal guy."

"Thanks."

"So when you do magic, you make it seem—"

"Really real?" Eddy said.

She couldn't have been standing in the kitchen doorway for long. During the weighty silence of Daniel's buildup to magic, Sean would have heard her turn the knob. "Um, door's closed, you knock first?"

"That would've messed up the magic." She came in and snagged a stool. "I knew Daniel was going to show you what he's learned so far. He showed me yesterday, while you were with Geldman. He levitated a straw!"

"About an inch," Daniel said.

"That's more than Sean can do until he gets a mentor. Which will be when?"

Same question she asked every day. He gave the same answer: "Sometime."

"I thought you were going to ask Professor Marvell this morning."

"He'll let me know when the Order decides."

Sandwiched between them, Daniel mouthed, *Tell her.*

Sean mouthed back, *Not now.*

Daniel frowned and said out loud: "Why not just tell her? It's not like it's your fault."

Great, that made Eddy lean around Daniel so *she* could frown at Sean. Now that she'd gotten the whiff of a secret, he might as well give it up. "All right. I'm not getting a mentor this year, because I'm not allowed to learn any practical magic, so why bother. Marvell changed his mind, or the Order changed its mind, and he told me at that meeting I had with him and Helen."

It was gratifying, actually, how Eddy gaped. "Why would they change their minds?"

Sean would have given a noble shrug and spared her illusions about Marvell, but Daniel spoke up again: "We think Marvell might not trust Sean, because Orne picked him for his apprentice. And Mr. Geldman thinks that's the Order's reason, too."

"But Professor Marvell's known about Sean and Orne all along," Eddy protested.

"Right," Daniel said. "But when it came down to training Sean, maybe he got cold feet. Marvell's a lot harder on Sean than on me. This morning he landed on him for asking a question about the summoning. Like, Sean thinks the summoning's his claim to fame when really he was just a—" He looked at Sean.

"An extension cord," Sean said.

Eddy's jaw slackened again.

"An extension cord between Bishop's spell and Nyarlathotep's energy," Daniel explained. "In other words, Sean didn't do crap. That's not what Marvell said, but that's what he meant."

"And what's Geldman got to do with this?"

Sean took that one: "Yesterday he agreed that Marvell hates Orne so much, it could affect how he thinks about me."

"You were complaining to Geldman about the Professor?"

"We were just talking."

"And whenever you talk to Geldman," Daniel said, "the important things come up."

Eddy pushed off the breakfast bar. Her wheeled stool glided backwards to a gentle impact with the prep island. She was still frowning, but not at them. "I don't get it. Professor Marvell was totally cool with Sean before."

She didn't get it, because Sean hadn't told her about the root rot Helen had discovered in his family tree. Crazy. He'd told her every stupid thing he'd done during the Servitor crisis, but now he was ashamed to tell her about his ancestors, who were totally not his fault?

Although Marvell seemed to think otherwise. . . .

"They'll be cool again," Daniel said. "Meanwhile it's not fair Sean can't learn practical magic."

"Nothing we can do about that."

Daniel propelled his stool to the island, next to Eddy's, opposite Sean's. "I can do something. I'm going to teach him what Geldman teaches me."

If Sean had realized Daniel was bent on full disclosure, he would have blown his brains out his ears trying to do telepathy: *Dude! It's too soon to tell her about that!*

Amazingly, Daniel's blasphemous opposition to Marvell didn't stir up Hurricane Eddy, just a brisk chilly wind. "I don't know," she said. "It sounds like the Professor was too hard on Sean today, but that doesn't mean he's wrong about him waiting. Besides, you keep saying, Marvell, Marvell, but wasn't it the Order's decision?"

"Marvell's in charge of the study program, so—"

"So maybe you guys shouldn't go behind his back. Especially if Helen agrees with him. Does she, Sean?"

Daniel looked surprised by Eddy's reaction, which showed Sean still knew her way better. "Yeah, Helen agrees," he said.

"All right, then."

Sean expected Daniel to fold. Instead he said, "I don't want to sound like an elitist jerk, Eddy, but you're not a magician. Neither's Marvell, not all the way. Until last week, I would've agreed with you, but now that I'm learning magic, there's no way I'd want to give it up. Sean, you know what I mean?"

Sean's memory of the summoning and dismissing spells had never lost its keenness. After watching Daniel touch the power, his longing for that rush had resurged. "Yeah, I feel that way, too."

Eddy had glanced at Sean, but her eyes returned to Daniel's. "You make magic sound like an addiction."

"Not an addiction—that's running away. Wanting to do magic is running toward something. It's what I feel like I have to do. Like, if you're a bird, do you fly?"

Sean got Daniel's point before Eddy did, or at least, he blurted it out first: "Sure you do, because you have the wings for it. Well, unless you're an ostrich, and your wings don't work anymore, but then you have killer strong legs, right?"

Daniel gave him a dubious look. Eddy sat chin down and brows knit. Finally she said, "Magic is wings for you and Sean."

"And your wings are your superhero brain cells."

"Or supervillain brain cells." But Eddy smiled. "I can't hate you for wanting to help Sean. I guess if you're unbelievably careful, you can teach him a few things. *Minor* things. *Safe* things."

Daniel couldn't appreciate how big a victory he'd scored. Sean, knowing, played the one Perfect Movie Moment worthy of it: "Dude, you are so my brother, my captain, my king."

To judge by his deep bow, Daniel understood the honor Sean bestowed. *"Fellowship of the Ring,"* he said.

"Ten points."

Of course, Eddy still had to do her Gandalf Stormcrow imitation. "If the Professor and Helen find out—"

"We'll be unbelievably careful not to let them," Daniel said.

"Yeah, well. What magic were you doing, mind-moving that pencil stub? If Sean tries a trick like that, he might put your eye out."

"Daniel can borrow goggles from the construction guys," Sean said.

"Or a welding mask," Daniel added.

"Go with the mask," Eddy said. She headed for the door, calling back over her shoulder, "You guys better move if we're going to play any tennis before dinner."

Sean trailed her as far as the basement stairs before realizing Daniel hadn't come along. He poked his head back into the kitchen. Daniel stood at the breakfast bar, spinning his pencil stub. With a finger, not with magic. "Hey," he said. "That was really a great speech."

Daniel didn't look up. "I meant it, Sean. About magic being our wings."

"Right. You coming?"

"In a minute."

Daniel sounded down. Maybe he was having a post-magic reaction, like a mini-hangover, and so Sean left him to spin it out in peace.

8

How they decided Daniel should "tutor" Sean was this: Tuesdays and Thursdays, they'd grab an hour after theory class; Mondays, Wednesdays, and Fridays (Geldman days for Daniel), they'd grab an hour after dinner. Eddy was cooler about the unauthorized lessons than Sean had expected—the one additional warning she issued was not to use the library. Marvell or Helen could show up anytime, or other Order members looking to consult the Arkwright tomes.

Daniel and Sean ended up using Helen's fabled "dungeon," which Eddy had discovered during a solo prowl of the unfinished basement. In the farthest, darkest corner a bulkhead opened onto stone steps that descended into a brick-lined half cylinder of a wine cellar. In Endecott Arkwright's day, its floor-to-ceiling racks must have held enough booze to get all of Arkham drunk, but now there was only the low reek of ancient vinegar and a few bottles so new, they hadn't even collected dust. The rest of the racks had become spider condos, fully occupied. Under a single dangling lightbulb, Daniel and Sean arranged a folding table and two rickety chairs borrowed from the upper basement, and they were all set for magic lessons.

Daniel said the dead-air silence of the cellar was perfect for gathering energy, and soon he was spinning whole pencils and levitating sheets of paper to the ceiling. All Sean spun were his wheels. The experts who said he was a potential magician, Marvell and Helen, Geldman, even Orne, they'd change their minds if they could see him struggling simply to access ambient energy, supposedly Azathoth's freaking bounty. After nine sessions with Daniel, he still hadn't come up with anything more productive than the Jedi hand-out-eyes-closed trick, which did zip for the (obviously) non-Jedi Sean.

At the opposite end of the bell curve, Daniel had devised what Geldman called an access metaphor: a way of visualizing ambient energy so that he could absorb it. The irony was that ocean-phobic Daniel visualized energy as these deep-sea brine pools he'd read about. They were saltier than the surrounding water—so densely salty, a submarine would float on them! What if that heavy brine (ambient energy) flowed through the lighter ocean (the rest of the world) in streams, and what if Daniel could swim down and let his hands float on the heavy water, so its salt diffused into his palms? Bingo, access metaphor! He just had to visualize the swimming as intensely as possible, which was why his shoulders rotated—swam—when he was in collection mode.

But the more Daniel practiced, the less his shoulders moved. His process was becoming internal, invisible, which was the goal. Around nonmagicals, an energy-gathering magician didn't want to look like he had a movement disorder. Around other magicians, to broadcast gathering could invite a preemptive strike. But even without a physical "tell," it was hard to fool keen magicians, who could sense when others tapped into ambient energy.

That last tidbit of Geldman lore gave Sean hope, because he *did* know every time Daniel gathered energy. The air thickened as before a storm, and he felt the change of pressure in his ears. When Daniel spent energy, the object that received it would brighten, like Mom's paintings and the glass crow her ghost had somehow influenced, but the glow Daniel created was a minute flicker in comparison, then gone.

Sean got that his own access metaphor had to grow out of some innate quality of his magic. The problem was that his magic didn't seem to *have* any innate qualities. Geldman said most magicians, including Source-users, found effective symbolism in the elements. And so Sean had tried Water and Earth, Fire and Air. Water, Daniel's inspiration, did nothing for him. With Earth, he envisioned quakes, drifting sand, mudslides, all big nopes. Fire gave him a mild tingle of connection when he imagined lava zigzagging through the cracks in volcanic rock. Air, again a mild tingle when he imagined it as heated gusts.

But the tingles weren't enough, because they left ambient energy too vague for Sean to grasp. Daniel wouldn't let him give up. If Sean kept trying new visualizations, he'd eventually hit the right metaphor. Easy for Daniel to say. He'd found his way in already.

One day, when the Order would be meeting in the library all afternoon, Daniel persuaded Sean over lunch to hit the dungeon for an extra-long session. Sean had agreed—how could he not when Daniel was so willing to put in the time?—but considering how unlikely he was to have a magical breakthrough, it seemed too bad to waste an afternoon like the one speeding by outside the kitchen windows. Even the guys hustling drywall into the carriage house looked energized by the rare summer combo of bright sun and low humidity. Drywall meant the interior framing was done, and the plumbing, and the electrical work: The building's skeleton and arteries were finally in place, its wire nerves taut. Throw the main circuit breaker. The Order's new headquarters would light up. It would live.

The image of wire nerves struck Sean as one of those quirky

jerks his brain generally took on its stumble from No Idea to Got It. A second jerk came when Daniel flipped the switch at the bottom of the wine cellar steps. A retina-searing flash exploded from the dangling lightbulb before blackness reasserted itself. "Shit," Daniel said.

It was so *not* shit. Lightning—

"Sean, you okay?"

Lightning strike! That was what it felt like when he'd stepped into the summoning pentagram and Nyarlathotep's energy had surged into him. "Sure," he said. "Bulb just popped."

"I'll go get another one."

Daniel fumbled up the steps. Sean stayed put, his back to the weak illumination of the main basement, his face to the wine cellar darkness. The tingles of energy he'd struggled to harvest so far had come from the image of white-hot lava zigzagging through rock. Lightning was white. Lightning zigzagged. And the almost useful images of hot air? Lightning made the air it traversed expand, bang, thunder.

Lightning was electricity in its flashiest form, but electricity was everywhere. You could generate it by shuffling across a carpet. It hummed in the wire nerves of the Arkwright House and in the battery of his cell phone. If ancient people had known more about it, wouldn't they have added electricity to their list of elements?

Daniel brushed by Sean with a lit flashlight—an ordinary battery-powered one. Detective O'Conaghan had a flashlight that ran off magical energy. Magical energy behaving not like water or earth, fire or air—

Light refilled the wine cellar. Daniel tucked the spent bulb into a rack slot. "That's better."

"I think I've got it," Sean said.

Daniel brushed a web and its spinner off his chair. "Got what? One of these Shelobs?"

If there was a spider on Sean's chair, it was squashed meat—he'd crashed down without checking. "An idea."

He'd tried to keep excitement out of his voice, but from the way Daniel leaned across the table, he'd picked up on it. "For your access metaphor?"

"Maybe. Give me some room."

Daniel leaned back and locked in, arms crooked behind his chair.

Sean looked up at the lightbulb, but the juice zipping through its filaments wasn't the magical energy he needed—actual electricity could only help him as an image. He left his face tilted to the glare but closed his eyes.

"That's right," Daniel said. "You want to start with black space, a blank. Now put whatever you want into it."

Sean imagined lightning first. No tingle. Maybe the bolts were too sporadic. He tried a Tesla coil that veined his black space with its violet discharge. No tingle, but the image felt more . . . appropriate? A better match for the ambient energy in the wine cellar? Geldman had taught Daniel it was crucial to match the intensity of the metaphor to the intensity of the available energy. At first Daniel had thought too big: waterfalls, flooding rivers, tsunamis. He'd had to scale back to the heavy-brine streams. It made sense. At this distance from the cosmic center, filtered through every interdimensional barrier between it and the Arkwright House, Azathoth's output was background radiation. The trick, then, would be to scale back electricity to approximate it.

He stared at the lightbulb again. Glass shell, vacuum, a filament heated by electrical current until it glowed. Reflecting its glow were the threads of a spiderweb spun between the fixture cord and the ceiling.

Filaments.

Threads.

Spider-line made of energy instead of silk. Electric webbing, with Azathoth as the spider that had cast it all the way from ultimate chaos. Picture the Outer God as a mindless but busy creature with infinite spinnerets. It spurted strands that arced in every direction and tangled without pattern. Nyarlathotep was the clever spider who'd weave portions of the tangle into orderly webs, but forget about Nyarlathotep. For now Sean had to keep his mind on the raw electric silk until his mind's eye saw it clearly.

Between one breath and the next, it saw.

It saw, and he realized the difference between his clumsier imaginings and the one that could work for him. A gossamer web shot through black space, its strands radiating from innumerable points beyond his darkness. Where he'd messed up was picturing ambient energy as tangled; though the strands crossed each other at every angle, no one strand touched another. What he couldn't figure out was how an innumerable number of the innumerable strands pierced him through and kept going without imparting their energy. He should have been filled to the brim with magic.

Sean grabbed at the silk with the imagined hands of his imagined pincushion body, but they passed through the strands without changing their course or absorbing more of a tingle than his discarded metaphors had yielded. He opened his eyes and lost the whole damn symbolic complex, as Geldman would say. Minus the damn.

Daniel still pinioned himself to his chair. "So?"

Sean groaned. "The way that bulb blew? It made me think of lightning, and that made me think of trying electricity as a metaphor. I got as far as this electric spiderweb shooting at me from everywhere. Going right through me, too, but it didn't leave its energy. I should've gotten enough juice to put the whole house in orbit!"

"That's okay. Ambient energy's always passing through us, but we can't hold on to it until we consciously claim it."

"I was trying. You know, grabbing for it."

"You just have to figure out the next part of the metaphor. Like, I was trying to dive into my streams at first. Geldman said, be more subtle."

How subtle did you have to be to grab web? Hold on, though. Spider silk wasn't his real access metaphor—electricity was. A matrix of electricity kind of *like* spider silk, so call it silk lightning. And to catch lightning—

You used a lightning rod.

A lightbulb must have appeared over Sean's head, because Daniel said, "You've got another idea?"

"Maybe."

"All right, but go easy." Daniel's laugh was short, a little anxious. "Like I said, I don't dive. I just touch the surface of the heavier water. You, trying an electricity metaphor? Talk about a scary combination."

"You listen to Eddy too much."

"Not sure that's even possible."

"No worries. I don't want to blow anything up. Especially not my own head." So Sean would skip his first idea of a battery of lightning rods on castle parapets (the full Frankenstein) and go with a single rod.

He closed his eyes and imagined the silk lightning into his black space. The irregular matrix re-formed in seconds, again pinning him in its center. Maybe he should pause the process and give his actual collecting metaphor further thought? Daniel would be cool with that, and he'd tell Eddy how cautious Sean had been, which would rock her world. One problem. This close to doing magic again, there was no waiting.

Sean imagined his right hand. Then he imagined his right hand holding a lightning rod. Instantly lightning arced to it, and white-hot pain jolted into his imaginary arm. He dropped the imaginary rod and opened his real eyes. Thank you, Jesus, his real arm was still there, unscorched. He'd expected to see his hairs frizzled, at least.

They weren't, but they *were* standing straight up, and there *was* heat in his hand and forearm. It set his nerves vibrating between pain and pleasure and his muscles thrumming with contained energy. Though it was nothing like the sense of superhuman strength Nyarlathotep's lightning bolt had conferred, he finally had some magic in him again.

"You gathered, right?" Daniel said. "You must have, yelling like that."

He'd yelled? Sean flexed his right arm. Its feverish vibration grew uncomfortable. "You have the lucky pencil?"

"Hold on, I should." And yes, Daniel produced the stub he'd used for his first demonstration. He set it in the middle of the table. "Go for it."

"You're not wearing goggles."

"I won't tell Eddy if you don't."

Besides, it wasn't like Sean would even get the stub off the table. Intention came next, feeding on the energy he'd collected. He concentrated on spinning the stub in a circle. On letting the thrum in his arm flow out to push the worn eraser, to flick it. Push the eraser end. Flick.

Flick!

His release of magical energy didn't feel any more spectacular than a good hard sneeze, but the stub not only spun—it also whirled off the table like a runaway helicopter rotor and hit the back wall of the wine cellar and popped into flame as it fell among some yellowed wine labels on the floor, which it set on fire.

Daniel shoved off his rickety chair so hard, it skidded into the spider condos. Sean's went over with a crash. Then they were both at the mini-conflagration, Daniel stomping it out, Sean kicking debris away from the smoking ashes. The danger averted, Daniel squatted, prodded something, and jerked back his hand. "Ow!"

"What? What is it?"

"It's that metal band that held the eraser on. It's melted. Still freaking hot, too."

"I melted it?"

"Well, it sure wasn't me."

Sean squatted next to him, and for a few seconds they hung over the silvery wad like two cavemen awestruck by a meteorite. Daniel recovered first and punched Sean's shoulder. "Impressive, man!"

Sean returned the celebratory jab. "Shit, I was only trying to make it spin."

"It spun, all right. Told you to take it easy."

"I thought I was."

"Guess you better take it super easy next time."

No kidding. He'd held the lightning rod for less than a second. Maybe he needed a smaller one? Something more like a kebab skewer? "It rocked, though, the feeling."

"I suppose it did," a voice said that didn't come from Daniel. It didn't come from Eddy either, not this time, not even close, being masculine and deep and full of the Back Bay. It was Marvell's voice, and Marvell was standing by the one wine-bearing wine rack, not looking amused in the least.

Sean stood and faced him. Daniel did, too, jaw working so hard, it kept notching a dent into his foam brace.

Marvell looked away from them long enough to select three bottles from the rack. "It's Dr. Benetutti's birthday," he remarked. "The meeting wanted to offer her a toast, and I volunteered to brave the spiders."

No way, was there, that Marvell hadn't caught them out? That Sean could come up with an excuse for being in the wine cellar?

They were chugging wine. No, no open bottles. They were sharing a joint. That would explain the smoky smell, and Daniel looked like a headlight-frozen deer, so he wouldn't protest.

Never mind, because tucking the bottles under his arms, Marvell added, "I doubt Helen wants anyone practicing magic down here. Particularly not you, Sean."

"Okay, Professor, well—"

Marvell ascended a step. "I suggest you clean up and put the furniture back where you found it. Our meeting should be over at four. At five I'll expect to see you, Sean, in my office at MU."

Just him, not Daniel?

"Sean?"

His throat was dry as the ashes underfoot. "I'll be there, sir."

Bottles clinking, Marvell exited. Speaking of bottles, would it make Sean's situation any worse if he copped some wine for himself and drank it before his sudden appointment?

"Dude," Daniel said, voice low and shaky.

Sean slumped against the wall. "I'm so screwed."

"I hate that."

"How I'm screwed?"

"Yeah, that, too. But I mean the way Marvell acted so cool when he's got to be really angry. I can't stand that shit."

"Me neither."

Daniel scraped at the ashes on the floor. "I'll get a broom."

"I'll get the chairs." Sean grabbed Daniel's. Daniel picked up the one Sean had knocked over back when, fire panic aside, things had been going great.

In the main basement, Daniel said, "Look. I'll go and talk to Marvell first. I'm the one who offered to teach you. It's just as much my fault."

"I could have said no."

"But—"

"Get the broom, okay? I'm going alone, like he wants."

"But you'll tell him I started it."

Sean threw the chair back into the musty corner where they'd found it. Wood cracked, and he was glad. "I'll figure it out when I get there," he said.

9

Helen's office was in the glass-and-steel addition to the university library. Marvell's was not only in the original building but in one of the four corner turrets to boot, a prime location if you liked stone walls, vaulted ceilings, and Gothic windows so heavily leaded, they excluded more sunlight than they admitted. Even his desk was Goth, walnut aged to a dull black sheen, with hunched gargoyles taking the place of legs. The two guest chairs matched the desk; the desk chair didn't. In its sleek ergonomic embrace, Marvell looked smugly comfortable, like a medieval interrogator ready to haul a confession out of some poor slob before calling in the guy with the ax.

An ebony screen cordoned off the anachronism of digital gear. Sean almost knocked the screen over when he sat on a guest chair and started butt-skating off its slick horsehair seat. Marvell watched him resettle himself over the wire rims of reading glasses. Then he took off the glasses and said, "I was surprised this afternoon, Sean."

"Sir?"

"That Daniel Glass would let you talk him into teaching you magic."

Nice how Marvell assumed that Sean had initiated the tutoring sessions, but if Daniel hadn't insisted on getting his full share of the blame, Sean would have let the assumption ride—it sucked to sound like a snitch. "I didn't ask Daniel to teach me, Professor. He offered to."

"Really? You didn't hint?"

"No, sir. He offered on his own."

"Did you tell him the Order doesn't want you practicing magic yet?"

"Yes, but anyway, he's just showing me what Mr. Geldman teaches him."

Marvell didn't doff the cool mask that had bugged Daniel, but in it his eyes narrowed. "Apparently you and Daniel were too engrossed to notice, but I was on the cellar stairs a couple minutes before you hurled that pencil into the wall. Before it burst on fire. Before it started a bigger fire in the trash. If fire had gotten to the wine racks, tinder dry as they are—"

"It didn't! We put it out."

"Is that the point?"

To hang his head would be the smart move. To say, *No, Professor, because if I hadn't been trying to do magic, there wouldn't have been any fire to begin with. And blah blah, I was wrong, blah blah, I'm sorry, blah-blah blah-blah-blah, it won't happen again.* Rubbing his right forearm, the one that had vibrated with magic, Sean had a weird sensation that, the magic spent, it was missing crucial muscles and nerves. Forget about the shamed-dog speech. "Yes," he said. "It *is* the point. That we put the fire right out. That I did magic and nothing really bad happened."

Mask finally slipping, Marvell glowered. "Something bad *did* happen. After destroying the pencil, you told Daniel you'd only meant to spin it on the table. Therefore you lost control, entirely."

"I didn't *lose* it, Professor. I just didn't know how to use the energy yet. How much I'd need, how much to let go."

Marvell rolled his eyes toward the vaulted ceiling. "Amazing that you didn't know, considering your teacher has studied practical magic a whole week longer than you have. There's nothing more hazardous than a neophyte leading a neophyte. Especially when one of the neophytes has little capacity for discipline."

That slap stung. "But you haven't given me a chance to show any discipline!"

"No? What about the agreement you made with me and Helen? There was an excellent opportunity to show restraint, but you couldn't go a month without breaking it."

"Maybe because it wasn't the right agreement, Professor."

Marvell rapped his desk with his folded reading glasses. If he did that often, he had to go through a dozen pairs a year. "The Order decides case by case how students should be trained. Each young magician has different needs and abilities. What will work for Daniel won't necessarily work for you."

"I know, Professor, but you wrote it yourself in *Infinity,* how once a magic-capable person finally does magic, like me and Daniel both have now, he's got to keep doing it."

"I wrote that such a person would *want* to keep doing it, which isn't the same thing as *having* to. We're back to control, Sean. Back to patience. Back to trusting the Order—"

"But the Order doesn't trust me, or at least you don't, Professor. You want to know why Daniel offered to teach me? He thought you were being unfair, setting him up with a mentor but not me."

"Daniel doesn't know your background."

"But you do. Even Mr. Geldman thinks you're holding me back because of Orne, and Orne's not something I can help, and that's why it's not fair."

At the mention of Geldman's name, Marvell had frozen, glasses poised between the lift and the smackdown. With exaggerated evenness, he asked, "Are you saying you've discussed your status as an Order student with Solomon Geldman?"

Great, now he'd dragged Geldman into this mess. "No. I mean, me and Eddy were just hanging out at the pharmacy, and Mr. Geldman wanted to talk to me privately. He wanted to make sure I wasn't mad at Daniel for getting a mentor ahead of me."

"And somehow the conversation turned to the Order's lack of trust in you."

Yeah, somehow. What had Daniel said? Whenever you talk to Geldman, the important things come up. "I guess because I was worried about it."

Marvell slipped his glasses and some scattered pens into a drawer. While clearing his desktop, he also cleared all irritation from his face, so that his cool mask fit perfectly again. "To be honest, Sean, you should be worried, but not about me or the Order. Though it's not our reason for holding you back, your lineage *is* troubling—I challenge you to reread Phillip's history of the Witch Panic and keep a good opinion of Redemption or Patience Orne."

"I never had a good opinion of them!"

"Knowing you're related to the Ornes hasn't softened your judgment, now you've had time to think about it?"

"No, sir."

"Well, I'm glad to hear it. Her involvement with the dark arts aside, Patience Bishop Orne was probably a psychopath. And no, I'm not suggesting you're one. If I thought that, you wouldn't be here."

Thanks for the vote of confidence.

"As for Redemption. By all accounts, he was intensely curious, enthusiastic, impulsive, strong willed. He tried to curb those tendencies so that they served his Puritan faith, but it was all up once he discovered magic. One bit went out of his mouth and no new bit went in, because restraint was the last thing *his* mentors worried about, Patience and Enoch Bishop."

Bits grossed Sean out, how horses slobbered over them, how they had to pinch, come on. "So you're worried I'm like Redemption."

"Curious, impulsive, stubborn, enthusiastic, yes."

"Last summer you were all for curiosity."

"When controlled, it's an excellent quality in a magician. The same holds for enthusiasm and strength of will."

Sean had to say it: "Wouldn't part of a mentor's job be to teach me control?"

"Before anyone can teach you to control magic, you need to learn self-control. Think of it as a muscle. Yes, a mentor can refine how you deploy that part of your strength, but only if you've already built the muscle up."

"I can do that, but—"

"Then prove it," Marvell said. He added, "Otherwise . . ."

The way Marvell paused after drawling that *otherwise,* was Sean supposed to crack and blubber, *Whatever you say, sir*? Screw that. He could stand as much suspense as Marvell wanted to dish out.

But instead of being awed by Sean's Spartan silence, Marvell twisted it into a win for his side. "Stubborn again. Then I'll have to make this conversation unpleasant."

It had been pleasant before?

"If you can't accept the Order's rules, it won't be able to work with you. It will have to withdraw the offer of magical training."

"Send me home?"

"I'm afraid so."

Dad might be only semi-reconciled to Sean studying magic, but for Sean to get kicked out for breaking the rules? Capital offense. As for Eddy, she might not leave enough of his ass unchewed for Dad to get a nibble. "I don't want to go home," he conceded.

"No one in the Order wants that. Helen, in particular. After last year, she feels a strong connection to you."

It was a dick move to bring up how badly Sean could disappoint Helen. He had to think about Daniel, too, who already blamed himself for the wine cellar blowup. If Sean got expelled because of it—

Sean didn't hang his head, but he did roll out the shamed-dog routine, after all: "I guess I jumped the gun, Professor. I should have told Daniel no thanks on the tutoring. You're not going to come down on him, are you? He was just trying to be a friend."

"I understand that. So no, I won't give him the hard time you've made me give you."

"Okay, well. I'm sorry, and no more practical magic until you—"

"Until the Order, Sean. Honestly, I'm not calling all the shots here."

Maybe not, but he sure seemed to like pulling the trigger. "No practical magic until the Order says okay."

"And the other things we agreed to?"

The way his head was thudding, it took Sean a minute to remember them. "Um, don't talk magical business out of the wards. If I see Orne's aether-newt again, tell you or Helen. If Orne tries to contact me some other way, same thing."

"You've stuck with those rules so far?"

"Yes, sir."

"And you'll keep sticking with them?"

Did Marvell want Sean to sign an oath in blood? "Yes, sir."

"Then let's shake on it again."

He gripped the hand Marvell extended across the ebony gleam of his desktop, then used the momentum of leaning forward to get on his feet. "I better go, Professor. They'll have dinner ready at the House."

Marvell gave him the warm smile that had Helen and Eddy fooled, but it softened just the lower half of his mask, leaving his gaze icicle-pointy. "Let Helen know we've worked things out, and tell Daniel I'll talk to him before class tomorrow."

Lucky Daniel, but that was still getting off easy. Sean felt like he'd been in the turret office all day, not the twenty minutes Marvell's cathedral spire of a clock had ticked off in its niche by the door. He had one foot on the medieval flagstone of the office, the other on the Victorian parquet of the hallway when Marvell added, "One last thing I need to make clear. Even if the Order finds it can't further your magical education, it will continue to supervise you."

"What's that mean?" Sean asked cautiously.

"It means even if you are no longer with us, we'll keep track to ensure you don't take up with an unauthorized mentor or try to continue with magic on your own."

Split between centuries, Sean sorted out the threat: "You'd try to stop me from getting another teacher?"

Marvell shook his head. "We wouldn't *try*, Sean. We *would* stop you."

"From doing any magic, ever."

"That's what our mandate to protect the public would require. I'm sorry to sound harsh, but you've got to realize magic isn't a toy. In the Order, we take our responsibilities seriously. You need to start doing the same."

In other words, screw up again, and Sean could land himself an early appointment with the ax guy. "I've got you, Professor," he said, and then he got both feet in the same century and moved them, fast, breaking into a run long before he hit the library exit.

10

That night, Eddy grilled Sean until he'd given up every detail of his meeting with Marvell. Two things kept her from killing him: First, Daniel was a major conspirator in the tutoring scheme. Second, she herself was a minor conspirator. Forced to split the verbal whupping three ways, she ended up giving herself the biggest smacks. "I knew better than to let you guys do this," she groaned.

Seeing Eddy upset seemed to bother Daniel more than the idea of facing Marvell. "Yeah, but how could you have stopped us?"

"I could've told Helen. She'd have talked you off the ledge without involving Marvell."

"Don't be so sure," Sean said. "Helen thinks he's Professor Godly. She'd have told him."

"Nobody's Professor Godly to Helen," Eddy said, defending her own goddess. "Anyhow, forget them. I should've talked you out of it myself."

"I'm the one who brought up tutoring Sean," Daniel said. "That makes it my fault."

Normally Sean would have let them fight for the blame, but Daniel kept giving Eddy's shoulder these awkward pats, and you didn't pat Eddy when she was mad. "Hey, let it go. We're all still here, and I'll just have to wait to learn magic, that's all."

"Man, I'm sorry."

"Don't be. If it's anybody's fault, it's—"

But Sean couldn't say "mine," after all. Magic went gene-deep for him—it was natural he'd want to do it. And Marvell had promised him a mentor, and Sean wouldn't have almost torched the wine cellar if Marvell had stuck to that promise. If anyone was to blame, it was Marvell.

Sean left the sentence hanging and took off for his room. It wasn't five minutes before Eddy knocked. He yelled he was in bed. For a couple minutes more, she whispered outside the door with Daniel. Then they left him alone.

But they must have gone straight to Helen, because first thing next morning *she* was knocking on his door. Sean let her in. "My turn to make breakfast," he said, like he'd been about to hurry to the kitchen and knock out a ten-course brunch buffet.

"Cheerios and strawberries?" Helen said.

"Um, Rice Krispies and blueberries."

"I guess that can wait a few minutes." She settled on the window seat, which gave him no choice but to park on his desk, facing her. At least he was in shadow, while a shaft of sunlight spotlighted every freckle on her face and kindled her hair to spiky auburn fire.

"Eddy and Daniel talked to me last night," Helen said.

"I figured. Did they have a humongous debate about who was more to blame for me being an idiot?"

"A moderately humongous debate. Mainly they were worried about how angry you seemed when you cut out of the discussion."

"I was sick of going over it. What's there to talk about? I'm done."

Helen swung her feet up onto the seat. "'Done' doesn't sound good."

"It's true, though. I'm done with magic until Professor Marvell gives the go-ahead."

"Ah."

"What?"

"He's the one you're angry with. Theo."

"Maybe."

She ducked her chin and looked up at him from under raised brows.

Sean had to give. "Well, he *is* the one in charge, right? And he decided I couldn't do practical magic right after you told him me and Orne are related."

"It's not that simple, Sean."

"I can do complicated."

"Theo only proposed the delay. The decision was the Order's. A majority of members agreed that your introduction to magic had been too abrupt, and you should take a step backwards."

Helen thought she was telling the truth—the steadiness of her gaze proved it. Should he tell her about Geldman's suspicions? About Marvell's own admission that he thought Sean was like Redemption Orne? Impulsive, stubborn, too curious for his own good. Bound for the dark side right out of the action figure box, might as well just hand him the red light saber. "You're sure, Helen? The Order doesn't think I'm, like, too dangerous to train?"

She smiled. "You're too dangerous for *Daniel* to train. Burning up my wine cellar."

"We had the fire out in five seconds."

"I know. And the only Orne-related danger the Order's worried about is the danger he poses to *you*. Did you ever think . . ."

When she hesitated, Sean took the bait. "Nope. That's my problem."

Helen wrinkled her nose at him. "Bullshit."

"Wow, thanks."

"Did you ever *think* that the more magic you do, the more Orne's going to want you? Ever think that's why Theo might be applying the brakes?"

"But how's Orne going to know I'm doing magic? Me and Daniel only did it here, inside the wards."

"But you go outside the wards every day. Doing magic changes your energy, Sean, in ways Orne or his newt could sense."

"I didn't know that." But knowing it now didn't negate Marvell's dick behavior in the Office of Doom, especially the way he'd lobbed that twenty-megaton threat when Sean was halfway out the door.

"Well, you know now. Theo's on your side, Sean, same as me. Part of that is sometimes seeming overprotective, harsh, because we're afraid for you."

Was Marvell afraid *for* him or *of* him? Sean almost asked Helen the loaded question, but Daniel had come out of his room and started down the stairs, to meet Eddy halfway up, from the sound of their voices. "Better go make that breakfast," he said.

"Right, I hear the hungry horde's on its way to the kitchen." Helen accepted the hand-up Sean offered. She gave him an earnest look. "You're all right, then? Or better at least?"

Helen always made things better, so Sean could give her back an earnest nod.

"Good. I'll help you, ah, cook."

"Pour the Krispies?"

"Wash the blueberries."

"Deal."

By Sean's watch, Daniel's pre-class meeting with Marvell lasted seven minutes, just long enough for Marvell to lecture him about the stupidity of a noob teaching a noob, which was the very pinnacle of magical stupidity and a half-assed scheme he'd never imagined Daniel capable of. Needless to say (though Marvell had said it anyway), repeat stupidity would be grounds for Daniel's expulsion from the summer program.

The word "expulsion" was to Eddy like holy water to a vampire, and now both Sean and Daniel had doused her with it. After she'd recovered from the second scalding, she snarled, "No way I'm letting you guys screw up again." Daniel blanched at the ferocity in her voice, but Sean helped him convince her that further screwing up was in neither of their game plans.

That night, as if to get things back to normal, Helen offered to "chaperone" them to a movie. Eddy and Daniel were in. Sean begged off so he could write Dad about the wine cellar incident—better Dad find out from Sean than from Marvell, who couldn't have informed him yet, or Dad would have Skyped, steaming.

When the rest had gone, Sean was alone in the Arkwright House for the first time. That made the place feel bigger, older, and much more likely to ooze ectoplasm from its walls, however well repaired. What was a little Spackle to a ghost? He tried to write in the common room, but without Eddy and Daniel holding their latest book club meeting or arguing about a Scrabble play, it felt too empty.

He went downstairs to hole up in the kitchen, where at least there were snacks, but the closed library doors lured him over. He slipped inside and fumbled on the overhead lights. The sudden brilliance didn't surprise old Endecott with his feet up on his desk, or Mrs. Endecott embroidering by the fire, or even Helen's uncle John climbing a stack ladder in search of just the right tome. The only ghost around was the spectral aura Mom had somehow infused into the stained glass crow.

Since he'd figured out Mom's secret gift, the crow's halo glow had kindled every time Sean entered the library, lingering as long as he was alone in the room, winking out the second anyone else appeared. He smiled up at it. Mom, or whatever part of her the glass held, was company enough; the other ghosts could stay away, thank you.

However, in case Endecott popped in later, Sean set up his laptop not on the dais desk but on the computer station nearest the crow. He opened an e-mail screen and typed "Hey, Dad." Great start. Too bad he didn't know what should come next. The library was almost too quiet for concentration, the way its noise wards squelched any whooshes from passing cars, any footsteps or chatter from campus pedestrians, any distant buzz from the highway. The open windows admitted only the fiddling of crickets and the halting staccato of some night bird as lost for notes as Sean was for words. "Hey, Dad," was too cheerful. "Dear Dad" was too formal. How about just "Dad"?

Maybe he should light up the *Founding*. It was more likely to inspire him than a stupid blank screen. Sean climbed onto the dais and flipped the switch hidden under the sill. It powered up slimline fluorescent fixtures Dad had mounted between the stained glass and the Plexiglas shield that protected it from weather. *The Founding of Arkham* brightened, and the crow amplified its halo to match, and Sean gave it a thumbs-up—

And was rewarded with a caw. Far off, on the edge of audibility, but a caw, all right. A second and a third followed faintly. Simultaneously, the crow's beak gaped.

Sean dropped onto Endecott's desk as the crow flew from Nyarlathotep's upflung hand to the right edge of its window. The wooden frame between the left and center windows proved no barrier; the crow passed through without a missed wing flap and began circling the governor and minister. They remained motionless, merely painted glass. Same with everything else in the *Founding*.

And the crow's flight was smooth, free of the jerky stammers of supernatural movement you saw in horror movies. That almost made it scarier, except why should Sean be scared while the crow still bore Mom's aura? So what if things in her paintings had never moved. Maybe, transplanted to the Arkwright House, her magic drew extra energy from Order members, like the ones who'd met in the library yesterday. That made sense. It had to.

A stronger caw flirted with his eardrums. The crow was calling him, and if it was from Mom, might it not speak for her?

Because he should have been eager to answer that question, Sean made himself haul a stepladder onto the dais. As he positioned it under the center window, the crow stopped circling to hover above the minister's head, an inky reverse of the haloed dove saints wore in old-time paintings. What if he'd been wrong about the crow? What if an Order magician had enchanted it as a joke? What if Nyarlathotep, the real one, had sent it to summon Sean to a second face-to-face? After thinking the crow belonged to Mom, the first alternative pissed him off. The second made his heart and stomach lurch.

Sean climbed a rung on the stepladder.

The crow perched on the minister's shoulder. Was that its equivalent of a step toward him?

He climbed another rung. Another. His eyes were now level with the crow's.

In a harsh avian accent, a lot like Boaz's, it croaked: *Touch me.*

Instead Sean touched the window sky, cool opalescent glass that retained his fingerprints.

Touch me, touch me, touch me, the crow insisted, bobbing its head with each syllable.

It could be Mom. Or a joke, or Nyarlathotep, or—

A trap Marvell had set to catch Sean doing magic?

That thought triggered a surge of anger that swamped any fear of the Master; worse, that polluted any wonder and longing for Mom. Any fool with a stepladder could touch a few cuts of glass lead-bound into the shape of a bird. There was nothing magical about it. Or if there was, Sean didn't give a crap.

With his left hand, he gripped the ladder top. His right he lifted to the crow. Its hum had strengthened—he felt it with his fingertips still an inch from the glass. More, the hum had developed thuds and pauses, like a heartbeat.

He reached through the inch of air and touched the crow, and it pulsed lightning into him.

And then—

He was the crow.

11

He. Sean. Was the crow.

But not the glass crow. No, he was a real one with real nerves and real muscles that suddenly didn't know how to keep him perched on the minister's shoulder, or how to fly, or how to do anything other than misfire and spasm. It was a good thing the minister was also real now, and that he had enough control over his hands to catch Sean and lower him gently to the turf. Real turf, too, not streamer glass: it was thick and soft and starred with clover, just the thing if you had to lie on your feathered side and flail a helpless wing and claws.

"Don't struggle," the minister said. He sounded amused, but without any meanness to it. "The first transition's always startling, especially if you pass into a nonhuman body. Or construct, I should say. You're no more a crow than I'm the Reverend Benjamin Tyndale, first pastor of the first church in Arkham. We're two minds meeting in a fabricated world, thinner than the glass it's seeded inside, though you'll find it feels as wide and high and deep as our own."

Sean lay still.

"When your mind finishes merging with the construct, you'll be able to walk, talk, even fly. I thought of merging you into one of the other humans, but I thought you'd like the crow better."

As his panic subsided, Sean *felt* the merge. He was no longer trapped in the crow's skull, imperfectly connected to its body; like a warming plasma, his will spread through the web of its nerves until he owned the finest fiber and so the whole. He hopped onto his thin-toed feet and ruffled his feathers into place, sleeking both wings with his beak. Then it hit him. Whoever occupied the minister construct didn't sound like Mom. It didn't sound like Marvell, either. No, it couldn't be Marvell, because he wasn't a magician, and whoever had created a whole world inside the *Founding* had to be crazy powerful. One magician came to mind at once. Sean opened his beak. He caw-spoke: "Mr. Geldman?"

The minister settled cross-legged on the turf. "That's a reasonable guess, but I'm not Solomon Geldman."

Don't let it somehow be Marvell—

"I'm Redemption Orne," the minister said.

Of their own accord, Sean's wings propelled him into the air. Startle response? He glided to the ground a few yards from the minister. "I don't believe you," he croaked.

Unoffended, the minister smiled. "Why not?"

"This place, it's inside the library windows?"

"Yes."

"Well, the windows are inside the Order's shield—the wards go out to the property lines."

"Oh, I'm aware of that."

"Then you can't be Orne. You're—someone in the Order pretending to be him."

"Why would a member of the Order of Alhazred pretend to be a renegade?"

His wings jerked again, but he checked the flight impulse.

"Because you're testing me. You want to see if I'll break the rules and talk to Orne. Now that Helen Arkwright's found out about him. Now that they've told me."

"And what exactly did Ms. Arkwright discover?"

If the minister *was* Marvell, it was a pretty good ploy to pretend he wasn't on a first name basis with Helen. So was pretending not to know about her genealogical research. "She wanted to figure out which magical line I came from. She traced me back to somebody named Constance Cooke."

"And where did she go from there?"

"She knew you had an uncle named Cooke and a daughter named Constance, who died when she was a baby. Except then Helen found some letters. One was from your uncle to Pastor Brattle. I guess it thanked Brattle for faking Constance's death record. See, because when Cooke adopted her, he wanted to say he found her on the doorstep or something, not that she was related to you and Patience. Witches and murderers."

The minister stood and walked away. For all their apparent reality, the other Puritans remained inert as wax figures. So did Nyarlathotep in the woods to Sean's left and the Indians on the hillside to his right. In fact, everything but Sean and the minister was inert. He looked up at swallows hanging motionless in the sky, down at a line of ants struck to tiny statues as they climbed a yarrow stalk. The eeriness of it lifted the feathers on his nape, and he flew after the minister and lighted near him on the brink of the hill. Below them was the mouth of the Miskatonic and the *Mayflowery* ships and flocks of seagulls, all frozen in place. The minister wasn't looking at the scenery. In fact, his eyes were closed.

Standing half as high as the minister's knee, Sean had to crane his short neck to make out the tight-lipped sadness of his face. Could Marvell fake that kind of emotion? Would he even bother to try? Or was this the real Orne, in which case, Sean had just been pretty insulting. Not that he should care, but—"Um, Reverend? About the 'witches and murderers' thing."

Maybe-Orne looked down. "I was neither a witch nor a murderer when I had to leave Constance behind. Patience was both, however, and I did become a witch soon enough." He extended an arm toward Sean, like a falconer to a falcon. "You can't think I'll hurt you, now that you know we're kin."

If maybe-Orne—probably-Orne—had wanted to twist Sean's neck, he could have done it while he was flapping helplessly on the ground. Besides, he'd break his own neck if he kept craning it. Fluttering up, Sean dropped onto the minister's forearm. He sank claws into the thick wool of his coat sleeve but spared the skin underneath, for the moment.

No hood appeared, no jesses around Sean's ankles, no suddenly conjured cage.

"Ms. Arkwright has beaten me to it," Orne said, "but I did intend to tell you about our relationship. I've known you were a magician since soon after you were born. Your father was out pushing you in a carriage. I was one of those strangers who exclaims over every baby, and since I'd persuaded a plausible young woman to play my wife, your father didn't object. I gave you a finger to grab, as babies will. Even though I'd hoped to feel it, your latent magic startled me. Then, of course, its strength was a delight."

Going after a baby, with a fake wife? That was hard-core stalkerage. "How did you persuade her?" Sean said.

"Her?"

"The woman."

"Oh, a mild ensorcellment. I removed it right afterwards and let her go with an extra hundred dollars in her purse. Puzzling over where the money came from was the only aftereffect she might have suffered."

"You pay people for ensorcelling them?"

"I think it's fair to give compensation. But aren't we getting off track, Sean?"

With so many tracks to pursue, Sean wasn't sure he could jump off one without landing on another. "My dad would freak if he knew you'd done that. He freaked when Helen told him you were my great-grandfather times ten."

"I'm sorry to hear it."

"Yeah, he went up to my mom's studio and stared at the window he made for her. He wouldn't tell me what was up, but I could tell it was something bad."

Orne lifted his eyes to the horizon, where low cliffs declined to sandy marshland and apricot clouds barred a lemon sky. "I know that window well."

Stop there. "You know what window?"

"The one in your mother's studio. The Crusader, the sick pilgrim, the lady in her garden."

"Dad's never put photos of that window on his Web site, or even in his portfolio."

Orne shrugged. "I've seen the window in situ. Last December, during the two weeks you and your father were away."

At Grandpa Stewie's in Vermont, Christmas vacation. "You broke into Mom's studio?"

"The Order put wards on your home, but they left the carriage house undefended. I spent those two weeks mostly in your *father's* studio. He'd finished restoring the *Founding* windows, and now it was my turn to work on them. I suspected you'd come study with the Order. What better way to keep in touch than to make us a sanctuary within its very sanctum? The Arkwright House was still under repair, and I gambled the *Founding* would be installed *before* the Order put up strong wards. My gamble paid off. Since the windows were again part of the house, the wards didn't detect my seed world as foreign magic."

"Nobody in the Order knows the window's, like, enchanted?"

"You're the only one to whom it's shown its magic."

"The crow glowing." A hollow ache started in Sean's middle, where he supposed his crow stomach must be. "I thought that was my mom. Like her ghost had put the same magic in the crow she used to put in her paintings."

"Its energy felt like hers?"

"Yeah."

"Not surprising. The magical signatures of blood relatives are often similar. But now that you know Kate wasn't responsible for the crow, you must be disappointed."

Try "majorly pissed off," now that he imagined Orne in the carriage house. Orne staring at Mom's window. Orne handling the paintings she left unfinished when she'd died, still humming with *her* magic. Sean flapped from his arm and touched down on the nearest soldier. His armored shoulder proved too slippery for comfort. He flew to the foremost Indian, who showed no reaction to claws gripping his bare skin. "I could tell Helen and Marvell," he cawed. "Tell them what you've done to the *Founding*."

Orne approached slowly. "Yes, you could."

"I've got to tell them, in fact. Besides, it's creepy enough you spying on me with the aether-newt. Like how you showed it to me before I came here, to rub it in."

"Rubbing anything in wasn't my intention."

He flapped to a higher perch atop the Indian's head. "Anyhow, the newt's not the worst thing, or even this window. Helen and Marvell told me how our relationship could matter to you. How an apprentice and master with blood ties can make a stronger psychic bond."

"Correct."

"They might even merge their magical energies."

"A synergy is possible."

"And in a synergy, the master's boss. He can steal the apprentice's energy. Make the apprentice his slave."

This time what tightened Orne's lips looked like anger. "I'm not surprised Marvell would tell you that, but he's dead wrong. I want you to be my apprentice, but I don't want to control or enslave you. I promise you that, Sean. I take my oath upon it."

As if Orne's words charged the air between them, Sean's hide tingled. The sensation startled him, then grew pleasant, soothing, and part of his mind asked why he shouldn't believe Orne. Another part focused on a lightbulb popping in a wine cellar, on sparks and lightning, on electricity, all the images he had used to visualize ambient energy. Would another magician's energy—maybe *directed* energy—also feel electric to him?

He beat his wings as if to shed water, and the charged air around him dissipated. "That's magic!" he croaked. "You're trying to 'persuade' me, like you did that woman."

Orne blinked as if he, too, were coming out of a trance.

"You're trying to make me believe you're all right, the Order doesn't know what it's talking about. And then what? You stick a hundred bucks in my pocket to pay for it?"

"No," Orne said. Low, weary. "I wasn't trying to ensorcell, but I *was* using a magical tone meant to calm you, and even that was wrong. If I can't earn your trust without tricks, I don't deserve to." He walked toward woods that in the real world were confined to the left window of the *Founding*. In what Orne had called a "seed world," there were no such divisions. Orne could walk, and Sean fly after, from one "window" to the others. At the edge of the woods was a granite outcropping. Orne selected the flattest boulder for his seat.

Sean made for a pine that had sprouted amongst the rocks and grown up twisted by their rough embrace. One of its branches afforded him a perch level with Orne's shoulders; it also gave him a direct sight line to Nyarlathotep, whose golden eyes remained fixed on the spot where the crow *had* been. Sean steeled himself to see the god turn his head, and smile, and beckon his old minion over.

But Nyarlathotep remained motionless, the one waxwork that didn't "fit" in the diorama, unless you took the longer view that he could "fit" anywhere he chose to. "Does *he* come into the *Founding*?" Sean tried to whisper, but his crow voice refused to be hushed.

"I couldn't have created this seed world without my Master's assistance," Orne said. "But he doesn't need the window to watch you. The Order's wards can't thwart his glance. No wards can."

"So he *is* watching me?"

"Possibly, among a billion other items of interest. You don't have to worry he'll interfere as he did last year. The Master's made me his official agent with you."

"Like, his recruiter?"

Orne studied his upturned palms. "You've got a long road to walk before it leads you back to the Master, whichever fork you follow."

"What are the forks? I come over to you or I stick to the Order?"

"Just so. About sticking to the Order, the thing that troubles me is how that will subordinate you to Theophilus Marvell. I find it odd that a magical society should be led by a paramagician, especially when his position gives him so much say about how students are trained."

"Does it? I mean, he says the whole Order votes on stuff like mentors."

"Possibly an Order committee does—the *whole* Order is a very large and scattered group. Even so, I imagine they take Marvell's advice, which lately has been that the other new student is ready for a mentor, while you're not."

"How do you know about that?"

"From Solomon Geldman."

Sean did the Boaz slide on his branch. A tuft of needles halted him. He gave the tiny cones at its base a sharp pecking. "Well, maybe you're the one to blame. Marvell's afraid I might be a throwback to you."

The contempt in Orne's voice thickened. "Oh yes. He's afraid, and so you have to prove that you can be controlled, and not by your superior inability, which would at least make sense. He'd have you submit to an inferior."

Sean laid off the innocent pinecones. To hear somebody tear Marvell down was sweet. Probably too sweet. "The Professor's not my inferior. Everyone says he's one of the biggest Mythos experts, and how all his research—"

"I don't dispute Marvell's accomplishments. He can be of use to you as a scholar, but he's not a magician, or even the most acute paramagician—Geldman tells me that Ms. Arkwright already surpasses him there."

"She does?"

"She was able to find the dismissing spell for you, under Enoch Bishop's very powerful blotting ward. Marvell knows he couldn't have done that. But so long as Helen Arkwright defers to him, he'll save his envy for others, including his students."

"He's not holding Daniel back."

"He's allowed him a mentor, but he may be withholding other things. However, we can safely leave Daniel Glass to Geldman. You are my concern, and how Marvell's thwarting your impulses toward magic. Counterproductive, I say—nothing's more likely to twist them."

"So you think I need a mentor right now."

"Yes."

"You?"

Orne turned his palms up again, as if to show Sean he had nothing to hide. It was like the old stage magician's gag: *Nothing in my hands, nothing up my sleeves.* But even though stage magicians weren't really magical, they always had something hidden somewhere.

He caught himself sidling between two needle tufts, a crowish anxiety dance. "So Professor Marvell says you suck. You say he sucks. You both say you're on my side. How do I know which to believe?"

Orne didn't flinch from the cawed challenge. "Eventually you'll decide which of us you want to trust."

"What's *wanting* got to do with it?"

"Perhaps everything. In the meantime, you watch and listen to him. You watch and listen to me. You weigh us in your balance."

"I can watch Marvell easy enough, but not you."

"We can meet whenever you like, here."

"No, we can't. I do have to report what you've done, and the Order will shut the window down. Take it right out, if they have to. Marvell pisses me off sometimes, but I can't let you stay inside the wards. It'd be like catching a spy and then letting him go."

Sean had braced for Orne to try his persuasion trick again, but his voice didn't go magically electric. It didn't even rise. "That all sounds reasonable."

"It does?"

"Certainly. At the very least, there's Ms. Arkwright. How unchivalrous if you didn't consider her privacy and safety."

"Well, but—" Sean chafed his beak on the pine branch. "You don't want to talk me out of ratting?"

Orne laughed. "Do you *want* me to talk you out of ratting?"

Sean looked toward the lemon and apricot horizon and into the unexplored woods. He lifted the wings he'd just started to use and felt a breeze tantalize them toward flight. "No, but shutting down your seed world, I don't know, it seems like a huge waste of magic."

"When I explain how the seed world can work from now on, you'll see you don't need to shut it down to protect your friends."

The horizon. The woods. The breeze. "I'll listen. Not promising anything, though."

Orne pointed at Sean. "Your crow is the portal into this fabrication. Until today I was its controller. Remember how the crow perched on Tyndale's shoulder before telling you to touch it? That's because I knew once you touched the portal, your consciousness would flood the avatar and push mine out. I'd need a new avatar—fittingly, Tyndale."

"Okay, so?"

"Now you're the new controller. I'm merely your guest."

Too cool to be true, ergo bullshit. "I don't know how to control anything."

"Here's how to start: I've been able to cast my mind into the crow from a distance, but that's a discipline you'll acquire only with time and practice. For now you'll have to physically touch it. Once inside the crow, you become the keeper of the seed world. No other magician can enter without your permission, and when you want a guest gone, you can dismiss him."

"You can't be in the seed world when I'm not?"

"Not unless you call me in, then leave yourself without dismissing me."

"You couldn't just enter through the minister?"

"Tyndale's not a portal. There's only one, the crow. Now that I've surrendered it to you, you're the only key, as it were."

In his own body, Sean would have sighed. As the crow, he emitted a gargle. "I never even heard of seed worlds before today. You could tell me anything."

"I could. But I'll only tell you the truth."

"How do I *know* that?"

Orne's face—the face of his avatar, anyhow—made the short

trip from unsmiling earnest to deadly serious. "Sean, if I lied to you about this, I'd throw away my best chance to gain your trust. My only chance, probably. Isn't that true?"

He bobbed his head.

"So I can't lie. Nothing's more important to me than your trust."

"Why? What do you want from me, if it's *not* the synergy thing?"

"I didn't say I wouldn't welcome a synergy, only that it wouldn't be the master–slave relationship Marvell described. But that's far in the future, if it's ever feasible at all. Think about our shared blood. Think about companionship. Think about learning magic without the Order's timid constraints."

"Is it? The Order, I mean, timid."

"The Order of Alhazred is reactionary, prejudiced, with a police mentality." Orne paused. "Some of its members, not all. But its founders built on fear, and Marvell is Henry Arkwright's true descendant, not Helen. Her mind is open, her magical sensibility pure. I'd like to meet her as a friend one day."

Orne had good taste, anyhow.

"But speaking of Ms. Arkwright." Orne's voice grew urgent. "She and your friends will be back soon. You don't want them to find you as you are now."

Sean looked down at his puffed breast feathers. "A bird?"

"No, in the library, seemingly catatonic on a stepladder."

Right, wasn't that how he had to look outside, in the real world? "How do I get back?"

"Look over there."

Orne pointed south from their vantage on the hill. Tall headlands marched down the seacoast. Kingsport didn't exist yet, but there was a big-nosed and bearded cliff that had to be a less eroded King Neptune, and there was the Giant's Causeway, rock slabs like humongous stairs. And there, on the tallest cliff, far above them, was the Strange High House, only so far it was just a stone foundation.

"Now find the moon," Orne said.

Floating low over the ocean was a silver crescent with a hot-air balloon lodged between its horns. No, it wasn't a balloon, but the blurry shadow of a palm and five splayed fingers. "A hand!" Sean squawked. "Inside the moon!"

"Your hand, pressed to the glass where you touched the crow. Fly straight into it, and that will return you to your body and re-set the window, everything back to normal."

"How do *you* get out?"

"You or I say a dismissing word, and I'll be returned to my body. I've chosen one easy to remember but not so common you might dismiss me accidentally."

"What's that?"

"First, here's how you can call me back into the seed world. Enter it yourself and then perch on Tyndale's shoulder. If I'm able to come, I'll do so within ten minutes."

It all *sounded* simple enough. "I might never call you."

"It's your decision, Sean. Now, here's the dismissing word."

"Ready."

Orne produced a slip of parchment from inside his right cuff. One word was inked on it: *Nevermore*.

Like Poe's raven quoth. "That word doesn't worry you?"

Laughing, Orne rose and stood with feet apart, as if bracing himself. "Go ahead, Sean, and don't linger after I'm gone. Good-bye for now."

Quoth Sean, then: "Nevermore."

If Orne got a jolt on his way out, it didn't show in his avatar, the Reverend Tyndale. He instantly beamed into his usual posi-tion and became just another incredibly realistic wax figure. Sean flew at his face to see if he'd dodge, which Tyndale didn't.

There was no time for more tests. He flapped for height, then stroked the air hard southward, beak pointed at the moon-cradled hand. Either it only looked far off or else his intention of leaving beamed him right to it—a dozen wingbeats, and he plunged into his own palm. His entrance into the seed world had merited magical lightning. Not so his exit. One second he was the crow. The next he was Sean, dizzy, clinging with both hands to the stepladder and staring at a *Founding of Arkham* in which his crow rose from Nyarlathotep's hand and Reverend Tyndale knelt in gratitude for the newfound land.

12

Sean's dizziness passed quickly, and good thing. Headlight beams lanced the window from a car pulling into the driveway. It had to be Helen's. Unless it was Marvell's, because he had rigged the *Founding* after all and was coming to expel Sean for talking to Orne.

He scrambled off the ladder and whisked it back to the bookshelves. It was too late to run for his room, but that didn't matter—it was Eddy and Daniel and Helen who came in the back door.

As though he'd had an uneventful night, Sean walked out of the library yawning. "Oh, it's you guys."

"And you were expecting?" Helen said.

Kinda sorta Marvell. "You guys. The movie any good?"

"Fairly suckulent," Eddy said. "But the frozen yogurt was great."

Daniel handed him a paper bag stained with chocolate. "We brought you some. I hope it's not too melted."

"Hey, if it is, I'll drink it. Thanks!"

"No problem. I'd hang out while you do, but I'm ready for bed."

"Me, too," Eddy said.

"And me three," from Helen, but she hung back while the others jogged upstairs. "You okay, Sean?"

Not so much, actually. He had the jitters like he'd chugged two quadruple espressos. It was either a side effect of being a crow, or it was guilt. His urge to show Helen what Orne had done to her pet window was abruptly, surprisingly strong, and he might have yielded to it if his bag hadn't started dripping vanilla yogurt and fudge sauce onto the marble floor.

For Helen, it was a perfect distraction. "I was afraid of that. Eddy ordered you double hot fudge. Do me a favor and get that to the kitchen?"

Sean put a hand under the sodden bag bottom. "Right, and I'll clean this up, too, Helen."

"You sure? You look a little pale under that tan."

"Must be the ghost I saw earlier."

"Not seriously."

"Totally not seriously." Unless you counted Orne, who should have been one by now.

With a last apprehensive look at the spattered marble, Helen followed the others. Sean wiped up the spill with paper towels from the first-floor bath, then carried the offending bag to the kitchen. The soupiness of the sundae wouldn't have put him off; the jitters did. He poured the glop into the sink and spray-chased it down the drain. Only a cherry survived the hosing; wedged in the drain, it glowered up at him. Gradually the jitters subsided. On their heels came the kind of caffeine comedown that yelled for more, a return to the great high. Which had been what?

Being in the window. In the seed world, sparring with Orne. At least he'd let Sean get a word in edgewise. At least he'd given

him magic, big magic and a wild new existence in it. With everyone in bed, Sean could go back to the library and into the crow.
He didn't have to call Orne. He could explore on his own, fly
around. Fly!

Better not. Not when it was so much like a drug, it left him
with a hangover. Not until he'd thought about it.

Not until he'd *talked* about it. Thinking stranded him alone
in his brain, which was already overstuffed with secrets. Man, it
was a full-time job simply remembering who knew what. Marvell and Helen and Dad and Geldman knew about great-et cetera-
grandfather Orne, but Eddy and Daniel did not. Marvell and Helen
and Eddy knew about Daniel teaching Sean magic, but Dad didn't
yet. Nobody but Sean and Orne knew about the seed world.

He needed someone who knew *everything*. Marvell was out.
Helen? More than the melting yogurt had stopped him from con-
fiding in her just now. She would have felt duty-bound to tell
Marvell, and because Dad relied on her and Marvell concerning
anything magical, he was also a no-go. Geldman might keep
Sean's story to himself, but what was he really all about, with his
connections to both the Order and Orne? Daniel, no. Sean
couldn't risk dragging him into more trouble.

That left Eddy, and what was wrong with him that he'd thought
of her last? Even before they'd taken their pirate–spy vows of eternal secrecy, he'd known he could tell her anything. In kinder-
garten, he'd told her he was the one who put the dead squirrel on
the teacher's desk. She'd talked him into confessing, but she hadn't
betrayed him. So what if she'd sworn she wouldn't let him and
Daniel screw up again. Maybe he could convince her it wouldn't
be screwing up to keep his access to the window. Or say he told
her everything, and she decided the secret was so dangerous that
if he wouldn't tell the authorities, she'd have to. In that case, he
ought to trust her judgment. He couldn't remember a time when
it hadn't been better—or at least, safer—than his.

In appreciation for its company, Sean spared the cherry a gnashing death in the disposal and gave it a decent garbage can funeral. Then he headed to the second floor and Eddy's room. It wasn't midnight yet. She might be up reading or surfing or writing in her journal.

A thin wash of light snuck under Eddy's door, but she didn't respond to the one-finger knocks that were all Sean could risk, Helen's room being across the hall. Probably she had earbuds in. He tried turning the knob. The door was unlocked. He pushed it open a little and whispered "Yo, Eddy." Still no response, so Sean stuck his head inside.

No Eddy. She couldn't be showering, because both second-floor bathrooms stood open. That left the common room.

He climbed to the third floor, but the common room was dark, and ditto the flanking bathrooms. Could she have snuck back down to the first floor or gone outside? Could she be in Sean's room, waiting for him?

Sean had taken two steps down the hall when Daniel's door opened and in faint light, like from a bedside lamp, Eddy backed out. "No, really," she stage-whispered. "Not tonight, but we could bike down to the harbor—"

"Shh. Sean."

"He's not in his room. We'd have heard him come up."

Sean took one long step back, into the common room. Obviously he wasn't welcome at the moment.

Daniel came out into the hall. "Yeah, well, maybe we wouldn't have heard him. Maybe we were distracted."

"*Maybe* we were distracted?"

"Speaking for myself, totally."

"Here, too. But I wouldn't be scared—"

"I'll think about it, okay?"

Eddy leaned into Daniel, slipping her arms around his waist, inclining her face to his.

Wait—

And Daniel kissed her. On the mouth. Long and serious.

Holy. Shit. Sean stepped out of his flip-flops and pushed them under a chair. Barefoot, he slipped from the common room and edged along the wall to the shadowy stairs. He was halfway to the second floor when the sound of someone else's bare feet, light, running, made him turn around and pretend he'd been walking up all along, no biggie, guy cruising casually to bed, guy who hadn't seen or heard a thing.

Eddy swung around the newel post and bounded down three steps before she spotted him. She jolted to a standstill, one hand clutching the railing, the other dangling her sandals. "God!" she said, a second too late. "You scared the crap out of me."

For once in their lives, let him be smoother than her. "Just returning the favor," he said. "I thought you were going to bed."

"I was talking to Daniel."

"Oh. Well, I wanted to tell you something, but—"

From the way her shoulders rose and fell, Eddy finally got that deep breath she'd been after. "No. We can talk. I'm not tired."

"You sure?"

"Yeah, come on. Let's go down to the kitchen. That way we won't bother Helen."

"Good idea."

Eddy slipped by, and the air she stirred carried to him the scent of Daniel's cologne.

Sean fanned it away before following her.

~⚞~

The first can of iced tea Sean gulped got him over the Eddy–Daniel shock. After popping the second can, he told Eddy everything about Orne. He'd expected the seed world to bother her more than his relationship to Redemption and Patience, but it was the opposite. "Helen's sure about this?" Eddy asked for maybe the millionth time.

"She says she is."

"God. But maybe it shouldn't be a big surprise."

"Because?"

Eddy shook her head. "It explains so much about why Orne is chasing you. I've got to look up that synergy bond Marvell told you about. I can ask Helen, right? She said it was okay for me to know about you and Orne?"

"If not you, who?"

"Yeah, but you didn't tell me for how long? Like, three weeks."

Sean rolled the iced tea can between his palms, but it had already warmed up too much to cool them. "They also said I could take my time. I had to work out how I felt about the whole thing."

"And so you've done that?"

Sean looked out the window at his elbow. Orne's newt couldn't be hovering near it, but it could be flitting around one of the sodium lamps on Pickman Street, along with the moths and bats. Anyway, it couldn't overhear him. "I've worked out enough to know I'm not going to swallow everything Marvell says about Orne. Not without checking into it myself."

Eddy had picked at the polish on her left thumbnail until it flaked. "How do you do that? You can't go back into the window again."

So here came the tricky part. "Well, maybe I could—"

As if to be ready to lay into him, Eddy laid off her nail. "No," she said.

"Listen first."

"You listen! You want to get kicked out of this program and put on the Order's blacklist? You can't go near that window again, and you've got to tell Helen about it tomorrow. If you don't, I will."

She had clamped her arms across her chest, which meant the

discussion was over, her way or the highway. Sean had never actually chosen the highway, but over the years he'd built up a mental picture of it: cracked blacktop zigzagging through desert until it smashed into a fever-red horizon. Traveling down that road, you were bound to rip up your tires, run out of gas and water, shrivel into a skeleton as you dragged yourself toward a convenience store mirage always another mile ahead. But if the alternative was sitting still while your opportunities did the shriveling? "You mean it," he said.

"That I'll tell Helen? Come on, Sean."

"Then I'll have to go back into the window tonight. And call Orne to talk to me. And stay there until Helen and Marvell come yank me out."

So yeah, he was actually pulling onto the highway ramp, and from her gape, Eddy couldn't believe it. "What's that going to accomplish? You'll still lose the window, and you'll get caught and lose the program, too."

"I might not lose the window. If they move my body away from it, I might be stuck inside. I'm not Orne. I can't do the remote jump yet."

"You are freaking nuts."

No, out of nowhere, he was freaking mad. "Eddy, will you try to get it? Why do you think I'm telling *you* all this? It's not, oh, so you can save me from my stupid damn self. It's because you're the only one who might understand. Or maybe Daniel might, but I don't know him like I know you."

She colored at Daniel's name; it wasn't Sean's imagination. Neither was the barely there ghost of Daniel's cologne wafting from her heated face and the hands chafing her elbows. "Daniel might understand better than me," she said.

"Because he's a magician?"

Eddy nodded.

"I don't think so. As well as you, maybe, not better. You've got too many years on him, putting up with me. Watching my back. And me doing the same for you. Trying, anyway."

"Yeah, trying." Eddy smiled, the corners of her lips shaking. "Usually screwing up."

"If screwing up's how I fly, you've got to let me screw up." And that was profound enough to tattoo onto his inner wrist, like a crib note he could refer to whenever he forgot the answers to the real-life quiz. "Look. Even before I found out Orne was my ten-times-great-grandfather—"

Eddy was clearly still adjusting to that idea, from the way she sucked in air.

"Even before I found out, I wanted to know more about him. I kept the last e-mail he sent me." Sean pulled out his wallet, then remembered he'd burned Orne's message the night before their drive to Arkham, ripping the page along its worn seams and dropping each smudged fragment into the candle flame. "No, I got rid of it. But I carried it around a long time."

"It was like Buddy's letter," she said, half to herself.

"Huh?"

"This letter Zooey keeps. Never mind. What else?"

"Marvell wants me to ignore Orne. Except that's not the exact right word."

"Maybe renounce him? No, refute him, like Beelzy!"

Sean might not know much about *Franny and Zooey,* but the Beelzy story, yeah. He remembered that one. "But I don't think I should refute him, Eddy. I think Orne keeps coming back at me for a reason. I've got to find out for myself what he really is. Say Marvell's right about one thing, that I'm like Orne. I'd be finding out about myself, too."

"Marvell's wrong. You're not like Orne."

"Wait, *who's* wrong?"

"Don't start again how I'm his fan girl. I never said he couldn't make a mistake."

"So he could be making a mistake not letting me do practical magic. He could be wrong about Redemption Orne wanting to use me. I'd bet anything the story's way more complicated than that."

Eddy began to swivel on her stool. "You'd bet anything," she said.

On second thought, "anything" could mean *everything*, which was what Nyarlathotep wanted, and what Sean hoped Orne didn't expect. "No, but a lot."

"So, you'd bet Orne's told you the truth so far. That you control the window. That you can keep him out, so he's not spying through it."

"I'd bet that much."

"But it *would* be a bet. You don't know it."

"I believe it."

"Hand me my tea."

Sean did, and she drank the can dry. Then, in place of spinning herself, she spun the can on the island top. Was she playing roulette, like if it came to rest with the tab top facing her, the answer was yes; with the bottom facing her, no? "If I don't tell Helen," Eddy began.

"Or Marvell."

"Or Professor Marvell. If I don't tell them about the window, you have to let me watch whenever you go into it. Plus, didn't you say you could hear the crow from the library?"

"Yeah, from the dais."

"Then I get to listen, too, if I can. That includes if you call Orne into the window. I'll be like your chaperone."

"You think Orne's going to try to kiss me?" Uh, not the best choice of a crack, after what he'd seen upstairs.

And Eddy's color rose, even as she cracked back, "Kiss a crow?"

"Right. Gross."

"Get serious. If I'm going to keep my mouth shut, I have to be sure I'm not letting you walk off a cliff. I can be more objective about Orne than you can—he can't pull any I'm-your-ancestor crap on me, and I'm not magical, so he can't lure me with promises of greater power and all that."

"Kind of embarrassing, somebody eavesdropping."

"Not eavesdropping, because you'll know I'm there."

"I bet Orne will know, too."

"You should tell him, in fact."

"But then he won't spill any evil plans."

"Sean." Eddy drew out his name in an exasperated drawl. "Do you think he's going to spill evil plans to *you*? Look. You want to figure out whether Orne's trustworthy. That's what I want, too. But if it looks like he's getting anything over on you, I'm going straight to Helen. Ditto if you go near that window without me. So, deal?"

It was as good a one as he could have expected. "Deal. But if you decide you have to go to Helen, tell her that you just found out about the window. I don't want you getting in trouble, too. And, same reason, we shouldn't tell Daniel."

Eddy looked down before nodding. "You're right. Except, in a way, that's leaving him out."

She spun her iced tea can again. Looking for a new yes or no? Sean was looking for one, too, on the question of whether to blow his entire up-front-honesty budget in one night. The can slewed to a halt with its tab top to Eddy, and to him. He'd take that as a yes. "Sometimes you have to leave a person out."

"For their own good."

"Or because that's just how it is. Like—" He'd better get it over with. "Like last year, I didn't expect to tag along when you were dating a guy. And I won't expect it now, even though the new guy's halfway decent."

Breathing faster but still sounding breathless, she said, "You were on the stairs."

"No. I was in the common room. Saw you come out of Daniel's room. Saw him kiss you. So I was trying to sneak down again before you guys caught me."

"Yeah, well." Never a coward in the end, Eddy met his eyes. "You caught us first." Then, reading his stare right, she threw the empty can at him, a painless hit to the chest. "And no, not that. God, Sean."

He'd caught the can, and he held on to it. "How would I know? And if you had, so what? I mean, if you like him that much." Because, knowing Eddy, she would have been prepared and all. Right? Damn, Sean wasn't up to being the chaperone around here.

Eddy was fishing around in her back pocket. For a second, the flat square she produced scared Sean with its resemblance to a condom wrapper, but then he saw it was blue cardboard folded over white onionskin. "The fortune from Geldman's?"

"I'm as crazy as you were with Orne's e-mail, carrying it around all the time." She offered him the blue square.

Sean took it and slipped out the onionskin. The words on it looked like they'd been typed with an old-fashioned manual, some letters lighter than others. It read:

Inside there's someone more eager to see you
with every meeting since your recent first. Such
affinities of the soul do exist, even in these
crowded and cynical days. Be aware that a heart
will be yours to take, if you discover you have a
similarly inclined heart to give.

It took him three readings to make sure he'd translated the Geldmanese correctly. "So Daniel thought you were hot right off, and you could grab him anytime you wanted?"

Eddy took back her fortune. "Close enough."

"Looks like whenever Mr. Geldman shoots, he scores."

"I like Daniel a lot."

"More than Joaquin and Greg?"

"Duh, yes."

"Because they didn't like *Franny and Zooey*?"

"Maybe. Partly. We have a lot more things in common than one book, you know."

"Like, other books."

"More than that."

"But he's afraid of water."

Eddy snatched her can back so she could nail him again, this time on the head. Bad target choice, didn't hurt at all, and the can skittered across the floor, flinging tea drops she had to clean up. After tossing her wad of paper towels, she said, "People can get over phobias. But even if he doesn't, I'll still like him. I'll just do water stuff with you."

"Good to know I'm useful."

"You're not—?" Eddy stopped, for once defeated by a word.

And, for once, Sean wasn't. "Jealous?"

"I don't mean you-want-to-date-me jealous," she said quickly.

"I don't mean that, either. Just, yeah, it would suck if you got so into somebody, you never hung out with me anymore."

"That's not going to happen, Sean. Especially not with Daniel. He's your friend, too."

"Right. So you guys can leave me out when you're messing around—"

"Thanks for the permission."

"—and me and you can leave Daniel out when we're dealing with the window. Because, really, that's for his own good."

"You're right. Keep the risk to ourselves."

"Keep it to me. Remember, something happens and you have to tell, you didn't know about the window until *that minute*."

"Well—"

"Come on, Eddy. What's the point of you losing the gig with Helen? If I get thrown out of the Order, I'll need you inside the MU Library to look up stuff in the *Necronomicon* for me. You know, the full Giles."

"Giles? No way. I'm so Buffy."

"Right. You're lucky if you make it to Xander."

Now she went for *his* empty can. He hoisted both it and the half-full one over his head, and she had to settle for punching him in the ribs. A pulled punch, though, so Sean dumped only one glug of tea into her hair, fair all around.

13

The next day Eddy informed Daniel that Sean knew about their new relationship. Mercifully she didn't say he'd caught them in a lip-lock, because Daniel was embarrassed enough without the graphic details. During a break in class, he admitted she was his first girlfriend. The accident, rehab, et cetera. "Dude," Sean said. "You're ahead of me." Which was the truth, considering that over the past three years he'd only made it to a second date twice and a third date once. Plus Geldman had never predicted romance for him. At least not in a fortune stuffed into a cardboard clamshell. At least not yet.

Soon Eddy and Daniel got comfortable enough around Sean to do some mild PDA, and he got comfortable enough not to mind it, so *that* was working out all right. Sean's trips into the seed world were working out all right, too. Eddy came up with a cover story in case Helen or some eerily nocturnal Order member wandered into the library while they were at it. Sean's dad had used this new putty while restoring the *Founding* windows, see, and he wanted Sean to check how well it was holding up, and she was there to hold Sean's ladder. They had to do it in the middle of the night because dumb-ass Sean had forgotten to check the putty earlier and he was supposed to call his dad first thing in the morning. And she was wearing a stethoscope because—

Well, she'd just have to hide the stethoscope if an intruder showed up. Why she actually needed it was to listen to what was going on in the seed world. Without it, she couldn't hear anything unless her ear was squashed to the glass, and even then the sound was muffled. A quick visit to a nursing supply store had solved the problem.

His early trips into the window, Sean kept his distance from Reverend Tyndale. Eddy had insisted he learn how far the seed world extended before inviting Orne back in. Though he grumbled for form's sake, it was fun to explore on the wing, and his adjustment to crow form grew shorter every merge. The first night, with no Orne to catch him, he plummeted to the ground. Eddy's panicked "Sean, Sean!" reverberated through the seed world like the shout of Goddess Almighty. Up on a second stepladder and casting a horizon-to-zenith shadow on the southern sky, she even looked like a goddess, and Sean lay in claws-up awe until he realized his apparent death was causing the divine ruckus. By then he was able to hop to his feet and take flight.

He discovered that unless he aimed for the exit point, he could fly without bounds in any direction. He first flew south, over future Kingsport Harbor, then inland over Indian villages scattered through otherwise solid forest. Flocks of birds loitered motionless in the air he plied. In a clearing, deer paused in mid-bound, and on a promontory, a bear stood guard over a sea in which stalled whales spouted fountains of ice. From two points farther south, he glimpsed smoke rising as if from clustered chimneys. One braided column had to rise from the Plymouth Colony, another from a baby Boston.

His next flight was along the wilder north coast. The third

night he ventured into the forest, an animate cathedral with column trunks, vaulting branches, and sunset-edged leaves that formed a gilded ceiling over the dusky groves. Animals abounded except in the wedge of wood nearest Nyarlathotep. Maybe this wedge was the Master's particular chapel within the cathedral, for the only congregants were the crows and owls and whip-poor-wills that crowded every branch, gargoyle still. Lonely over being the only "living" creature in the seed world, he pecked some of the other birds. They never stirred. He pecked hardest at a crow perched above Nyarlathotep, as if ready to fill in for his missing minion. He couldn't rouse it or knock it off its branch, and Eddy yelled at him to stop—apparently she could see crow-Sean whenever he was in a part of the seed world represented in the *Founding*.

On the fourth night, under the condition he'd leave the window the second she rapped, Eddy agreed to let him call in Orne. Within a minute of his perching on Tyndale's shoulder, Orne arrived. The first thing he did was to take Sean on his wrist. The second was to discover Eddy's looming thunderhead of a shadow and the dark disk of her stethoscope hovering like a companion satellite below the crescent moon. When Sean had explained what the shadows meant, Orne spoke to her directly: "Miss Rosenbaum, or shall I call you Eddy, as I did when we chatted online?"

"Eddy," she said shortly.

"Excellent. And I admire your ingenuity with the scope. It will let you join our conversations. I wish you could simply enter the seed world along with Sean, but that's impossible, as you're neither a paramagician nor a magician."

The shadow shrugged. "I can still see and hear you, Reverend. If you try to snow Sean, I'm pulling him out of there."

"Frank as ever. I'll endeavor to make pulling unnecessary."

Eddy momentarily appeased, Orne sat on his favorite boulder

at the edge of the woods. Sean retook his perch in the twisted pine. "Paramagicians," he said. "So you mean Professor Marvell could get in here?"

"Only if you invited him."

"That's not happening. I wish I could bring Helen, though. It'd be nice to have someone along."

"I thought you might feel that way. It's why I made another avatar construct. Have you noticed the crow perched just above the Master's head?"

"Um, yeah." Noticed and pecked the hell out of it.

"That's the second avatar. If you find another magician you want to introduce to the seed world, have him or her hold on to any part of your body while you enter. Then, when your avatar touches that particular crow, your guest will transfer into it. To be dismissed, as I am, by the trigger word."

Nevermore, Sean was almost stupid enough to say aloud. Almost. "I'd have to really trust that person."

"Obviously."

Daniel was the only one who came to mind, and Daniel was as much out of the running as Helen, given they'd decided not even to tell him about the seed world. "I doubt I'll use the second avatar anytime soon."

"Don't worry. There's no expiration date."

Sean changed the subject to his now-forbidden struggles with practical magic. Orne was especially interested in his access metaphor. "You bring me back to my first essays. Lightning was also my guide into magic."

"Seriously?"

"Yes, but you have the advantage of understanding the nature of electricity, as I didn't in those days. I hope you've toned down your metaphor? Lightning's a powerful image!"

"I've got it down to tiny threads of lightning, like spider silk, coming from everywhere. I couldn't grab the threads, though, so I thought, what about a lightning rod?"

"What havoc came of that?"

The heavenly rumble was Eddy snorting.

Sean told the story of the vaporized pencil and the meeting in Marvell's office. He'd expected Orne to condemn Marvell for once again oppressing magical youth. Instead Orne shook his head. "I don't often agree with the professor, but in this case, he's right."

Sean almost did a 360 around his branch.

"Why so amazed?" Orne said. "I'm sure Daniel meant well, but how can he safely teach what he's just begun to learn?"

Was Eddy going to defend her boyfriend or what? Not a rumble out of her, so it was all on Sean. "Right, but he wasn't stupid. He warned me to go easy."

"Did he know how to gauge the energy you accessed or how to help you create safe images in the first place?"

"He tried."

"This is a situation where trying isn't enough. You see that, don't you?"

In fact, staring down into the concern in Orne's eyes, Sean did see it. "So I shouldn't try to do magic until I have a real mentor. Like Marvell said."

"You're doing magic by being here in the seed world, but it's safe because an experienced magician designed the mechanism, and the mechanism itself supplies the energy for your transitions."

"Does that make *you* my mentor?"

"No, only a friend like Daniel, trying to help you along until you're assigned a mentor, or choose one." When Eddy moved restively but said nothing, Orne added: "I can offer you this world, and perhaps another key."

"A key besides this crow?"

"Yes. Let's see if I can find one." Orne walked over to the governor, who stood untroubled while God-fearing Reverend Tyndale rifled his pockets like an expert wallet snatcher. What Orne came up with wasn't a wallet but a long-barreled antique key with brass curlicues for a top.

Sean flew to the arm hefting the massive key. "What's it open?"

"That's irrelevant. The important thing is you could use the image of a key to collect energy in a controlled fashion. Benjamin Franklin himself realized that trying to capture electricity with rods was too dangerous, so he's supposed to have tried a key instead."

"Tied to a kite!"

"You shouldn't need the kite. Imagine you're holding the key so only the tip of the bow is exposed." Orne demonstrated, leaving nothing visible above his fist but the little brass knob that topped the curlicues. "At the same time imagine your hand's a perfect insulator. Only what you expose of the key will collect energy, which you can then harvest with your free hand."

"Getting just a tiny bit of magic?"

"About enough to spin a pencil, as you meant to do."

"And the more key I poke out, the more magic I grab."

"You'd experiment." Curlicue by curlicue, Orne exposed the bow of his key. "Slowly, cautiously. Remember, this is a *thought* experiment for now, conceptualizing your tools for the future."

Unless Eddy really did have godly vision, she couldn't see the gleam in Orne's eyes that Sean caught from a couple feet away. Or maybe the gleam wasn't conspiratorial, just a reflection of the sunset.

In any case, when Sean had Nevermore'd Orne out of the seed world, Eddy only warned him once not to test the key idea. Orne had scored points by semi-backing Marvell, but mostly she was excited to think he might have hung with Benjamin Franklin.

Sean didn't have to look far for a key to model his imaginary one after. An antique monster stuck out of the china cabinet in Helen's dining room. He borrowed it the next morning, and since they always ate in the kitchen, no one missed it.

Orne was a genius. After a week of practice, snatched half hours in his room or on the beach while Eddy and Daniel were off together, Sean had mastered spinning pencils, levitating feathers, and making mini grit vortices by twirling a finger over the sand. He played it safe, though, and never extruded more than the knob tip of his psychic key—his harvesting image—above his fist.

By Sean's third meeting with Orne, Eddy was comfortable enough to let them out of her sight for a few minutes. They walked under the trees of Nyarlathotep's "chapel," and in a harsh crow whisper, Sean told Orne about his success with the key image. Orne didn't commit himself in words, but he smiled approval. Then he showed Sean another wonder of the seed world. Just a few crow hops inside the wood was a chestnut tree. Orne patted its trunk. "From the library, looking at the left window, you can see this chestnut. It's the tree that has the artist's signature embedded above its roots."

Orne didn't mean a written signature but an amber glass rondel bearing the impression of a horned owl. That was how Plantagenet Howell had marked all the windows he'd designed and fabricated. "But you can't see the signature from the seed world?"

"Come this way." Orne circled the trunk to a gap that accessed the hollow interior. "Too small for a man. Perfect for you."

Sean proved it by stalking into a miniature cavern complete with woody stalactites and shelving mushrooms; the floor was compacted leaves that smelled like plum cake. A honey-gold shaft of light drew his eyes to a tiny window opposite the gap: the rondel! That shaft became the only light as Orne knelt before the gap. "Go to the signature," he said.

Up close, Sean could make out the impressed owl. "I'm there."
"Tap it."

Sean pecked the rondel. The amber glass went clear white and impressionless. He peered closer and let out a wordless caw. The rondel now acted like a wide-angle lens through which he could see the entire library, from the fireplace to the conference table, from the double doors to Eddy on her stepladder, one hand applying the stethoscope, the other pressed to his (real body's) back. More, he could hear the ticking of the mantel clock, the creak of the ladder as Eddy shifted her feet, her muttered, "Come on, come out of the damn woods."

He pivoted to the gap entrance, in which Orne was a single eye. "It's a spy-hole!"

"Your window into the library. You could use it to check on things if Eddy wasn't on sentry duty. And when you master casting your consciousness into the seed world from a distance—"

"Then I could spy on the library. Even on Order meetings. Wait, does that mean you can spy on them?"

"Not in this body, which is the only one you call me to. I designed the spy-hole that way, so you could be sure the Order was safe from me."

"But not from me?"

Orne's laughter echoed in the hollow tree. "Does the Order need to fear you? Come, let's get back into Eddy's sight."

Poor Eddy. When Sean told her about the rondel spy-hole, she was back on the teeter-totter about Orne. On one end of the tilt board was her determination not to believe a word out of his mouth, and on the other end were the words out of his mouth. It *seemed* like he'd deliberately made a spy-hole only Sean could use. But what if his whole story was a lie and he could still sneak into the seed world in Sean's crow or that second avatar he'd pointed out? And even if they put a surveillance camera on the *Found-*

ing, couldn't Orne trick them? Have a dozen ways in, a hundred spy-holes? "Maybe it's time to talk to Helen," she said.

"Not yet."

"Why?"

"I feel like I can trust Orne. I mean, he's trusting me. Marvell sure doesn't. You know he's put a padlock on the wine cellar?"

"No, Helen did."

"He must have told her to."

"Paranoid."

"Ask Daniel. He knows how Marvell looks at me in class, like I'm a time bomb. And look, I don't even totally blame him. But I'd rather hang out with someone who's not scared of me. Somebody who'll actually answer my questions."

"But are his answers the truth? Plus we've got to cut down on these late-night chats, or I'll be so exhausted, Helen will know something's up. And you'll keep falling asleep in class, which isn't helping you with Marvell."

Sean agreed to an hour a seed world session. So the next trip, right off, he spit out the question he'd been swallowing, afraid there was no good answer. "So, not judging, but while you were watching your line for magicians, didn't you kind of stalk some of them?"

Orne lay stretched on the ground. "If you mean I watched certain descendants closely, yes."

Sean had been doing this stiff-legged crow strut on the turf beside Orne, not because he was on edge, just because it was fun. He paused by Orne's cocked elbow. "And if they turned out to be magical, did you contact them?"

"Before you, there were three who'd have made strong magicians." Orne spoke in a lazy drone. "The first was Constance, but I never approached her. She'd been raised to dread her parents. The second was her son, Thaddeus. I didn't meet him until he was forty and a Congregational minister much more comfortable in the job than I'd ever been. I didn't disturb him. It takes more than raw ability. Disposition is vitally important. A certain dissatisfaction with the mundane. A capacity for recklessness."

"You think I've got those?"

"I know you have."

"And that makes me like you."

"Very much like me."

Point for Marvell? Point for Orne? Points for both? "Who was the third descendant?"

Orne plucked a stem of cloverlike blossoms from a nearby shrub. He twirled it, then nibbled a blossom. "You'd like this, I suppose. Quail do."

Who cared about quail clover? The way Orne stalled, Sean had the answer he'd expected. "The third one was my mother."

"Katherine Krol, as she was then." Orne sat up and offered Sean his right arm. When Sean hopped onto his wrist, he lifted him so they could look each other in the eye. "As with you, I watched her from infancy. As with you, when she was sixteen, I made contact."

"With an ad in an old book?"

"No. I vary my method to suit the target, if you'll allow me to use that word."

"You already did," Eddy said from on high.

Orne smiled at her cloudy shadow. "You've been so quiet, Eddy, I forgot you were there."

"Never mind me. Tell Sean."

Orne propped his arm on an up-bent knee to steady Sean's perch. "Kate's school hosted an art show, at which her paintings won the top prizes. I left a note on one saying I was interested in buying it, and her father phoned me the next day."

"My granddad Stewie."

"An understandably cautious man, but my credentials were

enough to get me invited to the house. I owned a gallery in Bur-
lington, you see."

"Since when? Since you knew my mom was into painting?"

"No sooner than that, I confess."

"So you only bought the gallery to stalk her."

Orne sighed. "I don't fully understand what you mean by *stalk*,
Sean. For me, it implies violent intent, like a tiger stalking prey."

Or a lion. "What I mean by it is sneaking around after someone because you're all crazy obsessed."

"So obsessed you do them harm in the end."

"Maybe."

"Then *stalk* doesn't apply to my relations with Kate. I helped
her sell her paintings, earn a scholarship to an excellent school
of design. If any harm was done, it was to my own plans."

Eddy was so into this conversation, she couldn't just lurk.
"How?" she boomed, and "How?" Sean echoed.

"By the time I talked to her about becoming a magician, she'd
already chosen another passion. She—"

"Wait," Sean croaked. "You told my mom you were her great-
great-times-nine? You told her about magic and the Outer Gods
and all?"

"I did. And then I took back the telling."

"What—?"

Orne raised his left hand. "Give me a chance, Sean. I'll finish
the story. Briefly for now, but with all points covered."

Sean clapped shut his beak.

"Kate had great magical capacity. She had curiosity, drive, and
courage. But her curiosity was for this world, and her drive was
to wake people up to what's gorgeous in a pebble, if that was what
she decided to paint. And for that, she had all the courage she
needed."

If Orne had never told the truth before, he was telling it now.
"Since I was real young, I knew Mom could see stuff other people

didn't. She put this glow in her paintings, and they hummed. I could feel it, like they were alive, buzzing."

"I could feel it, too," Orne said. "From the start, in a stuttering manner, Kate put magical energy into her work. Full immersion in magic she didn't want, but I was able to give her two gifts. First, I taught her how to consistently access and transfer energy. Second, I obliterated the memory of what I'd told her about our relationship and the magical world. All she kept was the trick of channeling magic into paint, and I imagine she thought of that as technique, not sorcery. She went to Rhode Island for school. I closed my gallery and, as far as Kate knew, moved to Prague to open another. Occasionally we'd exchange letters. Postcards. Maybe you could find me among her effects as Samuel Grimsby, and your father would recognize that name as well."

Eddy coughed, distant thunder. A crow's throat couldn't get tight, obviously, or Sean would have been coughing, too. Instead he hunched his wings and tucked his beak into his breast feathers.

Orne set him on the turf. "It must be time for us to go. Eddy?"

One more roll of thunder, then "Yeah, pretty much."

No, it couldn't have been an hour. "But afterwards, you still watched her?"

"No. Kate had made her choice. And after you were born, I had you to watch. Say the word, Sean."

There had to be a hundred more questions he should ask. He couldn't put any into words, though, so he cackled: "Nevermore."

Orne vanished.

Eddy rapped on the glass-to-her, sky-to-Sean. He shook himself, then arrowed for the palm in the crescent moon. He popped through into his own body, whose throat was tight beyond tight, almost closed, and whose face streamed fucking tears.

14

After escaping from Eddy's solicitude, Sean spent a sleepless night trying to figure out why Orne's story had shaken him to tears. He couldn't remember Mom mentioning a Samuel Grimsby, but "Grimsby" had been out of her life for a while by the time Sean was born. Besides, kids didn't care about old guys from their parents' pasts, so even if she'd talked about him *around* Sean, he likely wouldn't have paid attention. Funny. If Grimsby/Orne hadn't helped Mom get into the Rhode Island School of Design, she probably would never have met Dad. No Mom and Dad, no Sean. At least, not the same Sean. For good or bad, that made Orne responsible for his existence a *second* time.

Head aching, he finally dry-swallowed aspirin and dozed through dawn. The headache followed him to breakfast, and he was ready to thank any god, Outer or otherwise, when Marvell called to cancel theory class. Helen gave Eddy the day off, and then she and Daniel decided to hang out on the beach until he went to Geldman's at three. Sean tried to beg off. Eddy wouldn't let him. Fresh air would be better for him than lying around. Besides, she wanted to kayak, and she needed a partner.

Well, minus his ocean phobia, *Daniel* could have been her partner. When they got to Arkham Harbor, Sean was glad he'd squelched the snarky comment—Daniel had to be genuinely terrified of the water or he'd be stripping down to his mandatory neck brace and jumping in like everyone else who'd ditched work this sweltering Friday. The swim beach on the south side of the jetty was a refugee camp of umbrellas, sun shelters, coolers, and folding chairs; on the north side, off the launch beach, kayakers rolled to cool off from their treks through the parking lot. With only a light breeze to drive it, the incoming tide was languid enough for Daniel to hike to the end of the jetty. Weird, if you thought about it. You'd think he'd sit on the boardwalk under a café awning, safely away from the water, tall drink in hand. Daniel Glass, preppy man of mystery.

He wasn't close to winning Weirdo of the Day, though. While Eddy fussed with her deck rigging, an unbeatable contender slouched down the launch beach toward the waterline. The guy wore a Windbreaker zipped to his jawline, and a knit cap, and leather mittens. Seriously, mittens, the kind where you could pull back the top layer to expose fingerless gloves, but he had the top layers in place, as if a blizzard were raging and he feared frostbite. He also wore wraparound shades, probably a good thing—his freakishly flat nose, wide lipless mouth, and receding chin didn't leave Sean eager for a look at his eyes.

The guy passed five yards away, but even at that distance he gave off such a reek that Sean had to cover his nose. The smell was a compound of dried cod, and sick sweat, and a cheap sandalwood cologne that made the whole even worse than its parts. He scrambled upwind to escape the foul wafting, and he wasn't the only one. By the time the guy flopped down at water's edge, he had half the launch beach to himself.

Had he passed out from heat exhaustion? No, because he lifted himself on his elbows and gazed without apparent chagrin at the way the mild surf lapped his enormous sneakered feet. In fact, he scrooched closer, so the wavelets broke to his knees, soaking his jeans.

Whoa. How about just wearing flip-flops and shorts? Or, sad to think, how about just taking his meds?

Sean pushed his kayak into the water and paddled over to Eddy, already afloat. He poked his chin toward the guy. "Crazy alert."

"Where?" Eddy looked, and frowned. "Oh. I've seen him before, a bunch of times."

"Here on the beach?"

"No, when I go to the pharmacy to meet Daniel. I call him Mr. Haddock, because of the smell. You caught it, right?"

"Hell yeah."

"He hangs around outside Tumblebee's. Jess, the owner? She can't stand him—he drives away business, but she doesn't know how to get rid of him. I mean, what are you going to say? 'Oh, sir, could you move along, you're gagging my customers?' I feel bad for him, but I feel bad for her, too. I hope Daniel doesn't see him."

"How come?"

"A couple times we thought he was following us back to the house. Both times he turned the other way on Water Street, but it freaked us out."

And there was Mr. Haddock again, dabbling fully clothed and staring off into the distance. Or maybe, hard to tell with his shades, he was staring specifically, creepily, at the jetty, on which Daniel had dwindled to a stick figure among the stick-figure fishermen. Damn, the guy's feet were a size 20, easy, and that wide mouth looked like a snake's, or a shark's. Sean wondered what kind of teeth he might keep in there.

Eddy prodded Sean's arm with her paddle. "Stop staring."

"What if—?"

"We've got enough what-ifs in our lives already, in case you hadn't noticed. Let's get going."

Yeah, they had plenty. There were the what-ifs about Orne, and about the seed world, and about Marvell and the Order, and that didn't even begin the list of what-ifs about magic in general. Sean snuck a last look at Mr. Haddock, who still sloshed in the surf and stared, maybe, out along the jetty. Unless he had his eyes closed behind the wraparounds. And what kind of eyes—?

But Sean shut down that speculation fast and paddled seaward after Eddy.

❦

Sean and Eddy stuck close to the concrete wall of the jetty, following its long curve to the end. Daniel waved from atop a plinth that supported the jetty's light mast—he had the prime perch to himself today, because most of the fishermen had clumped together closer to shore. "Somebody caught a big dogfish!" he yelled. "You guys better watch out."

"Thanks!" Eddy yelled back. "Seen any great whites?"

"About fifty before you showed up. You must have scared them off."

"Damn straight."

Beyond the jetty were the remains of the old breakwater, most of which was underwater as high tide approached. Most, not all. The rocks closest to the jetty still protruded a few inches, and Eddy and Sean skirted them on their way to see what might be scrounging a meal on the man-made reef. Eddy spotted black sea bass and tautogs chowing down on mussels and barnacles. Sean glimpsed a sixty-pound striper; well, a thirty-pounder; okay, maybe fifteen. But still, plenty big enough.

Other kayakers joined them above the breakwater. To everyone's excitement, so did a pod of seven harbor porpoises. They swam around and under the kayaks, now and then poking their blunt-nosed grinning heads out of the water as if they thought floating humans were as good a show as they were. More kayakers arrived, along with some Jet Skiers. Fishermen crowded against the guardrails to toss baitfish to the porpoises, jetty strollers to take pics, and the bigger their audience, the more wildly the porpoises cavorted, some leaping clear of the water, which was unusual for this smallish species. From his plinth, Daniel had the best view of anyone, and he about fell off laughing when a porpoise leap soaked Sean to sputters. Soon afterwards, as if in search of even more admirers, the pod headed toward the swimming beach. The kayakers followed them by sea, the fishermen and strollers by jetty top.

"You guys go," Daniel called down.

"Are you coming?" Eddy called back.

"No, I can see fine from here, and if I climb down, I might lose my spot."

Eddy started inland, swift as a porpoise herself. Sean pursued her for a few strokes, then paused to strip off his drenched T-shirt. After redonning his life vest, he turned to see if Daniel was still laughing over his soaking, but Daniel wasn't looking at him. Or at Eddy. Or at the porpoise pod. In fact, he'd turned his back to the action and was gazing seaward, or rather, down at the breakwater. What was up with that? Something exciting, to judge by the only other person left on the end of the jetty, a boy maybe nine or ten, who stomach-balanced on top of the guardrail, feet kicking precariously in the air.

Sean paddled back toward Daniel. Rounding the jetty end, he saw what the big deal was: Two new harbor porpoises, considerably bigger than the others, loitered by the breakwater, tails down, heads thrust high into the air, and damned if they weren't checking out Daniel. "Dude, you've got fans!" Sean said.

If he heard, Daniel didn't answer. The porpoises' beady stares seemed to have mesmerized him. The kid on the railing had also frozen in fascination, but he soon thawed sufficiently to try scaling the plinth for a better view. He was skinny enough to have shared its summit with Daniel, if his flip-flop hadn't blown a crucial toehold. At the sound of his desperate scrabble to recover, Daniel whipped his head around and bent over to avert the danger. Too late: the kid peeled off the plinth, missed a grab at the guardrail, and plummeted headfirst onto the exposed teeth of the breakwater.

The splash and a sickening crack of skull on rock startled the two big porpoises. As Sean stroked for the fallen kid, one of them blundered against his kayak, nearly flipping it; by the time he'd recovered, the porpoises had vanished, the kid had sunk out of sight, and a woman was screaming "Brendan!" from the jetty above. He glimpsed Daniel's white face, a fisherman skidding up beside the woman, beach-bound kayakers looking back. But Sean was the closest, so he rolled into the water, tried to dive after the kid, and was buoyed right back up by his life vest.

While he was tearing at its straps, water exploded over him. It wasn't a porpoise this time, but backsplash from someone who'd dived from high overhead, off the jetty. Sean dashed salt out of his eyes and peered into the depths just off the breakwater. He made out frog-kicking feet, khaki shorts, a halo of dark curly hair. He looked up. Daniel wasn't on the plinth. He wasn't among the jostling crowd drawn back to the end of the jetty by the woman's escalating screams. A man standing by picked up something white, familiar—a foam neck brace.

Sean squirmed free of his vest. He couldn't toss it into his kayak, which had already drifted off. Who cared, with the kid drowning and with Daniel inexplicably in the water, already so far down that the gloom had swallowed him up. Daniel, who was too phobic to stick a toe in the baby end of a pool, forget the ocean.

Daniel, who had dived like a pro, as straight and forceful as the punch of a knife.

Sean sounded like a whale with Ahab after it. The water remained warm for only the first few feet, clear and bright for only a few more. He dived belly parallel to the side of the breakwater, seaweed brushing him, a point of reference anyway, but too soon his ears popped and he could barely make out the weed he clung to. Without scuba gear, Sean couldn't go deeper.

He pushed off the breakwater and swam for the surface. The whine of an approaching motorboat greeted him as he broke into sweet air. Harbor police? He didn't have time to look before he dived again. It was useless, but he couldn't float in the warm water zone, sun on his face, while Daniel and the kid were down in the dark cold.

From the murk Sean couldn't reach, two white ovals rose. They resolved into faces, Daniel's, Brendan's, and they approached him fast because a blunt-nosed and grinning porpoise was on either side, the two big ones, each with a flipper locked under a human arm and flukes going like mad. Daniel kicked like mad, too, his free arm wrapped around Brendan's torso. For Sean to try helping with the carry could only slow things down, so he got out of the way and did his own kicking back up to the sun.

The first thing he saw, with huge gratitude, was the harbor patrol motorboat nosing toward the spot where Daniel dog-paddled, supporting an unconscious Brendan. The porpoises had vanished again, and who could blame them? Up on the jetty, Brendan's mom (had to be) stood silent now, another woman embracing her, but the rest of the crowd made a racket, including cheers as a harbor officer jumped into the water and another slipped him a backboard, onto which Daniel helped the first officer maneuver Brendan. Damn, the kid had this huge blood-streaming gash on the side of his head, and Sean thought he saw

the white of bone poking from his right forearm. He swallowed
bile. Daniel had blood on his cheek and neck, but it had to be
Brendan's, because Daniel seemed fine, not even out of breath
after his wild dive.

And there, at last, was Eddy, several lengths ahead of the other
kayakers en route to the accident scene.

A Jet Skier reached Sean first, towing his errant kayak. She
steadied it while he climbed back in—shaky with reaction,
he needed the help. "Are you all right?" she asked.

"Yeah. Thanks for catching my yak."

"No problem. That was crazy! But the guy who brought the
kid up, he's some kind of free diver, right?"

"I don't know. The porpoises helped him, though."

"Porpoises?"

"Two. Bigger than the ones you were following. They helped
carry the kid."

Eddy paddled up, red with exertion. "Where's Daniel?" she
panted.

And that was a great question. The officers had gotten Brendan aboard, and their motorboat was racing toward the harbor-
master's pier. Had Daniel gone with them?

"Daniel's the rescue guy?" the Jet Skier said. "He swam over
that way."

She pointed toward the launch beach side of the jetty. Eddy
took off without another pant. Sean thanked the Jet Skier again
and gave chase.

The tide had turned, leaving more of the breakwater exposed.
Eddy negotiated the jagged rocks with deft thrusts of her paddles
and swivels of her hips. By the time Sean had made his slower way
through the gauntlet, he saw there'd be no catching her. She was
twenty yards ahead, churning water alongside the jetty in her race
after a swimmer *she* had no chance of catching. Daniel was halfway to the beach, stroking like an Olympian. Two dorsal fins

flanked him, the big porpoises no doubt. Sean hadn't been joking, after all, calling them Daniel's fans; what were they now, his bodyguards?

Sean's arms were still a little shock-wonky when he started inland. He was just picking up speed when someone called to him off the jetty. "Hey! Hey, your friend's stuff!"

He back-paddled, slowed, looked up to see Mr. Haddock slouched over the guardrail, weirder than ever the way he'd pulled his Windbreaker collar over his chin and his cap down over the top of his wraparound shades. Awkward in his mittens, he brandished the neck brace someone else had picked up earlier, and a pair of Top-Siders, also Daniel's. "Your friend's," he called, and his voice was as weird as the rest of him, thick and slurpy. "Left them up here when he jumped in."

"Oh, thanks." Sean steered his kayak to the jetty and caught the brace and shoes. By the time he'd stowed them, Mr. Haddock had turned from him, shades aimed shoreward—Daniel-ward?

The smell of dried cod and sweat and cheap cologne wafted down from him.

Sean paddled in earnest to get away from the stink. Far ahead, Daniel approached the beach. His porpoise guard stuck with him until he made shallow water and started wading; then they dived out of sight. Eddy was a quarter of the jetty back, Sean a half, when Daniel ran up the sand, ignoring some onlookers who seemed to question him. He hit the parking lot still running and vanished among the close-packed cars.

Eddy deserted her kayak at the tide line to run after him. Sean took the time to haul it out of the surf and to strap both kayaks onto their carriers. A guy helped him haul the yaks to the Civic in exchange for news of the accident but was discreet enough to return to the beach when they saw that Daniel had indeed stopped at the Civic. He sat on the backseat, driver's side, legs out the door and wet red polo wrapped like a towel around his neck. Eddy squatted beside him, saying "Daniel, are you all right?" as if for the hundredth unanswered time.

He bent forward, clasping both hands over his nape.

Sean squatted opposite Eddy. That way, if Daniel suddenly keeled, they could both catch him. "Did you, like, wrench your neck?" he asked. "Because I got your brace back. Your shoes, too."

Daniel shook his head, and it did seem to move without a hitch, no grind, no pop. "I'm okay," he said, muffled. "I don't need the brace."

Since when?

Eddy touched Daniel's bare left foot. He jerked it back and draped it over the right one, curling both sets of toes—crazily long ones, and yes, scarred like his fingers. Then he swung his legs into the Civic and muttered, "Let's just get out of here."

Fast as they could, Sean and Eddy racked the kayaks and stowed the carts, then Sean piled into the driver's seat, Eddy into the shotgun. Lately, she'd been riding in back with Daniel, but with him still clutching the back of his supposedly okay neck, she must have figured he wanted space.

The sunbaked parking lot had left the Civic stifling. Sean started it up and dialed the AC to HIGH. He zigged and zagged around illegally parked cars and turned left on Harbor Street. Eddy made him pull over by Saltonstall Park, under the first available shade tree. "We're not going to the house?" he asked.

"Not yet." She twisted to kneel on her seat. "Unless you want us to, Daniel."

He let go of his neck, but still clutched the shirt tight around it. "No."

"Can we talk about the accident?"

Daniel sighed. Nodded.

Sean knelt on his seat, too. "That kid did a full body plant on the breakwater."

"He was alive, though," Daniel said. "At least I think he was.

And the officers started CPR the second they got him out of the water. Then I—I had to go."

"I bet he'll be all right," Sean said. "Even if you're knocked out, your throat kind of closes up when you go underwater. You don't drown right away. We learned it in lifeguard training."

"He broke an arm, though. And cracked his head bad."

Eddy looked at Sean, raising her brows. Right, she hadn't seen how the kid fell. He told her the story in skeleton form, then said to Daniel, "Whatever happens, you did as much as anyone could have. More! Man, I couldn't dive half as deep as you did, not without scuba gear."

"I had to try," Daniel said.

"You didn't try, dude. You did it. You saved the kid. You and the porpoises. You're heroes." Sean turned to Eddy. "These two big ones that came up after the pod swam toward the beach? They helped him lift the kid to the surface. I don't know if anyone saw that but me."

"Did they, Daniel?"

"Yeah. I guess the stories about them are true, how they'll rescue people sometimes."

"You had to swim down forty, fifty feet. How'd you—?" Sean shut up before he started sounding like a cop: *How'd you dive like that when you're terrified of water, huh, Daniel? And how'd you swim to shore like you're in training for the Olympics, no biggie, go this fast and far all the time?* "Well, anyhow. You're the hero, dude. If you'd hung around, you'd be topping the evening news."

"Last thing I want is to be on TV."

Sean shut up. So did Eddy, until Daniel looked up at her and shrugged. "Go on. Sean wouldn't ask. You do it."

She shifted her knees on the car seat, as if bracing herself. "You said you have a water phobia, especially about the ocean. You weren't afraid of it just now."

"I've never been afraid of it," Daniel said.

"You never nearly drowned when you were a kid?"

"No." Daniel twisted his shirt scarf tighter. "Before I came to Arkham, I used to dive and swim all the time, in our condo pool, if nobody else was around. And in the ocean, at our summer house. We've got, like, fifty feet of beach, but it's private."

"Then why did you lie to us? Why wouldn't you swim here?"

"I couldn't, not if I wanted the new treatments to work."

"Treatments for the car accident?"

"There wasn't any accident."

Eddy clutched the headrest until Sean thought her nails would punch through the vinyl. Whenever Dad put that kind of grip on something, he was fighting off the impulse to punch somebody. No way Eddy would punch Daniel, but her voice was tremblingly tight: "What's wrong with you, then?"

Daniel had major balls, not to drop his eyes from hers. What he did drop was his shirt. "This is what's wrong," he said.

Darker red stained the red cotton. Darker red, fresh, still trickled down Daniel's neck, so it hadn't been Brendan's blood on him, after all. The five long parallel scratches on each side of his throat made it look like he'd stuck his head in a toothy machine, a harrow maybe, and wounded himself while pulling free. There could have been a rusty old harrow on the bottom of the harbor. But would it make scratches that quivered like these? That fanned out from Daniel's neck when he breathed in and fell when he breathed out. That, if you looked closer, weren't bleeding from inside the slits but from the skin that seemed to have torn and retreated from their stiff edges.

So, if you didn't have to wear a foam brace to support your injured neck, why would you wear it? To hide something. Like a vampire bite.

Or gills. Definitely. Gills.

15

Not that Sean would have expected Eddy to belt out a B movie scream at the mere sight of someone's gills, but the scream would have been less unnerving than the way she went the color of skim milk and slumped down silent in the passenger seat. Was he supposed to know what to do next? The best he could manage was to look straight at Daniel—at his face, not at the quivering slits in his neck—and to keep his voice out of the soprano range. "So, that's like, you're not hurt?"

"Nothing that's going to kill me." Daniel leaned forward as if to peer at Eddy over the seat, but he chickened out and fell back. *Did she faint?* he mouthed at Sean.

Sean shook his head.

Without turning to look into the backseat, her voice a rigid monotone, Eddy said, "Do you want to tell us about this, Daniel? Because we should go to the house first."

"No. I have to go to Geldman's."

"Hey, man," Sean said. "You could skip one lesson."

"Not for a lesson. I need him to—" Daniel raised a hand to his neck, not quite touching the slits. "—start fixing this."

"Fine," Eddy said.

Geldman's Pharmacy, your one-stop spot for everything from stomach aches to gill repairs. Sean twisted around and started driving.

~~✺~~

One glance at Daniel, and Geldman led them all into the white corridor behind the counter. The door through which he ushered Daniel opened on what looked like a Victorian doctor's office. Before closing it, he asked Sean and Eddy to wait in the back parlor. They'd barely settled into the accommodating armchairs when Cybele appeared with tea. She poured two cups from the same pot, but the one she placed before Eddy held a much darker brew than the one she placed before Sean. When the girl had gone to assist Geldman, Eddy pushed her cup away. Rejection caused the tea to steam forth the fragrance of poppies, which seemed to lure Eddy into draining the cup while having no particular effect on Sean. His own tea tasted like plain old orange pekoe. Apparently the sedative air freshener the green candles exhaled was all he needed to calm down, and there were plenty of greenies among the legions of never-diminishing white.

Eddy's tea brought back her color. More important, it melted the silence so unnatural in her that Sean didn't mind when she immediately began grilling him. "Daniel never told you about why he really wore that brace?"

"Ah, no."

"Hinted?"

Perhaps because Boaz sensed something crowish about Sean these days, he came to his defense. Eddy had taken the armchair beneath his perch, and he beat his wings until her hair blew in all directions. "Hell no!" he croaked. "He'd have told you, wouldn't he, wouldn't he? Let you kiss a fish, hell no!"

Eddy went red. "Shut up."

"Let you kiss a frog? Hell no! No prince under there, just fishy frog."

"Shut up!"

Sean tossed his new bro a scone from the tea tray. Boaz caught it, shook crumbs onto Eddy's head, then flew upstairs with his prize. Finger-combing scone out of her hair, Eddy muttered, "Dumb-ass bird."

"Hey, don't dis my people."

"It's the truth, though? You'd have told me if you'd known?"

That Daniel was the Creature from the Black Lagoon? Which he wasn't, but whatever he was. "Eddy, I didn't know. Sometimes I wondered, the way his neck never seemed to bother him. And that water phobia thing. If he really had that, why'd he like going out on the jetty so much? And, thinking back, he had this book Geldman lent him."

"The one with the pictures of mermaids? But weird ones, more like frogs than fish. The name was something about Atlantis."

Someone rapped gently on the parlor door. When Geldman entered, he said, "You're thinking of *On the Mysteries of the True Atlantis off Novo-Anglia.*" He stepped aside to let Daniel come in, his neck lightly bandaged, his wet clothes exchanged for a white shirt and gray slacks that, somewhere between Geldman's closet and Daniel, must have magically tailored themselves to fit their borrower.

"That's the book," Eddy said.

Geldman wheeled over his desk chair and nodded Daniel onto it. "A colorful but misleading title. The gentleman author was mistaken about his subject, which wasn't Atlantis but Yehanithlayee. Well. I need to prepare a draft for Daniel and call Helen Arkwright."

Geldman left the parlor. In the dancing light of the candles, Daniel's Frodo hair looked wilder than ever, but his face was beyond calm, like a prisoner's who was resigned to whatever judgment the court meant to throw at him.

And Eddy started the throwing: "You know what pisses me off, Daniel? Maybe you had to wear the collar in public, but why'd you have to wear it around us? Why'd you have to lie about a car wreck? I've told you all about the Servitor. You should've realized we could handle weird situations."

"That wasn't something weird about yourselves."

True, because the Servitor hadn't infected them with tentacles or anything. "Good point," Sean said.

Fixed on Daniel, Eddy ignored Sean. "Sure, you'd be nervous at first, but after we'd hung out for a while? And especially after you and me got together."

"You're right, Eddy. I should have told you."

Smart man, but—

Eddy wasn't relenting yet. "And what does having gills mean, anyway? You can't be like the mermen in Geldman's book, because there's—" But she didn't say the rest: *There's no such thing.* According to the kind of people who'd use that catchphrase, there was also no such thing as a wizard, or a Servitor, or a stained glass window that held a whole world in suspended animation. No Orne. No Outer Gods. No magic.

Daniel reversed her unfinished assertion: "There is such a thing. As merpeople. In a way."

Still in beach gear, shorts over a bathing suit, Eddy chafed her bare arms. His own shorts and T-shirt salty damp, Sean shared the chill, but it was his aching temples he rubbed. That place Geldman had mentioned. Yeha-something. "Yeha—"

"Yehanithlayee," Daniel said. "The True Atlantis. A city under the ocean."

"And it's in New England?"

"It's near here. Off Plum Island."

Plum Island was north of Arkham, off the coast between New-buryport and Innsmouth—

Innsmouth.

From the clenching of Eddy's jaw, she remembered at the same moment Sean did. "The underwater city in Lovecraft's story," she said. "Where the Deep Ones lived."

Daniel nodded.

And, according to Lovecraft, the Deep Ones were amphibi-ous monsters just anthropomorphic enough to hook up with humans, and the results were human at first, until they started morphing into something like those *True Atlantis* merpeople after all. "You're a Deep One, that's what we're getting at?" Sean said.

Daniel touched the side of his neck, where a little blood had seeped through the bandage. Then he nodded again.

In the quiet that followed, the sound of Boaz hopping across the floor overhead was harsh as hailstones on tin. Sean kept look-ing at Daniel, and Daniel kept looking at Eddy, which proved he was a much braver man than Sean, who didn't dare check out her face until her response told him how hard she was taking the con-fession. The way the corner of Daniel's mouth twitched, this sec-ond bout of Eddy silence was killing him. Finally he ventured a low, "I'm sorry, Eddy."

And after all their suspense, Eddy just sounded tired: "I'm sorry, too. You should've told me."

They'd already played that blame game. "Look," Sean said. "I've read 'The Shadow over Innsmouth,' but I don't know shit else about the Deep Ones. And maybe 'Shadow' is wrong about them? Helen's always saying how Lovecraft was a member of the Order, but he used to drive the other members nuts by writing 'fiction' about Mythos facts. And then he'd drive them nuttier by changing some facts to suit himself. Maybe you've got the real scoop?"

Tough question or not, Daniel looked glad to be off the "should have" hook. "Well, Lovecraft wrote that after the Feds found out monsters had taken over Innsmouth, they put half the residents in detention camps and then torpedoed Devil Reef, where their underwater city was supposed to be. But Geldman was around here in the '20s. He says the real reason the Feds went to Innsmouth was reports of bootleggers. The Order got wind of the raid ahead of time. It knew about the Deep Ones in Innsmouth, so it warned them to lie low. All the Feds really carted off were a few truckloads of whiskey from Canada. That was the fact Lovecraft didn't like, how the Order had allied itself with the Deep Ones. I guess he wished the government *would* wipe them out, and so that's how he had things happen in the story."

"So, wishful thinking?"

"Looks like it." Daniel smoothed his borrowed trousers. "It's crazy complicated, though. I've read 'Shadow' over and over. In the end, the guy that rats on Innsmouth to the Feds? He finds out he's a Deep One himself. He's freaked out at first, but then he starts liking the idea, and he dreams how Yehanithlayee wasn't destroyed, just a little damaged. The Deep Ones are still down there, and when he changes, he can go, too, and live in glory. That's how he puts it, 'in glory.' What are you supposed to think about that?" He glanced again at Eddy.

Sean also dared a glance. Changing the subject from bad boyfriend behavior to the Deep Ones themselves could have gone two ways—either to boost Eddy's Irritation Threat Level or to distract her. Sean considered it a win that she had shifted forward in her armchair, forehead corrugated with concentration. "The Order helped the Deep Ones?" she asked.

Daniel matched Eddy's forward shift with a sideways scoot of the desk chair, halving the distance between them. "Geldman says the Order respects them as fellow magicians—all Deep Ones are magical, I guess. Plus they're native to Earth, like humans—you can't say they don't *belong* here as much as anyone does. And if humans messed with them, they've got the magic and tech to mess back a lot harder. Eventually the Order told the government enough to make them leave the Deep Ones alone, and now the Order and government are kind of partners in keeping them secret. That's about all Geldman's told me so far. I'm grateful he told me anything."

"Why?" Eddy said.

"My father doesn't want me learning about my Deep One half."

Eddy beat Sean to the big-money word in that sentence: "Half?"

"Sure. I'm half human, too. A hybrid. How Deep Ones and humans could, well, interbreed—that's one of the genuine facts in Lovecraft's story."

"Then Deep Ones and humans must be the same species, or at least subspecies! Otherwise, they couldn't have children."

Daniel's laugh was sharp edged. "Way, way back, they were probably related, yeah. There's something more going on. Geldman explained it to me and my father. Deep One DNA is mutable. Not just the usual way, through mutations—in a Deep One sperm or egg cell, it can rearrange itself to mimic human DNA, boom, now the species are interfertile. But the rearranged Deep One DNA still has these dormant trigger genes. The hybrid looks human until the trigger genes kick in and start rearranging the DNA back to Deep One. Usually it starts at twenty, twenty-five years old, but it can start earlier. Like with me."

"How early?" Sean said.

"When I was fourteen, this happened." Daniel held up both hands and spread his fingers wide. From their bases to the first joints, pinkish skin stretched. Fine capillaries infiltrated the translucent webbing; when Sean squinted, he could see them pulsing. "It's the same between my toes."

"But you only had scars there this morning," Eddy whispered.

"This is how my hands looked just before I came to Geldman. See, the Change is mostly a biological process. It moves slow. Geldman's treating me with magic, which moves a lot faster. But if I immerse myself in water, especially seawater, his magic's blown, and everything reverts to where it was before his treatments."

"So today, when you jumped in after that kid," Sean began.

When he faltered, awe-smacked by the double courage of Daniel's action, Eddy finished: "You knew what would happen."

"Well, you both saw. The water ripped open the skin that was starting to seal my gills. That let me breathe through them while I dived. But now—" Daniel dropped his hands to his knees, closing the fingers tight, hiding the webs. "The Change has started again."

Eddy got up and sat on the edge of the tea table, another move closer to Daniel. Candle flame licked the tuft of her braid without setting it on fire, but for his own peace of mind, Sean pulled the offending candelabra toward him. "So Geldman's treatments are to reverse your Change?" he said.

"Reverse it. Keep it from starting again. I take, like, five different potions every day, and they have to be made fresh, so Geldman's going to teach me how to compound them for myself. I'm already helping Cybele make my, um, cologne."

The cologne that had teased Sean's memory for so long with its scent of fresh-mown grass and herbs. "It's Cybele's Number One! The stuff Helen put on her Servitor burns."

"Close, but that's a healing balm. Mine's liquid, a spray." Daniel coughed, eyed Eddy. "And it's not really cologne. It's a deodorant. If I didn't use it every day, I'd smell like a Changer, and nobody'd want to come within a mile of me."

It was Sean's turn to jolt forward from the cradling cushions of his chair. "You'd smell?"

"I'd reek, like a dead fish."

"And, um, like gym clothes that've been smooshed in the bottom of your locker too long?"

"You could put it that way."

Eddy realized where Sean was heading. She scowled at him. "You're thinking about Mr. Haddock."

Why not, with his stink and his flipper-sized feet and the way he zipped his Windbreaker collar up over his neck, maybe for the same reason Daniel had worn the brace? "He fits Daniel's description, how you can't come within a mile of him."

Daniel sighed. "Yeah, you and Eddy might as well know it now. Mr. Haddock's a Changer, a hybrid turning into a Deep One. I was pretty sure, and Geldman confirmed it. He's been watching the guy, too, how he shows up at Tumblebee's whenever I'm due at the pharmacy. How he follows me sometimes when I leave."

"He really does?" Eddy said. "We weren't just being paranoid?"

"Not according to Geldman."

"And he was at the beach today," Sean put in. "Watching you on the jetty. He's the one who gave me your neck brace and shoes from off the jetty. He knew I was your friend."

Eddy hugged her upper arms to her sides. "I didn't like Mr. Haddock before. Now I'm really creeped out."

Daniel's lips tightened. "I guess I must creep you out, too, then."

She stared at him blankly.

"Because if it weren't for Mr. Geldman and Cybele, I'd look

and smell like Mr. Haddock. Or worse. By now, I'd be totally Changed."

The way Eddy flushed and stammered, she hadn't at all realized how Daniel might misunderstand her. "No, Daniel! I didn't mean because he was a—a Changer. I'm creeped out because of how he's following you. What's that about? Does Mr. Geldman know?"

"He says Changers come to Arkham pretty regularly. Some do business at the pharmacy. Mr. Haddock hasn't come to see him for a while, but he has in the past. Geldman says he's sure the guy doesn't mean any harm. He supposes Mr. Haddock could have spotted me by chance, and now he's curious about me, a hybrid who's not from Innsmouth."

Daniel had been reaching for Eddy's hand, little stretches toward it, little jerks back. When she finished the reach for him and clasped his hand firmly, webbing and all, his tension-hitched shoulders relaxed.

Sean gave them a minute before he couldn't stand it anymore and had to ask, "But how did Mr. Haddock even know you're a bro? Since you don't look or smell like him."

"I don't know," Daniel said. "Maybe the way any magician can pick up on another one. The energy signature thing."

It could be, but Daniel didn't sound convinced or convincing. Probably he was just worn out, exhausted by the adrenaline rush and exertion of the rescue, the anxiety of revealing his big secret. Sean felt ready for a three-day nap himself, not for processing any more information, even if Daniel wanted to give it. The questions swarming in his head would have to wait. Eddy and Daniel continued holding hands. (Did Daniel's webbing feel all rubbery?) They were getting cool with each other again, and they were both cool with Sean, and they were all cool together. He leaned back and closed his eyes. So, Daniel's father hadn't told him he was half Deep One. The Deep One half had to come from his mother.

Who'd died from leukemia. Or had it been from something else, some Deep One blood disease the human doctors hadn't known how to treat? . . .

Another soft knock on the parlor door heralded Geldman's return. He gave Eddy and Daniel plenty of time to drop hands before walking in with a steaming mug for his patient and Helen right behind him, come to herd all her pain-in-the-ass lambs home.

16

Daniel rode back to the Arkwright House with Helen. Sean and Eddy rode back in the Civic, picking up pizzas for dinner on the way. They had to eat their share alone; when they arrived, Helen and Daniel were already locked in her office. An hour later, the door remained shut. Sean paused outside long enough to hear Daniel's voice, raised, angry, but Eddy hissed at him from the stairs, and he had to abort the eavesdropping mission.

Another half hour passed before Daniel pounded up to the common room to join them. He veered toward the couch, as if to sit next to Eddy, then went instead to a chair at the game table, where his elbow knocked the tiles on a half-played Scrabble board into gibberish. Through clenched teeth, he said, "So you called me a hero."

His glare arrowed past Eddy to Sean. Not that it wasn't true, but when had he called Daniel that? Oh, at the beach, after the rescue. "Ah, yeah?"

"My father just called me everything but a hero. Helen phoned him. I'm not blaming her, that's her job, and I'll bet she's sorry, the way he hit the ceiling. How could the Order let me near the ocean? Like I'm a kid they could pen in behind a toddler gate. Then he started on how *I* should've known better, wasn't I listening to Geldman?"

"Man, I'm sorry."

"So I told you guys I got to Arkham the same day you did? I came to the Arkwright House the same day, but I was living in this apartment near the pharmacy for three months before that, getting my treatments. My father wants me to go back there. I told him no way, not when my friends are at the House, first friends I've made since the Change started. Of course, then he had to know all about you and Eddy. Especially about Eddy, the minute I let out she's a girl." Daniel abruptly shut up.

"It's okay," Eddy said.

"It's not okay. He made me admit we were going out."

"So?"

So Daniel got fascinated with the messed-up Scrabble game. He started arranging tiles on a rack. "He said I was crazy. He said you'd be crazy, too, if now that you knew what I am, you didn't blow me off completely."

It wasn't magic that set Sean's skin prickling but his own shock and Eddy's vehement headshake. "Daniel," she said. "He didn't tell you that."

"He did, all right. He can't believe I'd—" A tile fell from Daniel's fingers. He racked it, looked at whatever word he'd made, then pushed the rack over. "He can't believe I'd act like my mother did, tricking a normal person into being with me. He said, maybe it's in the Deep One genes."

The prickles in Sean's nape turned to stabbing needles. After a few seconds, Eddy walked to the game table like there were eggs underfoot. Sitting opposite Daniel, chin up, eyes too bright, she didn't touch him as she had at Geldman's. "It sucks that your father said that."

"You think?"

"I know. But what did he mean, your mother tricked him?"

Daniel chewed at the webbing between his thumb and fore-finger. It must have hurt, because he winced and rubbed that hand on his thigh, on Geldman's gray slacks. "You want to hear the long story, after everything you've already heard today?"

"Whatever you want to tell me. Us. The truth."

"Maybe you want some pizza first?" Sean suggested. "We already had ours."

"No. My stomach feels like it's upside down. Maybe a Coke."

Sean brought him a bottle from the kitchenette refrigerator, then returned to his recliner, figuring it was enough for Eddy to be at the table, Daniel didn't need to be crowded.

Daniel drank half the bottle. Then he said, "When the Change started for me? My father paid for specialists, and second opinions, and third opinions. The docs finally agreed I had some kind of rare genetic anomaly. They sent me to a medical geneticist who got excited when he found case histories like mine. My father stopped taking me to him once he found out all the case history patients had ended up in asylums, no cure. Then he took me to plastic surgeons instead, and they cut away the digital webbing. And to dental surgeons, for implants."

"Something happened to your teeth?" Eddy said.

Daniel pulled a tight grin, flaunting his perfect grille. "These are fakes. Implants. My own teeth fell out when new ones grew in behind them. Shark teeth. The dentists pulled those out and plugged these in. Well, not these exact ones. I've had the implants redone twice, because you know about sharks, how they have spare teeth lined up in their jaws? So do I now. They shove the implants out of the way, or grow around and stick out over them."

Sean swallowed. "That's got to hurt."

Daniel shrugged. Now that he'd gotten started, he plunged on: "The worst part is how my father always knew exactly what the

Change was. He'd seen it before, when it started for my mom, and in the end she told him the truth. Okay, so he couldn't tell the doctors. But he didn't tell me either, not until my gills emerged. He couldn't get any doc to remove those or even cover them up— they said the connections between the gills and my lungs were too complicated. It didn't matter. They couldn't 'cure' anything for long. The webbing grew back. The teeth grew back. My ears were shrinking. Even my bones were changing, like, my fingers and my toes getting longer."

"You had to be scared," Eddy said quietly.

"I was, but it was funny how I remembered my mom before she went away to the hospital. She'd started wearing a scarf around her neck, gloves all the time, even this mouth guard. Obviously, right, I had the same thing she'd had? I thought I'd die from it, too, but at least it was a connection to her."

Sean's speculation at Geldman's had been correct: Daniel's mother hadn't died from leukemia. It sounded like she'd died simply from Changing. Bad, but he could understand the connection thing. "After my mom died?" he said. "I thought every stomachache I got was cancer, same as hers."

Daniel gazed at him for a long time. Then he looked back down at the Scrabble chaos. "I know. I'm sorry."

"Yeah. But." Sean paused for another swallow. "So after your gills showed, that's when your father told you about the Deep Ones?"

"What little he knew. Eventually he admitted my mom hadn't gone to a regular hospital. It was a sanitarium. She was going to stay there where no one could see what was happening to her, especially not me. And my father was going to find the cure for her. Only my mom got tired of waiting. She gave up. She hanged herself."

Eddy pressed a hand to her mouth, muffling her "No."

Sean kept swallowing, and it kept getting harder.

Daniel slogged on, monotonous: "She killed herself. My father said he wasn't letting me get to that point, it didn't matter how crazy the solution was. And a crazy solution came up pretty soon afterwards. The medical geneticist had kept digging on his own. He ran into stories about the Deep Ones. Legends. What most doctors would toss as paranormal bullshit. He followed up on the legends until he found the Order, and the Order sent him to Geldman. Dr. Bremerton—that's the geneticist—he's a member of the Order himself now. He contacted my father about Geldman's offer to treat me magically, and my father agreed, and I came here."

He stopped and looked at Eddy. She still had her hand over her mouth. He slogged on again: "Geldman's treatments were working fine until today. All I had to do was keep from immersing myself in water, especially salt. A quick shower's all right, or rain. Not immersion. That's why I didn't jump in right away after the kid fell. I waited to see if Sean could reach him."

"You jumped in soon enough," Sean said.

Eddy dropped her hand gag. "And you had to. Geldman must get that."

"Oh yeah, *he* does. He believes in karma, even if he doesn't call it that. Help someone, your magic gets stronger and purer. Hurt someone, it gets twisted. The porpoises did a lot, though. They're supposed to be Deep One allies, according to the *True Atlantis* book. Maybe they were hanging around the jetty because they recognized me, and that's why they helped me with the kid."

"Or they were there because of Mr. Haddock?" Sean said.

"Maybe."

Instead of sinking her marine biologist teeth into the idea of porpoise allies, Eddy stayed focused on Daniel's situation: "Geldman needs to talk to your father, then. To make him realize you *were* a hero."

She'd meant well, but Daniel reverted to the scowl he'd

brought into the common room from Helen's office. "All my father cares about is for me to be normal. He'll take me being a magician if he has to, but I better be a human magician."

A soft click from Eddy's throat shut him up. He shook his hair, still ocean tangled, over his eyes and looked at her through the curtain. "Not that I don't want to be human, too. All the way, down to the genes, if Geldman can eventually pull that off."

Sean puzzled over Eddy's flush until he brightened up and realized that Daniel was hinting at kids. Really? Daniel was thinking that far into the future about him and Eddy? And was she, too? He gave his throat a thorough clearing. "You think Geldman could get rid of your Deep One DNA?"

"He doesn't know if he can. Right now he's just thwarting the trigger genes."

"If anyone could, though."

"That's what I'm hoping."

Eddy went for Daniel's hand, and again Sean wondered about the feel of the webbing (rubbery? *clammy?*), but she didn't twitch an eyelash. For a minute it looked like they'd all get back to the equilibrium Helen had interrupted at Geldman's. Like Daniel had said, it hadn't been Helen's fault, but Sean's gut tightened a little when she walked into the common room looking too sober for his comfort.

"Daniel," she said. Soberly. "I told your father you'd call him after you've had a chance to absorb what happened today."

"I'm sorry I took off—," Daniel began.

"That's all right. It was probably better you did. Could you come out here for a minute?"

Daniel and Helen retreated down the hall. Eddy glare-pinned Sean to the couch. As if he were going to eavesdrop again. As if he'd have had time to get set up. Two minutes after leaving, Daniel came back into the common room, and Sean heard Helen walking downstairs.

"My father," Daniel said. He took a deep breath. "Dr. Bremerton, the geneticist I told you about? My father wants him to come to Arkham and make sure Geldman knows what he's doing."

Questioning Geldman's magic was like asking Everest to prove it was a mountain. "Hasn't your dad seen you since the treatments?" Sean said.

"Plenty of times. He's being an asshole."

"Kind of," Eddy said. "But give him some credit for being worried about you, Daniel."

"Maybe I would if he wasn't such an asshole about it. At least Helen's fixed it so it's not totally obvious my father's checking up on Geldman. There's going to be a meeting tomorrow night, her and Marvell and Dr. Bremerton and Geldman. Just to get everybody up to date, is how she put it to all of them."

In Sean's opinion, Helen had pulled some win out of a losing situation, but Daniel flopped out on the couch, a forearm across his eyes. "I ought to be in on the meeting," he said. "I told Helen so, too."

Eddy moved to the empty recliner instead of the foot of the couch, even though there was still plenty of room for her skinny butt. "What did Helen say to that?"

"No."

"Just no?"

"She said if I was there, people couldn't speak freely. So instead they get to talk behind my back and then not tell me shit."

"You think they're hiding something from you?" Sean said.

"I *know* my father and Dr. Bremerton are. Helen, too, probably. I can't tell with Marvell and Geldman. It's like, their mental wards are too strong for me to get through."

Eddy paled, and her voice sharpened: "What do you mean, you can't get through mental wards?"

Daniel rolled over, putting his back to them both. A few seconds later, he rolled flat, arms by his sides. "Sean," he said. "You asked how Mr. Haddock could tell I was a Changer."

"Right."

"Deep Ones live underwater, so how do they talk to each other?"

"Like whales, singing?"

"Partly. They're also telepaths. Mr. Haddock knew what I was by reading my mind."

"Could you read his mind back?"

"Of course he could," Eddy broke in. Red was creeping up her neck, like mercury rising in a thermometer. "He just said his father and Bremerton and Helen are holding back. To know that, he must be able to read them." She paused. "And he must be able to read us. We're not trained paramagicians, like Marvell. We're not wizards like Geldman."

The reestablished calm was shaking at its foundations, and Sean finally got why. "But if Daniel could read people's minds well enough to know they have secrets, couldn't he read the secrets, too?"

Daniel rolled upright. "I'm not fully telepathic yet. It's more like empathy—I can sense emotions, and I can usually tell if someone's lying. That's all."

"That's still a lot, Daniel," Eddy said. Her voice had frozen to an ice shard. "That's the second big thing you didn't tell us."

Daniel squirmed before he said, "It's all one package, Deep Ones, telepathy."

"No, and you know it's not. You're the one who split them up. And you could have told us you were telepathic—"

"Empathic," Sean chipped in desperately.

Eddy ignored him. "You could have told us about it without even mentioning Deep Ones. You could have just said telepathy was part of your magic."

"If I'd told you guys right away, it would've scared you off," Daniel pleaded.

"So instead you go around secretly reading our emotions. That's like wearing X-ray glasses and looking through our clothes. Or worse. Looking all the way to our bones."

"I don't know," Sean said. "Looking just through clothes would be worse."

"Keep out of this."

Not this time. "Besides, X-ray glasses suck as an example. You wear those on purpose. Daniel can't help being empathic. And he's right. If the first thing out of his mouth had been 'Hi, I'm an empath,' we *would* have freaked. We couldn't have acted normal around him. Well, as normal as we ever act."

Eddy had turned to him bristling, but he'd made the rare shot she couldn't rebound. "All right. But it still feels weird, I'm sorry." She vaulted out of her recliner; the momentum carried her to the door, from which she looked back at Daniel. "Anyway, I don't care if you sensed all along that I liked you. I don't care if you sense how much I like you now. I just don't like realizing you had so many secrets. So if you have any more, maybe make a list for me, will you?"

Daniel hadn't gotten his mouth all the way open before she took off down the stairs. Empathy must have told him to let her go, because he slumped back on the couch. "Thanks for the help," he said sincerely.

"You know she'll get over it, right?"

"I'm hoping so."

"You can't, like, feel it?"

Daniel worked up a quizzical smile. "Kind of. And she did use the present tense."

"Huh?"

"She said 'how much I *like* you.' Not 'liked.'"

"What is it with girls, anyway? They're all, pay attention to their feelings. Then they find a guy who *has* to pay attention, and they flip."

"Yeah, but nobody wants to feel like an open book. Especially around closed ones. What about you?"

"What about me?"

"Well, first time we met, you *acted* friendly, but you *felt* jealous."

Hell no, Sean almost said. But memory said *hell yes.* He shrugged.

Daniel continued, "I thought you were Eddy's boyfriend, or else you wanted to be."

"You were off the mark there."

"I know it now."

"It was just how tight we've always been. When there started to be other guys—"

Daniel's brows went up.

"Hey, not *many* other guys. But I still didn't want her to dump me as her best friend."

"She's not doing that, Sean."

"I know. We're cool."

"She wouldn't have dumped you for anybody. That's not how she flies."

"I know. I guess I worry about stupid things sometimes."

"Tell me about it."

Sean laughed, then Daniel joined in, then they both sat silent. It was an okay silence, and if Daniel was taking advantage of it to read Sean's feelings, big deal. Mainly what he felt was *wiped.* Funny, though, how Daniel had said it was Eddy who flew a certain way, when it was Sean who'd been doing all the flying—

Flying. The window. The crow-in-waiting over Nyarlathotep's head, the one Orne had prepared for a guest magician—

That was so not something he needed to think about. Naturally he opened his mouth and said, "Hey, about the meeting tomorrow. How they're not going to let you sit in."

"Don't get me started on that again." But Sean had already turned on Daniel's ignition. "If it were only Helen, she'd have let me in. I didn't want to say it in front of Eddy, because you know how she is about Marvell—"

"What's Marvell got to do with it?"

"Helen talked to him about the meeting before she came up. He's the one said it wouldn't be appropriate for me to be there."

Surprise? Not. If Marvell would go control freak all over Sean, why not all over Daniel, too?

And all the more reason why, wiped or not, they might have work to do tonight. "We saved you pizza. Let's go nuke it. Besides—" Sean paused.

"Besides what? Wings? Breadsticks?"

"No. Just something I've got to show you in the library. About tomorrow. If you really want to hear what they say about you."

Maybe the more Daniel's huge eyes protruded, the harder he was doing his empathy number on you. They were popping now. "Pizza sounds great," he said.

"And?"

"Whatever else. Especially whatever else."

Whatever else, then, if they could pull it off.

17

Over the rest of the pizza, Sean matched Daniel's confessions with two of his own: how his magical line ran back through a dozen generations to Redemption Orne and how he'd been meeting Orne in the *Founding* windows. Daniel seemed relieved that he wasn't the only one with strange ancestry, but he out-Eddied Eddy in his doubts about the seed world. In the end, it was the fact that she'd actually helped Sean keep exploring it that persuaded him to give the "guest avatar" a try.

Sean climbed the stepladder to the left window, while Daniel stayed on the dais, ready to connect with Sean's ankle. Their first two attempts, Sean passed into the seed world alone. Evidently Daniel had to really grip Sean, not just touch him. The third attempt, he held on tight, and Sean popped them both into their respective crows. Daniel's collapsed off its branch, narrowly missing Nyarlathotep's pointy crown. He twitched and flailed the way Sean had during his initial transfer; then, just before Sean had gotten panicky enough to summon Orne, he hopped up, comfortably crowish and ready to fly. They took a spin over the bay that would become Arkham Harbor, not a jetty or danger-ous breakwater in sight, just waves caught in mild mid-swell. It rocked having someone to cruise with, but they couldn't go far-ther that night. He still had to show Daniel the hollow chestnut tree and the amber rondel that, beak-tapped, turned into a lens overlooking the library. Crowded wing to wing, they found they could both peer through the spy-hole and, presumably, hear everything said at the conference table.

The seed world was awesome, Daniel squawked, and the spy-hole was, like, fate. Sean croaked agreement. But when they popped out, Sean on the stepladder, Daniel clutching his ankle, the obvious problem occurred to them. To spy on the library, they had to be about as blatantly visible to the meeting attendees as two people could get.

Daniel's eavesdropping hopes were fizzling unless Sean could remote-connect with the window the way Orne did. Out in the hall, Sean used his mind key to gather ambient energy and then *intended* it through the closed library doors and across the room, where he imagined it settling on the glass crow like an invisible hand. Daniel touched the targeted door panel and said it was get-ting hot, but nothing else came of Sean's effort except a rotten headache.

While he was resting for another try, Eddy came downstairs. She'd gone to Daniel's room to apologize. No Daniel. She'd gone to Sean's room. No Daniel *and* no Sean. Add one and one, and you got the two of them screwing around with magic somewhere.

The way Eddy had reacted to Daniel's earlier secrets, Sean couldn't blame him for spilling right away about their seed world trip. Her response was relatively mild: Sean shouldn't have gone into the window without her around, and he shouldn't have taken Daniel with him, and they were both going to get their asses ex-pelled if they weren't more freaking careful. However, she didn't say a word against their eavesdropping plan. Sean made the mistake of asking why the unprecedented disregard for authority, and she blew up, though quietly, so Helen wouldn't hear. God, hadn't Eddy kept her mouth shut a million times when Sean was up to shit? (Yeah, but—) And, God, didn't he think Daniel had a right to know what they said about him during the meeting? (Yeah, but—) And finally, what was she, some kind of knee-jerk protocol droid, unable to think things through for herself? (Nope, not a chance.)

That settled, Eddy sat down and considered the problem of remote-accessing the seed world. Sean couldn't touch the crow portal from inside the library, and apparently the hall was too far from the windows or the doors too sturdy a barrier. What if Sean touched the window from *outside,* in the garden?

It was a great idea, except for Dad's security window. There were six inches of air space between it and the stained glass that held the portal. Eddy pointed out that six inches was a much shorter distance than twenty-five feet, and so they borrowed an extension ladder from the carriage house to experiment. After climbing to the level of the crow, Sean had to lean sideways to position his fingers on the Plexiglas above it. Eddy steadied the ladder. Daniel held his ankle from the ground. Scared of melting the Plexiglas or, worse, blowing out both it and the stained glass, Sean exposed only the top knob of his mind key. That gathered too little energy, so he exposed the top of the topmost brass curlicue micron by micron, until enough silk lightning had leaped into it for him to fashion an imaginary hand he could intend toward the crow. *Yes.* It passed through the Plexiglas and sparked on glass and lead, and he and Daniel were crows again for the few seconds before Sean flew them back out of the seed world.

Damn, this could work.

Details, though, Eddy said. She went inside the library while Sean extended his arm across the security window. The trees along the rear of the property kept streetlamps from backlighting the

Founding, but when the fluorescents between the stained glass and Plexiglas were on, they faintly illuminated Sean's arm, and Eddy could make it out, no problem.

Well, yes, problem. Helen was sure to light up the *Founding* so the meeting could admire it.

Thanks to working for Joe-Jack, Sean had a solution. He flipped off the library circuit breaker and hunted up a screwdriver, with which he detached the light switch wiring. Helen wouldn't try to illuminate the *Founding* until after dark, so no way she could get an electrician to fix Sean's sabotage before the meeting.

After high fives all around, they went to bed. The house ghosts, ever polite, continued to avoid Sean's dreams, but other interlopers showed up: the kid with his scalp split; Mr. Haddock; the True Atlantis merpeople, who were really Deep Ones. Scariest was Daniel's mother, who had a bathrobe sash knotted around her neck, or else a towel, or else strips of pillowcase, you know, stuff you could get in a sanitarium. The noose made her gills bleed, and the blood dripped down her squamous arm onto Sean's sheets until he would have woken to a sodden red mess if she hadn't stayed a dream.

But she *had* stayed a dream, and when he jerked awake with a gasp, the only thing dampening his sheets was his own sweat.

Dr. Richard Bremerton arrived Saturday around three o'clock. Weirdly, he looked like a younger, taller, skinnier, and more hyperactive version of Geldman. Sean, Eddy, and Daniel had gone biking after lunch. When they braked in front of the Arkwright House, Bremerton loped down the steps, introduced himself to Sean and Eddy, then examined Daniel's Jamis with bike-geek intensity. That done, he hustled Daniel up to Helen's office to examine him. Marvell showed up at five, and he and Helen joined Bremerton in interrogating all three of them about the accident at the harbor. Sean mentioned Curious Changer (their new name for Mr. Haddock because, come on, it wasn't cool to disrespect Daniel's people, even if he didn't want to become one of them). That slip earned them some extra grilling before Helen sent them out for burgers and a movie.

They got the burgers but skipped the movie. At dusk, they parked the Civic out of sight on High Street, snuck into the back garden, and put their ladder up. While Sean and Daniel crouched in the lilac bushes below the *Founding*, Eddy watched the library from a low branch of the side garden beech. It was full dark before she returned to whisper that yeah, Helen had tried to switch on the *Founding* lights and given up with a shrug. Bremerton and Marvell were looking over papers at the conference table. Geldman had just walked in. It was go time.

Sean climbed into position. Eddy slipped underneath the ladder to hold both side rails, her back braced against the house. Daniel gripped his left ankle, fingers clammy with sweat. Sean tried not to think about their webbing, or about how Marvell would go ballistic if he caught them. *See, Professor, my dad wanted me to make sure the security window was holding up—*

"Sean," Daniel whispered. "Everything okay?"

"Yeah. Getting there." Sean hooked his right arm around the ladder and closed his eyes. As anxiety yielded to concentration, the silk-lightning matrix formed in his mental black space. It wound around him. Through him. He envisioned his mind key, exposed exactly as much as the night before. The energy it absorbed he twisted into the wiry image of a hand that could breach the Plexiglas, and then he reached for the crow. Reached! Touched. Changed arms for wings that carried him through the dusk-coppered air of the seed world. He wheeled at once into the cover of the wood, where Daniel lay twitching at Nyarlathotep's feet. They were both where the people in the library couldn't see them, though sharp eyes might spot the absence of his crow. No help for that—they'd have to hope the dark windows wouldn't attract notice.

Recovered from his transition, crow-Daniel hopped inside the chestnut tree and went for the amber rondel. His pecks had no effect, and he sidestepped to let Sean tap it into a lens. Then, scrunched together, Sean's wing over Daniel's feathered back, they each managed to put a beady eye to it. Marvell was in his usual big-shot seat at the head of the table. The others stood at the sideboard, getting coffee. Geldman turned first and looked straight at the *Founding*, straight at the left window, straight at the signature rondel, and it was no accident, because he hoisted his cup as if to salute Sean and Daniel. "Why isn't your window lit, Helen?"

"The switch is broken. Every time I think we've fixed all the electrical quirks in this house, something else blows."

"Give her some of your candles, Mr. Geldman," Bremerton said, sitting to Marvell's right.

"Perhaps I will, for emergencies." By selecting the chair next to Bremerton's, Geldman put his back to the *Founding*.

"Shit," Daniel croaked. "I thought he saw us."

"Dude, he did. I almost bailed."

"But if he's not going to tell—"

"Shh. He can probably hear us, too."

Geldman's chair tipped onto its back legs, returned to all four, like a curt nod.

Helen sat to Marvell's left. "We'd better start. Mr. Geldman, you examined Daniel right after the accident?"

"And found what I expected to. He'd immersed himself in seawater for ten to fifteen minutes, which counteracted my treatments. He's back to where we started four months ago. You would agree, Dr. Bremerton?"

"It's incredible. All that progress gone. Gills reopened, digital webbing regrown. His gums are tender, too—I'm afraid the Deep One dentition is pushing out over his implants."

"My interventions, being magical, are subject to instantaneous reversion. However, I've restarted the treatments, and so Daniel's Change will begin to abate again."

"Well, this immersion shouldn't have happened in the first place," Marvell said.

Helen sighed. "That's Mr. Glass's take on the incident."

Marvell patted her forearm. "I'm sorry you had to take the brunt of his wrath, Helen. But can we blame him for being upset?"

"No, but it's not like Daniel dived off that jetty on a whim. He knew his gills would reopen and so he'd be able to bring up the injured boy. Today's paper says the boy will recover."

"That's good to hear."

"It also asks the rescuer to come forward. The boy's parents want to thank him. And yet, the way Mr. Glass talked to Daniel, you'd think his action was a spoiled brat's, not a hero's."

All Sean could see of Geldman was the hand he rested on the conference table. Its fingers rose slightly as he spoke: "Mr. Glass is more likely to set Daniel back than the immersion."

"Yes, he can be a bit overzealous," Bremerton said. "Still, you have to deal with the parents your patient's got, not the ones you might like."

Marvell smiled. Helen didn't. Sean felt Daniel's rib cage bellow.

Geldman's fingertips described circles on the tabletop. "There's wisdom in accepting the unchangeable. However, more things can be changed than we commonly suppose. To return to Daniel's condition, Dr. Bremerton, you can assure Mr. Glass this reversion's done no lasting damage. The Change—the program of the xenogenes, as you put it—will yield to magic as before. Give me a year, and Daniel will look as human as even his father could ask."

Like Sean, Bremerton must have caught Geldman's emphasis

on the *look*. "He'll have a human phenotype, but his genotype will remain hybrid. In Mr. Glass's eyes, tainted."

"Deep Ones probably talk about the human taint," Helen said.

"No," Geldman said. "They value the addition of complementary human traits to their genetic pool. Otherwise, there'd be no Deep One–human hybrids. There don't absolutely need to be, you know."

Marvell scowled. "The Order does know, which is why its policy is to discourage new outbreaks of hybridization."

"The Deep Ones don't look on mingling as a disease process, Professor. Or a social ill. They see it as an aesthetic, even a spiritual, choice."

"I know that, too. And *they* supposedly know, per the terms of the 1930 treaty, that mingling's not a viable choice in the current state of human—"

"Ignorance?" Geldman suggested.

"Human understanding," Marvell said. "Leave it at that."

"Certainly, as we're here to discuss Daniel Glass, not the timetable for global enlightenment."

Sean wasn't sure what Marvell and Geldman were arguing about, but he was already on Geldman's side. "Your boss kicks butt," he muttered to Daniel.

Daniel didn't answer. He jostled Sean to get closer to the peephole.

After a few seconds, during which Marvell gulped coffee and Helen flicked anxious glances at him, Bremerton restarted the conversation. "Anyhow, I don't doubt your prognosis for Daniel's immediate future, Mr. Geldman. As for the long-term effects of your treatments, I'm still afraid we could see reduced efficacy over time. Maybe toxicity, neoplasms, metabolic disturbances."

"Not impossible," Geldman said. "Which is why I welcome your long-term involvement."

"Right now, I'm more worried about Daniel's mental state. He doesn't need anyone making him feel like a dumb kid when he's been doing so well here, getting out, making friends. That can't have been easy, all the years his father isolated him."

"Sean and Eddy are bright spots," Helen said. "They've already accepted Daniel's differences, which many people might even regard as monstrous. But they're—" She nodded at Geldman. "Enlightened, you'd say?"

"Since last summer, they've begun to be, even in my broader sense of the word."

Man, Sean needed fingers to stick into his ears before his head swelled too much.

"I take it Mr. Glass isn't entirely pleased with Daniel's new friends," Marvell said.

"Why do you say that, Theo?"

"He suggested Daniel move back to his own apartment, didn't he?"

"More like demanded," Helen admitted. "But Daniel refused. The situation with him and Eddy—"

"There really is a situation?"

"They've started dating."

"You didn't tell me that, Helen."

"I didn't think I had to. You must have seen they like each other."

"I don't see them together as much as you do. But never mind. That must be over, now Eddy's found out about Daniel's problem."

Helen blinked.

"You assume too much, Professor," Geldman said. He went to the side table to refill his cup, then wandered across the library, sipping and perusing the shelves. Bremerton scraped his chair around to see what Geldman was up to. Marvell didn't draw delicate circles on the tabletop; he drummed on it, hard, until Geldman spoke again: "Whereas most people are open only to the reality they desire, Eddy is open to reality as it is. Her chief aversion is for falsehood of any kind. As soon as Daniel started telling her the truth, he started winning her back."

"I believe it," Helen said.

Geldman halted in front of the dais and gazed up at the *Founding*, not at anything in particular this time (like the rondel and Sean and Daniel behind it) but as if in thoughtful abstraction. Even so, Sean fought the urge to draw back from the peephole.

Daniel didn't stir a feather.

"And Daniel," Geldman continued. "He's very much like Eddy. Since it's only a disguise, not a medical necessity, that neck brace chafes him more in spirit than in body. If we're sincerely concerned with his well-being, we'll tell him all the truth we know and give him the means to find out more."

"No," Marvell said. "I couldn't allow that."

"Why not?"

"Well, for one thing," Bremerton said, "Mr. Glass has insisted we not tell Daniel anything about his grandfather Marsh. Or discuss his mother's, ah, suicide."

"Which wasn't a suicide," Helen said, shaking her head.

Daniel's crow eyes had fixed on the peephole lens until they popped like his human ones, and his whole body shuddered under the race of his crow heart. He wing-elbowed Sean to the side. Sean yielded. He couldn't see the library anymore, but he could still hear.

"Look," Marvell said. "We know so little that—"

"We know Aster Glass didn't hang herself in a sanitarium," Geldman told the *Founding*.

Told Daniel. Jesus.

"But we have no idea what she did after she left it."

"We have an idea who might know."

"So you want to go quiz Marsh about his daughter?"

"No."

"Then what?"

"Tell Daniel his mother walked out of the sanitarium alive. Tell him his grandfather Marsh didn't die years before he was born. In fact, Marsh has a very lively interest in Daniel, as the presence of his agent proves."

"We're not—"

"We *are* sure about the agent, Professor," Geldman said in as stern a voice as Sean had ever heard him use. It got slightly softer, slightly more distant, as if Geldman had returned to the conference table. "I've seen the Changer every day that Daniel's visited me. I've watched him trail Daniel back home. Sean spotted him at the harbor yesterday."

"All right," Marvell said. "We'll assume the Changer's a spy. But we can't assume he's from Marsh."

"I know this fellow. He's been to the pharmacy many times for his employer, who does happen to be Barnabas Marsh. But putting Marsh aside, let me point out one last thing. I've designed Daniel's treatment to spare his nascent telepathy. It remains empathy for now, but empathy is enough for him to tell that we're lying about some things, by word or by omission. That's slow poison. I say we stop administering it."

It was like Daniel had figured—felt. His father was lying to him, and Marvell knew it, and Helen and Bremerton and Geldman. The lies were huge, too—no wonder the feathers on Daniel's nape and back had risen.

"Mr. Geldman," Marvell said. "We simply aren't authorized to tell Daniel about his mother and grandfather."

"He's not a minor," Bremerton said. "Technically we *could* talk to Daniel about the other side of his family. But for now we'd better respect Mr. Glass's wishes. Daniel remains financially dependent on him. Emotionally dependent, too, in ways that are just starting to change. Besides, the Order's not on good terms with Daniel's grandfather, is it?"

"When it's necessary to deal with Innsmouth, we go through

Barnabas Marsh, but it's never been a pleasant experience. I don't see how it could do Daniel any good to meet him."

"I don't know about that, Theo," Helen said. "But I'm with Dr. Bremerton. Daniel's got enough on his plate, starting his studies, making new ties. It could be too much right now, finding out his grandfather's alive, and maybe his mother."

"Highly unlikely she's alive," Marvell said.

"I don't see why she shouldn't be," Geldman said. "However, working with the Order as I am on this case, I will accede to its wishes. I'll say no more about Aster and Barnabas Marsh."

Yeah, sure, because he didn't have to. Daniel half flapped, half hopped out of the tree trunk. By the time Sean followed, he was on the wing. He blundered against Nyarlathotep's uplifted arm, recovered, gained altitude. Did the Dark Pharaoh smile? Sean didn't have time to decide between fact and paranoia. He flew after Daniel, straight up into the dusk sky. Damn, Daniel was an arrow streaking toward the zenith, paying no attention to Sean's frantic caws. Exactly how high did the sky go in the seed world? Would Daniel hit an invisible ceiling, splat, or would he keep going until the air got too thin to support his wings, too thin to breathe? Sean veered from vertical flight and beat hard for the crescent moon, which cradled a palm that was hazier than usual, barely there. His real flesh pressed the Plexiglas shield, not the stained glass itself, but the exit connection still worked fine: He soared between the horns of the moon and into human Sean on the ladder. Something jerked his left foot off its rung— Daniel staggering back into himself. He let go of Sean as the whole ladder lurched. Good damn thing Eddy was there to wrestle it back to stability and hold it firm while Sean scrambled down.

"What happened?" she whispered. "Where's he going?"

Daniel had wandered zombie stiff toward the back gate. "We better go after him."

"First help me get the ladder back to the carriage house. I hope they didn't hear it scrape when you guys came out of the window."

"The library's soundproofed, remember?"

They hustled the ladder back to where they'd found it. Luckily Daniel's zombie shuffle hadn't quickened, and they caught up to him as he crossed Pickman Street and collapsed on the curb. Eddy hunkered down next to him. Sean stood guard, watching for pursuit from the Arkwright House. Marvell and Geldman had walked to the meeting. Bremerton was staying the night. Nobody ought to be coming out the driveway unless they'd been busted—

Daniel muttered something. "What, Daniel?" Eddy said.

Daniel coughed. His voice remained thick, but the second time, Sean heard him all too clearly: "I'm going to Innsmouth."

Couldn't blame Eddy for sounding confused, since she hadn't heard a word of the meeting. "Innsmouth? Why?"

"They can't keep me from going. I'm walking if you or Sean won't drive me."

"When?"

"Now."

Oh hell. Sean turned. Daniel's tight-stretched mouth and far-focused eyes told the story: Anyone who tried to stop him was in for a fight. They didn't need to have it on the curb, though. "Hey, come to the car. Before someone sees us."

"You're driving me?"

"I'm with you whatever you decide to do, okay? Let's talk about it first, that's all."

And Daniel's eyes came into focus, first on Sean's sneaker, then on his face. After a few seconds, he must have sensed Sean's sincerity, because he nodded like a rational human being.

So, maybe, they wouldn't be heading toward Innsmouth at midnight. Because if Lovecraft had been even a tiny bit accurate in his description of the town, midnight was not the best time for a visit.

18

They sat in the Civic until just before their curfew, then huddled in the common room to continue the great Innsmouth debate. First Sean had to tell Eddy about the meeting, and good thing he got that done in the car, because her indignation over Mr. Glass's lies and the ongoing cover-up packed some decibels. Even Helen didn't entirely escape her outrage, though Marvell (damn straight) got the worst of it. She could halfway understand them not telling Daniel about his grandfather, but to let him go on thinking his mother had killed herself? That was the most messed-up thing she'd ever heard.

With Marvell crossed off Eddy's hero list, Geldman jumped straight to the top. He had to have known Sean and Daniel were inside the *Founding*. Orne might have told him about the seed world, or else he'd sensed it for himself. Either way, while seeming to go along with the Order and Mr. Glass's demands, he'd provoked Marvell and the others into revealing the truth.

They all agreed that lying to Daniel about his mother had been dead wrong. The question that kept them up until 2 A.M. was how

Daniel should follow Geldman's lead about Barnabas Marsh. Daniel insisted on going to Innsmouth, ASAP. Sean argued they should wait for the right moment, like broad daylight, after they'd left notes about where to search for their bodies. Eddy held out for exhaustive pre-trip research until it was clear that logic wasn't going to budge Daniel. By then they were so tired, Daniel grudgingly conceded that no one was up to driving to Innsmouth that night.

They reconvened the next morning, an encouragingly bright Sunday, and Daniel talked them into an immediate trip. They told Helen they were going to hike in the state park at Ipswich and loaded the Civic with a convincing array of coolers and backpacks. On the way out of Arkham, they stopped at the pharmacy for Daniel's potions and so Sean could leave a note with his crow bro, Boaz. He wanted to mark the envelope, DO NOT OPEN UNLESS WE GO MISSING, but Daniel nixed that. Geldman would probably mind-read their destination right away, no call for Movie Moment melodrama. Though kind of lamenting the missed opportunity, Sean kept his message brief: *We're going to Innsmouth. If we're not back tonight, do whatever you think you have to, thanks. S & D & E.*

If Geldman read Sean and Eddy's intentions, he said nothing about it. Whatever he might have said to Daniel in the exam room stayed in the exam room.

The scale out front, reticent for once, dispensed no fortunes.

Back in the Civic, Eddy used her laptop and Tumblebee's Wi-Fi signal to run a search for Innsmouth. Most results referred to Lovecraft's story rather than to the actual town, and the only tourist information was on fan Web sites—the official town page was skeletal, with a conspicuous lack of charming seaside photos and chamber of commerce hype. However, it did have a map and directions. A search on Barnabas Marsh produced an Innsmouth address of 4 Washington Street, the fact that Marsh was mayor of the town and owner of the Marsh Metals Refinery, and a phone number. Daniel refused to call it. He didn't want to warn Marsh his long-lost grandson was coming. That way, Daniel figured, he might startle something out of him.

Did they *want* to startle somebody who was probably a Deep One? Probably Big Boss of the Deep Ones, since he was the Order's contact? Sean kept his qualms to himself. Sleep hadn't taken the edge off Daniel's anger, so let somebody else piss him off. Like Marsh if he wouldn't see them.

Route 1A took them through Ipswich and into Rowley, where they hit the only snag of their trip. According to the map, their turnoff would be a road marked TO INNSMOUTH & INNSMOUTH HARBOR. They couldn't find it. Eddy made Sean pull into a gas station for directions. The old guy at the register grumbled about "those damn Lovelace fans" who were always stealing the damn Innsmouth sign. No use replacing it—it'd be gone by the next weekend. Anyhow, the Innsmouth road was just north of the gas station, to the right. The one without a sign.

It was reassuring that Lovecraft geeks routinely visited Innsmouth without being sacrificed to Dagon or even getting a selfie with Deep Ones to post on their blogs. Maybe it was because of the treaty Marvell had mentioned. Like, if the Deep Ones didn't harass visitors, the Order wouldn't harass them.

They pulled back onto 1A. A kiwi-green Volkswagen Bug passed them and took a squealing right onto the signless road, probably geeks in a rush to see infamous Innsmouth. Sean didn't try to keep pace with the Bug. The road ran through a salt marsh, two narrow lanes frequently punctuated by age-grayed timber bridges, and neither road nor bridges had guardrails. No way Sean was going to immerse Daniel again by plunging the Civic into a bog. He poked along at twenty miles an hour until they left the marsh for undulating dunes. There sand blown across the blacktop was the big hazard, and he dared to up their speed to twenty-five. A couple miles into the monotonous landscape of stunted pines and bayberry, beach roses and dune grass, they started to pass brick foundations poking out of the sand like the jaws of primordial whales. Eddy speculated that a slow tsunami of dunes had engulfed the houses. That was what happened when people clear-cut the coastal forest, but she still felt sorry for the homeowners who'd fought sand until brooms weren't enough, and shovels weren't enough, and fences sank in the gritty flood.

As they began glimpsing the ocean, Daniel spoke for the first time in an hour. "My mom took me somewhere like this when I was four or five. My father was gone on business, so it was just her and me and wrecked houses in the dunes and a beach with nobody on it. We stayed in a tent for a week. There was a man, older than my father. She didn't tell me who he was, but he walked with us every day, up and down the beach. He rode me on his shoulders."

"You think it was your grandfather?" Eddy said.

"Maybe. My mom said not to tell my father about him, or about our beach trip either. I remember that."

Sure enough, the dunes gave way to the kind of lonely beach Daniel had described. The road bottomed out in a shallow parking lot drifted with sand. From there it climbed more solid ground, a rocky rise that crested over an abrupt river valley, a long crescent of bay, and a town that looked like Kingsport or Arkham must have looked a century before. No scenic pullover here, so Sean swerved the Civic as far onto the shoulder as he could, and they emerged wordless to check out Daniel's ancestral home.

❧

Lovecraft had written that Innsmouth was falling apart, with caved-in roofs, boarded-up buildings, and crumbling steeples; with rotting wharves, a silt-clogged harbor, and nothing left of the old lighthouse but the foundation stones. If he'd seen that kind of dilapidation for himself, then the townspeople had gotten busy since his visit. True, there didn't seem to be any new houses, and there were many vacant lots, especially in the harborside neighborhoods. But the remaining buildings were either in decent shape or under restoration—most streets had a house or two surrounded by scaffolding, and new shingles and fresh roof decking were everywhere. As for the clogged harbor, it was deep enough for the tugs and barges tied up at one new pier and the fishing boats and cruisers tied up at a second. No rotting wharves, either, but the ancient breakwater did have only the blackened base of the former beacon, topped now by modern jetty lights.

Eddy pointed out landmarks she recognized from the town Web site map: the Manuxet River, which cut the town in two as it rushed in churning falls to the harbor; New Church Green, where Lovecraft said the Esoteric Order of Dagon had its headquarters; and the town square, actually a town semicircle. Daniel pointed to a neighborhood well back from the water, where the houses were big enough to qualify as mansions. Washington Street had to be in that area.

Daniel was too restless to enjoy the view for long, and so they headed into Innsmouth. From the overlook to an iron-bedded bridge flung over the river gorge, the road was smooth blacktop. Beyond the bridge, the semicircular square opened out. Someone with brain cells (or a sore butt) had paved over all but a few decorative strips of the original cobblestones. The strips marked off a central parking lot, two dozen slots that the Civic shared with a battered pickup and an SUV. The kiwi-green Bug that had passed them earlier stood in front of J. Waite, Groceries and Produce, ignoring the NO PARKING signs posted the length of the sidewalk.

Besides the grocery, Sean scoped out a drugstore, a diner, a five-and-dime, and three fish dealers. The shops were in two-story brick buildings much older than their jaunty striped awnings. Capping the row was a three-story building with the marble portico of a bank or library. "Your map say what that place is, Eddy?"

"Town offices, refinery offices, and post office all in one. And that's the refinery." She pointed to an industrial block on the edge of the gorge. Its buildings loomed above a chain-link fence crowned with razor wire: classic redbrick New England factories with mile-high smokestacks and huge windows that glared in the noon sun, as white as acid-blinded eyes.

Sean turned off the Civic, killing the AC. Rolling down his window let in humid air thickened with fish stink, but since they were parked opposite the fish dealers, he didn't put that down to Deep One infestation. "The refinery office would be closed on Sunday?"

"Nothing else is."

And plenty of people were out shopping, too. One clump were obviously fan tourists, two geeky dudes and a Goth couple trying to look cool while simultaneously taking pictures like crazy. Most of the apparent townies looked normal. A handful looked, to varying degrees, like Curious Changer: mouths stretched too wide, feet and hands too big, eyes shielded with wraparound shades (or worse, exposed and way bigger and more protuberant than Daniel's). They dressed in clothes too warm for summer but perfect for concealing mutations in progress; the universal fashion statement was neck covering, whether a turned-up collar or a scarf or a bandage, like the fresh gauze Geldman had wrapped around Daniel's gills that morning. There was also a Changer gait: a bent-kneed shuffle, as if the Changers' joints were getting rubbery, their feet too floppy for easy land locomotion.

And, of course, there was the smell. When a normal woman and a Changer approached the adjacent pickup, the Changer brought with him a stench distinct from the purely fishy one the dealers' shops exhaled. Sean's nose worked: fish base, yeah, and sweat, and a skunk-musky nastiness. He had to close the Civic windows and restart the AC, with the exhaust fan on.

The Changer getting in on the truck's passenger side paused, bent, and stared into the Civic, throat bellowing under a saggy turtleneck collar. Great, had he empathically overheard Sean's disgust? If so, why was it Daniel his frog eyes locked on?

Daniel stared right back, and the Changer climbed into the truck. When it had driven off, Daniel said, "He could tell about me. That I'm a Changer, too."

Eddy scanned the crowd, frowning, in full alert mode. "Could you tell how he felt? Angry?"

"No. Just curious."

Sean caught his own eyes darting, like Eddy's, in all directions. The normal townies paid little attention to the Changers. Sure, you had to factor in familiarity, but shouldn't some of the normal people act more like the fan tourists, whose nonchalance was an obvious mask for their nervousness? Even weirder: since they'd arrived in the square, sparks of magical energy—directed, intended energy—had been nipping Sean's skin like minute gnats, barely noticeable except that there were so many nips, and they kept coming. People were doing magic all around them, and his sense was that the magicians were the *normal* adults more than the Changers. Like that woman who kept passing the Civic, sparking him every time. There: she stepped from building-shadow into an alley-fall of sunlight, and for a second, she went out of focus, blurring at her edges. Did that mean she was wearing an illusion, and if she was, did it hide something worse than a Changer?

He turned to ask Daniel if he'd felt anything similar, but Daniel was getting out of the car. Eddy looked at Sean, and sighed, and said, "We've got to do it sometime."

"Where are we going? If it's to Marsh's house, shouldn't we drive?"

"I'm letting Daniel take the lead on this one."

And so Eddy exited the Civic, and so Sean exited, too.

As he swung his door shut with a faux-confident bang, the kiwi-green Bug swung a door open and disgorged two enormous sneakered feet followed by the rest of Curious Changer. Coincidence? Sean's ass.

As Curious slouched toward them, he said, "Get back in."

Eddy cracked her door.

"No," Daniel said. "If he's from my grandfather, like Geldman said—"

Curious stopped a yard from the Civic and bobbed a lopsided bow. "Yours in Father Dagon and Mother Hydra," he slurred.

Daniel stepped around Sean and up to the plate: "Yours in the same, I guess. You're the one who's been following us?"

"Just you," Curious corrected.

"Okay, so why?"

"Old Man Marsh said to." Curious deposited himself on the hood of the Civic. Sean might have imagined his butt giving a rubbery squelch, but he wasn't imagining the stink, only compounded by a cologne not made by Cybele.

He retreated upwind, to Eddy's side of the car.

Curious glanced their way, shrugged, turned back to Daniel. "I'm Abel. Work for Old Man Marsh."

Maybe Daniel was immune to Changer smell. Anyhow, he held his ground. "You're talking about Barnabas Marsh, my grandfather."

"The same. You didn't think he forgot about you?"

"I thought he was dead. That's what my father told me."

Curious—no, *Abel*—slurped air, apparently his version of snorting. From his standing vantage, Sean could see under his raised collar. He had deep creases in the sides of his neck, gills like Daniel's minus the rawness, and they quivered when he spoke. "Well, your father lied."

"Yeah, I get that now."

"Old Man Marsh, dead. Not too likely. So, you've come to see him?"

"Yeah."

"I've told him you're here. I'll walk you over to the house."

Abel slouched off. Daniel followed him like a sleepwalker, but he snapped out of it when Eddy grabbed Sean's elbow—Daniel must have felt her alarm as acutely as Sean felt the bite of her nails. "Wait," he called to Abel. "What about my friends?"

Abel barked a laugh. "They're welcome to come along. Old Man Marsh knows they're here. He's ready."

Eddy went to Daniel at once. Sean locked the Civic, wondering whether they were as ready as the Old Man, and what exactly it was that the Old Man was ready to do about them.

19

Abel led them from the town square to Federal Street, which climbed Innsmouth's tall westward hill. The higher up they went, the bigger the houses got. At the halfway point, they passed New Church Green. On the far side of its central park was a gray stone church with a squat tower, supposed headquarters of the Deep Ones. Sean asked if the Esoteric Order of Dagon still met there, and Abel nodded and sneered, revealing yellowed mouth guards. Okay, maybe he didn't mean to sneer—in stretching his wide mouth even wider, he couldn't help but look nasty, especially if you knew what kind of teeth the guards hid. The Green was deserted except for a Changer on a park bench. Unlike Abel and most of the downtown Changers, this dude wore no hood or cap. Probably he couldn't find one to fit his grotesquely elliptical head. He'd molted all but a few straggling hairs; his scalp was mottled and scabby, and his ears curled in on themselves like desiccated leaves about to drop. When his unblinking eyes met Sean's, Sean looked away fast. "I guess the church doesn't give guided tours?"

Abel gave him another sharky smile. "No, and best you stay out of the Green. It's no place for strangers."

So Lovecraft had gotten that part right.

Washington Street stood at Innsmouth's highest point in more than geography. It featured residences with lots so extensive, it took only four of them to fill the street. Wrought iron fences enclosed terraced gardens; white marble steps made the long climbs from sidewalk to houses. And yeah, the houses were mansions. They were all in this style, Empire something, that Joe-Jack hated, what with the mansard roofs (he called them bastard roofs) and the center towers that were so hard to scaffold for repair work. Abel walked past the first three lots, chanting: "Here's Gilman, and here's Eliot, and here's Waite." The fourth house he introduced as "Marsh."

It was the biggest of the big, three stories with a tower that sported a pope's-hat roof. Just the hat for the Changer in New Church Green, if you ditched the porthole windows and the widow's walk. "Marsh," Abel repeated, pride in his slurpy voice.

"My grandfather's house," Daniel said.

"Go on up. I'll be waiting out here to take you back to your car."

Daniel unlatched the iron gates. Each had a decorative shield with the initials o-m picked out in gold. That had to be for Obed Marsh, the guy who'd first invited the Deep Ones to party in Innsmouth way back in the 1800s. After tracing the letters on one shield, Daniel shoved the gates back so hard, their hinges rained rust flakes on the marble steps. From his grunt, Abel didn't appreciate this abuse of his boss's property, but Daniel had already taken off, and he kept his lead on Sean and Eddy all the way to the porch steps, where either his energy or his courage ran out. They pulled up, panting, in time to turn with Daniel toward the view. Innsmouth fanned out below the Marsh House from hilltop to harbor. Across the glinting bay stretched Plum Island.

South were the marshes and dunes they'd driven through, along with a misty hint of Arkham's cliffs. North, more marshes, more dunes, and another misty hint, this time of Newbury and a small airfield. Normal civilization, not far off, really. They could drive to it in less than an hour.

"It's too late not to do this, isn't it?" Daniel said. He turned to Eddy.

"Not if you don't want to."

"Half of me says go inside. The other half says run like a bitch."

"We can do either one," Eddy said. "Your decision."

Sean looked down the marble steps. Lounging on the lowest one, Abel scratched one huge sneakered foot with the heel of the other. Would he try to stop them if they bugged out?

What Abel might do wasn't the question. "If we run," Sean said, "you won't find out what happened to your mom."

"Maybe I don't want to know?"

"Dude, you thought she killed herself. What could be worse than that?"

"He's right," Eddy said. "If you can do it, go in."

"You'll come, too?"

"No, I'm going to wait out here with Abel." She dashed up the porch steps, and in a Perfect Eddy moment, she spun around, pumping her fists high overhead, ready for the big match.

There was nothing Sean and Daniel could do after that but follow.

The doors of the Marsh House had arched tops, etched glass windows, and a brass knocker shaped like whale flukes. Daniel plied the flukes; the rap summoned a young woman dressed in an old-time maid's uniform, black dress and white apron and rubber-soled shoes polished to a high sheen. Her mouth was a little too wide and her eyes a little too popped, but she didn't yet smell like a Changer. Before Daniel could speak, she said that Mr. Marsh was expecting them—would they mind waiting in the parlor?

Daniel sat, fidgeting, on the couch to which she led them. The way Eddy sat beside him, crouched on the edge of her seat, she looked ready to broad-jump over the low table set with tea and pastries for which none of them seemed to have an appetite. Sean sat in a gilt and velvet armchair, but not for long. The parlor boasted several cabinets of curiosities, all begging him to have a look. One held taxidermied birds, including a raven that reminded Sean too much of himself in the seed world. The next held trays of pin-skewered beetles and butterflies, the next two exotic weapons and jewelry that Captain Obed Marsh must have brought home from his South Seas adventures. Coolest was the fifth case, which contained three large statues. The middle figure was Cthulhu himself, three feet high including his pedestal, carved in silver-veined green stone. Flanking him were two ivory figures reminiscent of the "merpeople" in the *True Atlantis* book.

Sean read the handwritten labels at the feet of the ivories. The one on Cthulhu's right was *Dagon, Indonesia, 18th c.* The one on his left was *Hydra, Indonesia, 18th c.* They were the god and goddess Abel had mentioned, human except for some decorative scales and fins. If the Deep Ones looked like them, they were way prettier than the Changers he'd seen so far.

"Sean," Eddy said. "Stop snooping around."

"I'm not. You don't put stuff on display if you don't want people to look at it." And beside a pair of pocket doors was a final intriguing case—no, it was an aquarium, the frameless acrylic kind, but its top was sealed, and there weren't any visible filtration or heating systems. Moving closer, he saw that what he'd taken for massed corals was a glass sculpture in every shade of water from colorless crystal through Caribbean blues and greens to deep-sea blacks. It melded the aqueous rainbow into an organic cityscape whose curved terraces grew seaweed and sponges and whose towers were impossibly stretched and filigreed. The sculpture was illuminated by fixtures hidden in the aquarium base, which vibrated slightly, agitating the tank water so that the glass-refracted light danced like sunbeams through waves.

No fish lived in the aquarium—how could they with no way to feed them? It was all about the sculpture, with the water adding a depth air couldn't. Besides, this city was *supposed* to be underwater—a brass plate named it Y'HA-NTHLEI. Sean wrestled the crazy syllables with his tongue, and what came out was the "Yehanithlayee" Daniel had talked about, the Deep Ones' lair off Innsmouth.

Sean was about to call Eddy and Daniel over when a gasp from the next room startled him silent. He eased close to the pocket doors beside the aquarium, which weren't quite shut. Another gasp reached him, raspy, and a whoosh like wheels on carpet, followed by soft footsteps receding and a welling of Changer stink. He backed off—Old Man Marsh had to be coming at last.

Marsh did come, from the opposite direction. Sean had made it back to his seat when an undertaker strolled into the parlor from the front hall. Or not an undertaker, but with his black suit and noiseless black shoes, the guy could have played one on TV. Though his slicked-back hair was graying, making him more than old enough for the Change, he didn't look or smell like a Changer. Nor did he zing Sean with magical sparks or blur at his edges when he crossed into the parlor sunlight.

Which argued against an illusion.

Unless the guy was really, really good at it.

In which case, he was a major magician, maybe in Geldman and Orne's league.

Daniel stood, followed by Eddy, Sean a distant third.

Marsh made straight for Daniel and extended a (normal

no-webs) hand. "Good afternoon, Daniel. Abel told me you were coming."

Daniel didn't reach out, probably because he was staring so hard at his grandfather's face, he didn't notice his proffered hand until Eddy nudged his elbow. Then, as if his forearm weighed a ton, he lifted his own hand. Marsh clasped it, then turned it palm up and uncurled Daniel's fingers with his thumb. Also with his thumb, he touched Daniel's fresh webbing and traced the red scars above it. That blatant examination made Daniel jerk away. "Abel, your spy," he said.

Unoffended, if you could trust his bland smile, Marsh offered his rejected hand to Eddy. "I won't pretend Abel hasn't informed me of your name, Miss Rosenbaum. Welcome to Innsmouth."

Eddy shook. Sean was next. "Mr. Wyndham."

He returned Marsh's grip. Skin to skin, he caught a faint buzz. If it wasn't his nerves-revved imagination, it might be magical energy gloving Marsh's paw in not only the appearance but the feel of humanity. Plus he had no smell. Zero. Not of a fish, not of a skunk, not even of a masking cologne like Daniel's.

And Daniel's cologne interested Marsh, because after he'd seated himself in the twin of Sean's armchair, he sniffed his right hand, delicately, like you'd sniff expensive wine. "Solomon Geldman's work, your scent?"

As if he didn't want to mention Cybele, Daniel nodded. Sean approved. They were here to get information out of Marsh, not vice versa.

"There's a remarkable magician," Marsh said. "I was proud to hear he'd taken my grandson as his apprentice. Of course, you go to him for more than instruction. Well. Better Geldman than the butchers your father employed."

"You mean the doctors, sir?"

"I mean the butchers. Look at the scars they've left on your fingers. Yanked your teeth, too, and put in those fakes. Tell me they had the brains to leave your gills alone."

"They didn't know what to do about those."

"But Geldman does." Marsh draped one arm over the back of his chair and planted his right ankle on his left knee. The movie-still attitude made Sean think of the actor who'd played Straker in that old *Salem's Lot* movie. Marsh sounded a little like him, too, deep voiced and classy, only American classy instead of British. "Your reversion from the Change was going smoothly until the other day. Eli Glass must have thought he was beating us. What he couldn't impose on your mother, he'd impose on you."

Angry as Daniel had been at his dad, he stiffened. "It's not like that. I don't want to Change."

Marsh's dark eyes drifted from Daniel to Eddy. "Since recently?"

"Since always," Daniel said tightly. He didn't cut his eyes toward Eddy as Sean did, but he probably felt the flame in her cheeks.

"No offense. But I've seen what happens when our kind get involved with uninformed humans, as your mother, Aster, did. I don't approve of the blanket prohibition against intermarriage that's in our treaty with the Order of Alhazred, but human partners must know all the consequences. They must consent free and eager. There are plenty who will, you know, but your father wasn't one of them."

"My mother didn't tell him she was a hybrid before they got together?"

"She didn't tell him even when she started to Change. At first she pretended she knew nothing about her 'illness.' Eventually, she had to tell the truth, though, and then she agreed to go to the sanitarium, so you wouldn't see her Changing, Danny."

"Don't call me that."

"Why not? She did."

Daniel's voice rose: "That's why I don't want to hear it from you."

Kit had been Mom's name for Sean. After she'd died, even Dad hadn't used it. Until last summer.

"Have it your way," Marsh said. "Daniel's as good a name, but it's not your only one. You've got a Shin-yay name, too." He nodded toward Eddy and Sean. "That's our name in our own language, *S-h-n*-apostrophe-*y-e-h*."

Daniel's left hand squeezed the right so hard, it had to hurt. Then he blurted: "My father said my mother died of leukemia. Then he said she killed herself. Then I found out she didn't die in the sanitarium. She left it. Do you know what happened next?"

Eddy slipped her arm through Daniel's. Marsh held his movie star pose, but Sean saw his shoulders rise. "Well, what else would she do, Daniel? She came home."

Someone tapping magic electrified the air. Was it Daniel, straining his empathy to make sure Marsh wasn't lying? "To Innsmouth?"

"To this house. For a while."

"Then—did she die?"

Marsh laughed softly. "Daniel, now. We don't die that young or that easy."

"You can get killed, or kill yourselves."

"Don't you remember your mother at all? Aster wasn't the quitting kind. Once she'd wrapped her mind around leaving you and settled into the Change, she did all right."

"She's alive," Daniel said.

"Of course she is."

It hadn't been "of course" for Daniel, not after his father's lies. He sucked in a huge breath and held it, bent over his knees. If he did a face-plant on the table, it would be right into an elaborately iced cake—he'd drown in the frosting, gills or no.

"Daniel," Marsh said. He broke his pose and leaned forward.

Daniel sat back, safe from the cake. "Where is she?" he got out.

"She's gone to Y'ha-nthlei. You know of the place?"

"I've read about it. A city underwater, off Devil Reef."

"In the chasm *beneath* the reef, to be exact. Much deeper, secret and secure."

Sean cleared his throat. "It's like that sculpture over there?"

"Yes. That shows our family's property below."

Daniel went to the aquarium. Eddy turned to Marsh. "Lovecraft wrote that the Feds imprisoned Innsmouthers and torpedoed Y'ha-nthlei. But Geldman told Daniel that didn't happen."

"If you're faced with one assertion from Howard Lovecraft and another from Solomon Geldman, believe Geldman. His statements may be tricky, but essentially they're true."

Without turning, Daniel said, "How long's my mother been down there?"

"Since she completed her Change."

"Does she ever come up?"

"Once or twice a year, maybe. Aster likes it better below."

"You don't, Mr. Marsh?" Eddy said.

"Oh, I like it fine, but I've got business to look after air-side. The town, the refinery."

"And dealing with the Order?"

"When someone's got to." Marsh lifted the silver teapot that had been cooling its heels since the maid brought it in. You'd think the tea would have been cold, but maybe Geldman had taught Marsh some of his tricks, because the amber liquid he poured, one and two and three cups full, was steaming. He handed one cup to Eddy, one to Sean, left the third for Daniel, Sean supposed.

Daniel remained at the aquarium.

Not wanting to deal with the fancy creamer and sugar bowl, Sean gulped his tea straight. His throat was dry, and he didn't want his voice to crack when he asked the touchy obvious question: "Mr. Marsh, so. You're a Deep One yourself?"

"Thank you," Marsh said.

"Sir?"

"For the compliment. My illusioning skills suffice to fool most humans, but I don't expect them to fool other magicians. Not for long."

"Count me as almost fooled. Some people in the main square, I could kind of tell they were illusioning themselves. You, the only hint I got was when I shook your hand. The magic sparked me then."

"Count me as totally fooled," Eddy said. "I was starting to think Daniel's grandmother might be, um, Shn'yeh? Not you, sir."

"And thank you, Miss Rosenbaum."

"Is that who's in there, my grandmother?" Daniel asked, his voice sharp. He'd stepped from the aquarium to the pocket doors—he must have noticed the Changer smell.

As if Marsh had been expecting the outburst, and why not, the telepathy thing and all, he merely redirected his gaze. "No, Daniel. She's like Aster, spends most of her time below."

"Then who is it? Another one of your spies?"

"It's your cousin Tom. Your aunt Elspeth's boy. But you won't have heard of Tom and Elspeth. Why should Eli mention them while he pretended we were dead, your grandmother and I, and, in the end, your mother?" He walked toward the pocket doors. "Don't mistake me. I'm not saying your father's a bastard, though you may think he's one at the moment."

"You know what I think."

"That's a fact, and you know what I feel. I'm glad you've come. And no, I couldn't go to you. Aster didn't want me interfering with Eli. She knew you'd eventually show up in Innsmouth. The place our people first pulled out of the sea, we all come back to it. Biological imperative, you could say."

Like salmon returning to their birth streams? Only Daniel hadn't come to Innsmouth to spawn. Even though Eddy had come with him.

That was a line of thought Sean had better cut short.

Daniel had stared at the floor while Marsh was talking. What he finally lifted weren't his eyes but his right hand, to slip its fingers into the gap between the doors. "I want to know what could happen, if I stopped Geldman's treatments."

"What *would* happen, no *could* about it."

The one Daniel glanced at was Eddy. "How old is my cousin?"

"Twenty-five, and yes, he's been Changing for a while. He's come to the last stage, when things get rough and a Changer needs looking after."

Daniel gave the door beside him a tentative pull. Well oiled, it slid without a squeak into the wall—the simultaneous groan came from the darkened room beyond, maybe a second parlor, maybe a dining room, though who'd ever want to eat in a room that exhaled such a reek? It was worse than the Servitor's stench in a way, because at least the Servitor had smelled like one thing, itself; this was the ultimate Changer amalgamation of fish and putrefying skunk and human misery.

When Daniel gave another tug, widening the gap to a yard, Marsh gave the other door a shoulder shove that propelled it all the way into the wall. The room he revealed looked like the twin of theirs, but with the heavy draperies drawn and no fixtures lit except for a pair of sconces that bracketed the fireplace. A wingback chair loomed on the hearthrug, with a folded wheelchair nearby.

"Go on in, then," Marsh told Daniel. "I told Tom you were coming. He's willing to meet you."

Willing maybe, but was he able? With the doors open, the sound of his gasps and gurgles made it to where Sean and Eddy sat. If Tom wasn't already on a respirator, he needed one.

Daniel eyeballed Marsh, who eyeballed him back without a blink. Magical energy was condensing between them, probably telepathic challenges and defiance, but listening to Tom, Sean couldn't concentrate on it. At last Daniel broke the staring match by walking into the second parlor. Marsh stepped in after him and pulled the pocket doors back out. He left a gap wide enough to walk through, from which he nodded at Sean and Eddy before receding into the dark.

"What should we do?" Eddy said. She'd risen on one knee so she could see over the sofa back. With Marsh's retreat, she slid down and gave Sean the rarest of all Eddy looks: the anxious one that meant she really didn't have an answer.

"I think Mr. Marsh left the doors open so we could go in, too."

Eddy folded up as tight as Tom's wheelchair, knees clamped together, shoulders drawn forward. "What if we were wrong to help Daniel come here?"

"He would've come anyway."

"Maybe he should have come alone. Now we've seen and heard things he might wish we hadn't. I don't know if we should look. At his cousin, I mean."

Because that could be looking at Daniel's future, the one Geldman was trying to prevent. "I want to look," he said.

"God, Sean, this isn't a freak show."

Anybody else saying that, it would have rocketed him through the roof. But Eddy knew him. She'd earned the privilege. "Yeah, I might have been like that before the Servitor. It's different now, because we know reality's weirder than anything in a book or movie. You said it when we came to Arkham—we've got to learn to face that. And Daniel's in the same boat, even if he's further along than us."

Eddy stayed folded. "Weird stuff's worse when it's somebody you know."

"Yeah, but you know me, and I'm weird."

"You're still human."

"So? Look at Mr. Marsh. He's not human, but I don't know, he doesn't seem like a bad guy."

"He looks human."

"If looking human's all it takes, Nyarlathotep's cool in a whole bunch of his avatars."

Eddy gave herself a final scrunch, digging her chin between fisted hands. "I know it's—," she began, but talking with her cheeks punched in made her sound like a Munchkin. She sat up. "I know it's stupid. But this is Daniel."

The guy she was probably falling in love with. "I think it'll help Daniel if one of us sees. I'm going in, Eddy. You don't have to."

She picked up a sofa pillow. Her fingers sank deep into it. Then she hurled the pillow at the chair where Marsh had sat, and, soft as the thing was, it would have put a hurt on him if he'd still been there. Sean grabbed it as it bounced back toward the china-laden table. "You don't have to go in," he said again.

Eddy stood. "Yeah, I do."

Sean parked the pillow, and they went into the second parlor together.

﹌

Somebody had switched on a floor lamp that threw a truncated cone of light over the wingback chair but left Daniel and Marsh in shadow. They faced Tom, who continued to rasp and gurgle. And stink—as shallowly as Sean was breathing, the back of his throat burned. To control his nausea, he fixed his eyes on the portrait above the fireplace and made up his own little docent lecture about it. Life size. In oils. From back in the days when people dressed like Dickens characters. Dude in a bay window overlooking Innsmouth, complete with the harbor and Plum Island and beyond both a reef of jagged black rock. Dude pointing at the ships in the harbor, or maybe at the reef. And smirking. He had to be Obed Marsh, sea captain, merchant, and Deep One collaborator, but not a Deep One himself. He had died at a normal human age, but his descendants would live for centuries, including this Barnabas, who'd been Old Man Marsh since the 1920s.

Sean and Eddy had taken each step in unison, and they halted together a few feet from the chair. Daniel had disappeared behind it, as if to kneel in front of his cousin. Marsh motioned them to come forward but to the side of the fireplace.

It would be close enough, maybe too close. While Eddy followed Marsh's direction, the raw magic pulsing from the chair made Sean hesitate. It wasn't because the energy was so strong, but because it felt so messed up, one second an airy sucking at his skin and the next a zap of static discharge. Between that and the smell and the respirator soundtrack, he would have run if it hadn't been for Eddy. He'd talked her into this. He couldn't leave her—or Daniel—to see it through alone.

His eyes on the carpet (which was scarier than Geldman's, with fleshy red carnivorous-looking flowers), he made it to Eddy. It wasn't reassuring to hear how fast she was breathing or to see the quake in her knees. Screw it. He raised his eyes to the guy in the chair, who looked a lot like Daniel, actually, as Daniel might look in a few years. The impression faded as Tom began to blur and jitter, one second in full-color focus, the next graying into a humanoid smear with parts that overlapped all wrong.

Either he was a ghost, or he was a living magician whose attempt to illusion himself had gone haywire.

The illusion theory won out when the illusion dropped. Eddy's breathing didn't hitch; while Sean was hanging back, she must have already seen the real Tom. Sean's breath clogged in his throat, and the wall thrust into his back. It was covered with thick-flocked wallpaper but hard underneath, something that wouldn't collapse while he took in the person in the chair.

That Changer in New Church Green? Compared to Daniel's cousin, he'd barely started to morph. Sean's brain struggled to make sense of Tom by imagining that someone had merged a shark with a frog, then flayed it, then stuffed the flayed-off hide with a human whose bones and muscles were bending and breaking, straining and tearing, in order to fit in his new skin. Tom's head, stretched elliptical, had no hair (though it did have a fin-like ridge that ran from forehead to nape and then out of sight down his back) or ears (unless you counted the pinkish drumheads where ears should have been) or nose (apart from two tight slits of nostrils). His eyes had migrated toward the sides of his head, where they bulged from telescoping orbits. A milky cataract covered the left eye. Maybe the film was an "under construction" shield that had already fallen from the right eye, which was all shark-black pupil edged with a narrow blue iris. Neither eye had a lid to blink. More mobile, the lipless mouth gaped from drumhead to drumhead. The teeth were serrated arrowheads. The chin receded into a neck as wide as the head, slashed on either side by five gill slits that flared with every hissing exhalation and oozed a viscous yellow fluid onto the towel around Tom's sagging shoulders. Where the human skin hadn't split and peeled away from his emerging gray-green hide, a similar fluid swelled pustules to bursting, then hardened and flaked like orange resin.

Was it this gunk that put the extra kick in Tom's stink?

The rest of his body hid under an oversized T-shirt and jeans. Enormous mitts covered his hands, and sacklike socks his feet. It was only a partial mercy: Sean could still see the convulsive flex of crazily elongated fingers and toes.

Though Daniel had done some Changing himself, Sean gave him huge credit for having the courage to put his hands over

Tom's mitted fingers and still their jerks. His face was blank. His lips shaped silent words. It looked like he was trying telepathy, and maybe it was working. At least he didn't seem to be mouthing the same thing over and over. As far as Sean could tell, Tom's gasps weren't an attempt at speech but the sound of air bellowing in through his mouth and out through his gills. As if in sympathy, Daniel's gills flared beneath his bandage.

Marsh sidled to Eddy and Sean, deftly herded them into the first parlor, and shut the pocket doors. The maid must have come in while they were gone, because the food and tea things had vanished. Eddy's missile was back in its former place on the sofa, too. She snagged the pillow, not to hurl it at Marsh as he settled into his armchair but to hug it to her belly.

"You both did very well," Marsh said.

Because, what, they hadn't passed out?

"Is he in pain?" Eddy asked in a strangled voice.

"Tom? Well, he's not comfortable, obviously, but we have medicines to ease the transition. If he were stranded in your world, it would be another story."

"He won't die?"

"A caterpillar doesn't die when it changes into a moth."

Eddy sniffed. "That's not the same. Humans don't naturally turn into Deep Ones."

"But hybrids aren't human, not altogether. That includes Daniel, miss, and it always will include him, no matter what Solomon Geldman does."

Tears busted through Eddy's dam, but she let them run unswiped down her face. "You wanted us to see Tom so we'd be scared away from Daniel."

"Exactly wrong. I wanted to see if you had the nerve to look at the truth and still stick by him. His father already hates what he is. He doesn't need friends doing it, too."

"I'm not going to hate him."

"Good, then. You, Mr. Wyndham?"

"Not even a chance," Sean said. "I mean, I might get freaked sometimes, but why should I hate him? You guys aren't evil, are you? Deep Ones. That other word you said."

As you'd figure from his old-school outfit, Marsh carried a cloth handkerchief, which he handed across the table to Eddy. "Shn'yeh," he said.

"Right. You're not monsters. You're just another species."

"Tigers are also another species."

"Tigers are cool."

"Except when they eat you."

"Shn'yeh eat people?"

"I can't guarantee it's never happened," Marsh said. "But it would be an aberration, and very few of us would approve."

"That's all right, then. I mean, sometimes people eat people. You know, Jeffrey Dahmer."

Normally Eddy would have said "Jesus, Sean" by this point, but she remained muffled behind Marsh's handkerchief. "Miss Rosenbaum," he said. "If you'd like, there's a powder room in the main hallway, the door under the stairs."

Eddy nodded and took off.

Marsh watched her go, shaking his head the least you could and still get caught at it. With an equally quashed sigh, he turned back to Sean. "Where were we?"

"Eating people, sir."

"And we don't do that. We don't particularly want to kill people, either, or take over the world."

"That all works for me."

"We do at times mix with humans, but as I said earlier, it's disastrous to do so with uninformed partners. Look what's happened with my own daughter. She had no business marrying Eli Glass, and she's not the only one who has to pay for the mistake. Daniel's paid. He's still paying."

As much as Sean wanted to stay diplomatic and open minded, the idea of Deep Ones hooking up with humans was squicking him out. Maybe it happened only when the hybrids were still human looking, like with Aster and Eli Glass? Though to have hybrids in the first place, 100 percent Deep Ones would have had to mate with 100 percent humans, right? "You said something about the treaty you've made with the Order."

"Not something you've heard of before?"

"Not the details."

"The Order of Alhazred likes secrets. We do, too, of course. I hate to admit it, but things got out of hand in Innsmouth back in Obed's time, and they stayed out of hand until the Order intervened. Some folks thought Innsmouth wasn't enough of an airside foothold in this part of the world—if our magic was strong enough to let us hide in plain sight, we should keep expanding. Others of us saw how you humans were getting new weapons, new ways to communicate and travel, even underwater. At the same time, most of you were as primitive as ever about accepting strangers. Take Howard Lovecraft. Smart fellow, with a heart that pulled him toward the truth of the worlds, but at the same time the truth scared him silly. If he felt like he had to bad-mouth us in his stories, what would the rest of you do in real life? Or try to do and force us to make a damn mess."

Eddy returned and sat beside Sean, her face shiny from scrubbing, her mouth set. She must have paused at the door long enough to hear Marsh's history lesson, because she said, "You and the Deep Ones against expanding, Mr. Marsh, you were glad when the Order came in?"

"Well, I can't say *glad,* but we saw how the Order could help us control the troublemakers. Frank Gilman and I negotiated for our side. We'd been to college at Miskatonic, and we both knew Henry Arkwright. Long as he and the Order promised not to interfere with us Deep Ones, long as they'd mediate for us with the government people, we were willing to make concessions. We'd stay in Innsmouth, not try to take over any other human towns, and we'd keep rambunctious types from coercing humans to mix, or attacking them if they tried to settle here. The second part wasn't that hard. By 1930, any family that wasn't all right with mixing had already left. New people? We don't build to lure them in, neither houses nor jobs nor much by way of sightseeing. The few who do give us a try can't help but feel we're clannish, unwelcoming. They don't stay long. And while they are here, magic keeps them from seeing too much or remembering anything inconvenient."

He was talking about purging memories, like Orne had done with Mom. "I've heard about that kind of magic."

"Have you now? Mind manipulation's a tough study, but it's one some of us have had to learn."

"You could make us forget what we saw in the other room?" Eddy said.

Marsh leaned back. "I could make you forget Tom. I could make you forget Innsmouth. I could even make you forget what Daniel really is. Then, as long as Geldman keeps him from Changing, you could go on not knowing."

Eddy didn't respond, so Sean said, "Could you go back even farther, sir?"

"Farther?"

"In somebody's memory. Like, to a year ago."

Eddy got him. "Back to before the Servitor? To before we even knew about magic?"

"That would be more complicated, but possible. Is that what you want, miss?"

"That would be the easy way out," Eddy said, almost in a whisper.

"But for how long? And do you think that's what Daniel would want?"

If Eddy had an answer, she didn't get to give it. The pocket doors shooshed open. Marsh stood. What the hell, Sean did, too. It was easier than craning his neck to look over the back of the sofa.

Daniel shooshed the doors closed, then leaned against them.

"You had a long talk with Tom," Marsh observed.

"I tried," Daniel said. He sounded like the conversation had wiped him out, but not in an entirely bad way. "I think we mostly understood each other."

"It will get easier. Telepathy's new to you."

Eddy, too, stood and faced Daniel. "You're glad you saw Tom?"

Daniel nodded, then said to Marsh, "He's met people from Y'ha-nthlei."

"Quite a few," Marsh said. "Including his aunt Aster, as I'm sure he told you."

"Yes."

Marsh waited. He knew what was coming next. No big psychic trick. Damn, even Sean knew.

"I want to meet her, too," Daniel said. "I want to meet my mother."

20

By meeting his mother, Daniel didn't mean *sometime*. He meant, like, *yesterday*.

"I understand your eagerness," Marsh said, "but it's not possible."

Daniel didn't yell or beg. He also didn't back down. "If you say I can't see her, then you *don't* understand."

"Daniel, Aster doesn't know you're here. She doesn't know you're studying in Arkham, or about Geldman's treatments, or even that you've begun the Change."

"I started years ago. All this time, you've never told her?"

On the sofa next to Eddy, Sean considered retreat; though Marsh's illusion held firm, having Daniel in his face made his shirt collar heave as if from invisible gills. "No," he said. "So I've got to tell her now, and you've got to give her a chance to get used to the idea."

"What idea?"

"That you haven't come back the way she's always trusted you would, ready to Change and go down to our deep home. It'll be a shock to her."

"That I'm still human?"

"That you might stay human. Think about it."

It seemed that Daniel started to. At least he shut up.

Marsh's collar heaved. "You think I'm the only one standing in your way? Truth is, I'm probably the one least opposed to you meeting Aster. I was telling your friends about our treaty with the Order. Most folks have come to accept it. The restrictions don't chafe much, and they see the benefits. But others oppose it on principle. They think the Order has no right to interfere with us. Some in our own family feel that way, Daniel."

Daniel said nothing.

Marsh took advantage of his silence. "And what's got the anti-Order folk really stirred up is how the Order's interfering with you. With Abel going to Arkham every day, people got curious. Those porpoises at the harbor jetty? Most were natural beasts, commanded to distract onlookers, so the two Deep Ones illusioned as porpoises could have a good look at you. Maybe test your telepathy and talk. They'd already seen you living with the Order and going to Geldman's. They'd sensed you weren't Changing anymore. They put it all together, and they're saying it's too much, the Order of Alhazred helping you throw the gifts of Mother Hydra and Father Dagon back in their faces."

Daniel glanced at the pocket doors. "Tom said that, too, how the Change is a gift."

"The way you're fighting it is the biggest insult you could give around here. At least the anti-Order folks haven't spread the news. They don't want Aster to learn you're a traitor—their words, not mine. Unless you accept the Change, they're not going to welcome you, Daniel. You shouldn't have come to Innsmouth—in fact, I've been worried Arkham's too close. You called Abel a spy? A body-guard is more like it. Speaking of which, he's waiting to take you to your car. You've got to be back in Arkham before the Order misses you. We can't have people saying that when Daniel Marsh Glass shows up, trouble follows on his heels."

No, that wouldn't be great public relations. "I'm ready whenever," Sean said, and Eddy made her willingness even clearer by standing up.

Daniel still held his ground. "When can I come back and meet my mother?"

"I'm not sure, Daniel."

"It'll be harder for me to come when Sean and Eddy leave at the end of the month. I'll still be in Arkham, but I don't know how to drive. My father thought I was too sick to learn."

"Transportation won't be a problem. Abel could drive you here. But you might want your friends with you?"

After a moment, Daniel nodded.

"I doubt I'll be able to arrange things before September. What about the winter vacation? Maybe your friends could come back?"

"I could," Eddy said.

"Me, too," Sean added.

"Why don't we work toward that, then?" Marsh extended his hand to Daniel. It looked human down to the manicured nails, but could shaking with an illusioned hand seal a bargain?

Maybe wondering the same thing, Daniel hesitated. When he did take Marsh's hand, though, he held on to it. "I've got one more question."

"That's?"

"Once my mother took me to a beach like the one outside Innsmouth. Dunes and ruined houses, nobody around. Nobody but a man who'd ride me on his shoulders while he talked to her. He didn't come in a car or boat. He swam in to the beach. Then he swam out again and dived and didn't come back up. I should have worried he had drowned, but I remember just accepting it, the way my mother did."

Marsh smiled as he gently extricated his hand from Daniel's. "That was Innsmouth Beach, you're right. And that was me come to see you. It's good you remember, Daniel."

Daniel gave a jerky nod and walked out of the parlor. Seconds later, the heavy front door slammed.

Eddy took a couple running steps after him, but stopped when she got to Marsh. "What should we do now?"

"Go back to Arkham. Stay away from Innsmouth. Get Daniel to do the same until I can smooth his way."

Sean joined her. "What if we can't keep him away, Mr. Marsh?"

"Well, then I guess you'll have to decide how far down you want to dive with Daniel. I'm just warning you, it could get much deeper than clapping eyes on Tom."

As he walked toward the pocket doors, and Tom beyond, the maid clacked in to show Sean and Eddy out.

~~~

Maybe Sean only imagined that watchers lurked behind every curtained window they passed on their walk down Federal Street, but it was a fact that three more Changers had parked on benches in New Church Green, and that the two least Changed started trailing them. Whenever they got close enough to add their stink to Abel's, Abel made a jabbing sign with his left hand, and they fell back a few pavement squares. In the town center, they slouched against the grocery store wall while Abel hustled Daniel into the shotgun seat of the Civic. From the twitch of his lips, Daniel wasn't catching any warm cozies from the Changers, and he glared back at them until the Civic rolled out of the parking lot.

In his kiwi Bug, Abel followed them to Route 1A. When they passed the gas station, he executed a screeching U-turn, waved out the window, and plunged back onto the road to Innsmouth. Marsh must have given him the night off from babysitting.

"Go to the gas station," Daniel said.

"I've got enough gas to get to Arkham."

"I know. Do it."

"Why?"

"So we can sit in the parking lot until Abel's out of the way. I want to go back to that beach."

"Dude, that's so not a good idea."

Stretched out on the backseat, eyes closed, Eddy said nothing, which was what she'd said the whole drive out from Innsmouth.

"I don't know what kind of idea it is," Daniel said. "I'll figure that out when we get there."

"You can figure it out in the car."

"Go back or let me out. I'll walk it."

"Right, sure. I'm going to let you do that."

"Go back," Eddy said, eyes still closed, hands folded across her diaphragm like a tranced-out oracle's. "What is it, five o'clock?"

"Four thirty," Daniel said.

Actually 4:40 by the Civic's clock. "Your grandfather said stay away."

"From Innsmouth."

"The beach is part of it."

"Sean, just go the fuck back," Eddy said.

The oracle didn't explain her command. Daniel's eyes bored holes into the side of Sean's skull. "Okay. But we're not hanging around for the sunset. And if Abel's hiding behind a dune to catch our asses, you guys can talk to him."

However, no one challenged their return—they had the road to themselves all the way to the sandy parking lot at Innsmouth Beach. The tide was receding; at its high point, it had deposited long cairns of seaweed studded with shells and crab carapaces, blue and peekytoe and horseshoe. Keeping to the shoreward side of the cairns, Daniel walked north. Eddy followed on the seaward side and far enough downslope so that the waves washed over her bare feet. Sean took a middle route, tramping through the heaped ocean debris for the distraction of hearing it crunch. He would have headed south, away from Innsmouth. Obviously Innsmouth was what Daniel wanted to see, because he climbed the last high dune and planted himself among the grasses at its top. Sean joined him. The breeze had strengthened enough to keep down the greenhead flies, and they were able to sit in peace and enjoy a postcard-ready view of the harbor and town and Plum Island in the distance.

Eddy stayed on the beach and played this game she'd invented when they were kids. Like the flock of sanderlings that skittered ahead of her, she danced at the shifting seam between water and land, trying to keep one foot in each element. Her score was perfect until a bigger wave surged to her knees. Even though Sean didn't call it, she accepted the loss and trudged up the dune to stand behind them.

Daniel pointed north. "See that black line a ways out, opposite Innsmouth?"

Sean spotted it, a broken arc of rock like the ridged spine of a sea serpent. "That's Devil Reef?"

"Yeah. When we camped here, my mom always watched the tide go out and the reef come up. She told me mermaids lived under it and came out on the rocks in the moonlight. I don't remember seeing them myself, but I bet she did. I bet some swam over to visit her. Crazy. She was telling me the truth, and I didn't know it."

"The city down there," Sean said.

"Y'ha-nthlei."

"If it's like the glass version, it's the most awesome thing ever."

"No wonder my mom stays there most of the time. That vacation we took, she must have been thinking about going deep. Already wanting it."

Eddy's feet dislodged sand, making it cascade in rivulets around them. She remained silent, so Sean said, "I bet your mom didn't want to go deep back then. Not while you were a little kid."

"I was still pretty young when she left."

"That was after she started Changing. Anyway. Now you know she's alive and okay. And your grandfather's alive, and he's a pretty cool dude."

"He's as bad as my father in one way. He won't take me to see her."

"He will eventually."

"How long's *eventually*?" Daniel fingered a tuft of dune grass. "If people in Innsmouth are down on me for not Changing, I don't see how my grandfather's going to win them over. It sounds like Changing's part of their religion."

Defying the sand butt her wave-spumed shorts threatened, Eddy sat next to Daniel. Not girlfriend close, but not on the other end of the dune either. "What do you want to do, Daniel?"

He flattened his tuft of grass to the sand. "I want to go look for my mom. I want to go to the reef."

The back of the sea serpent humped as the sea shrank from the reef. It didn't look inviting, not even compared to Innsmouth. "You know that would be too dangerous," Eddy said.

"No, I don't. See, Eddy, I never got the feeling anyone in Innsmouth wanted to *hurt* us. Not even the Changers that followed us back to the car. They were pissed at me, but it was like you'd be pissed at a relative who'd screwed up. They made me feel ashamed, not afraid."

"You don't have anything to be ashamed of. You weren't insulting them by trying to stay human. You didn't even know about Deep Ones when your Change started."

Daniel tugged at the wiry grass so hard, it sliced the tender web between his thumb and index finger. He sucked the welling cut. "But I know about them now. They want me to stop the treatments. So does my grandfather. So does Tom. I got that much from what he thought at me."

"Tom wants you to end up like him?" Sean said.

"Didn't you get it? He's not dying. When he gets through the Change, he'll be stronger than ever. He'll live hundreds of years."

"Do you want that?" Eddy said, maybe too calmly.

Daniel palm-scrubbed a drop of blood that had smeared his chin. "All I want is to talk to my mom, and I'm scared if I wait, something will happen to stop me. I bet the Order has agents in Innsmouth, to make sure they're sticking to the treaty—if Marvell finds out we came, he'll tell my father. Sean, you heard him at that meeting. He thinks it's the Order's duty to do every damn thing my father wants."

No getting around it: if Marvell could keep Daniel from meeting his mom, he would. "Could you swim out to the reef?"

"Easy, but I'm not Changed enough to go down into the chasm where Y'ha-nthlei is. Scuba divers couldn't, either—you'd have to have one of those diving suits or a sub, it's so deep. But if I hung around on the reef, Deep Ones might come up, and I could tell them who I wanted."

Eddy scooped sand. "And then they'd deliver your message to Aster, no problem?" She tossed her handful down-dune. "We already know the anti-Order crowd's keeping her in the dark about you."

"The more reason for Daniel to tell her the truth," Sean said.

"Mr. Marsh is going to do that. He's going to arrange for Daniel to meet her."

"Yeah, *eventually*. And over my father's dead body," Daniel said.

"You really don't think you can talk to your father?"

"Eddy, he told me my mom was dead. He told me she killed herself." Daniel spread his fingers, flaunting his scars. "He let the doctors do this."

She looked away, then up again, biting her lips. After a long brave gaze into Daniel's eyes, she nodded. "All right. Talking's out."

The lower the sun sank, the longer the shadow Devil Reef cast eastward over the gold-spangled ocean, but Innsmouth cast a far longer shadow toward the reef. More than ever, Sean didn't want to go near the town after dark, or out to the rising sea serpent. "Dude."

Practicing with Deep Ones must have kicked Daniel's telepathy up a notch. "Yeah," he said. "You guys couldn't swim out to the reef with me."

"And no seawater for you, anyhow. We'd need a boat."

"If we went back for the kayaks, Marvell or Helen could stop us."

Kayaks out that far, at night, maybe versus Deep Ones? Not happening. "I'm thinking a motorboat. And what happens if we go to the reef and no one shows up to party? Is your telepathy up to phoning Y'ha-nthlei?"

"I seriously doubt it."

"Well, didn't Lovecraft write about some kind of iron charm you could throw off the reef to summon Deep Ones?"

"Yeah, but was he right, and do we have one?" Eddy said.

"Geldman would know. In fact, he's probably got Deep One summoning charms in stock."

"We can't ask Geldman," Daniel said.

"How come?"

"He told me this morning. The hint about my grandfather was all he could give me. If I went to Innsmouth—if we went—we'd be on our own."

The thing about wizards that sucked? They didn't do helicopter mentoring. Unless—

Unless aether-newt surveillance wasn't the same thing. "Never mind Geldman, then," Sean said. "What about Redemption Orne?"

Orne's good behavior in the seed world had advanced him so far with Eddy that she shrugged instead of exploding.

"Why not?" Sean said. "At least he doesn't have to worry about going against the Order."

"You'd have to go back to Arkham and into the window," Daniel said. "I'm not risking it."

"Risking what? The Order can't lock you in the wine cellar."

Eddy interrupted with an urgent hiss of a whisper: "Listen."

She pointed into the air above them, which, though empty, wasn't silent. A high-pitched piping, insectile, insistent, descended to circle Sean's head, sounding louder in one ear, then louder in the other, around and around in mad stereo. He swatted at the invisible and yelped to find it wasn't quite intangible—his fingers passed through a chill viscosity that left them dry but tingling.

"You okay?" Daniel said. Eddy floundered across the steep face of the dune to Sean's other side.

He shook the tingle from his hand. "I guess. I thought—"

The piping had stopped.

It started again near the foot of the dune, where the air condensed into mist and the mist into a bubble-skinned caterpillar with ten suction-cup feet on ten stumpy legs. With an egg-shaped head minus nose and mouth but plus diamond-pupiled eyes and fleshy-feathery ear fans. And more fleshy-feathery fans down its back, and winking spheroids along its sides, and tails, five of them, the longest wickedly barbed. The creature hovered a few inches above the sand, and, of course, it flicked the barbed tail, because flicking tail was what newts did best.

Eddy had seen the thing before, when Afua Benetutti had puffed silvery dust over it. Daniel stared. "That's?" he whispered.

"An aether-newt, yeah," Sean said. "And it's got to be Orne's. It must have heard us talking about him, how we wanted to ask him something."

Double flick.

He still wasn't sure whether that meant yes or no or "Dude, eat me." Before he could try Eddy's plan of asking whether it was an aether-newt and seeing how many times it flicked, the newt corkscrewed out of sight into the dune. The sand above its point of entry swirled faster and faster until it glowed with heat like the blast from an opened kiln, and like silica in a kiln, the swirling sand melted.

Daniel jumped to his feet. "That looks like something that's going to blow up."

Why would Orne's newt try to kill them? *It* wouldn't, but what if Deep Ones also used aether-newts? The anti-Order kind of Deep Ones who thought Daniel was a traitor?

Eddy and Daniel had taken cover on the other side of the dune. Sean was about to dive after them when the liquefied sand didn't so much explode as burp out a gleaming length of newt. No longer ethereal, it plopped onto the dune and shook its new shell of articulated glass plates. They rang like chimes as it slithered down the dune to the beach. There it twisted its forebody back toward Sean and beckoned with its newly crystalline ear fans.

Sean yelled the all clear and slid after the newt. When Eddy and Daniel had joined him, they converged on a tidal flat where the newt was treading a circle into the damp sand. That done, it extended its longest tail into the pristine interior and with the barb began to write not in mystic runes but in crooked English caps. Squatting, Eddy read out the words of the message as they appeared:

> SEAN
> COME TO
> ISLAND VISTA MARINA IN NEWBURY
> ROUTE 1A NORTH ACROSS PARKER RIVER BRIDGE
> MEET OUTSIDE SHIPS STORE
> I CAN HELP
> RO

Task completed, the aether-newt ballooned until its temporary exoskeleton cracked and fell to the sand in tinkling shards.

It went airborne, ethereal again, and, clearly expecting an answer to carry back to its master, bobbed before Sean's face. Through its shimmying and shimmery form, he could see Daniel's tense expression, and Eddy's. *I CAN HELP* had to mean help Daniel meet his mother, since that's what they'd been talking about when the newt appeared. Also, Orne wanted to meet at a marina, and what could you get at a marina?

Boats, baby.

"That thing must have been following us all day," Eddy said.

Why not—they'd been outside the Order's wards since leaving the Arkwright House. Outside the wards and talking about magical stuff, which was against Marvell's rules, but a super-minor offense compared to the one they were considering. "Daniel, you want to take him up on the help?"

"I don't know, but would it hurt to find out what he's actually offering?"

Eddy circled Sean and the newt, like she wanted to examine the creature from all angles. "That would mean you'd meet Orne, Sean. Face-to-face for real."

Implied question: Was he ready?

Evidently Orne thought he was, and so far today, meeting long-lost relatives hadn't produced apocalyptic results. The operative words being *so far*. He looked into the newt's diamond-slit eyes as if they were lenses and he was delivering his lines straight to the cameraman. "Okay, Reverend. I'll come to Newbury. Quick as I can."

The aether-newt flicked a last double and faded to nothingness. If it had to travel to communicate with Orne, it was on its way.

"Sean," Daniel said. "Thanks. Really."

"No problem." He hoped. "We better get moving."

Daniel led the way down the beach, but Eddy hung back to collect some of the glass plates the newt had shed and, with one, to scrape away its message to Sean. "Smart," he said when she caught up with them.

"Well, this does look like the kind of place Deep Ones might come to get a moon-tan."

"What are you going to do with the armor thingies?"

"Save them for your dad. How many windows have aether-newt glass in them?"

Dad. It was late to call him in England. Besides, it would take too long to explain going to meet Orne when he hadn't even mentioned the seed world yet, or the crow construct, or how Orne had known Mom, and how without Orne, she might never have met Dad. Without Orne, no Sean. Without Aster, no Daniel. Speaking of Aster Marsh Glass, she'd be the third long-lost relative of the day. No, the fourth, counting Cousin Tom.

Marsh had warned they'd have to think about how deep they wanted to dive with Daniel. Sean couldn't ask Dad or the Order for advice, or Geldman either, per Daniel. He'd have to rely on himself or on Orne. Well, which of them was likelier to know whether deeper with Daniel meant a pothole or an abyss?

Not Sean. So, yeah, Newbury. "You remember the name of that marina?"

"Don't worry," Eddy said grimly. "We'll find the place."

21

It was a twenty-minute drive to Newbury. At the Parker River Bridge, Sean pulled over to let Eddy take the wheel. She and Daniel would go hang somewhere until he called for pickup. "Or backup," Daniel said.

"I won't need it."

"Sure? You guys rode shotgun to my grandfather's."

"Yeah, but you'd never met him before. I've at least half-met Orne."

"Okay. We won't go far."

They drove over the bridge and didn't slow down when they passed the marina on the other side. In Eddy's place, Sean would have crawled, trying to spot Orne. Walking across, he refused to play that game. The view helped. The name Island Vista Marina wasn't wishful thinking—down the last stretch of the river, in the hazy near distance, was Plum Island. Loitering as dusk came on, he watched kayaks pass under the bridge and motorboats chug upstream. Then he got his procrastinating ass to the marina.

It was a big place, with winter storage racks, a service department, and ten floating docks. The parking lot swarmed with fishermen stowing tackle and parents packing up kids; he threaded through their trucks and SUVs looking for the ship's store, which turned out to be closed. Sean peered through the door at bait tanks and ice chests. No one was inside.

Along the store wall facing the river was a covered deck furnished with picnic tables and rocking chairs. Sean climbed aboard. So much for his hope that he and Orne could talk there: A young guy lazed in a rocker like he was there for the duration. With his white shorts, blue-striped tee, and tousled blond hair, he looked like a model for those catalogs that catered to the summer-house-and-Labrador-retrievers crowd. He even had Top-Siders propped on the railing and a cardigan draped over the back of his chair. And not a drop of oil or fish blood on him. Dude, surreally? Sean claimed a table, but once Orne showed, they'd have to find a more private spot. Wait, the guy stood. To leave? "That didn't take you long," he said.

Sean glanced toward the parking lot, expecting to see a female model (with Labrador), just arrived for the photo shoot. He saw the same fishermen and families.

"Sean," the model said.

Sean's tongue stuck to the roof of his mouth, and all he could do was stare.

"Yes, it's me," the model said. "Did you think I'd look like Reverend Tyndale?"

Too late for politeness, heart racing, Sean jumped up. "I'm sorry. I guess I did kind of expect him, except without the Puritan outfit. Who are you supposed to be?"

"Supposed to be?"

"I mean, who's your illusion of?"

One corner of Orne's mouth quirked upward. "Do you sense an illusion?"

"No, but I didn't sense Mr. Marsh's either, and he must have a lot to cover up."

"Indeed. I'd like to think my illusions are as seamless as his. However, I'm not wearing one at the moment." Orne's face grew serious. "I wanted to honor our first in-person meeting by coming without disguise."

"This is what you really look like. Really."

"That's right."

Orne's eyes were blue, like Sean's—like Dad's, for that matter. But Sean and Dad had a lot of gray in their blue, while Orne's blue was pale and pure. Like Mom's. Damn, why did he feel lightheaded, and why wouldn't his heart slow down? "You got here before me. I thought you'd have to come from Arkham. Or can you, like, teleport?"

"No," Orne said. "But as you discovered at the beach, my newt's been with you today. It was also with you during that accident at the harbor, and afterwards, when you learned Daniel's secret. I worried how that might have affected you, so I went to talk to Geldman. He said Daniel had found out his grandfather was alive, and now all three of you were heading to Innsmouth. I followed my newt, to be available if you needed me. But let's sit down."

By that he meant Sean had better sit down, and he was right. Sean took the rocker beside Orne's. Orne sat again, and from the cooler he'd stowed underneath his chair, he pulled two bottles of spring water. The one he handed Sean had an unbroken seal— Sean was still leery enough to check before he drank. He must have been dehydrated; by the time he'd drained the bottle, his heartbeat had slowed and he'd figured out why learning the model was Orne had made his brain cramp. "You're too young," he blurted. "Lots younger than my dad."

"I took the Communion of Nyarlathotep when I was twenty-three," Orne said. "My body stopped aging after that."

That made sense because who'd sign up for immortality if it meant you'd end up as shriveled as a mummy? "That's an even better deal than being a Deep One. I guess they keep aging, just slower than humans."

"Much slower. Daniel has relations in Y'ha-nthlei centuries older than I am."

"I don't think he's thought about that yet."

"Good. He has enough to deal with. From what Raphael over-heard on the beach, Daniel's learned his mother's alive and Changed."

"Raphael's your newt's name?"

"Yes."

"Like the artist, not the Ninja Turtle."

Orne grinned as if he got the joke. "Like the archangel, actu-ally. But Raphael didn't spy on your meeting with Barnabas Marsh. He'd have sensed its energy and resented the intrusion, and rightly so. Did something happen there I should know about?"

With the sun dropping fast, the Parker River mirrored a lemon-and-apricot sky like the one in the *Founding*; against the reflected glow, the last of the dock-bound boats were black silhou-ettes, vaguely sinister. "Marsh let us meet Daniel's cousin Tom, who's almost finished Changing."

"That must have been unnerving."

"Yeah, but Daniel got over it pretty quick, and he wants to meet his mom next. Only Aster doesn't know Daniel's started to Change, or how his dad's trying to stop it. Marsh wants time to, like, prepare her. Besides, there are these Deep Ones who think Daniel's a traitor, and Daniel's supposed to be patient while Marsh talks them around. But Daniel thinks he's got to get to his mom fast, before his dad stops him."

"Daniel wants to go out to Devil Reef on his own?"

"With me and Eddy. But what good's going if we don't have a summoning charm?"

"You won't need one. If Daniel—one of their own—goes to Devil Reef, Deep Ones will come." Orne set his rocker in gentle motion. "Speaking of the reef, what did Marsh tell you about it?"

"Nothing, really. It's freaky, out by itself in the deep water. I never saw anything like it."

"That's because it's artificial."

"A piece of old breakwater?"

"No, more like a giant doorstep. The Deep Ones built it above the opening to the abyss that harbors Y'ha-nthlei. That was thousands of years before Europeans came and proved they couldn't curb their curiosity as the Massachusetts and Wampanoags had. Pirates and smugglers tried to hide booty there. After enough of them disappeared off the reef, they gave it up as cursed, and 'cursed' remained its safeguard until people stopped believing in such things. Later Innsmouth patrolled the reef. It still does, to keep off the sport boaters and divers who want to explore the place. It's posted as private property—officially, the Marshes own it. Also, since the Order intervened, the state and federal governments are aware of the situation in Innsmouth. They back up the Marshes if anyone wants access to the reef, scientists included. You know, people with submarines and sonar."

"So the abyss doesn't show up on any charts?"

"None the public can access. Devil Reef appears as a small seamount with nothing interesting at its base. The Deep Ones do their part, of course. Marsh tells me there are extremely strong wards around the city entrances. Including organic ones."

"You mean live wards?"

"Shoggoths. They block the ways in like corks and simulate the ocean floor around them, perfect camouflage. I'm assuming that if a diver were to poke the floor and find out it was protoplasmic, not rock—" Orne made a hand-puppet maw and snapped it shut on his index finger. "It's not likely a diver would get that close, though."

And if he did, one gulp, gone. "They really have shoggoths?"

"Since the Elder Race of Antarctica declined, Deep Ones are the only species on Earth that keeps them. They communicate with the shoggoths through telepathy, use them for construction, transport, hunting, defense, same as the Elder Race did. But the Deep Ones obviously have superior control over the creatures. Otherwise, the whole world would know about them, whatever was left of it."

The coolest thing was how Orne discussed crazy stuff (telepathy-operated shoggoths!) as if it were normal. "I hope they don't let shoggoths up on the reef."

"Oh no. The Deep Ones guard the upper reef themselves."

"Nobody notices?"

"They go illusioned as any sea creatures about their own size."

"Like the porpoises at the jetty. Did Raphael see them?"

"It did, and I through it."

"Marsh said two of them were anti-Order Deep Ones. The others were real porpoises. I couldn't tell the difference."

"Nor I, at that distance. If you go out to the reef, remember that any porpoises or sea turtles swimming around your boat might not be porpoises or turtles. Same for seals pulled out on the rocks. What's more, any *real* animals of that sort could be Deep One allies."

So say a kayaker came along and thought, screw the KEEP OFF signs, he was stopping at Devil Reef to hunt for pirate treasure. What was there to be afraid of? Porpoises were playing around his bow, and gray seals were lolling on the reef, all sleepy and peaceful. So he tied up his kayak and climbed the slick rocks, only to have the seals stampede him into the water and the porpoises grow webbed hands to pull him under. "Then we should forget about going to the reef. I mean, if it's suicide."

"It's far from that. The Deep Ones realize disappearances would draw exactly the attention they want to avoid. And they're much less prone to homicide—or human sacrifices—than we are, truth be told. If the reef watchers can't drive off trespassers, they alert the Innsmouth patrol boat, which can also call in Coast Guard support. Marsh say it's never had to."

If the patrollers looked like the Changers in New Church Green, it was easy to believe they didn't need backup. "Okay, but if the Deep Ones don't stop us, the patrol boat will. Either way, we don't get to the reef."

Orne rocked steady as a metronome. "Just you and Eddy, you'd get turned back. Daniel would complicate things. Since he's a hybrid of Y'ha-nthlei stock, most Deep Ones would be reluctant to bar him. But this other group you mention?"

"The anti-Order guys. It sounds like they're against any interference with Innsmouth, and the way Geldman's helping Daniel is the last straw. They don't want Daniel around unless he decides to Change."

"Then they certainly wouldn't want him out on the reef."

Sean caught the rocking bug from Orne. "What would they do to stop us?"

"Well, I doubt they'd intentionally hurt any of you. Daniel's of their blood, and you and Eddy are his friends. But they might try an intervention."

"Like, sit in a circle and guilt-trip him out of his humanity addiction?"

Low laughter. "There's an image. But I doubt they'd just talk. I'm afraid they might try to kidnap Daniel."

"And duck him in seawater and force him to Change?"

"I'm afraid so."

While Orne gazed at the river, Sean snuck a closer look at him. For sure, his pale blue eyes were like Mom's. His nose was like Grandpa Stewie's, medium length with a convex curve, and his hair was the same pale blond. Mom's hair had been a darker blond, while Sean's was plain brown. So really, their fingers were the only things Sean and Orne had totally in common: extra-long and thinnish. Pianist fingers, Mom used to say, though Sean was more a kazoo guy. Maybe magicians needed long fingers as well, the better to wrap around a staff or wand.

Orne stopped rocking and angled his chair toward Sean's. "We could talk all night, but talk won't solve Daniel's immediate problem. The safest thing would be to wait for Marsh to pave your way. I'm tempted to say that's all you can do."

"But?"

"But Daniel might be able to get to the reef and talk to his mother, if you and Eddy stand by him."

"We'll stand by, all right. Not screwing up is going to be the hard part for me. *You* know that."

Orne smiled, with the quirk. "I know your potential, too, and I've brought something to help you with any Deep Ones you meet. I've also got you a boat, which we'd better look at before it gets dark."

~⟞

In the farthest berth on the last dock was a Boston Whaler Montauk, the 170. "My uncle Gus has a 190," Sean said. Click. "Or maybe you knew that?"

"Yes, Raphael went with you to Harwichport this spring. I heard you were always out on the water, and at the wheel."

"Gus has been teaching me and Eddy."

"A former navy man, that's reassuring, and good to know Eddy can drive, too. So you think you could handle this particular boat?"

Sean climbed aboard and checked out the console and the outboard, a Mercury four-stroke so spotless, it had to be right out of the box. In fact, the whole boat looked brand new. "It's pretty much the same."

"The draft's a little shallower. Useful what with the shoals around Plum Island."

The shiny newness continued in the boat's safety gear: ring and throw bags and three life vests. There were also two long-handled fishnets and two gaffs. The gaffs were the only used-looking items, but they had sturdy shafts and rustless hooks, wickedly sharp. From the dock, Orne remarked, "For defense, but only in extremity. If things turn ugly, run—this boat will go faster than even Deep Ones can swim."

"How about their patrol boat?"

"You won't outrun that, but Marsh runs the patrol—the worst his people will do is turn you back. Look in the equipment locker, in case I've forgotten something."

Sean found repellent for mosquitoes and midges, which they'd sure as hell need coasting through the marshlands at night, and greenhead repellent, which they wouldn't need unless they were still out at daybreak. If they were AWOL that long, poor Helen would freak. They'd already miss curfew unless they canceled the reef trip. He pushed the thought away and cataloged the rest of the locker. Binoculars. Bottled water. Cheese, crackers, and Oreos. First aid kit. Flashlights. Batteries. Flares. A spare key for the Montauk in a floatable box. And a navigational chart showing Plum Island Sound and Innsmouth Bay.

"The marina owner marked that for me," Orne said. "It shows the deepest channels through the sound. He wrote down the tide times, too. You'll have the least trouble with shoals if you're traveling up to two hours on either side of high tide. Which means you'll want to start no later than an hour and a half from now."

"Okay. Is it costing you a ton to rent the boat overnight?"

"I'm not renting it. I've bought it, and I've paid for summer docking and winter storage here at the marina. I'll have uses for the boat as well, but the keys on the console are yours, and you're welcome to take the boat out whenever it's idle."

Sean jumped back onto the dock. If Grandpa Stewie or Uncle Gus had given him part ownership in a boat, he'd have hugged the crap out of them. Hugging Orne wasn't an option. How about shaking hands? Or just saying thank you, except even then, what did he call Orne? Grandpa Redemption? Nope. Grandfather? Too Victorian. Stumped, Sean settled for plain and awkward: "Thanks. It'll be great, when we can go out for fun."

"Which tonight won't be, I'm afraid, if you do decide to go."

"I guess we have to, now you've done all this."

Orne sat atop a piling. "Having the means doesn't require you to use it."

"Well, do you think we can manage it without anyone getting hurt?"

"Hurt to the body, hurt to the mind, hurt to the heart. Too many kinds of hurt to calculate, whether you take Daniel to the reef or you tell him I couldn't help after all."

"I don't want to lie."

"What do you want, then? Why is it important for you to help Daniel?"

Orne looked at him with such urgent expectation that Sean had to put his back to it. He wrapped his fingers around the cool steel railing of the Montauk. "He's my friend. He's more than that to Eddy. Or it was getting that way before all this Deep One stuff. And his father's an asshole, and Marvell's an asshole for going along with him. They don't understand. It'll kill Daniel not to see his mom now he knows she's alive."

"And you understand that as Marvell can't. As even Mr. Glass can't."

He leaned into the railing, and the whole hull shifted toward the opposite side of the berth. That put dark water under him, water that flowed toward the sound without taking along the livid reflection of his face. "Well, what if I found out Mom was alive? I know she can't be, that's the difference between me and Daniel. But what if *somehow*. I'd get to her no matter what."

Orne remained silent so long that Sean turned to see if he'd crept away. He still sat on the piling, gazing downstream. "You were about a month old when I determined you were magical. The next day I left for a long trip. Very long, in fact." Orne raised a hand before Sean got his mouth open. "I don't mean to entice you about my destination. I only want you to know it wasn't lack of interest that kept me from checking in on you and Kate. Also, why would I need to check in? You were well, and well protected. Anyhow. I didn't come back for six years, and then it was to learn that Kate was very ill. Terminal cancer. I went to Providence at once, and I took Solomon Geldman with me."

The dock lamps had flickered on, and their orange light gave Orne's face a drawn and jaundiced look. Sean wasn't immune—his hands and arms had turned a matching saffron. "To treat her?"

"He'd agreed to try. He examined her, but we'd come too late. She'd passed the point of intervention, even magical."

"But I've seen what Geldman can do, like with Daniel!"

"Daniel isn't dying, Sean. When death has seeped soul-deep, there's no saving a mortal, and if anyone can detect that irreversible turn from living into dying, it's Geldman. I couldn't doubt him or waste any more time. I knew the only solution for Kate was immortality, and the Communion of Nyarlathotep was the only way she could achieve it."

Orne's statement punched through muscle and guts to the curve of Sean's spine. "Then why didn't you tell her about it? Why didn't you give her a chance?"

Unflinching, Orne said, "I did, Sean."

"You couldn't have, or she'd be alive. No way she'd have left if she didn't have to."

"Left you."

"Me and Dad and everyone."

"Would it have done any good if she'd stayed with you but left herself behind?"

"What's that even mean?"

The air between them sparked—Orne had charged his voice with magic: "Stop talking. Listen."

Coercive warmth flooded the knotted muscles in Sean's shoulders and arms, making them slacken. He could fight the mental manipulation, yell for Orne to stop, as he'd done in the seed world, but to accept, to relax—

"Listen. You want to know how it was."

He let his arms hang at his sides, pleasantly heavy.

"Your father had taken you out for the day," Orne said. "There was a hospice volunteer, an older woman, staying with Kate."

Sean remembered casseroles covered with triple layers of foil, small patting hands, and lilac perfume. "Mrs. Amati."

"She opened the door for us. Kate recognized me as her old mentor Samuel Grimsby, I introduced Geldman as a colleague, and we talked until Mrs. Amati, with a bit of persuasion, fell asleep. Then I returned to Kate the memories I'd expunged, the ones about our true relationship and the magic in her. I said I'd heard how sick she was, and so I'd brought Geldman, the most capable healer I knew. She let him touch her hands, look in her eyes, sample the force and scent of her breath. He needed do no more before he bowed his head and left the room. I understood. So, without explanation, did Kate. There was no cure, she said. I contradicted. I told her about Nyarlathotep and his Communion. It took hours to answer her questions because I had to make her understand exactly what the Master would give her and exactly what he would demand in return; how taking the Communion would preserve her, but it would also change her and ally her with forces even I couldn't explain in full. She weighed her options, finely, to the point of exhaustion."

"She said no."

As Geldman had done, Sean imagined, Orne bowed his head. "She said no."

"She was wrong. I would have made her say yes."

"That's why I'd made sure you weren't there. No sight of you. No sound of you. Even the little trucks and plastic dinosaurs you'd left on the couch were dangerous, but Kate got over them."

What if Mom *had* become like Orne? When he was little, Sean probably wouldn't have known the difference. Dad would have freaked out if she'd told him the truth about her miracle cure, but he'd never have separated her and Sean the way Eli Glass had separated Aster and Daniel. What about Nyarlathotep, though? Join his gang, and he wanted everything. He'd told Sean as much to his face. What did *everything* mean, specifically? Looking at Orne, you couldn't see where he'd given *anything* up.

It hurt Sean's head to think about it, actually hurt, a grind of pain around his eye sockets. Maybe that was because he was squeezing his eyes shut so damn hard. He blinked to refocus on Orne. One thing he knew: "If my mom had changed in some scary way, so she thought she had to leave me and Dad? I'd still be like Daniel. I'd go after her as soon as I knew how."

After another long silence, Orne said, "Come back to the deck. I've one more thing to give you."

⁓

It was a tin whistle without the finger holes, except it was made not of tin but of a reddish gold engraved with a tight spiral of hieroglyphs. To Sean, the symbols looked like tiny mouths more or less open, with more or fewer teeth and the occasional flapping tongue. Maybe there were some eyes in there, too. Orne said the workmanship was Egyptian, but the script and language were nonhuman.

"The whistle's a magic-modulator," he said. "You collect energy and *intend* to breathe it out through the instrument, which will convert it into sound. Music."

Funny how Sean had thought earlier he was more a kazoo guy than a pianist—however precious, the whistle reminded him of one. When Orne blew into it, high-pitched tones emerged, each lingering until the air vibrated with an eerie harmony, the first tone fading away, then the second and so on. But when Sean blew into the whistle, nothing came out. Nothing went in, either. Instead his vigorous exhale puffed out his cheeks and burst free around the mouthpiece in a great fart imitation. He tried again. Same result.

"You're putting out plain air," Orne said. "Unless it carries magical energy, it won't enter the whistle. You've been practicing with the key as your collection image. Relax and use it here. Gather as usual; a tiny amount will do. Center the energy, then send it out with your breath."

It took Sean a few tries before he could consistently produce one tone per puff. For his last attempt, he built up a decent magical buzz, enough to levitate a pencil. That charged breath emerged as a shrill bleat.

Orne winced, then applauded. "Someone nonmagical wouldn't have heard that at all. But Deep Ones have keen ears for magical sound. That blast would have gotten their attention, and because it expresses your potential, it would have earned you respect as a fellow magician. A stronger blast yet could serve to warn or distract or deter, depending on whatever secondary intention you added."

"Could I hurt Deep Ones with this?"

"You might if you put enough energy and malicious intention into your breath. Avoid anger; think self-protection. And how much key did you expose that last time?"

"Just the little knob on top."

"If you have to expose more, do it bit by bit. I don't want you injuring anyone, yourself included. You'll have noticed that doing magic gives you a headache?"

"Yeah. It was real bad after I did the summoning last year."

"That's because you still have to use personal energy to shape and deploy the ambient energy you gather. Try too much at once, you could incapacitate yourself."

"Knock myself out?"

"Exactly. Be very careful, Sean. This whistle should be new to the Deep Ones. They won't know how powerful a weapon you wield, but much will depend on your confidence. Remember their telepathy, and *think* that the whistle's dangerous, as it could be. *Believe* that you're ready to do whatever it takes to defend yourself and your friends."

Sean slipped the whistle and its red-gold chain over his head and under his shirt. Like the One Ring, it was heavier than it looked, but it rested cool and comfortable against his breastbone. "How do I get this back to you?"

"No need. It's a gift."

"It's too much!"

"You should indulge me, Sean. As many grandchildren as I've had, I've never gotten a chance to spoil one."

"Thanks! But I don't even know what to call you yet."

"If you're still most comfortable with 'Reverend,' so am I."

"Okay. Then thanks again, Reverend. Really."

Orne headed for the deck steps. Halfway down, he turned and added, "And go slow through the sound. The moon's new tonight."

It was, a fingernail trimming. New moon, dark of the moon. "That's what it was when I summoned the Servitor."

"True. I didn't think of that."

"Is it a bad omen?"

After studying the slivered moon, Orne shook his head. "You first proved your mettle that night. I'm betting you'll prove it again."

"You're still testing me?"

"Does a father grade every step a child takes?"

"I hope not."

"Well, he doesn't. Mostly he just watches. He watches the child walk away. He watches for him to turn back."

Except it was Orne who walked away, while Sean got out his phone to call Eddy.

22

Orne was right about the whistle. When Sean demonstrated it, Eddy heard nothing, while Daniel grimaced and suggested tuning that sucker. The Montauk was what impressed him. Sean promised future boating lessons, but tonight he'd have to drive while chart-savvy Eddy navigated. Since Daniel was the empath, he'd watch (and feel) for company, on or under the water. Jobs assigned, Daniel settled down on the rear bench, Eddy untied the docking lines, and Sean pulled them out into the Parker River.

They left the dock shortly after high tide, which gave them plenty of time to get through the sound at its most navigable. The Montauk ran smooth and high, a sweet ride of a boat; with Eddy calling their course from the bow, they glided between Plum Island and the mainland marshes without any serious flirtations with shoals and mud flats, rocks and submerged pilings. Aside from the clouds of mosquitoes and midges that repellent kept at bay, the only creatures they saw were fish purling the surface, two night herons, and a great horned owl that swooped across the bow, making them all yell. Well, making Sean and Eddy yell.

Daniel sat as silent as the owl's wings, only his head moving as he guarded their wake.

They were rounding the southern tip of Plum Island when harbor porpoises appeared to surf the Montauk's bow waves, three port, three starboard. Daniel leaned over the rails to feel them out. After a few minutes, he said, "I think they're real porpoises. I don't pick up any magic from them."

"But I'll bet they're Deep One allies," Eddy said.

Sean kept his eyes forward. The chart showed a reef between the last shoals and Sandy Point on Plum Island. At high tide, the reef would be well underwater, but he wasn't taking any chances. "I don't care about the porpoises as long as they don't attack us."

"They're just riding along now."

"Not those two," Daniel said.

"What?"

"A couple took off toward the point." Daniel scuffled to the stern. "And something's on the beach over there."

Eddy joined him aft. She'd hung Orne's binoculars around her neck, and she used them now. "Gray seals, pulled out for the night."

"Can I look?"

Sean watched the binoculars change hands. Then he had to look forward again as the Montauk entered Innsmouth Bay. At the mouth of the sound, the surf ran about a foot; beyond it, the ocean was a sheet of barely rippled glass. To starboard he made out a long concavity of mainland with clustered lights at its midpoint: Innsmouth. A lesser string of lights marked the harbor breakwater. To port was open Atlantic, where, a mile and a half out from town, a sea serpent humped its jagged spine clear of the water. Someone profoundly brave or stupid had dared to spear it with lamp-topped harpoons, one on each end of the beast. "Devil Reef," he called over his shoulder. "Check it out."

"Can't," Eddy groaned. "We're too busy checking out stuff back here."

"The patrol boat?"

"Maybe we're going to wish." Eddy stepped over to the console, without the binoculars, which Daniel still trained on Sandy Point. "Those two porpoises swam to the beach where the seals are pulled out, and then a bunch of the seals dived into the water and came back up porpoises. They're after us."

Under his life vest, Sean wore the Windbreaker he'd brought from Arkham. With little wind for it to break, he'd started sweating. "Deep Ones?"

"Unless you think seals can shape-shift."

"You're sure they did?"

"We'll find out when they get close enough for Daniel to read. Or else you could run for it on principle."

Run for it where? They could go south along the coast, toward Arkham, or north along the ocean side of Plum Island, either way buzzing past Devil Reef as they left the bay. Too bad they had to actually land on the reef and hang around waiting for helpful Deep Ones to show.

Or had helpful Deep Ones already showed? They shouldn't assume their pursuers were the bad guys.

Daniel either read Sean's mind or had the same idea. "No use running. We *want* to meet Deep Ones. Slow down and let them catch up."

Eddy looked dubious, but Sean cut speed. It was probably better to contact Deep Ones while they were in the boat, not sitting ducks on the rocks. He kept the Montauk putt-putting gently toward Devil Reef. Deprived of their bow waves, the real porpoises dived out of sight. The maybe-fake ones came on fast, their triangular dorsals slicing the water in a tight V-formation. Like the two fake porpoises off the Arkham jetty, these were bigger than usual. Sean itched to accelerate, but that would only make them look scared or guilty.

They'd covered half the distance between Plum Island and

Devil Reef when the porpoises reached them. Instead of coming alongside the Montauk, they fell into single file and circled it at a few yards off. Daniel handed the binoculars back to Eddy and drifted from gunwale to gunwale, face blank, bending far over the railings to stare at their pursuers. His lips moved as if in soundless conversation. Then he said, "They're Deep Ones. They're talking to me."

Eddy relayed the binoculars to Sean and went to Daniel. "What're they saying?"

"Look!"

But "look" was what Daniel was saying. He also pointed at the surrounding swimmers. A few seconds before, they'd had the sleek gray backs and broad flukes of porpoises; now their backs were silvery green, armored with palm-sized scales or plates and sporting a single fixed fin that ran from their hairless heads all the way down their spines. And they had legs that frog-kicked, and arms that oared, and webbed hands and feet. Sean let the Montauk glide to a stop and stepped from the console to the railing opposite Daniel's. Watching the Deep Ones, he began to notice differences in their coloration and unique notches or splits in their dorsal fins. Most distinctive was a swimmer with black scale-plates on one shoulder and a semicircular dip in the middle of the fin, scalloped like a giant shark bite. He counted from him (or her?) and got up to seven before Shark-Bit came back around.

"They're getting closer," Eddy said.

Slowly, spiraling inward. Metal glinted on their dorsal fins and their ankles and wrists. Deep Ones didn't go absolutely naked, then. Some wore broad gold bracelets and anklets; all of them had piercings in their fins, stuck through with gold rings along the upper edge and gold beads or disks elsewhere. Shark-Bit rocked the heaviest cuffs and anklets and the most fin piercings, and he (or she?) was the one who first swam into the sphere of illumination thrown by the Montauk's all-round light.

Sean went back to the console in case of trouble, but he could see Shark-Bit from there. *She,* not *he,* from the underbelly that appeared as she rolled in the water—white and scaleless with two small but obvious breasts. She dived briefly, and then her head broke the surface six feet from Daniel, giving them all a good look at her face.

The shocking thing was how unshocked Sean felt. Seeing Tom Marsh had prepared him. In fact, it had overprepared him, because Shark-Bit wasn't half as nasty. Her Change was complete, and the human-fish-amphibian features of her face had blended into a whole that, however alien, made visual sense. From the top of her elliptical skull to her collarbones, she was covered with finer, more iridescent scales than the ones on her back and upper shoulders. The dorsal fin started at mid-forehead; dozens of gold rings and studs pierced it there, making it look more like a tiara than a part of her body. Well, if Shark-Bit was going to have any piercings, she had to put them in the fin—she had no ears, just two flat drumheads behind her frog-goggly eyes. No nose to speak of, either, just the two slitted nostrils that flared pink as she breathed air instead of water. Her lipless mouth was an upside-down *U* filled with serrated teeth, and her gills, five on either side of her thick neck, flared pink like her nostrils, then on closing made a soft wet sound like smacking lips.

The other six Deep Ones had stopped spiraling inward, but they still swam a circle around the boat: a guard picket to keep the Montauk from advancing or retreating while their leader parleyed with Daniel. At least it looked like they were parleying, eyes locked, her mouth quivering, his forming silent words.

Eddy eased along the railing to Daniel's side and casually slipped a hand through the back of his belt. It was a good move, because it wouldn't take much to turn his precarious lean into a dive overboard. If Daniel started tipping, Sean would grab him by the life vest. They'd keep him as high and dry as Geldman had ordered, even though Shark-Bit had swum close enough to hang on the gunwale with her face only a couple of feet from Daniel's.

She smelled nothing like a Changer. What odor Sean caught was salty, oceanic. That made sense. Fresh live fish didn't stink, after all. Another thing, now that he could see her hands clearly: She didn't have fingernails but rather claws, black hooks two inches long. Eddy had to have noticed them, too, what with one set gripping the rail right beside her left hip. Though she shifted the hip away, she kept her grip on Daniel's belt. "Is it her?" she whispered.

Daniel didn't answer.

"Daniel. Is this your mother?"

Sean hadn't thought of that, but if Marsh had headed straight to the reef to tell Aster about her son's homecoming, she might already be up looking for him.

Daniel backed to the console, Eddy retreating with him. As for Shark-Bit, she hoisted herself so she could peer at them over the railing; the turrets of her eyes swiveled from Eddy to Sean, then back to Daniel.

"Is she your mom?" Sean muttered in Daniel's ear.

Daniel rubbed his head as if it ached like a bitch. "No. She's Elspeth Marsh. Tom's mother. My aunt."

"Aster's sister?"

"Right. We're all related, though. People from Innsmouth. People from Y'ha-nthlei."

"Dude, reminder, you're from New York."

Daniel's laugh was ragged. "That's where my father's from. But I'm Innsmouth through my mother. The Innsmouth is what counts."

"That's not true," Eddy said sharply. "I know you're mad at him, but your father's as important as your mother. Your human side, I mean."

"The Deep One side is stronger. It takes over."

"Is that what your aunt's been telling you?"

Shark-Bit—Elspeth—blew out air in a watery snort, but it was Daniel who attacked Eddy. "She didn't have to. I've known it since the Change started for me. I'm the one's been cut and had my teeth pulled. I'm the one Geldman's experimenting on. Because that's what he's doing, Eddy. He's never tried treating the Change before."

Seeing Eddy's lips turn white, Sean shoved in: "Come on, chill. You want it, don't you, the treatment?"

"I don't know."

Eddy had flashed from white to scarlet. "You wanted it before you came here."

"I thought his cure could last. My grandfather says no, Tom says no, they all say no." Daniel swept his hand in a circle that included Elspeth and the swimming Deep Ones. "Even Geldman doesn't *know*. He admitted it at that meeting."

"So what do you want now? You still want to see your mother?" Eddy jerked her chin at Elspeth. "Will *she* go down and tell Aster you're here?"

Elspeth snorted again, which sounded more like *no way* than *yes*.

"That's not what they came for." As if his telepathic conversation with Elspeth had left him too tired to stand, Daniel slid down the side of the console, butt to deck, knees to chest. "They think it's blasphemous, trying to stop the Change, but they're not mad at *me*. I didn't know any better. It's my father's fault, it's the Order's fault. It's even my grandfather's fault, because he didn't keep me from leaving his house this afternoon. They—" Another comprehensive sweep of Daniel's hand. "—they feel sorry for me. I can feel it. They want to help."

Not just tired, Daniel sounded drugged, like Elspeth might be one of the Deep Ones who'd studied up on mind manipulation. Sean closed his eyes. His skin prickled to magic that enveloped the boat, but he could pinpoint no particular surge. "Then they should go get your mom," he said. He scooted a foot over to nudge Eddy's. "Right?"

She nudged back. "Right. Ask her, Daniel. Who better to talk to you than your mother?"

Daniel shook his head. "I already asked. They don't need her to talk to me. Talk's not the point."

"Well, what is?"

"Keeping me away from people who are hurting me and holding me back. They can't take me to Y'ha-nthlei yet, I'm not ready. But they've got other safe places where I could Change."

"Where they could *make* you Change," Eddy said.

No reaction. Then Daniel bobbed a single nod.

"Drive, Sean," Eddy said. She sidestepped to the aft bench and pulled a fish gaff out of stowage.

Elspeth didn't miss the move. She hissed, and Sean had to agree with her about the escalation. "Hey, we don't want to start a war here."

Eddy reversed the gaff so the wicked hook pointed away from Elspeth, but that was as far as she was willing to go toward peaceful negotiations. "It's up to them whether it starts or not. I'm going to be ready, that's all. Now, get us out of here."

"To the reef?"

"Forget the reef. They'll have reinforcements there. South, Arkham."

Daniel didn't protest the flight plan. He'd again locked eyes with Elspeth and sunk into telepathic chat, or brainwashing. Sean eased the Montauk into motion, hoping that would make Elspeth drop off the gunwale and that he'd be able to nudge through the circling Deep Ones. Yeah, right. That would have been too easy. Elspeth hung on tight, and the swimmers only broke their circle to converge on the boat. As two hauled themselves up beside Elspeth, the Montauk yawed.

Sean spun the wheel to compensate and punched the throttle wide. As the bow lifted, a fourth Deep One peeled off it. The other three hung on, Elspeth flinging a leg over the railing. Eddy gave her knee a crack with the gaff pole, and she jerked the leg back. Another Deep One nearly clambered on board before Eddy rammed it in the chest. It dropped into the churning wake through which the other Deep Ones frantically butterflied. That left two boarders to get rid of. Sean put the Montauk through some ripping swerves, but while he managed to fling Eddy to the deck, Elspeth and her buddy clung as tight as ticks. Daniel slid away from the console, tried to get up, fell across Eddy's legs, and that was pretty much it for her. She managed to swing the hook end of the gaff as Elspeth twisted eel-like into the boat, but Elspeth caught the shaft and wrenched it from Eddy's hands. With the same arm swing, she hurled it overboard. Elspeth's buddy also slithered aboard and lunged at Sean. It was like getting tackled by a giant toad, an iron-pumping toad, with slick hide and underneath it two hundred pounds of solid muscle. Sean went down between the console and the port hull.

Left hip smarting, he dragged himself into the bow. Buddy ignored his retreat—unimpaired by his claws and webbing, he'd taken over the console and brought the Montauk to a smooth stop. Damn, that meant the others would catch up and join the party, if it wasn't over by then. Eddy was raging in the stern: "No! He doesn't want to! Let go!" And Elspeth was hissing back at her like a mixed grill of cats and cobras. And Daniel? Passed out? Gagged?

Silent.

Not silent. The wordless gasps were his.

Sean had to get up. And do what, exactly? From the bow, he couldn't get at the remaining gaff, so his only weapons were the binoculars Eddy had handed off to him. They'd have made a decent bola, if they hadn't flown off his neck somewhere. What sat on his chest now was a wispy aether-newt, Raphael, which prodded with its barely tangible snout at something under Sean's shirt.

That would be Orne's whistle.

Sean reached through Raphael and fumbled it out. Buddy didn't notice—he'd gone to help Elspeth. Whistle clenched in his left hand, the newt whisking away, Sean staggered to his feet. In the stern, the worst-case scenario was under way: Elspeth had wrestled Eddy away from Daniel, and Buddy was trying to wrestle Daniel off Elspeth's back, but yeah, Daniel had some Deep One strength, no budging him. Not, at least, until the other five swimmers arrived, and they'd closed to within a hundred yards.

First thing, then, was to get some distance between the Montauk and the swimmers. Sean swung around to the console controls and—

Elspeth's buddy had either taken the key or, more likely, tossed it into the ocean. Until Sean could get at the spare in the locker, now blocked by wrestlers, the Montauk wasn't going anywhere. Without magic, neither was Sean.

But he had magic, and Orne had given him a way to wield it, if he could stop panicking and concentrate. Fast: A Deep One was clambering up the transom.

Sean shoved the whistle mouthpiece between his lips. Instinct screamed to watch the fight and be ready for any move in his direction, but to gather magic he had to close his eyes. He could still hear Eddy's yells and the Deep Ones' ululant calls. He ignored them, pulled his darkness close around him, a black sphere, a black egg with Sean as the yolk. The sphere-egg seethed with magic, because waves of it pulsed from Daniel and the Deep Ones as if the audible noise they made was nothing to their telepathic tumult. Screw the waves. Ambient energy also crisscrossed the darkness, spiderweb, silk lightning. Sean didn't have the key for the Montauk, but he had his access image, the Ben Franklin antique, and he poked its crowning knob from his fist. Lightning arced to the brass, and he pinched the knob with his free fingers to take it into himself.

His first puff into the whistle was air that escaped around the mouthpiece. On his second try, magical energy burst out the business end of the hieroglyphed tube in that shrill bleating note that seemed to be Sean's signature tune.

The Deep Ones bleated, too. Sean opened his eyes. Elspeth had released Eddy. Daniel was a hammock slung between Buddy and Transom Swarmer, who clutched his ankles and wrists in their claws. It looked like they'd been about to swing him overboard, but now they stood frozen while he dangled and groaned.

Eddy, who wouldn't have heard the bleat of the whistle, crab-scrabbled away from Elspeth. Over a shoulder, she looked at Sean. She saw the whistle. *Do it again,* she mouthed.

When he closed his eyes a second time, his sphere-egg was there and ready. He key-captured lightning and intended it through the whistle one silken strand of energy at a time. Each strand emerged as a tone shrill in itself but chording with the others; each tone lingered in the air, and the Deep Ones stood with eyes swiveled skyward, their huge eardrums visibly vibrating in sync with the music. Daniel groaned again. Eddy, magic-deaf, pointed behind Sean, and he turned to see the remaining four Deep Ones hanging on the bow rails, as attentive as the ones on board. After the last tone faded, Buddy and Transom lowered Daniel to the deck. Eddy tried to crawl to him, but Elspeth stepped between them. She touched her slash of a mouth, swept her hand toward Sean, then swept it down toward Daniel.

Daniel knelt up between Buddy and Transom. Their claws had made a scratched mess of his arms and legs, as Elspeth's had made of Eddy's, but none of the wounds looked deep. "She says I should speak for her," Daniel said shakily.

Maybe if she'd done that in the first place, they'd have avoided the fight. Or maybe Sean could have used the whistle sooner, proving he deserved her attention. Never mind. Like Orne had said, half his job now was to believe in himself. That might be guidance-counselor-speak when dealing with other humans, but when dealing with empaths? Crucial tactic, baby.

Sean let his left arm fall casually across the console wheel. He kept his right hand high, displaying the whistle. Not twirling it or anything. Just letting the Deep Ones see he was ready to use it. Really confident guys didn't have to get all cocky about themselves, at least not in the movies. "Ah, okay. That's fine."

"She says she greets you, a fellow magician, in the names of Father Dagon and Mother Hydra."

Did he have any names to drop in return? Nyarlathotep would be impressive, but Sean hadn't actually signed on with him, and since their aborted interview, he'd left Sean strictly alone. Mostly, that was super. At this particular moment, an appearance by one of his flashier avatars would be welcome. "I greet her—," he began. "I mean, I greet you—" Then he ran out of steam. With respect? With all *due* respect?

"In whose name?" Daniel said.

"I don't have any gods in particular."

"Your pipe is of the Master of Magic's making, but if you won't name the Master, tell me who your mentor is."

In a way he did have one of those. "Redemption Orne," Sean said.

Daniel blinked. Eddy, too. But they both stayed cool with the half truth, and Daniel said for Elspeth, "We know Reverend Orne; the Master is his lord. It's the strongest allegiance, but dark. We'd think members of the Order of Alhazred would have nothing to do with it."

Elspeth had a grip on Daniel's mind, for sure, the way he was voicing not only her words but also her tone, which had shifted from neutral to sarcastic. "I'm not exactly a member of the Order. I'm a student, like Daniel."

Daniel retained enough of himself to scowl as he parroted El-speth's dismissive "And this girl?"

"She's Eddy. She's a student, too."

"She doesn't have any magic."

"Yeah, but you don't have to be a magician to study magic."

A minute passed during which Elspeth eyed Daniel and Daniel kept shaking his head, as if she was thinking something at him that he refused to say out loud for her. In the end, she shrugged, and Daniel gritted out, "Why did the Order send you two? Because you don't look like much and so would make good spies?"

Eddy glared. "We're not spies, and the Order doesn't have any-thing to do with it. We came because we're Daniel's friends. He found out his grandfather was alive, and then he found out about his mother, and he wants to meet her. That's it. That's all."

Weird as it already was for Elspeth to speak through Daniel, it got weirder when she used his own mouth to talk him down: "He'll meet her when he's begun to Change again. My sister wouldn't want to see him in this condition. Unnatural, shameful."

Much more Daniel bashing, and Eddy was going to lose it. Sean snuck in a suggestion: "Couldn't you just tell Aster that Dan-iel's here? Then let her decide whether she wants to meet him."

Elspeth again swept her hand toward him. Daniel said, "Is that the favor you'd ask from us, as a fellow in magic and Reverend Orne's apprentice?"

Two toots on the whistle to prove he was magical, and he got to ask for a favor? Sean transferred the whistle to his left hand so he could wipe the sweat off his right. "Yeah, let Daniel go to the reef, tell his mother he's there, and we're good."

"Then I'm sorry to say—," Daniel began for Elspeth. For him-self, he shouted, "Sean, behind!"

As Sean wheeled, one of the Deep Ones hanging on the bow railing finished climbing aboard. Ducking below the console,

Sean jammed the whistle into his mouth and blew a panic blast with the magical residue from his last gathering. It didn't produce much, one bleat, but that went straight into the sneak's face as he peered over the console top. Obviously it made a difference how close the target was to the whistle, because the sneak yowled and backflipped over the railing, raising a mighty splash. The other Deep Ones on the bow let go, more splashes; Elspeth and Buddy and Transom took steps back, then held their ground.

Wincing, Daniel bowed to the deck. Too obviously, the whistle hurt his ears as much as it hurt the fully Changed Deep Ones. This time Eddy was able to get to him, and she bowed her body over his.

The single tone faded fast. Sean dived into his darkness and snatched a brass knob's worth of lightning. Accessing the magic began to exact a payment, electric pangs shooting into his skull through his temples and eye sockets. Between practicing with the whistle earlier and using it to quell attacks, he was getting close to magical exhaustion.

He couldn't let the Deep Ones know that, though. He opened his eyes, stood up, faced Elspeth. A filmy Raphael hung between them, flinging all its tails to starboard; it vanished when Sean looked in that direction. Gliding dark and quiet toward the Montauk was a big red cutter with INNSMOUTH PATROL stenciled in white on its hull. And if that wasn't enough to make Sean slump with relief, riding the flybridge was Abel himself. Elspeth saw the cutter, too, but she didn't seem worried about it. Well, why should she worry? Abel and his patrol guys—five Changers in the cutter's bow—would just order her gang off in the name of Old Man Marsh, and away they'd go, living to get their dorsal fins in a twist another day.

Daniel and Eddy had knelt up and were watching the cutter's approach. Eddy got off a fist pump before Daniel shook his head like they were screwed. Didn't he see Abel?

Or did he see what Sean had missed at first? That Abel's hands were behind his back and bound to the flybridge railing. That three of the Changers in the bow were the ones from New Church Green. They weren't the cavalry. They were backup for Elspeth.

Her downturned mouth couldn't manage a smile, or else she'd be grinning at Sean big-time. She had to content herself with extending a long arm, fish-hide palm upward and eloquent: *Give me the whistle, then. You can't keep us all back.*

He sucked in air and the whistle mouthpiece, intended his gathered magic outward. This string of tones was like the second one he'd produced, just a little louder. Elspeth hissed and withdrew her hand. Daniel bowed again to the deck and Eddy with him. The resonating chord must have reached the cutter— the Changers batted hands at their shriveling ears, while Abel hunched his shoulders as high as his bonds let him. The chord couldn't last long, though, and the cutter came on in spite of it, turning so that it would reach the Montauk side by side, with its boarding ladder in play.

Sean had a minute, maybe two. He could gather and produce another chord like the fading one, but that would be it before the Changers crowded onto the Montauk. They'd get the whistle. Then they'd get Daniel.

No. He was the one who'd brought Daniel out here, into danger. So what if Daniel had wanted it? Sean had made it happen. Through Orne, he'd been the key.

And he *had* the key: Ben Franklin's, long shanked, ornate topped.

Reentering his darkness, Sean felt the key safely caged within his mental fist. Exposing more than the crowning knob was a bad idea, no telling what he'd blow up. Yeah, on his own, but he had the whistle now, which Elspeth claimed Nyarlathotep had made. If that was true, it could handle way more magical energy than Sean could ever puff into it.

Right?

Outside his sphere-egg, guttural voices drew close. The Changers on the cutter.

It had better be right.

Sean pushed out the whole top of his key. Through his darkness, through invading waves of Deep One telepathy, a torrent of braided lightning flashed into the brass. When he absorbed it into himself, pain seared his hand, shot up his arm, speared his skull through. Wicked as the pain was, the energy brought him exhilaration, too, the way it had at the summoning, but he couldn't hold on to it. In seconds it would fry his brain.

He opened his eyes. "Eddy."

She lifted her head from Daniel's shoulder. Daniel still clutched the sides of his head.

"Cover his ears," Sean gasped. Then he blew the whistle, willing the torrent of lightning into it, intending terror, intending *Get the hell out of here and leave us alone!* Thundercrack music exploded above the Montauk, the ride of the Valkyries on bad acid, adding up to a discord that made him slam his own hands over his ears as hard as Eddy was slamming hers over the backs of Daniel's hands, giving him double shielding, but he writhed anyway, Sean could see that.

Elspeth and the Deep Ones dived for the water like they meant to hit the ocean floor and drill into it. Every Changer dived, too, including two who stumbled out from the cutter cabin, but they surfaced before long, arms lashing and feet churning wide wakes as they fled toward Innsmouth. Sean got to watch their retreat while he hung over the starboard railing, throwing up everything he'd eaten for the last week. Emptied out, he kept hanging. Until the pain stopped ricocheting inside his cranium, straightening up was no more in the cards for him than it was for Daniel, who lay flat on his back, panting.

Eddy, on the other hand, had already found the spare key,

veered the Montauk out of the path of the drifting cutter, and maneuvered it close enough to jump to the boarding ladder. In fact, she'd already made it to the flybridge to cut Abel free and lay him down to pant it out like Daniel. Then she disappeared inside the cabin.

With Eddy on top of things, Sean dared to drop his forehead onto the railing and space for a while.

When he lifted his head again, the cutter had come to a stop fifty yards east, and Daniel had made it to the aft bench. He looked like he'd live, so Sean pushed off the railing and drove the Montauk over to the cutter. As he slowed to an idle beside it, Abel climbed down from the flybridge. Eddy stood at the main deck railing, next to a Deep One who stuttered into an undertaker a few times before he got his illusion to stick. "Quite a demonstration, Sean," Barnabas Marsh said. "I came in for some of it even in the cabin, but I'm glad you did it."

Sean wobbled to his feet. "They got you, too, sir?"

"I'm ashamed to say they did. I suspected Daniel might try to reach Aster on his own, so I joined Abel for this evening's patrol. Elspeth stopped the cutter. She wanted to talk, she said. My own daughter, but I still shouldn't have let my guard down enough for her partisans to swarm us. Well. I didn't rightly plumb the outrage over Daniel's situation, and so—" Marsh bowed his head. "—I'm indebted to you, magician to magician."

Daniel had come to stand beside Sean. "So am I," he said.

Mass adulation was more embarrassing than Sean had imagined it would be. "Dude, no problem," he said to Daniel. "Unless I blew your ears out."

"They're ringing like crazy. I can hear, though."

To Marsh, Sean said, "The magician-to-magician thing. Does that mean I could ask you for a favor?"

"For yourself or for Daniel?"

"After everything, I guess it's for us both. Let us finish what we came to do."

Marsh considered. "Repaying debts is part of the Shn'yeh code of honor. So is acknowledging when one's been beaten. I don't think Elspeth will interfere with Daniel again. Not immediately. She'll let him win this round."

"Does that mean yes, Grandfather?" Daniel asked.

"I hope so, Mr. Marsh," Eddy said. "I want to finish what we've started, too."

After a nervous minute, during which Marsh studied each of them in turn, he finally nodded. "I'll go talk to Aster now."

23

They moored the Montauk to a floating dock on the landward side of Devil Reef. Iron rungs had been hammered into the slick black rock; though rusted, they were sturdy enough to get Sean and Eddy and Daniel to the top of the reef. With the tide falling, it rose ten feet above the water and overlooked a gentler ocean-ward slope with a snug collar of tidal pools at its base. Gray seals lounged beside the pools. Real seals, Daniel said, but like the porpoises that had chased them earlier, they were probably Deep One watchdogs. If so, they'd gotten word to stand down, because after a twist of their rubbery necks and flash of their teeth, they went back to the more important business of scratching them-selves with their flippers.

Poised in the stern of the patrol cutter idling off the reef, Marsh was the only Deep One in sight. He raised a webbed hand. When Daniel returned the salute, he dived for Y'ha-nthlei. Abel manned the flybridge again. He shook his head from time to time as if he had water in his ears; otherwise, he appeared to have recovered from Sean's sonic assault. Same with Daniel, the occasional head jerk or dig at his ears. Sean had expected to see liquefied brains after that final blast. Luckily he seemed to have gotten the worst of it himself: a nag of a headache and a queasy stomach. He parked on a flat boulder and combatted nausea with tiny sips from his water bottle.

The adjacent boulder was big enough for three. He'd left it for Eddy and Daniel, and they took it, but left space for the nonexistent third between them. That was pretty cold after the way Eddy had wrapped herself around Daniel back on the boat. The emergency over, they seemed back to where they'd been in the dunes: not broken up but not totally together, either.

Nobody talked. Eddy had the binoculars, and she kept busy scanning the ocean in all directions. Sean fixed his own eyes on the stretch of water between reef and cutter. Presumably that was where Aster Marsh would emerge, if she came up tonight. Marsh had warned them she might need time to think about his news. Probably, too, Elspeth had gotten to Aster first, to complain about how her son and his friends had attacked Deep Ones who'd only been trying to help.

Sean patted the whistle hanging under his shirt, heavy and cool. Body heat didn't affect it, though magical energy did—his last desperate effort had left it almost too hot to hold. He wasn't sorry he'd used Orne's gift, but it worried him how much energy his key image could gather. The whistle had modulated it into a musical blow powerful but nonlethal. What if he'd deployed the same amount of energy unfiltered? Boom?

That or he'd have been unable to conjure any effective defense, in which case, Elspeth would have gotten Daniel. Crappy outcome, either way. Marvell was right, saying Sean was a hazard. Marvell was also wrong, not giving him a mentor. Sean had told Elspeth that Orne was his mentor, and it didn't have to be a lie. Not if he wanted to make it the truth.

"I still don't know," Daniel said, not shifting his eyes from the water. Eddy lowered the binoculars.

Daniel looked up at her, then at Sean. "Before things got crazy, my aunt was telling me—showing me—all this incredible stuff about the city down there. Caverns branch off from the abyss it's in, and they go on for miles, but there are these bioluminescent plankton and corals that light them up, no night anywhere except in the shoggoth pits. It's like another whole planet, animals we've never seen, thousands of Deep Ones. Shn'yeh. And with them, magic's normal. I can see why my mother stays below."

"You wish you could go," Eddy said.

Daniel took a deep breath, then said, "Yeah. A lot."

"And I don't blame you. *I* want to go."

"Me, too," Sean said. "Don't they ever let humans in?"

"No, only Shn'yeh, and only when they've Changed all the way."

That didn't seem fair, when the Deep Ones got to come up into the human world. "The Order should try to get along better with Innsmouth. Then they could set up, like, an exchange student program."

From Daniel and Eddy's silence, either the idea didn't go over or they had more personal stuff to worry about. After a minute, Daniel said, "Back on the boat, Elspeth kept insisting Geldman's treatments wouldn't work, that I'd end up stuck between human and Deep One, good for neither side. And she didn't play fair. She used mind magic to convince me. I guess you guys figured out what was happening? I hope you did, anyway."

"I did," Sean said, and Eddy nodded.

Daniel picked up an oyster shell studded with barnacles. "I know one thing. If the treatments start harming me, Geldman will stop. He made sure we understood that, me and my father.

Until then, he won't give up. He'll try to keep me human, as long—"

Eddy met Daniel's eyes but forced him to finish the sentence for himself: "As long as I want him to."

"And that's what you still don't know," she said. "Whether you want to stay human or Change to Shn'yeh."

Daniel tossed the oyster shell. "I'm both, right? Why do I have to pick one?"

"It'd be amazing if you didn't have to," Sean said. "I mean, if you could be human on land and Deep One in the water."

Voice of reason, Eddy said, "Right, but it doesn't look like you can just switch back and forth."

And that ended the conversation. Daniel found another shell to pick at, and Eddy rescanned the horizon. On the cutter, seal-like, Abel gave himself a good scratch all over, finishing with a scrub of his back on the flybridge railing. Going from skin to scales had to be an itchy business. It was one point against the Change, but Sean didn't mention it. The air between Daniel and Eddy was thick with their tension. It had the muscle to pull them together, or to shove them apart—no way he was blowing the equilibrium with dumb cracks.

"When I was doing the talking for Elspeth," Daniel finally went on.

Eddy's binoculars came down, but it was Sean who responded. "That was wild, right?"

"When she was *thinking* to me about Eddy, there were some things I didn't say out loud."

"Because she was cussing me out?" Eddy said.

"More like cussing me. She thought I should have learned from my mother how dangerous it was to love a human."

Stumbling over rocks would have made Sean's attempt to give them space too obvious, so he stayed put. He did commandeer the binoculars, though, which gave him an excuse to turn his back and study the coastline. Boat lights twinkled far off. Farther still, he made out the beacon of the Orange Point lighthouse, revolving like a restless Cyclops below the Witches' Burial Ground.

"Did Elspeth sense what I was feeling?" Eddy said.

"Yes, and she said you were a bigger fool than my father. At least he didn't know what my mother was when he fell in love with her. But you know what I am, and you still love me."

Sean braced himself for the sound of face-sucking, but it didn't come. He glanced over his shoulder. A whole person's worth of space continued to separate Eddy and Daniel, and they weren't even holding hands across it. Was he totally dense, or hadn't they just admitted they were crazy about each other?

It turned out to be a good thing they didn't get demonstrative—from his lookout, Abel called, "Coming up!" He meant the Deep One who'd surfaced right where Sean had imagined one would, midway between the patrol boat and Devil Reef. It swam to the cutter and climbed aboard, tall and broad backed, dorsal fin ringed and studded with more gold than even Elspeth had rocked: Old Man Marsh back from his mission. Daniel stood up and waved, but Marsh went into the cabin without responding. Had he scored such a complete failure with his daughter that he couldn't face Daniel?

Or was he getting out of the way of the Deep One who surfaced farther out, a crested head in black silhouette against the ripples it had created. This Deep One swam to the edge of the reef tidal pools. While it bobbed there, Eddy shifted to Sean's boulder, a tight fit that pressed them shoulder to shoulder, hip to hip; in the killer silence, he heard the rapid beat of her heart, unless it was his own heartbeat he heard, within his ears, inescapable.

Eerily lithe, the Deep One emerged from the water and crouched among the undisturbed seals. Slim waisted, breasted, a she, with fewer piercings than Marsh or Elspeth and only one gold wrist cuff. On the plus side, she didn't have a big bite scar on her dorsal fin. If that *was* a plus.

Daniel started down the side of the reef, nearly slipping.

The Deep One waved him back. She climbed the algae-slick rocks like they were a staircase, reaching the spine of the reef a few yards north of Daniel. There she crouched again.

There, one sleepwalker's step at a time, Daniel joined her, and crouched, and let Aster enfold his partly webbed hands with her fully webbed ones.

And that was how they stayed, gazes locked. The great thing about telepathy, they could say whatever they wanted, whatever had piled up over half Daniel's life, without worrying Sean and Eddy would overhear them. Even so, Sean yielded to Eddy's elbow pokes and scrounged around on the boulder until they'd both put their backs to Daniel and his mother. Like you'd expect out on the water, in the middle of even an August night, it was cool enough for Sean to wish they'd brought the space blanket from the Montauk's locker. There was no going for it now. They could only wait, hunched together, too aware of the soundless conversation behind them to attempt one themselves.

The memory that hit Sean in the absence of other distractions was old but unfaded. *He and Eddy sit next to each other on the bottom step of her front porch, seven and seven years old. Her mother, Rachel, sits on the top step and stares at the cell phone she's laid on her unopened book. It rings once in a while, but she doesn't pick it up. Sean doesn't ask which caller will be important enough to make her answer. Since early morning, when Uncle Gus and Aunt Celeste left him with the Rosenbaums, he hasn't asked a single question. He's eaten waffles and blueberries. He's helped Eddy draw a dragon on the sidewalk. They would still be working on it except they made the outline so big—spanning five squares of pavement—that they've run out of chalk for filling it in. Anyhow, they're kind of beat. Eddy leans against him, scuffing blue chalk from the dragon's wing into her bare soles. Normally Rachel would get on her for making a mess, but Rachel's like Sean today, mainly just waiting. Because Dad has been at the hospice place all night. Because that's where Uncle Gus and Aunt Celeste have gone, and Grandpa Stewie and Uncle Joe. Sean hasn't been there since Mom went to sleep and stayed asleep, breathing funny. That's okay. The next time they all come back from the hospice place, Mom will come with them.*

And he really had believed Mom would die and then get better, good as new. Seven was too old to believe in shit like that. Seven knew what dying was. It was never coming back, and never coming back was the worst thing, the black hole horror.

Or was the worst thing having a chance to live, to stay, and turning it down?

"Sean?" Eddy whispered.

Of course, just when a huge chunk of pain had lodged in his throat. He coughed it out.

"You okay?"

"Getting a freaking cold, maybe."

"Tell me about it." And Eddy really was shivering.

He put an arm around her and chafed her opposite shoulder. Her narrow bare feet smeared with blue chalk. All those years back, saying nothing (being a kid, not knowing what to say), she'd also waited. "Daniel will be all right."

"What if he decides to go with Aster? I mean, he can't this second. But he could give up the treatments. He could go stay with his grandfather while he Changes."

"His dad won't let him."

"He's eighteen. Legally, he can do what he wants."

"He hasn't wanted to go against his dad before."

"Before, he didn't know he had somebody else to go *to*. Soon as he found out about his grandfather—" She shut up. She sniffed.

Sean smelled it, too, the fresh brine and the faint fish and an elusive sweetness. Pulling apart, they stood and turned. Daniel had remained where he'd crouched, while Aster had slipped around him and approached their boulder. Sean was glad now they'd had the run-in with Elspeth's gang—it had gotten them over the shock that came from the sheer strangeness of a Deep One. Up close, as long as they weren't attacking you, Deep Ones were cool. They were their own species, not just a sharking away of humanity. Sean would even bet that, with the scattering of emerald green and turquoise in her scales and the extra height of her dorsal fin, Aster Marsh was a Deep One babe.

The thin rings of iris that surrounded her huge pupils were the same blue as Old Man Marsh's, and Tom's, and Daniel's. The Marsh blue. Sean worked not to blink while Aster appraised him. She then appraised Eddy for so long, he started getting nervous by proxy. Unnecessary: Eddy didn't falter. She didn't even flinch when Aster touched her cheek with one clawed and webbed hand.

Returning to Daniel, Aster touched both his cheeks and pressed her forehead to his. His arms rose as if to hug her. They dropped back to his sides. Brow connection unbroken, he started shaking his head. Sean's empty stomach rolled. Aster had to want Daniel to choose her and the Change. Maybe she was thinking to him how much his father and the Order sucked to put him through Geldman's treatments. How much Eddy and Sean sucked, compared to the friends he could have in Y'ha-nthlei. How selfish they were trying to hold on to him. Stuff like that, and you couldn't even blame her. She was his mother. She couldn't let go.

She'd let go before.

The Change had forced her to.

But his own mom hadn't saved herself through the Communion. She had let go instead.

But she must have been too sick to understand what Orne was offering her, and Dad, and Sean, everyone who loved her. There hadn't been time for Mom to get used to the idea of immortality. You couldn't throw that in someone's face all of a sudden without them thinking you were crazy, without them running scared—

"Sean," Eddy said.

He'd closed his eyes. Opening them, he saw that Aster had climbed back down to the tidal pools. Daniel was sliding after her. Seals humped away with indignant barks as he blundered through their cordon.

"He's going!" Though Eddy's voice stayed low, her words carried the sharp despair of a wail.

"He says he can't."

"Well, what's that?"

It was Aster diving, then surfacing a dozen yards off and looking back at Daniel. It was Daniel teetering on the edge of the reef. It was Marsh, come back out of the cabin, and Abel on the flybridge, both watching from the railings.

Then it was Aster swimming swiftly back to the edge. Daniel hesitated. She was going to pull him in!

She pushed him backwards, so he fell onto the thick carpet of seaweed that clung to the tidal rocks. He fell unhurt, but he stayed down while she dived again and this time didn't come up.

He stayed down, arm over eyes, chest heaving.

Trying not to slip and brain themselves on the rocks, Sean and Eddy took several minutes to reach Daniel. For another quarter hour, while the seals regrouped and the cutter chugged cautiously nearer, they knelt watch and listened to him choke out grief that Aster had gone and gratitude that she'd read his heart for him.

24

It was almost dawn when Sean guided the Montauk to a private pier in Innsmouth Harbor. Marsh would give it docking space until Sean or Orne came to retrieve it. The way Sean foresaw things going down in Arkham, it would probably be Orne.

Their cell phones were so packed with frantic messages from Helen and all their parents that they had to turn down Marsh's offer to crash at his house and start back without delay. Abel drove them to the Newbury marina in his kiwi Bug. They dozed through the stink, even Sean riding shotgun. In the backseat of the Civic, Eddy and Daniel fell asleep again. No invisible third person separated them now—his head lolled on her shoulder, her cheek nestled in his wild Frodo-in-Mordor hair. To keep from disturbing them, Sean blasted his obnoxiously loud *STAY AWAKE* playlist through an earbud instead of the car speakers.

Stopping for coffee twice, he did stay awake. He also made a brief call to Helen, which meant she and Marvell were waiting outside the Arkwright House when they pulled into the driveway. Another man stood, or rather shifted from foot to foot, beside

Helen. His curly black hair was a close-clipped version of Daniel's, which took any surprise out of how he went into full rant mode the second Daniel emerged from the Civic. Stalking across the gravel, poking the air with a forefinger, he snapped, "This was unacceptable! You know that. Absolutely unacceptable!"

Eddy was brave enough to get out and stand next to Daniel. Sean wasn't that much in love. He stayed in the car.

"Dad," Daniel said. "You drove from New York?"

"When Ms. Arkwright told me you were gone, what did you think I was going to do?" Glass was up in Daniel's face now and pointing at the fresh bandage Marsh had wrapped around his throat. "Tell me you didn't go into the ocean again." Then he noticed the fresh scratches on Daniel's arms and legs. His voice rose: "And did those things *attack* you?"

Daniel answered the second question first, semi-truthfully. "Nobody *attacked* me. And I didn't go in any water. We stayed in the boat until we got to the reef."

"Out on a reef? Are you insane?"

Helen approached Glass with bomb-squad wariness. He must have been chewing her out for hours. "We should go inside," she said. "Have Mr. Geldman come over to look at Daniel."

"Daniel's going inside to pack," Glass said—to Daniel, not Helen. "We'll go over to Geldman after. That is, if you want to, Daniel. If you're not ready to throw all our work away for those things."

Though his hands were shaking, Daniel kept his voice steady. "If I wanted to Change, I would have stayed in Innsmouth. And they're Deep Ones, not *things*. Unless you want to call them Shn'yeh—that's their right name, my grandfather told me. I met him. And I saw my mother."

Not even Glass dared to jump into Daniel's pause. His hands were shaking, too.

"I saw my mother," Daniel repeated. "She's not dead. You knew that, though."

"Daniel."

"She's alive. Changed. But she told me to come back here and stay human. She told me I'm not ready to Change. Maybe sometime. Not now."

The way Glass bowed his head must've convinced Helen his fuse had burned out, for the moment. She moved in and got Daniel by the elbow. "Come on. We can go down to the kitchen and talk over breakfast."

"Fine with me," Daniel said. "As long as Eddy comes."

Glass really looked at Eddy for the first time. Just like Elspeth, he said, "That girl?"

"Eddy Rosenbaum," Daniel said. "Remember I told you about her, Dad, when we talked after the harbor accident?"

Glass had apparently assumed that after learning his son's secret, Eddy would be long gone, at least as Daniel's girlfriend. He shook his head, then gave an exaggerated shrug. Helen took Daniel and Eddy by the elbows and went into the house. Glass followed.

That left Marvell to deal with Sean. During the confrontation between Daniel and his father, he had moved to block the driveway behind Sean's car, as if Sean might make a run for it in the Civic. Sean had considered it. But if Daniel could stand up to his father, he could stand up to Marvell. First step was getting out of the car, which he did. Helen would've met him halfway. Marvell's only move was to fold his arms across his chest as Sean trudged up to him. Then he said, "Solomon Geldman didn't see fit to inform us of your plans until after your curfew last night."

Good for Geldman.

"Right afterwards, of course, I called your father."

"What did he say, sir?"

"He told me to take your car key as soon as you came back."

"For how long?"

"Until he decides you should have the option of driving people into dangerous situations."

Sean detached the Civic key from his ring and handed it over. "What did he really say, Professor?"

"Until he comes to get it himself. He hasn't finished work on the church, but he's willing to fly back early if he has to."

"Why should he? I'm okay. We're all okay."

"He might have to come if the Order dismisses you as its student. I warned you under what circumstances we'd do that. Do you remember?"

"I remember that taking Daniel to Innsmouth wasn't one of them, sir."

"So you're telling me that's all you did. You didn't do any practical magic? You didn't have any contact with Orne's familiar or Orne himself?"

On their ride in from Devil Reef, he and Daniel and Eddy had agreed that they'd keep Sean's involvement in their adventure to a minimum and not mention Orne or the seed world. Instead of learning about his grandfather through the spy-hole, Daniel had gone to Innsmouth on the mere chance he'd find relations still living there. It was Old Man Marsh who'd lent them the boat. When they were harassed by the anti-Order Deep Ones, it was Marsh and Abel who'd driven them off. That was their story, and they were going to stick to it, mainly for Sean's sake, as he realized now. The only point that would get Daniel in trouble was how he'd spied on the Order meeting.

From where Sean stood, he could see the *Founding*'s Plexiglas shield and the stained glass beneath it, dark in the early morning shade. The only lies he *had* to tell were the ones that would protect Daniel and the seed world, and those were actually one big lie of omission—

Impatience and suspicion ground together into Marvell's voice: "Sean, those weren't hard questions. You used practical magic, yes or no. You had contact with Orne, yes or no."

When Daniel had faced down his father, it had been with the truth. Suddenly, maybe stupidly, Sean wanted to hit Marvell with some of the same. "Yes and yes," he said.

The truth punched Marvell's jaw slack. While he was recovering, Sean laid a hand on the whistle under his shirt, pressing its coolness into his skin. "Daniel's going to say his grandfather lent us a boat to go to Devil Reef. He's going to say Marsh's patrol cutter ran off some Deep Ones that wanted to kidnap him. All that's to keep me out of trouble. What really happened is Orne was watching us through his newt, and he had it invite me to meet him in Newbury. I did, and he offered to help. He got the boat for us so Daniel could go meet his mother. He gave me this."

He pulled the chained whistle over his head and dangled it between them. As it spun, the sun climbed over the Arkwright House and bounced light off the spiral of alien script, making its toothy characters glow like embers.

Marvell stepped back from the whistle. He stayed back while Sean told him how he'd used it to impress and intimidate the hostile Deep Ones. The first thing he said after Sean shut up was, "Why admit to all this?"

Why was he screwing himself, in other words. Great question, and to Sean's own amazement, he had an answer. "I don't want to get thrown out of the Order, Professor. I want to stay, and I want to come back next summer, and then I want to go to MU."

"So you confess to the very things that could get you thrown out?"

"So I'm telling you the truth. Like, just because Daniel went to see his grandfather and mother, he's not jumping into the ocean and Changing. Well, just because I met Redemption Orne doesn't mean I'm going to side with him against the Order. If he even is against it. I kind of don't think he is."

"'Kind of don't think,'" Marvell echoed.

Sean ignored the sarcasm. "I'm giving you the whistle to keep until I can use it better. To prove I trust the Order."

"And you do? You choose us over Orne?"

Another great question. "I'm not choosing anyone yet. But I want to stick to the Order for now, and I won't do anything to harm it. I can totally promise that."

Marvell took the whistle. He turned it in every direction and even pulled a tiny magnifying glass out of his pocketknife to scrutinize the script. He didn't try to blow the whistle, however. "You can promise not to harm the Order *knowingly,* perhaps."

"Can anybody do more than that, Professor?"

Marvell wrapped the whistle in a clean handkerchief before putting it in his breast pocket. "Well. I have to admit I'm impressed by your honesty, and by the pledge of Orne's whistle. You realize it's a hugely important artifact, worth a great deal of money?"

To tell the truth, Sean was starting to feel sorry he'd let the whistle go, but not because it was a priceless museum piece. Orne had given it to him, and look how it had saved Daniel. Still, he had something else from Orne, something he *wasn't* giving up. "I figured. That's okay. I know you'll take care of it for me."

"I'll get the archival process started at once. But before the Order can formally accept a loan like this, from a minor, I'll have to get permission from your father."

Hell yeah, Dad. "Could you let me talk to him first, Professor? I better call him right away, anyhow."

"Yes, you'd better."

He took a deep breath. "Should I, like, tell him anything about coming back early?"

Marvell touched his breast pocket, then the trousers pocket

where he'd stowed the Civic key. "No. I'd hate to interrupt his work. And as long as your wings are clipped, I think we can wait until the Order meeting in September to decide about your position with us. Barring any further troublemaking, of course."

It had worked? Marvell wasn't going to be a complete dick? "Thanks, Professor. No troublemaking."

Marvell had to be just a little bit of a dick. Though at first he hadn't been able to hide his excitement over the whistle, he'd slowly worked his way back to a stern glower. "We'll see. Well. Would you tell Helen about the artifact? She'll want to come to the Archives and have a look."

"Sure, Professor."

Like Marvell, Mr. Glass avoided being an absolute complete dick. Relieved that Daniel would continue treatment with Geldman, he gave him permission to go on living at the Arkwright House. In fact, he decided to stay a couple days himself. That he wanted to hang out with Daniel was great; that he probably also meant to scope the hell out of Eddy, not so much. Sean's call to England went as well as could be expected. First Dad yelled about Sean endangering himself and his friends. Then he yelled about Orne interfering again. It took an hour for Sean to calm him down to the point where they agreed to discuss everything when Dad got home, and then that they loved each other et cetera. Sean didn't say a word about how Orne and Mom had known each other. That would have to wait until they had a lot of time, face-to-face.

At first Eddy and Daniel were pissed that Sean had changed their cover story in midstream. Then Daniel said that maybe the truth—how Sean had been able to use the whistle—had impressed Marvell so much, he was afraid to let Sean out of the Order's sight. And Eddy said that giving Marvell the whistle was freaking brilliant. It had to be the most lustworthy artifact the Order had gotten in forever, and so they wouldn't want to risk an expelled Sean withdrawing the loan.

The two of them went upstairs to nap because Mr. Glass was threatening to take them out to dinner. Eddy leaned over the banister to fake-strangle herself at Sean. She'd better be careful. Daniel didn't *see* her miming anguish at the possible family party, but what did he *feel*? Hazards of dating an empath.

Helen went to the Archives as soon as everyone was settled. That left the first floor of the House, and the library, all to Sean. He was aching for sleep, and there were ominous rumors that Mr. Glass might invite him to dinner, too, but man up. He had one more thing to do before he crashed.

Onto the dais, up the stepladder, hand to the glass crow, and nothing went wrong: Sean entered the seed world flying. He flapped above the trees for the joy of using his wings again. South marched the cliffs and coves that weren't Kingsport yet; north lay the mouth of the Miskatonic but no Arkham, and farther north, the mouth of the Manuxet and Plum Island and a dragon spine of black rock the human settlers of Innsmouth would name Devil Reef. The Deep Ones themselves wouldn't call it that. They had to have a tongue-twister of a name for it. Maybe Daniel knew. Maybe Aster had told him already.

He could fly to the reef and see who'd lounged on it back in the day, but not now. Now he spiraled down to the minister and perched on his shoulder. Several minutes passed, enough to make him anxious. Then Orne animated the construct and took Sean-crow on his wrist. "Raphael told me about your battle."

"Yeah, well, Raphael helped, too. Reminded me of the whistle."

"You did very well. So did your friends. I'm glad Daniel's staying with the Order, and you and Eddy. I'd hate to see such a natural team broken up."

"I guess the wards kept Raphael from telling you about how Marvell chewed me out this morning."

Orne sobered. "Are you in trouble, Sean?"

"I don't think so. We'd made up a story to tell him and Helen, but then, I don't know. I felt like I had to tell him most of the truth. How I met you at the marina. How you helped us." With a caw, Sean cleared his throat. "I gave him your whistle to hold for me. Eddy says it got him so excited, he forgot about kicking my ass out of the Order, but that wasn't what I was trying for. I wanted to show I trusted the Order. I hope you're not mad—I can get it back. Marvell called it a loan to the Archives."

Slowly Orne's frown gave way to the ironic quirk of the lips Sean had seen on his true face. "Intentional or not, that was a masterstroke. You delivered one of the treasures of his enemy into Marvell's hands. How better to mollify him?"

"So it's all right?"

"Yes. As you say, we can get the whistle back if we need it."

"Anyhow, I'm still an Order student."

Orne lowered him gently to the grass. "I see."

"Maybe you don't. Because I didn't make any more promises I'd have to break, like I wouldn't have any more contact with you." Sean fluttered to Orne's shoulder. "Plus I didn't tell him about the seed world, and I'm not going to. We can keep talking in here. The only difference is I won't use the peephole to spy on the library. Since I *am* part of the Order, that'd be wrong."

Orne's shoulder shook, like he simmered with suppressed laughter. "I'm sure your place as student is secure, Sean. Marvell would never give up so promising a magician."

"That's what Daniel said."

"Then he's as acute as Eddy. Well, do you want me to close the tree trunk up, or do you want to test your will against opportunity?"

"I should probably test my will, huh?"

"An interesting question to ask a former minister. Is it better to remove all temptation, or better to withstand it?"

"Did you Puritan guys used to give out points for resisting stuff? Like, you got one point for not stealing something right in front of you, and two points for not stealing it if no one was watching, and three points for not stealing it if you really wanted it?"

Orne's simmer came to a boil, and he laughed aloud. "Let's leave open the peephole, the temptation, for now. We can worry about points later."

"Okay. Probably won't be any Order meetings before I go home, anyway." Going home. "I'll miss the window. I won't be able to talk to you without it."

"In an emergency, you could call on Raphael to bring me a message."

"Raphael will stay with me?"

"Unless you don't want it to."

"I decide?"

After a moment, Orne nodded.

"Then maybe it doesn't have to hang around *all* the time. Maybe it can just drop in once in a while so you know I'm okay."

Orne took longer to nod this time. Then he said, "The last time I saw Kate, when I told her about the Communion?"

Again, Sean wasn't going to blame Orne for not convincing Mom. He must have done all he could. "Yeah. I've been thinking about that."

"She wanted to know if you'd inherited our ability. I told her you had, and that you'd be strong. Then she asked me to make sure you had every chance to use your magic."

A shudder ruffled Sean's feathers from crown to tail.

"So you see, Kate wanted you to have the option of taking the road she hadn't. I'm going to keep my pledge to her and help you as far along it as you want to go. Whenever you need me to. As long as you need me." Orne set Sean on the ground and smoothed back his feathers. Then he said, "Nevermore."

His departure from the seed world was too sudden and too soon. Daniel had started calling Barnabas Marsh grandfather by the end of the Innsmouth trip, but now Sean had lost his chance to call Orne that. There was no use saying it to the inanimate minister and no time to call Orne back. Helen could return from the Archives, or Mr. Glass could wander into the library to snoop on what Daniel was reading. Next time. Or the time after. Mom had wanted him to have a chance at magic. She'd asked Orne to make it happen.

Sean arrowed to the palm shadow within the horns of the crescent moon and popped back into himself, crouched on the ladder, wingless.

But.

The glass crow hovered in its usual place above Nyarlathotep's casting hand, and it would mind his wings for him.

YOU'VE FOUND HIM

Theophilus Marvell left it to Helen to write the initial curator's report on Sean's whistle. That it might date back to Egypt's Old Kingdom had thrilled her—she was too young to have lost her awe for vast stretches of time, even if they were vast only in mortal terms. The script on the whistle was far more ancient than the instrument, and its gold alloy was sure to puzzle consulting metallurgists with its extraterrestrial components.

From the university, he walked to Geldman's. As Cybele filled his usual order, her lash-veiled gaze chastised him for entering the pharmacy under an illusion. But he was tired, unwilling to drop his mask until he meant to leave it off for a while, and that was not until a quarter hour later, when he turned onto Lich Street.

As on most fine summer days, gravestone-rubbers haunted its antique boneyard, too busy with their chalks to notice how Theophilus Marvell changed dark hair for blond and brown eyes for blue, how he shed twenty pounds and twenty years, to become Redemption Orne. The gray tabby sunning on his neighbor's porch saw the illusion break. She didn't flick a whisker, for she'd seen the sudden change many times before, and being a cat, she approved it.

Redemption unlocked Number Five, at the same time probing his wards. They were undisturbed, and in the shaft of sunlight that entered the front hall with him, even the dust motes seemed to have hung unmoving since his hurried exit the day before. It had been a mistake to show Sean the guest-magician avatar and the peephole. Knowing about them had allowed the boy to bring Daniel into the seed world, had allowed Daniel to find out about his grandfather, had precipitated the perilous trip to Innsmouth. Thank the Master it had all worked out well—Sean and his friends had come through the trial whole, and Redemption had even advanced his cause. He and Sean had met face-to-face at last and parted as de facto mentor and apprentice, for one could hardly call them less after the success of the whistle and Sean's decision to keep the seed world secret, a place where they might continue their "illicit" lessons.

Redemption set his pharmacy order on the hall table and smiled at the familiar candy-striped bag. Solomon Geldman, the eternal enigma. He'd helped plant doubt of Marvell (hence of the Order) in Sean's mind, but then he had used the special Order meeting to engineer Daniel's crisis, a mad complication to throw into their interwoven schemes. It had been an agony to sit still, illusioned as Marvell, while Sean and Daniel eavesdropped on the revelations that Geldman coaxed out of the other participants. Still, given the positive outcome, maybe Geldman had taken one of his cryptic longer views after all. Redemption would visit the pharmacy again that evening, try once more to puzzle out the enigma's motives, if only for both their amusements.

First he had to see to Patience and her donor.

Thank the Master again, the reawakening process had gone smoothly so far. Adrift in the dreams of Lethe Powder, supported by Geldman's reverse leech, Garth Lynx had proved a bounteous tap, and Patience's heart had begun to beat, her lungs to draw air, her cheeks and lips to blush the palest pink, like the blowsy petals of the roses in the dooryard, whose forebears she'd raised so long ago. In three more days, maybe four, Redemption could send Garth on his way with a harmless gap in his memory and money fattening his wallet. Then Redemption would slowly, safely, bring Patience back to full animation.

His buoyant mood lasted another three steps into the hall. On the fourth step, he felt the change he'd overlooked on first entering the house, for his palms began to prickle, the bones in his inner ears to vibrate. Say he was standing right next to Patience—in her current state between trance and waking, he'd expect to feel her resurging energy this strongly.

He was not standing right next to her.

He was not in the same room.

Or in the subcellar, or even in the basement.

Redemption grabbed the pharmacy bag and ran. He pelted down the basement stairs, plunged into the subcellar. With every step he took, his sense of Patience should have strengthened. Instead it grew weaker, and before he skidded off the last step, he knew that the time he'd thought he had, that three or four days? Time had fled from the chill space, as had the psychic scent of Patience's exquisite and exquisitely enjoyed nightmares. Replacing it was the copper tang of blood, because Patience had awakened, and Patience had left her alcove, and Patience had not been content to sip when she could quaff.

Garth Lynx wore an oozing choker of wounds where her feeding tentacles had battened onto his neck and gnawed their way down to the veins themselves. Multiple direct taps had meant a swift death for him, a swift glut for Patience. She'd also detached Garth from Geldman's reverse leech and tucked its proboscis back into its tank, where it lolled in its nutriment broth, happily brain-less and therefore untroubled by the carnage around it. Patience hadn't been content merely to tentacle-feed. Craving as always the salty-sweet taste of blood, she had cut Garth's left wrist with a scalpel from Redemption's surgical kit. His arm still dangled over the side of the gurney, its hand in a pail she'd set to catch his flow.

The pail contained only clotted residue.

Redemption knocked it aside and lifted Garth's arm onto the gurney. If he could take any comfort, it was in the wondering smile on the boy's gray face. He had remained asleep and dream-ing, had never felt her ravening, never seen her rub his blood on her face and throat, reveling in it.

But Redemption didn't want that comfort. He didn't deserve it. He was supposed to have started Garth toward as decent a future as money and the boy's talent could secure. Instead he'd have to put him into the furnace, piece by piece. He couldn't let Patience clean up her own mess. She'd probably hum over the work.

Redemption stamped the bloody pail to bloody plastic shards. Then he went looking for Patience.

Her energetic aura wasn't hard to track, for after such gorging it flared high. She was on the second floor, in her bedroom, already showered and dressed in clothes a few years outdated, which she would soon replace. When Redemption pushed through the half-open door, she didn't turn from the vanity mirror but smiled at his reflection as she continued combing out auburn hair damp-ness had darkened to vermilion. Her eyes were feverish with the glee of waking, and gluttony had swollen her belly to an obscene semblance of pregnancy. Most terrible were her teeth—they gleamed so innocently white, he had to fight an urge to pound them out of her mouth. Not that she would have stood for that at any time in her life and long undeath. "I know," she said. "You're angry about the donor."

"It was so unnecessary, Patience!"

"I suppose."

"You know it was! You knew I'd be back, I'd take care of you."

"Well, if you were so worried about him, you should have stayed with us. You must have realized I was waking up, and you certainly know how hungry I am when I do."

He bowed his head. "I thought I had more time."

"Perhaps, but you've awakened me often enough to know how uncertain the timing can be. Truth is, you were more worried about another boy than you were about that one in the cellar."

He lifted his head.

Patience had swiveled on her stool to face him. She never illusioned herself for him alone; therefore, she flaunted their Master's gift, eyes like his, three-lobed, three-slitted, white lava within the slits. "So I'm right. It's *our* boy, isn't it?"

Redemption took three heavy steps to the bed and sat, exhausted, in need of feeding himself. Sensing his emptiness, Patience came to sit beside him and rubbed the center of her left palm until not tentacles but a teat emerged. The blood that welled from it was gold, again like their Master's, Garth's donation transmuted. When Patience's cupped hand had filled with the shimmering liquid, she raised it to Redemption's lips, and he could not refuse the chalice. He drank every drop; then, soothed and roused by her bitter honey, licked her skin clean and sucked more directly from the teat. Wasn't it always so, wouldn't it always be, for ever and ever, amen.

When finally Redemption released the teat, intoxicated beyond the anger that he should have clung to, that he would have to find again later and turn on himself, Patience withdrew her hand. "It's our boy," she said again. "Sean Wyndham. Your mind's bursting with it. You've found him."

"I found him long ago."

"You know how I mean it. You've *found* him."

Redemption nodded. He took her bountiful hand and kissed the now-teatless palm, the wrist, the cool flesh above it.

Patience laughed like the young girl in the woods, as she'd been, like the young mother at her cradle. A third time, as if it were a spell, she said it: "You've found him."

And Redemption nodded again, to seal the charm.

Acknowledgments

Thanks to my agent, Craig Tenney, and my editor at Tor, Miriam Weinberg, for being my magical mentors and again helping me string words into story.

Thanks to Tor.com for hosting Ruthanna Emrys and me in our Lovecraft reread blog. Ruthanna's takes on the stories and our readers' amazingly erudite and entertaining comments continue to illuminate the dark canon for me, in all shades of eldritch light.

And thanks ever to my alpha and beta and omega reader, Deb.